THE WILD ROSES

Betrayal. Corruption. Obsession.
Is there a way out?

The Wild Roses

By

D. B. Carter

Dedication

To my dearest Rebecca and our three children, who always inspire me. Your love and support during the creation of *The Wild Roses* has been wonderful. When I think of you all, I know I'm truly blessed.

To Sarah, Hazel, Emily, Natalie, Janie, Leona, Sandra, Lorinda, Jamie and Daniel. Your encouragement while I've been writing this book has meant the world to me. Thank you all.

Other titles by the author

The Cherries: Faith, Hope, Happiness.
Does she dare?

If you would like to get in touch, then here is how to find D. B. Carter:

Twitter: @dbcarterauthor
Facebook: facebook.com/DBCarterAuthor
Website: d.b.carter.authorpage.co

Chapter 1

Pip stirred in her warm, comfortable bed and sighed, resigned to the inescapable fact that she was now awake. Minutes earlier there had been a gentle thud from the room next to hers and she could hear the whimpering of her little brother on the landing. Squinting her eyes, she turned on her bedside light, gently slipped from her cosy-blanketed sanctuary, and padded to her bedroom door; Daniel stood before her in the half-light, his cheeks glistening with tears.

"I fell out of bed," the boy sniffed, "but still I couldn't get to the bathroom in time."

Their mother's sleepy voice groaned from her bedroom, "I'm on my way."

"Don't worry, Mum," Pip whispered loudly enough to be heard. "Daniel's had a little accident, that's all. Go back to sleep, I'm sorting it."

"You're such a good girl." The disembodied voice tailed off and sleep once again consumed the speaker.

"Sorry," Daniel said as his big sister helped him out of his pyjamas.

"That's OK, lots of people have little accidents." Pip spoke with the quiet tenderness of an early morning secret shared.

She stood him in the bath and cleaned him with warm water. There were no pyjamas in the airing cupboard, though it was hard to be sure in the dark, but she found a t-shirt and some underpants, which sufficed for both warmth and decency. Daniel's skin had become cold to the touch.

"Oh, you're shivering," Pip sympathised. "Tell you what, why don't you come into my bed for a little bit, just until it's time to get up? Would you like that?"

"Yes please," he lisped through a gap in his front teeth and followed his sister to her bedroom.

"Why don't you scoot up next to the wall?" Pip suggested. She waited for Daniel to get into bed and climbed in after him. "This way, you can't fall out again." She turned out the light and cuddled him close, her body heat warming him through her nightshirt. She teased him, "Falling out of bed is silly."

"No it's not," Daniel giggled.

"It is, it's silly-silly-silly," Pip insisted, with ticklish little pokes and prods at the boy's midriff to make him wriggle with glee.

"No, you're silly," he retorted when the tickles stopped. "Your name's silly. Pip-Pip-Pip-Pip-Pip. Did you come from an apple?"

"Yes. The apple fell on Mum's head and she decided to keep me," Pip sighed. "Settle down, it's time to go to sleep."

"People don't come from apples," Daniel wisely observed. "But everyone calls you Pip."

"That's true, go to sleep."

"Except Granny and Grandad."

"Yes, except them." Pip stroked Daniel's hair. "Go – to – sleep."

Pip loved her youngest brother. In fairness, if pushed, she would admit to also loving her other brother, Matthew, but he was only two years younger than she was and had been consistently annoying for as long as she could remember; Daniel, however, was five and adorable, not fourteen and smelly. In truth, she felt sorry for Matthew having to share with their younger sibling, but she knew that her parents had half an eye on moving one of the boys in to her room as soon as she was able to get a place of her own. Not that was likely to happen any time soon, unless…

In the hubbub she had forgotten about her exciting news, which she was bursting to tell her best friend. Pip lay quietly, tingling with thrill, until a sleeping Daniel started to splay his limbs and she was inched back to the very edge of her bed. She told herself to try to doze at the very least.

Pip must have slept, because she jumped when her alarm went off. She turned over to switch it off and promptly fell off her perch at the edge of the bed, landing with a resounding bang. If the rest of the house wasn't awake before, they were now. She remained where she was on the floor, scrabbling to silence her clock which she had dragged down with her. With a sigh, she reached above her head for her radio and turned it on.

"And still in the charts, here's Sade and 'Smooth Operator'," announced the presenter with a degree of upbeat joie de vivre that very few things warranted at that time in the morning, particularly if you have been up in the night with a sad little brother.

Daniel's head appeared, looking down on her over the edge of the mattress.

"Now who's silly for falling out of bed?" he giggled.

~ * ~ * ~

"Sharon, hurry up! You want to have a proper breakfast before you leave!"

Roused by her mother's voice, Sharon sighed and peered at her alarm clock. Seven-fifteen already? She turned the chrome knob on her aged transistor radio and an enthusiastic male voice crackled to greet her, "And still in the charts, here's Sade and 'Smooth Operator'."

Still drowsy, she picked up her towel and radio and stomped into the family bathroom. Within a few moments, she was kneeling beside the pastel-pink bath and lathering her shoulder-length hair.

"Turn down the radio, love," shouted her mother, banging on the door, "I'm sure the neighbours don't want to listen to it!"

Eyes full of suds, Sharon thrashed around for the radio and managed to knock it into the bath. The soapy water distorted the music until she located the dial with slippery fingers and turned it to 'off'. She swore softly to herself, expressing her momentary opinion that her mother should be classified as a particularly unintelligent bovine.

She rinsed off her hair and returned to her room to blow-dry it, viciously brushing to build as much volume as possible. Dressed in her usual anonymous grey heavy-cotton A-line skirt and black polyester-wool blend jumper, which sported a thin silver pattern, she perfected her face with a little smear of pink lip gloss and the faintest hint of eyeshadow.

Lyn heard loud footsteps on the stairs and began to ladle hot porridge into a bowl for her daughter. She sighed as Sharon burst into the room and slammed the radio onto the mottled-blue laminate surface of the kitchen table.

"It's ruined!" declared the teenager. She flopped into a chair and poured a cup of tea from the pot in front of her. "It's your fault. I need a new one anyway, this one is ancient!"

Lyn closed her eyes and counted to ten before placing the porridge in front of her daughter with a patient smile.

"I'm sorry, love. Maybe Dad can fix it."

"Maybe Dad can fix what?" asked a male voice from the hallway. Sharon's father was a medium-height, wiry man of just over forty. He looked fit but tired as he walked into the kitchen, and he carried the almost undetectable stoop of a man who had done a lifetime of physically demanding work.

"Her radio, Bob," Lyn explained. "It seems I made her break it somehow."

"Let's have a look," he said, picking up the radio and causing a little trickle of soapy liquid to escape from somewhere near the battery compartment. "Well, there's your problem – it's got water in it."

"No kidding, Dad!" Sharon said. "That's possibly because Mum made me drop it in the bath!"

"Why did you do that?" Bob asked his wife.

"I didn't know she was going to do it!" Lyn said. "It's not like I hypnotised her to tie a rock to it and drop it off the bridge into the river."

After a moment's processing, the tension broke and all three laughed. Bob gently kissed his daughter's head.

"I'll take the back off it now and dry it out," he told her. "When I get home, I'll take a proper look at it."

Sharon nodded and silently spooned porridge into her mouth. A clatter from the letterbox in the hallway signalled the arrival of the post, and Lyn hurried to collect it.

"You know, Dad, most of my friends have radio-cassettes these days," Sharon ventured with her mother out of the room.

"They are a bit pricey, love."

"But think of the investment. I can record stuff off the radio rather than having to buy singles and play them on the record player in the living room."

"I'm not sure that you're supposed to do that, Sharon darling," Bob said, "and besides, I like listening to your music."

"Everyone does it. What's more, Lucy Barrow's dad has bought her a Sony Walkman."

"Who's Lucy Barrow?"

"She's in my A-level Home Ec. class. She's a bit stuck up, but she's OK."

"Well, her family must have a few quid, that's all I can say," Bob remarked, looking at his daughter's imploring eyes. "Maybe we can get you something for Christmas. I'll talk to your mum."

"You'll talk to me about what?" asked Lyn, walking back into the kitchen, reading the mail.

"Sharon was wondering about a radio-cassette player for Christmas."

"Have you seen these bills, Bob?" Lyn exploded. "We're still paying for new car tyres and you're promising radio-cassettes? We'll be lucky if we can afford a turkey at this rate."

"Steady on, love, it's not as bleak as that."

"Isn't it, Bob?"

They both broke off to look at their daughter, who was deliberately scraping the last of the porridge from the bowl as loudly as possible.

"It's OK, guys," Sharon said, "it was a silly suggestion. I know we can't afford it."

The doorbell rang.

"That's Pip!" she exclaimed, her mood instantly lighter. She kissed both her parents in quick succession and flung a large canvas bag over her shoulder. "Forget it, I'll see you both for tea. Bye."

"Bye, love," they chorused before the front door slammed shut.

"Maybe I could get one from my catalogue," mused Lyn. "Pay on instalments."

"And I'll have a look in the electric shop during lunch. Work's picking up, so I'll get overtime soon enough." After removing the batteries, Bob used a screwdriver to take off the back of the radio. He dabbed lightly inside with a piece of kitchen paper and peered knowledgably at the workings. "I should be able to get this going again, at least."

"My hero," Lyn whispered as she kissed him.

~ * ~ * ~

"Bus or walk?" asked Pip when Sharon appeared.

"Walk. It's a nice day, and who wants to get to school earlier than they have to?" Sharon glanced at her friend's shiny shoes. "Will you be OK walking in those?"

"I'll be fine."

Always stylishly dressed, Pip wore a black pencil skirt around her tiny waist, with a matching top and shoes; her short dark hair was perfectly coiffured, and her makeup was an excellent imitation of what she saw in the fashion magazines. Sharon was several inches taller, fuller-figured and less naturally coy than her petite friend, and (not unwittingly) drew the attention of even more boys.

"I have exciting news," Pip bubbled. "The career adviser says I've got a secretarial training place at Wilsons Packaging, when I've finished my course."

"Wow, that's great! Well done!"

"Thanks. Only just over six months of school left. Then, freedom! Think of me when you're slogging over your A-levels."

"I'll be busy missing you, that's what!"

The two girls had met, aged five years old, on their first day of primary school and had been best, inseparable friends ever since; both knew that the parting was going to be hard.

"Hey, six months is ages," Pip said, "so let's enjoy it."

"Yeah."

"I have other news... bigger news." Pip struggled to keep a straight face.

"Don't tell me that Tom has finally asked you out?"

"Yes!" squeaked Pip.

"Let's meet up with Gavin for lunch and you can give us the juicy details."

"Gavin? Do we have to?" Pip groaned.

"Don't be harsh. We're the only friends poor Gav has."

"Yeah, but he's not one of us, is he?"

"What, a girl?"

"No! I mean he's a geek who only talks about programming his computer… and you're in danger of giving him the wrong idea – he obviously fancies you."

Sharon was about to respond when she paused and slapped her forehead.

"I forgot to pick up my lunch! Shall we head up to town at lunch break and get something there?"

"Or we could go to the chippy on the industrial estate."

"Where you might bump into Tom? Philippa Raven, you are so transparent!" Sharon laughed at her friend's feigned innocent expression. "OK, let's meet in the foyer at lunch and walk up to the estate… and we'll give Gav the slip for one day."

~ * ~ * ~

When the lunch bell sounded, Gavin Knight hurried from his maths lesson to the sixth form common room, where Sharon and Pip would normally be sitting. The two girls had transformed his school life because his tormentors left him alone when he sat with them. To have a few minutes in every day with friendly voices (that were not a teacher or librarian) was a lifeline and Gavin adored both his saviours, but harboured no romantic delusions because logic told him of his limitations.

He sat alone in their normal corner of the common room for as long as he dared before realising that they weren't coming. Should he go and find the girls? Should he forget lunch and just go to the library? He rocked backwards and forwards in an agony of indecision, but at length he started to make a quick exit.

"Heads up!" someone shouted.

Gavin turned and was immediately struck in the face by a football. He reeled backwards, clasping his hands to his nose and lips, as his glasses fell to the ground. The familiar pungent smell and taste of blood filled his mouth and he sensed the fluid creeping from his nostrils. Pressing his handkerchief to his face with one hand, he squatted to feel around for his glasses with the other. Mocking teenage laughter filled his ears and the sting of tears filled his eyes.

"You spaz! You've got your greasy blood on my football!"

Managing to put his glasses on, he squinted at his tormentors and stood up. There was a clatter of plastic as his calculator fell from his old blue anorak and dropped to the hard floor. He panicked – he had worked for hours heaving crates around the cellar of the local pub to buy that Casio – but was too slow. A hostile Doc Marten boot cracked down on it and then kicked the shattered casing across the room. Gavin scampered after the device, snatched it up, and ran to the supervised sanctuary of the library. As he pinched his nose to stem the blood, he looked out of the window and spied the receding figures of Sharon and Pip exiting the school gate.

~ * ~ * ~

Sharon regretted not bringing Gavin because she spent much of her lunch time playing gooseberry. Tom, on his half-hour lunch break from the garage where he was training to be a mechanic, was maximising his opportunity to publicly make out with his new girlfriend, Pip.

"Got to get back to work," he said after surfacing for breath. "Walk me there?"

An ecstatic Pip looked at Sharon, who rolled her eyes with a smile and told them to go ahead. She had to get back for a double Geography lesson anyway, whereas Pip had typing practice and could easily slip in late and unnoticed.

A movement caught Sharon's eye as she passed by a light-industrial unit. Near the entrance, a young man was crouched beside a huge Honda motorcycle, lovingly cleaning the chrome until it sparkled in the autumn sunshine. He wore pale jeans and a faded red t-shirt which clung tightly to his muscular physique; Sharon's heartbeat quickened when she saw his bicep flexing as he rubbed the cloth back and forth. He glanced up and smiled.

"Hello, gorgeous," he said, bright blue eyes skewering her soul, "I've not seen you around here before. Where do you work, then?" He stood up, brushing his hands on the sides of his jeans.

"I don't work here, I'm just visiting a friend," Sharon replied.

"Oh, yeah?" he said almost as a challenge. He offered her a cigarette from a pack he plucked from his shirt pocket, and she found herself accepting. It was not her first smoke, she and Pip had both snaffled cigarettes from their mums' handbags as childish dares, but this was the first occasion she had been offered one as a woman, and it flattered her.

"Thank you," she said, her eyes involuntarily widening for a millisecond.

The young man flicked his silver lighter and held the flame out for her to light her cigarette. He then lit his own, and drew a deep breath, releasing it slowly and lengthily through his nostrils. Now he was standing up properly, Sharon realised he was well over six feet, with a broad chest and shoulders.

"Is this where you work?" she asked, giddy from the unfamiliar nicotine.

"At the moment. I'm a skilled toolmaker, so I'm in demand. I can easily pull in three hundred quid on a good week, so I go to whoever pays me."

"Wow!" Sharon was pretty sure her dad earned less.

"I'm Sam. Sam Grant."

"Hi, Sam, I'm Sharon. Sharon Wells." She held out her hand awkwardly, trying to seem mature.

"Not sure you'd want to shake my hand, Sharon. It's oily from working on the bike."

She nodded and let her arm fall back to her side. "I wouldn't mind, though. My dad's always making a mess working on some project or another. He works on his old Cortina every weekend – drives Mum mad."

"What model is it?"

"The Cortina? It's a mark three – er – GXL, I think."

"With a vinyl roof? Very nice. Good taste, your dad."

"Men and cars!" Sharon rolled her eyes.

"And bikes," Sam pointed out with a leg-jellying grin.

"I don't know much about them but yours is nice."

"Maybe I'll give you a ride sometime."

They lapsed into silence, both staring at the Honda.

"You still haven't told me where you work," Sam finally said.

"I don't." Sharon revelled in her brief enigmatic mystery.

"A lady of leisure, eh?"

"I'm in the sixth form," Sharon came clean, "doing my A-levels."

"Oh, A-levels? Bit of a brainbox, are you? What ones are you doing then?"

"Home Economics, Geography and – um – Human Biology." Sharon's eyes once again flashed when mentioning the last subject.

"Well, they sound very useful," Sam observed, with the return of that cheeky, heart-quickening smile. "Mind you, toolmaking's just what I'm doing for the moment. Long term, I've got a band – I'm singer and lead guitar. We're called Black Metal Armour."

"Wow! Should I have heard of it?"

"Not yet, but one day."

"Oh!" Sharon glanced at her watch and squeaked with embarrassing unsophistication. "I'm late, I have to go."

"I'll drive you. I've got a spare helmet."

To her own surprise, Sharon agreed. Sam walked into the building and returned with two helmets, a red one, which he put on, and a white one which he handed to her. He pointed to her legs.

"That skirt's not ideal but I reckon it's long enough to hide your blushes. Ever ridden pillion before?"

"No."

"Then climb on behind and hang tight onto me. And don't wriggle around."

Exhilarated, Sharon clung to Sam, feeling his warm flesh beneath the red t-shirt as the bike rapidly accelerated and decelerated through the town's streets. The journey took only a few minutes, but in that time, she found a new, sensual, primitive element of her personality that she could never acknowledge.

Sam revved the engine twice before he switched it off, catching the attention of a few straggling fourth-form girls who were making their way to the school's entrance. When Sharon dismounted and removed her helmet, they gave audible gasps of recognition and admiration before scampering off to spread their fresh gossip.

"Thank you," said Sharon, handing her helmet to Sam.

"You are very welcome." He flipped up his visor. "We've got a gig at The White Hart on Friday night, why don't you come?"

"I don't know…" Sharon wavered, "I've a pile of homework."

"Leave it, come to the gig. You know you want to," Sam enchanted her. "Wear something special and you can come on stage and do some backing vocals."

"But you haven't heard me sing!"

"I can tell your voice is good," he lied with a wink. "Anyway, you're so pretty that no one'll care about your voice. Come on, be at The White Hart for seven-thirty."

"OK," she too readily acquiesced.

As Sharon raced up the school steps, the Honda burst up the road with a roar. She wondered whether her heart was racing from running or because she was more excited than she had ever been before.

~ * ~ * ~

"What's this I hear about you turning up on the back of some bloke's motorbike?" Pip quizzed Sharon the moment they met at the school gates to walk home.

"Oh, just a boy I know giving me a lift." Sharon savoured her friend's ill-concealed fascination and decided to make her beg, until excitement and Pip's perseverance prevailed, and she told of her mini adventure.

"You're never going to go on Friday, are you?" Pip asked, tangibly incredulous. "The White Hart's rough from what I've heard."

"I am. Are you coming too? You can bring big strong Tom to protect you."

"Maybe." Pip was appalled by the prospect, but loyal to her friend. "I'll ask him later. What'll you tell your parents?"

"That I've been invited to a party – it's not exactly lying, is it? Anyway, I'm sixteen, not a kid. No, my big problem is finding something trendy to wear. I'm skint."

"You always are," Pip laughed.

As they walked on, deep in conversation, Pip suddenly spotted a familiar figure shuffling forlornly a little way ahead of them.

"That's Gavin! Let's catch him up and say sorry for deserting him at lunch."

Gavin's swollen face told them their decision had cost him dear, but he insisted they had nothing to reproach themselves for. However, after she heard about his prized calculator, Sharon resolved to solve that problem at the same time as she got a new outfit.

~ * ~ * ~

The following afternoon, Sharon cornered her sports master just before double games. While PE was still notionally compulsory in the sixth form, the school and the teacher were far from judicious in policing attendance. Nevertheless, she played safe by feigning period pains and asking to be excused. The embarrassed master readily agreed, and Sharon slipped unnoticed from the school gates.

When she was twelve, Sharon stole sweets from the corner shop and shared them with her best friend. However, Pip was outraged when she learned the truth, and made Sharon promise never to shoplift again. That promise was about to be broken, and not for the first time.

A few moments of cunning in the changing rooms of the department store meant Sharon was now the proud 'owner' of a short white off-the-shoulder dress; not tight, but leaving little to the imagination, it had the added advantage of being easily worn under her existing clothes as she walked nonchalantly through the exit.

The shoes were more complicated to obtain, but she knew a small independent store staffed by an older lady; Sharon managed to confuse her just enough to slip a pair of white stilettos into her bag unnoticed.

The calculator posed the biggest obstacle, as the more expensive ones were kept in a locked cabinet at the stationery shop. She waited until a young male sales assistant was free and played dumb, flirting with him just enough for him to leave the open cabinet unattended; a few seconds were enough for her to pluck a Casio from the small stack at the bottom of the cupboard. Nobody would notice its absence until the stock-take, and no one would remember her by then.

A surge of guilt came over her. When had she become a thief? In the past, she had lifted a few bars of chocolate, maybe a cheap set of bangles, and the occasional copy of Smash Hits magazine ("Shops expect that sort of thing, don't they?" she said aloud to no one in particular), but what she had just done was proper theft. Why and for what? Because a man she barely knew asked her to sing in a band? It was preposterous… but, there was no turning back. She couldn't return the stuff, could she? Then there was Sam; perfect, beautiful, powerful Sam. Sharon knew it was love at first sight – he was a real man and he would expect a real woman, not a timid schoolgirl. There was no choice; destiny called, and she was answering.

The autumn sun was slowly obscured by a black cloud with brilliant silver-gold edges, and she wrapped the old greatcoat that she wore tightly around her, shivering with excitement.

~ * ~ * ~

At his desk in his attic bedroom, Gavin crouched over his homework listening to the rain drumming on the roof. He paused from differential equations to blow on his fingers, partly to relieve writer's cramp but mainly because he was cold. There was a knock at the door and his mother came in with a cup of hot chocolate.

"Is that a new calculator?" she asked. "It's very smart."

"It's got everything – even Binary and Octal and Hexadecimal options."

"I don't know what any of those words mean, Gav, but I do know you're lucky to have such a kind friend who bought that for you. It must have been expensive."

"I think it was, at least thirty pounds. I felt a bit bad about it. I offered to pay Sharon back, but she wouldn't let me. She said she got a special price, but I don't know how."

"Well, maybe you could have her over for dinner, to say thank you?"

"She wouldn't come, Mum. I don't have friends like that."

"To spend thirty pounds on you? I think she might like you, Gav."

"Mum, girls don't like me like that, I'm too awkward," Gavin insisted. "She just felt sorry for me, don't read more into it. I don't think I'll ever find a girl who likes me like that."

"One day, a nice girl is going to be very lucky to have you as a husband. In the meantime, drink your chocolate and then come downstairs because the vicar is coming at eight-thirty to discuss the banns for your sister's wedding."

Gavin shrugged her hand from his shoulder and remained mute until she left. He returned to his work, but his glasses were too steamed up to see.

~ * ~ * ~

By midday on Thursday, Sharon was starting to panic. She had awoken in the thick darkness of the early hours of the morning with doubts cascading through her mind: was Sam serious asking her to the pub? Was it a date? Would she look foolish? What if her parents found out? These doubts were now a cacophonous maelstrom in her mind.

"Pip," she said when they met for lunch, "I need to go back up to the industrial estate. Come with me? You could see Tom."

"Definitely, but what about Gav? We can't leave him like last time."

"He can come too. Oh, and talking of Gavin, you still owe me for half that calculator."

"Twenty quid," grumbled Pip. "You might have asked me first. That's two Saturdays' pay. And where did you find the money for it anyway? You're always skint."

"That's my business. Just let me have the cash when you've got it."

"You've such a good heart." Pip fished in her bag, pulling out a pink envelope with her friend's name neatly written in the middle. "Here's the money – I hadn't forgotten."

"Thanks," Sharon said, devoid of guilt. "Oh, look, there's Gavin."

"Come up to the industrial estate with us, Gav," they chorused when they caught up with him.

"Yes, we both have people to see," added Pip.

Gavin acquiesced, and the three friends hurried through the streets to the comparatively broad open roads of the industrial estate. Tom was in his usual place in the queue to buy a pasty from a grimy trailer takeaway and within a few moments he had Pip attached to his face.

"Hi, Shaz," Tom greeted Sharon, breaking off from the kiss.

"This is our friend Gavin," said Pip. Her boyfriend gave a barely perceptible nod before turning away. She gave him a 'that was rude' glare and dug into his ribs, generating a faintly audible and not un-contemptuous, "Hi."

"I'm just going to see my friend," Sharon said. "If I'm not out by the time you leave, head back without me, OK?"

She left before they could reply, so Gavin, temporarily deserted, found a low wall to sit on and eat his sandwiches, while he flicked through a well-thumbed computer magazine. Consequently, he was one of the few men present who didn't watch the receding figure of Sharon, whose shapely form was emphasised by her tight pale jeans.

When Pip, at length, joined Gavin, they walked back to school together, making small talk but both worrying about their mutual friend.

~ * ~ * ~

Sharon soon arrived at the unit where she had met Sam, relieved to see his motorcycle sitting in the car park. Tentatively, she pushed on the door of the building and peered into the workshop.

"Hello?" she called out, stepping into the comparative gloom. The sound of machinery rumbled and whined from various points, but Sam was not amongst the operators. A small door to her right led into an office where a young blonde woman sat behind one of three grey desks.

"Can I help you?" the woman asked, placing the sandwich she was eating on the desk beside her typewriter.

"I'm sorry to bother you, I was looking for Sam. I'm a friend."

"I expect he's in the breakroom," the woman said as she stood up. She led the way through the long workshop towards a door at the far end. As Sharon followed, she became mesmerised by her sophisticated escort's bright red dress and matching high heeled shoes and by the way she walked, with deliberate slow steps, one foot placed perfectly in front of the other, inviting the eye to follow the sensual sway of her hips.

Sharon entered the breakroom and stopped short, immediately struck by countless pictures of half-naked women stuck on the walls; calendars, newspaper pages, and magazine centrefolds were taped to the crumbling plaster or pinned to the notice board. She wondered how on earth the secretary tolerated working in a place with such smut on display. Sam was sitting at a table, smoking a cigarette and reading the paper.

"I've found a long-lost little friend of yours, Sam," the blonde lady announced with a playful little wink as she left the room.

"Well, hello, Sharon," Sam beamed, his welcoming voice betraying no hint of surprise. "I thought you might be popping by. Want a cuppa?" He noted her eyes dancing around the images on the wall. "Shocking, isn't it?" He stood up, took her by the arm and led her out. "I work with some animals here, I really do. Not my sort of thing, but you've got to live and let live. Why don't I give you a tour of the place?"

Sharon nodded, pleased to be leaving the smut behind and reassured by Sam's averred disapproval. They walked through the workshop once again, stopping intermittently to look at a machine or say hello to a co-worker. When they passed via some large double doors into a small warehouse, the sudden silence was eerie, and Sharon realised her trainers squeaked on the shiny floor.

The storage racking stretched up to the metal roof and was filled with metal sheets, plastic pipes, cardboard boxes of components, and even an incongruous rusty bicycle. The natural light grew dimmer as they walked further inside.

"Sorry to bother you, Sam," Sharon said, "but—"

"Oh, you're no bother," he interrupted, "it's a pleasure to see you again. I've been thinking about you."

"Have you?"

"Oh, yes. I hope you've not come here to tell me you can't make it tomorrow?"

"No, not at all," she answered urgently and earnestly. "I just want to be sure you're serious about me be being invited."

"Very serious. I hope you'll sing too."

"But I won't know the words!"

"Don't worry, you'll be echoing lines or going la-la. There'll be another girl there on backing vocals, so follow her lead. Like I said, you're so pretty no one will care what you sound like."

"Did you mean it?" she asked.

Sam took Sharon by the arm and gently led her into the gloom between two tall stacks of racking. There, he looked at her full in the eyes for what seemed like an age, as if making some profound decision. Placing a hand to the back of her head he leaned in to kiss her. His breath was smoky but intoxicating, the pressure on her lips was perfect, and she found her eyes closing and her arms moving up to wrap as far as they could around his powerful upper body. Deeper, longer, timeless; she didn't know how long it lasted, but when the kiss broke, she continued to hold him for several seconds, as she didn't trust her legs to support her.

"Promise you'll come tomorrow?" Sam whispered, eliciting a nod. "Good. Now, we'd better get you back for classes."

As intense as the moment had been, it was now truly over, and they hurried to his motorbike.

~ * ~ * ~

"You're staying over at Pip's both Friday and Saturday night? I don't think that's a good idea. What about your homework?"

"I'll get it done, don't worry, Mum," Sharon replied, irritated by her mother's interference.

"Anyway, doesn't Pip work on Saturdays?"

"She does. I'll head to the library and do my homework until she's finished. Then we'll see a film. I think they're still showing *Ghostbusters*."

"You saw that months ago, Sharon. You seem to have money to burn!"

Bob was sitting on a kitchen chair and unlacing his work boots. He interjected, "What's the harm? The girls like to have a bit of fun. We did when we were her age."

"I want her to have the chances I never had. And getting good A-levels is important."

"Mum, I'm going to do my homework, now please get off my back about it!" Sharon stormed upstairs.

Lyn slapped the kitchen counter and screwed her face up, frustrated with her handling of the argument.

"She'll be OK, love," Bob said with his customary gentleness; he was always the soothing oil on her troubled waters. "She's doing well at school. She's smart, like her mum, and Pip won't lead our Sharon astray."

Lyn rummaged fruitlessly inside a drawer before slamming it shut.

"I miss smoking," she moaned.

"What did you mean about chances you never had?" Bob asked, fearing the answer. "Would you rather things were different?"

"I wouldn't change a thing, Bob," she laughed. "You're the best man I have ever known, and more than I ever deserved. No, I wouldn't change one solitary second. Now, come here and give me a kiss."

Unaware of her parents' conversation, Sharon walked up and down her bedroom wearing her new shoes, trying to move like the blonde woman at Sam's workplace; after several minor ankle twists and a leg cramp, she was getting the hang of it.

Elvis Presley's singing wafted up the stairs, meaning her mother had put her favourite record on the turntable. Elvis, Cliff Richard or Tommy Steele playing was a signal that Lyn was upset or troubled by something. Sharon's conscience prickled. Eventually the music stopped, and she heard her parents come upstairs to bed.

"Good night, love," they both called.

"Good night," she cooed back, "love you both."

Chapter 2

Pip was incensed. Her best friend had just dropped a bombshell during their walk to school on Friday morning.

"You're inviting yourself to stay for two nights and you're only telling me now?"

"You're right, sorry." Sharon was sheepish. "I panicked. I know what your mum's like – is it OK?"

Pip, soft-hearted, relented with a sigh. "Yeah, it'll be OK. Just don't forget I have to be up for work tomorrow by seven-thirty. I just hope Daniel isn't awake in the night again."

"I won't forget," Sharon promised. "Is your brother still wetting himself?"

"Yeah," Pip replied, pleased the topic had changed. "I hope he's not being bullied at school. I'll leave it to Mum, she says he'll grow out of it."

They walked on in silence until they reached the school gates.

"Well, I'm off to the delights of Human Biology," Sharon announced. "You've got a free, haven't you?"

"It's not a free," replied Pip in a passable imitation of the Deputy Headmistress, "it is a study period, for furthering your understanding of your chosen subjects. But yes, I'm off to work on my project."

"Swot!" Sharon called over her shoulder.

Pip found Gavin in the library, working hard on an essay and surrounded by textbooks and scraps of paper covered with his notes.

"Hi," she whispered, sitting at the cubicle next to him. She unpacked her files and tried to work but was unable to concentrate. "I'm worried about Sharon."

"Why?" he asked. "I hope she's OK, I'd do anything to thank her for the calculator she gave me – did you know about that?"

Pip was taken aback. Had Sharon not told Gavin that she had contributed half the cost? However, there were more important things to worry about.

"She's got herself involved with some bloke in a band. She's going to one of their gigs tonight and she's even going to be singing with them." Pip modulated her voice as the librarian glanced in their direction.

"That doesn't sound too bad."

"But it's at The White Hart. It's rough there. I'm going and Tom's coming with me."

"Sharon is sensible, and if she isn't, you are," Gavin reassured her. "In fact, you're the most sensible of us all, Pip."

"Thanks. That's the nicest thing anyone's said to me in a long time."

~ * ~ * ~

Sharon stopped off at the shops after school and acquired all the makeup she thought she might need to look good on stage. She hurried home, took her new dress and shoes from their hiding places, and packed them in a small overnight suitcase, along with her new cosmetics and some other essentials. Keeping her mother's protestations in mind, she also took her schoolbag and cantered down the stairs.

"I'm off!" she shouted. "See you Sunday."

"Bye, love," Lyn called, emerging into the hall from the kitchen, but the front door was already closing.

Sharon almost ran the half-mile to Pip's home, a mid-terrace '70s house built in a mock-Georgian style, with sandstone walls and white-squared windows. As the autumn twilight darkened about her, she rang the bell and stood impatiently until Mr Raven opened the door and genially ushered her upstairs.

Pip worked on Sharon's hair and makeup with an expert hand; vigorous back-combing and excessive quantities of hairspray, bright eyeshadow, and thick eyeliner, gave a smouldering, fashionable look.

"You could pass for twenty-one," Pip declared, standing back to admire her work.

Sharon put on her dress, luxuriating as its smooth, cool fabric caressed her skin. Pip glanced at her in the mirror and then turned around to look properly.

"I don't recognise that, is it new?" she asked running her fingers along the hem.

"Quite new, I suppose," Sharon replied, extracting the shoes from her case. She stepped into them and instantly became several inches taller.

Pip exhaled loudly.

"That's a bit raunchy!" she remarked. "You certainly look like a pop star now." She peered closer at the stilettos. "Are they new too? You'll break your ankle in them – I've never seen you in anything other than flats or trainers. I bet you'll wobble loads."

Sharon sashayed confidently up and down the room.

"I take it back," said Pip with genuine admiration. "Who knew that Sharon Wells was such a tart?"

"I'm not!" Sharon responded disproportionately to her friend's joke because it struck a nerve. Then she calmed and smiled. "Sorry – it's supposed to be sophisticated."

"Well it would be more sophisticated if you'd taken the price tag off the sole," Pip chuckled. "Come here and I'll pick it off for you."

She knelt on the carpet while Sharon rested one hand on the wardrobe to balance and lifted a foot off the floor. Like a blacksmith shoeing a filly, Pip scratched at the small white label, but froze in shock when she read the price.

"How did you afford these?"

"A present." Sharon realised she must have inadvertently taken something too expensive to easily explain.

"Who would give you these as a present? Not your mum and dad, that's for sure."

"I meant the money was a present!"

Realisation hit Pip. The dress looked new too, and it was a good brand. There was no way that her friend could have had the funds to buy them, even with ten Christmases of money gifts. She became aware of Sharon glaring at her.

"You are a self-righteous little prig!" Sharon snapped before Pip could speak. "You think I stole them, don't you?"

"No!" squeaked Pip, cowed by the aggression. "I'm sorry, I'd never accuse you of anything like that."

"Good. Now finish getting ready, Tom will be here soon," Sharon instructed. She turned away from her friend to put on her earrings and necklace.

Turning her attention to her own preparations, Pip finished her makeup and checked her own outfit in the mirror. Wearing a pair of tartan trousers, her shiny black flat-heeled shoes and a cream knitted sweater, she felt rather inadequate next to her newly glamorous friend, but they were going to a gig at The White Hart, not The Ritz.

Sharon took a long mackintosh that belonged to Pip and draped it over herself, partly for warmth and partly because she didn't want the Raven family to see what she was wearing. Outside a horn beeped and a car engine revved.

"That's Tom!" Pip declared. The two girls excitedly exited the house as quickly as possible and climbed into the pale blue Ford Escort, Pip sitting beside her boyfriend and the budding pop star sliding into the back.

Sharon ran her hand over the black moulded-vinyl seat beside her. She could see Tom's eyes, illuminated by the amber street lights, glancing from time to time in the rear-view mirror, but she couldn't be sure if he was looking at her.

"I like your car, Tom," she said softly. "Is it very fast?"

There was an unmistakeable pressure as he accelerated for a few moments.

"Not bad," he boasted. "You scrub up nice."

"Oh, this is what I wear when I don't care how I look."

Tom sensed his girlfriend's discomfort at the conversation.

"You look nice too, Pip," he said, placing his hand on her thigh and squeezing it, though his eyes still flicked lustfully back to the mirror from time to time. "Yeah, I like this car, but if things go well, I'm getting an Opel Manta when I turn eighteen."

"Oh, Tom, I'd be so excited if you got a Manta," Pip bubbled with enthusiasm. "I couldn't keep my hands off you."

"That's the idea," he said, eyes fixed back on the mirror. He could see Sharon smile.

~ * ~ * ~

Gavin was spending more time rearranging the food on his plate than eating it.

"Are you alright, dear?" asked his mother. "Got something on your mind? Have those bullies been at you again?"

"No more than usual."

Gavin's older sister, who was flicking through the pages of a bridal magazine chipped in, "I don't know why you don't just belt one of them."

"Karen!" their mother exclaimed. "Don't let me hear that kind of talk again, and certainly don't let your dad hear it. You know how he feels about violence."

Karen sighed, "Yes, I know, but we aren't talking about war, we're talking about thumping some thug who makes our Gav's life a misery."

"Hitting people is never the answer."

"OK, Mum." Karen rolled her eyes and diverted her attention to her brother. "So, what is the matter if it's not the bullies, Gav?"

"I'm worried about my friend Sharon. She may be in trouble."

"What sort of trouble?"

"I'm not sure really, but Pip seemed worried."

Gavin's mother reached across the kitchen table and held her son's forearm with a vice-like grip gaining his full attention.

"It is your duty to help others in life," she insisted, unintentionally melodramatic, "especially friends."

~ * ~ * ~

Pip wrinkled her nose as they walked into The White Hart. It was a utilitarian place with curious anachronisms such as wooden beams on the ceiling and blue linoleum on the floor around the bar, dark oak tables with plastic bucket chairs, and an old-fashioned bar skittles game between the modern jukebox and cigarette vending machine. There were several other patrons, mainly men, some leaning against the bar, others lolling in chairs, and nearly all of them adding to the smoky haze that already hung in the room. The three newcomers made their way to the bar and Tom ostentatiously opened his wallet.

"What will you have, girls?"

Pip asked for half a shandy, and Sharon, a Bacardi and Coke. Tom nodded and ordered them along with a pint of Guinness for himself and a box of matches. He wandered to the cigarette machine, sorting his change as he went, and fed some coins into the slot. With a loud clunk, the carton dropped into the dispensing tray; he tore the cellophane wrapping off while he studied the jukebox. The drinks were ready, so the two girls carried them to him.

"Where's your friend Sam then, Sharon?" Pip asked, glancing nervously around the bar.

"He'll be here," Sharon replied, less certain than she sounded.

"Fancy a tune?" Tom nodded towards the playlist displayed above the jukebox.

"It's all sixties stuff or Status Quo," Pip grumbled. "No Duran Duran or Spandau Ballet?"

Tom offered cigarettes to the girls, who both accepted, and took one himself. He struck a match, holding it out for them to use and then quickly lighting his own before the flame reached his fingers.

"What's wrong with The Quo?" he asked, glaring at his date. "We all like them in the workshop."

"Nothing, sorry," Pip panicked, scared of upsetting Tom on their first proper outing together.

"Here's a good one – Laura Branigan, 'Self-Control'," Sharon interjected, playfully holding out her hand to Tom until he dropped some coins into her palm. Having selected the track, she slipped Pip's coat from her shoulders, folded it over the back of a nearby chair and began bopping to the music. She took dainty puffs of her cigarette, anxious for a sign of Sam, and revelled in the stares she drew from the men in the bar.

"It's gone seven-thirty," Pip said, hoping that Sharon might decide to give up and leave. At that moment, Sam appeared through a door at the far end of the room, accompanied by a petite Asian woman and a huge young man, who Pip thought resembled an ogre.

"You look great, Sharon!" Sam declared.

The Asian girl, about eighteen by Sharon's estimation, nodded and smiled broadly. She wore an electric-blue blouse, a shiny black mini-skirt, and, most strikingly, a studded leather collar to match her purely decorative belt.

"You did well, Sam," she said, cocking her head to one side and surveying her new colleague. She held out her hand. "Hello, Sharon, I'm Tracy and I'll be joining you on backing vocals."

"And I'm Ed," said the ogre. "I play bass." At least six foot six tall, broadly built and with the complexion of a cauliflower, he seemed to dwarf Sam. The two men wore black t-shirts and jeans.

"Nice to meet you," Sharon said to her new bandmates. "These are my friends, Pip and Tom."

Poor Pip felt laughably tiny when Ed shook her hand. She didn't like the look of this band, nor the way her boyfriend was salivating over its two female members.

Tracy suddenly noticed the song playing and gave a sensuous shimmy. "Oh, I love this song! Did you pick it, Sharon? Great choice."

"We've been setting up in the function room next door," Sam explained. "Now that you're here, Sharon, we'll do a sound test. Let's get you another drink first, what would you three like?"

Sharon gulped the contents of her glass. "Bacardi and Coke, please."

Pip, who had hardly touched her shandy, declined, but Tom downed his Guinness and signalled that he'd like another.

"Careful, Tom," whispered Pip, "don't forget you're driving."

"I hope you're not going to be a bloody nag all night," he snapped back.

"I'm sorry, I just wanted to remind you, that's all."

"A big guy like Tom can handle another," Sam simultaneously flattered Tom and belittled Pip. He ordered a round of drinks for everyone and two further pints of bitter for the band members still setting up in the function room. "Come on, Sharon, we need to finish getting ready. Pip, Tom – are you guys OK waiting here until the gig starts?"

Barely giving them time to nod, he led Sharon by the hand into the function room with Tracy and Ed following, carrying the drinks. Tom, along with most of the other men present, watched Sharon and Tracy leave with more than a little lechery in his eyes but at length returned his attention to his girlfriend.

"This place is a dump," he said, with some justification. "Sharon seems OK, let's go somewhere else."

"I can't leave her!"

"We'll come back later."

Pip was torn. She hated the place too, but what if Sharon needed her? She shook her head.

"I'm not hanging around here," Tom said, palpably irritated. "The glasses are dirty and none of my mates are here. Some first date this is, Philippa, babysitting your friend in a dump!"

Pip began examining her glass with an expression of such utter disgust and revulsion on her face that she had the unintentional effect of making her boyfriend laugh.

"I can't leave Sharon here on her own. Please don't be cross," she insisted and implored, "please don't leave. Once the gig starts, it could be fun."

"OK," Tom relented, "let's give it a try."

In the function room, Sharon was introduced to the remaining band members. Frank, the drummer, was thirtyish and doing a poor job of hiding his receding hairline; he had a wiry build, thin unshaven features, yellowing skin and dead, grey eyes. By contrast, Darren the keyboardist looked like a child (though he was nineteen) and sported jet-black dyed spiky hair and heavy eye makeup; he rejected the urban 'tough-guy' look the other men cultivated, though he downed his pint with equal alacrity.

Tracy took Sharon's arm and led her to a quieter corner where she talked through the routines; most of the songs were familiar and those that weren't only required 'la-la-la' ("If you're not sure, just mime," seemed good advice). As they chatted, the occasional whine of an amplifier or twang of a guitar drifted across the room; Frank knocked over his cymbals at one point with a loud clatter, eliciting a round of applause from his bandmates.

Sharon detected a slight foreign accent in her new friend and was intrigued – being from a small rural town meant that the only non-white people she knew were a pair of Sri Lankan twins in the lower years of her school, and the owners of the Chinese takeaway on the high street.

"Can I ask, are you from China, or maybe Hong Kong?" she ventured, worried about seeming rude.

"No, Vietnam."

"How did you end up in this poky little town?"

A shadow fell across Tracy's features. "My mother and I fled our home after the war ended, but she passed away soon after we arrived in Britain. I was put in a children's home near here, which is where I met Ed."

"So, is Ed your boyfriend?"

"Sometimes. Well, he may like to think he is," Tracy giggled, the shadow lifting. "But no time for chat now, let's rehearse." She started to sway her body. "This is the kind of dance we should do, and we need to make sure we are synchronised."

The moves were basic and unoriginal – moving alternating knees forward and back, whilst swinging the opposing arm, with a slight wiggle of the hips in time to the music. Soon the two young women were in time, and Tracy broke off to give Sharon a prolonged hug.

"Nervous?" she asked.

"A bit." Sharon took a tiny bite of her lower lip.

"Me too. Let's get another drink."

"I don't know if I should. I've already had two."

"Three's the charm!" Tracy gave a conspiratorial wink. She called out to their fellow band members, "Which of you gallant heroes will get us girls another drink?"

Sam signalled to Ed, who hurried from the room.

"How old are you, Sharon, sixteen?" Tracy asked. "You look older tonight, but I can tell."

"Yes, but I can hold my drink," Sharon insisted. "To be honest, I was worried they may not serve us here."

"In this place? They'd serve a seven-year-old boy scout, if he had the money. Anyone younger than that wouldn't be able to see over the bar to order. I only asked because you seem interested in Sam, and I want you to understand what you're getting into. You seem a bit innocent."

"I know what I'm doing!" Sharon responded hotly, pride and indignation bursting forth. "I can look after myself."

"I'm sure you can, I didn't mean any offence, sweetie." Tracy lightly touched the younger woman's cheek with the very tips of her fingers.

"It's OK, forget it." Sharon cooled as quickly as she had flared up.

"I know we are going to be best of friends, Sharon."

Ed returned with a tray of drinks. He was accompanied by a young woman who sat on one of the chairs placed around the perimeter of the room and sipped a glass of cola. She wore large brown glasses, a bottle green shirt with a long suede skirt, a fashionable combination ten years earlier. Her long mousey hair framed an expressionless face.

"Who's she?" Sharon asked, taking her drink from the tray.

"That's Hannah, Darren's sister," Ed replied. "Chalk and cheese."

"OK, boys and girls!" Sam clapped his hands loudly. "It's show time!"

~ * ~ * ~

Pip and Tom had remained in the main saloon bar, making small talk and wishing the evening over as soon as possible. The pub had started to fill up as people arrived for the gig. Pip recognised several pupils from her school; most were fellow sixth-formers (some responsible for Gavin's misery) but others came from lower years.

"I don't believe it," she whispered. "That's Sally Thompson. She's only fourteen. I used to babysit her."

"Who are you to criticise? You're under age too," Tom huffed, uninterested, watching people arriving.

"And you," Pip retorted, hurt by his tone.

"Only for another six weeks."

Tom had recognised a familiar face and long red hair in the crowd but said nothing. The woman was walking towards the lavatories through the growing horde of patrons.

"I'm going to the Gents," he told Pip. "Watch my jacket."

Navigating his way to the toilets, he came to a small vestibule. To the left was a door marked 'Ladies' and to the right one marked 'Gents'. He took neither but stood in the little hallway and lit a cigarette. Sure enough, a few moments later, the door to the left swung open and his redhead emerged; her eyes widened with pleasure when she saw him.

"Oh, I thought I spotted you earlier," she purred. "I said to myself, there's Tom with his new young lady. Is she your little girlfriend, Tom?"

"What if she is?"

"Oh, it doesn't bother me at all. She looks very sweet."

"She is."

"But not much fun?"

"Not like you, Mandy."

"A bit like the bloke I'm seeing. Likes to splash the cash, but a bit of a disappointment in other respects."

Tom placed his arms round her waist, "Missing a real man?"

"Maybe," she teased, maintaining eye contact. "Tell you what, why don't I tell my little man I've got a headache and you tell your little woman some load of bollocks, and we meet at my place in half an hour?"

"I shouldn't leave her," Tom hesitated in a rare moment of selflessness, but couldn't resist the dainty morsel presenting herself, "but she shouldn't have asked me to this dump, should she?"

"Good boy. You know it makes sense."

She returned to the bar and Tom waited to finish his cigarette before following. As he rejoined Pip, he could see his redhead temptress making her excuses to a group of people seated at a table near the jukebox. A man stood up, seemingly offering to leave with her, but she shook her head, gently pushed him back in his chair, and kissed his forehead. With a little wave to her friends, she left, but not before a lingering glance at Tom.

"Pip, I've got to go," he said.

"Why?" She was startled.

"Bellyache. Probably the beer. We won't be coming here again – thanks a bunch!"

"But you know I can't leave!"

"I'm not asking you to, am I? You'll be OK with Sharon. Sam will see you two home safe." Tom saw Pip's eyes glisten with worried tears. "You already said you know some of the other people here. I've got to go! Here's a fiver in case you need a taxi home. It's a loan, mind, so I want it back."

"OK." Pip miserably took the five-pound note and anxiously twirled it into a tube, trying not to cry. "I'm very sorry the place was so horrid, and it's made you ill. You won't dump me, will you?"

"Stop making a scene! It's just bellyache. Look, why don't I pop by during your lunch hour tomorrow?"

Pip brightened a little.

"That would be nice. Twelve-thirty, at the front of the shop?"

Tom was already on his way out but gave a thumbs-up to show that he had heard. Pip set her barely touched shandy on the table, gazing at it suspiciously. If the dirty glass had made Tom ill, then better safe than sorry. She joined the group of fellow sixth-formers, smiling and feigning laughter, an isolated figure, waiting until the function room doors opened.

~ * ~ * ~

As soon as Ed started the familiar bass guitar for Frankie Goes to Hollywood's 'Two Tribes', Sharon knew the gig would be amazing. From her elevated position on the tiny stage, she could see the room full of gyrating bodies, but there was no sign of Pip. The programme was planned to give each band member a short break every so often without having to pause the performance in any way; during these rests, they downed more drinks, but adrenalin and excitement meant Sharon was buzzing rather than drunk. While Frank sang 'Golden Brown' with Darren accompanying on the keyboard, Sharon took the opportunity to try to find Pip. Before she got more than a few paces, Sam met her and pressed a fresh drink in her hand.

"No wandering off!" he shouted over the music. "Unless you need the loo?"

Sharon shook her head. "Trying to find Pip."

"She'll be fine, she's with Tom," Sam insisted, leading her back to the stage.

After the last song finished, Sharon found herself surrounded by people wanting to talk to her. She was asked out on four dates (which she declined) and several of her fellow sixth-formers said how great she was and how they never knew she was in a band.

"You look incredible," one girl told her. "It took me ten minutes to recognise you. I only knew when I spotted Pip – if she's here, you're bound to be too."

Pip! Sharon had forgotten about Pip. She made polite talk and scanned the people milling about the room but couldn't see her friend. Finally, as the last stragglers began to depart, two women remained: Hannah, who was still seated in the same spot she had been before the show started, and Pip, who was hovering uncomfortably by the door. Sharon beckoned her over.

"You were very good," Pip said when they embraced, "and you looked very pretty up there."

"Thanks, I'm so happy! Where's Tom? What did he think of it?"

"Tom left before it started. He wasn't feeling well. He lent us money for a cab home. Do you think you'll be ready to leave soon?"

"I'll check with Sam. Wait in the bar and I'll come and find you."

Darren and Frank were busy disconnecting and disassembling various bits of kit, while Ed and Sam carted assorted items out through doors behind the makeshift stage. Sharon hurried after them, down a narrow corridor of uneven whitewashed walls, emerging into a courtyard at the rear of the pub. The men were heaving the gear into the back of a Bedford van while Tracy and Hannah were standing nearby, casually sharing a joint.

"What's happening now?" Sharon asked Sam.

"Half an hour to load up the van and then back to my place for a debrief."

"I don't know if I can go," Sharon agonised.

"I expect all the band to be there. Are you in or out?"

"But I promised Pip we wouldn't be late home."

"Well, she can go, can't she? Everyone will crash at mine. Just tell her and Tom to head off."

"But Tom left. He wasn't well."

"Don't worry," Sam reassured Sharon, putting an arm around her shoulders and signalling Tracy, "I'll sort something out. You're coming to my place, yes?"

Sharon's defences were down.

"Yes, but I need to be sure Pip's OK. Maybe we could drop her off?"

"Leave it with me. Let me finish giving Ed a hand first."

Sam walked away, but Tracy was standing beside Sharon now, slipping her soft arm around her waist. She passed her the joint, "Here, try some of this. It's good."

"Well, this is a night for firsts," Sharon said as she drew the smoke into her lungs. Tracy kissed her cheek and they both giggled.

Pip's disapproving voice broke through the night air, "Sharon, what's going on?"

"Don't worry, Pip, Sam's organising getting you home. I'm going for a band debrief."

"I can't wait up for you, I've got work."

"It's fine, I'll crash at Sam's."

Pip grabbed her friend's arm and dragged her to a more private corner.

"What's got into you?" she asked, sounding like her own mother. "Smoking drugs and staying over with people you hardly know?"

"Stop being a prude, we've talked about trying pot!"

"Maybe so, but not here and not with strangers."

"But we aren't strangers, Pip," Tracy interrupted. "Why not come with us?"

"No thanks," Pip replied, tight-lipped and jaw set, "I have to get up for work tomorrow."

Sam arrived at her elbow. "Sorry to mess you about, Pip," he charmed, "but we've got to debrief. Let's get you sorted."

Pip allowed herself to be led away but looked back over her shoulder as she passed through the door to see Tracy, Hannah and Sharon in a happy huddle with their backs to her. Back in the main saloon bar, Sam suddenly picked her up and plonked her onto a bar stool, where she perched uncomfortably. Three men (or gorillas in Pip's opinion) were close by, looking at her much as the hungry wolfhound regards its owner's fillet steak.

"You don't mind seeing my young friend home, do you, gents?" Sam said. "I hear she's anyone's for a vodka and orange." He leaned close to Pip's ear and whispered, "That will teach you for interfering, little cow."

He walked out before a startled Pip could object. A clanging bell signalled Last Orders, and the noise increased as people flocked to the bar. The three men deliberately blocked her path, and Pip gazed frantically around until she spotted a group of her fellow students. "Help," she mouthed to a girl, who said something to her boyfriend. They began to walk over, but one of the three gorillas gave them a stare and they stopped.

"Do you think you could call me a taxi, please?" Pip asked the barmaid.

"You'll have a long wait," was the terse reply, as the woman struggled to deal with the flurry.

Pip felt the sting of tears in her eyes and fear filled her veins.

A familiar voice unexpectedly cut through the noise of the bar. "I'll see you home, Pip."

"Gavin? Oh, thank God! Yes please."

She moved to get off the stool, but one of the men barred her way as he faced up to Gavin.

"Hop it, sonny," he menaced, "I've just bought this girl a drink."

"There's been a mistake," Gavin replied calmly reaching past the man and taking Pip's hand. "She's only sixteen."

"So?"

"Sorry," said Gavin, his mouth dry, "I meant that she doesn't drink, and she doesn't know you. Can I pay you back for the drink?"

"Look, I don't know who you think you are, son but—"

"But nothing, Harry," interjected one of his associates, placing a hand on his friend's shoulder. He turned to Gavin. "You've got guts, lad, I'll say that for you, but push off now. We've had our joke with the girl, but I'd have seen to it that she came to no real harm."

Pip hurried from the pub, dragging Gavin behind her, closely followed by the remainder of their school group. When Gavin recognised his schoolfellows, his heart sank; however, to his great surprise, one of the girls kissed his cheek.

"You were great in there, Gavin, I'm proud of you. You were a real man," she told him with a withering glance at her own boyfriend.

"Yeah, well done, mate," said the owner of a blood-splattered football. He sheepishly held out his hand, and Gavin shook it with bemused detachment. "Don't worry, Pip, we'll all walk you and Gav to your homes."

"Thank you," she replied with a watery smile.

"But where's Sharon?" Gavin asked.

"She's gone to a post-gig thing at Sam's place. Don't bother going back to find her, she's old enough and ugly enough to make her own decisions. Come on, let's go, or it'll be midnight by the time I get home and I have to get up early for work."

~ * ~ * ~

Sam returned to the courtyard and gave Sharon the thumbs-up.

Hannah left to fetch her car while the other girls watched the loading of the van.

"Let's get a last drink for the road and let the boys finish up here," Tracy suggested.

Sharon nodded dozily and followed her into the bar. It was empty, save for the landlord, who was counting his takings at the till, and the barmaid, who was collecting empty glasses. Tracy hooked a finger into the front of her blue top and tugged it down as far as possible. Standing on the brass rail that ran a few inches above the floor by the bar, she leaned forward, and called to the landlord.

"Could my friend and I have a little drinkie? It's awfully thirsty work singing."

"Sorry, we've called time," said the landlord, without looking up from his tallying.

"Aw!" Tracy gave a sulky squirm on the bar.

"Pretty please," added Sharon, joining her friend's provocative pose.

The landlord glanced up and took in the display set before him.

"Well, I can't let you girls get dehydrated," he remarked, picking up two glasses and turning to the optics in the wall behind the bar. "On the house."

"My hero!" Tracy blew him a kiss. The landlord smiled as he placed the glasses in front of the girls, but then realised the barmaid was glaring at him and hastily returned to his counting.

"Hannah and Darren seem completely different," Sharon said. "You wouldn't think they were related."

"I know what you mean," Tracy agreed. "Hannah's great, though. She's our chemist, the person who gets our stuff. You know, like the pot we were just smoking. But she is studying chemistry for real at uni."

Sharon stumbled slightly, as the drink added its effects to the ones before and mingled with the cannabis.

"Time to go," Tracy decided. They walked out, arm in arm. "Are you sure you're happy going back to Sam's? You know what's on his agenda, yes?"

"Yes," replied Sharon, without the foggiest notion what her companion was asking.

"Good," said Tracy, "and you're fixed, yes?"

"Fixed?" Sharon asked in bewilderment.

"Fixed. On the pill or something."

"Oh," Sharon finally realised, "um, no."

Tracy tutted and nipped through the door to the toilets, returning a few minutes later with a small slim square box, which she pressed into Sharon's hand.

"Make sure he wears one, we don't want you getting knocked up."

Chapter 3

Pip fought the urge to quit her Saturday job by going back to sleep, and instead dragged herself to the bathroom. The warm shower washed the stench of stale cigarettes from her hair, gradually reviving her until she felt almost human. Back in her room, pressing together the poppers of her crimplene uniform and pinning on her name tag, her eyes lighted upon Sharon's overnight case and she once again plunged into an abyss of worry.

Downstairs in the kitchen she made tea and a round of jam on toast. Her mother, Julia, entered, wearing a fluffy mauve dressing gown and yawning.

"Kettle's still hot, Mum," said Pip, "I'd have made you a cup if I knew you were awake."

"Dad was snoring, which is typical on the one night when Daniel sleeps through," Julia sighed, peering out of the window at the dingy morning. Then she looked at her daughter's bare feet. "Put some tights on! You'll catch your death walking to work. The thick black ones you like are in the airing cupboard."

Grudgingly accepting that her mother was right, Pip put her half-eaten piece of toast on its plate and scampered upstairs. When she returned, she stuck the crisped bread back between her teeth as she scrunched up one leg of the tights, pushed her pointed foot in, and rolled it up to her thigh.

"For heaven's sake, Pip, not in the kitchen!"

Pip rolled her eyes and continued with the other leg, ignoring the loud 'tut' that accompanied her actions. She completed pulling up her hosiery with a wriggling jig.

"Sorry, Mum," she said, her mouth still full, "I'm in a hurry."

"I heard you come it at nigh-on one in the morning. Did you have fun?"

"Not really, it's not my scene."

"What about Sharon, did she enjoy herself?"

"I think so."

"Is she still asleep upstairs?"

"No, she made other plans. She met some friends and didn't want to keep me up late."

"That was thoughtful of her. Did she go back home?"

"I expect so," Pip said, knowing full well that Sharon's house key was in her overnight case.

"Is she still staying tonight? I thought we might get fish and chips."

"Sounds good. She said she'd be here." Pip stuffed the remains of her toast into her mouth and gulped her tea as she chewed. "Got to go, Mum, see you later!"

With a sting of irritation Pip realised Sharon still had her coat, so put on an old cardigan she had to hand, slipped her feet into a pair of shoes, and stepped out into the cool morning air. She tried not to shiver, her head full of the memories of the previous evening and dread for the day ahead.

~ * ~ * ~

Gavin woke later than usual and carrying an unfamiliar worry. He stared at himself in the mirror, combed his coarse dark hair into its traditional side parting and examined his hollow cheeks to see if he needed to shave. It was frustrating that, despite being nearly seventeen, his natural beard was little more than fluffy down that rarely required a razor's attention. He dressed in the same cords, shirt, and heavy-knit green jumper that he had worn the day before and went downstairs to breakfast.

His sister, Karen, sat at the old pine table, examining a large piece of blue card that had several circles of white paper scattered on its surface.

"Morning," Gavin yawned. "Still doing your seating plans?"

"Yup," Karen said, distracted.

Gavin shrugged and started to make his breakfast.

"Do you know if Uncle Sid is still talking to Aunty Beth?" Karen asked.

"No idea, but probably not. You know nobody's happy in our family without a feud."

Karen nodded distantly, then paused, frowned and looked up.

"Good morning, little brother," she hailed, as if he had just walked into the room. "Mum and Dad are on the warpath for you."

"Me? What have I done?"

"Coming home in the middle of the night," Karen said with mischievous delight. "Where were you anyway? Was it a girl?"

"None of your business."

"Be like that then," she winked. "Anyway, Mum said not to have too much breakfast because she is going to do bacon sarnies for everyone when you get down. What do you think of my seating plan?"

Gavin wandered over to have a look, but before he could pass comment, Karen exclaimed, "Yuck, you smell like an ashtray! You'd better change before Dad sees you, or at least have a good explanation."

"I do." Gavin returned to his breakfast and poured milk onto it from a stripy blue jug. He opened a matching jar and ladled three dessert spoons of sugar into his bowl.

"You'll ruin your teeth," Karen observed, "and you can't eat in here – I'm not messing up this seating plan for anybody."

"No probs," said Gavin, pouring orange juice into a glass, "I'll watch TV."

"Mum said no food in the living room, because Nana's coming over later. You'll have to go into the dining room."

This didn't please Gavin, as he knew his father would be working in there and was rarely in an ebullient mood when wading through paperwork. Nevertheless, he tucked the latest issue of *2000AD* under his arm and made his way to sit at one end of the old mahogany dining table.

He had barely read two captions of Judge Dredd before his father spoke, not looking up from his correspondence.

"Would you mind telling me where you were last night, young man? Your mother was worried sick and it's not like you to be out until the early hours."

"Sorry I worried you, I was at The White Hart."

"What on earth were you doing there? Not drinking, I hope!"

"No, Dad, I was only there because my friend Sharon was performing. Pip was worried about her, so I went to make sure they were OK."

"Pip was right to be worried, The White Hart has a bad reputation. Was there trouble?"

"Almost, Dad, but what good would I have been? I've never won a fight in my life. I hate the idea of hurting someone. Nowadays, I don't bother fighting back – it's over quicker that way."

"You know, back in the war, there was a corporal in our unit who was a violent man with neither fear nor compassion. I once saw him kill a man with a knife. It was war, we all had to do things, but he enjoyed it. One day, this corporal took a fancy to a local German lass, younger than you, and dragged her off somewhere but her grandfather went after them and knocked him clean out. Gavin, you could never be like our corporal, but if you had to, you'd do what the grandfather did. Do you see?"

"I think so, thanks, Dad. But there's something else that I need advice on. What should I do if I overheard something that someone needs to know, but would hurt them badly?"

"Eavesdroppers seldom benefit, son."

"It was an honest mistake. When I went to the loo at the pub, I heard a conversation in the hall outside. I couldn't help it."

"Ah, infidelity, perhaps?"

Gavin nodded, quietly astonished that his father hit the nub of the matter so quickly. "What should I do?"

"Tell the guilty party what you know. Let them explain any misunderstanding. If you haven't misunderstood, make it clear that they must do the right thing, or you may be forced to act."

"Easier said than done. I'm not sure how to find the guilty party."

"Let time take its course. And now, unless my nose is being tricked by the smell of stale tobacco smoke emanating from your clothes, I believe we have bacon sandwiches to go and collect."

~ * ~ * ~

Sharon awoke when the rays of late-morning sunshine rested in a narrow bright strip across her eyes. Two sensations struck her simultaneously, a painfully dry mouth and an uncomfortably full bladder; she strived to solve the first problem by attempting to create saliva, but that only highlighted the bitter taste and furry tongue which were the symptoms of her first real hangover. She turned softly in the bed and gazed at Sam's broad, muscular back; he was lying on his side, breathing deeply and showing no signs of stirring.

Gently, she moved the bed covers and sat up, swinging her feet to the floor and sensing the carpet fibres beneath her soles. A thumping headache announced itself and her hangover threw a sweep of mild nausea in for good measure. Eyes half closed, she walked towards the door but stopped when she realised she was naked. Her beautiful new dress lay crumpled on the floor, stained and dirty, and there was no sign of a dressing gown, but over the back of a chair was one of Sam's red lumberjack-style check shirts. She put it on, quietly turned the door handle, and crept into the hallway and then into the bathroom.

The extractor fan started up when the light turned on, its low grinding moan matching the throb in her head. After she had eased the urgent pressure in her bladder, she stood at the basin, washing her hands and peering at her reflection in the mirror.

"You're a woman now," she told herself. "Pip's going to be so jealous you beat her to it."

There were several toothbrushes of various colours standing in a mug by the taps, but she ignored them, instead squeezing toothpaste onto the tip of her index finger, which she proceeded to rub over her teeth, gums, tongue and the inside of her cheeks. Her mouth fresher, she scrunched her fingers through her hair and was relieved that it still looked presentable, thanks in no small part to Pip's expert preparations.

In the kitchen, she drank a long glass of water and stared out of the second storey window at the street below. Now more awake, she started to panic – she had got high on pot and hammered on rum, made a fool of herself on stage, deserted Pip, and slept with a man she hardly knew. Oh, how guilty she felt about Pip! And yet, what an amazing night it was, what new worlds had opened to her, and what excitement she had felt.

Was she a one-night-stand, whom Sam now expected to disappear and be forgotten? Surely not, or he wouldn't have asked her to the band debrief – but the band hadn't even discussed anything, they'd just drank and smoked; he'd got her high and then into bed. Was she a fool in a fool's paradise?

Her train of thought was interrupted by a "Good morning". Tracy had silently entered the kitchen, wearing only powder-blue briefs and a tiny cropped t-shirt which barely reached halfway down her stomach. Her long straight dark hair was tousled, adding to the impression that she was taking part in a glamour photo shoot. She gave Sharon a prolonged embrace, as if she was her oldest friend not seen for years. Given their mutual states of relative undress, Sharon experienced a mixture of surprise and exotic taboo, which increased when she felt warm breath followed by a tiny kiss on her cheek.

Back down the corridor, the bedroom door opened, and Sam emerged and went into the bathroom. His tight burgundy briefs emphasised both his powerful upper body and his muscular legs.

"Make some tea, will you, girls?" he called out before he closed and locked the door.

"Make it yourself, cheeky sod," Sharon muttered.

"That isn't very nice, is it?" Tracy rebuked. "The boys did all the heavy lifting yesterday, while we chatted and drank. Then Sam laid on food and beer here, and you begrudge him a cup of tea!"

"Sorry, I'm just a bit hungover, that's all," Sharon found herself apologising instead of making a snarky remark.

Tracy's smile returned. A few minutes later, Sharon carried a cup into the bedroom, where Sam was sitting up in bed lighting his first cigarette of the day.

"Thank you, gorgeous," he said taking the mug and sipping it. "Strong and sweet, just how I like it. Want a fag?"

"No thanks." Sharon's stomach lurched at the idea. "Tracy and I are going to make breakfast in a minute."

"Lovely job!" Sam rubbed his muscular stomach and gave it two hearty slaps. "I'm famished – but come back to bed first." His blue eyes twinkled invitingly.

Sharon smiled coyly and purred, "I can't, I have to help Tracy." She sashayed from the room, pausing briefly at the door to look back over her shoulder.

Tracy was squatting in front of the open refrigerator pulling out items and placing them on the top of the counter above.

"If we are going to be frying, I'd better put some clothes on," she giggled.

"I wish I could too, but my dress is in a bit of a state and I don't have any other clothes here."

"I may have something that will fit you in my room." Tracy eyed her bandmate, estimating her measurements.

"That would be great, thanks. I didn't realise you live here."

"Sometimes. I keep some bits and pieces in the spare room. Start heating the oil in the frying pan, stick some rounds of toast under the grill, and I'll be right back."

Sharon struggled. Firstly, the cooker was gas, whereas the one at her home was electric, and secondly, she had never cooked a fry-up in her life. Home Economics had trained her to make a lovely pineapple upside-down cake, but it appeared to draw the line at bacon and eggs. Thankfully, Ed wandered in, saw her struggle, and insisted that he be chief cook; soon the room was filled with the crackle and sizzle and smell of breakfast.

Tracy returned, wearing a black jump-suit. "I couldn't find much that would fit you, Sharon, but you can wear these to go home and pick up a change of clothes."

Sharon took the neon-pink jumper and tight jeans and hurried into the bathroom to change. It was clear they were never Tracy's clothes (at least a size too big and long), and she wondered who the previous owner was.

"I can't go home yet," she said when she got back to the kitchen. "My parents are out all day and my keys are at Pip's. I'm staying at her place tonight, so I'll wash these clothes and drop them back to you in the week. Is that OK?"

Sam's voice boomed from the doorway, making Sharon jump. "No, no, no, we need you tonight, Sharon. Band work."

"What kind of work?"

"Drumming up business. We're doing the clubs and pubs tonight, selling tickets for our next gig. If you're in the band, you've got to help."

"Am I in the band, really?"

"I think it's unanimous that you are." Sam grinned.

"I'll still need to meet Pip after work and go back to hers for my bag, and I'll need to think of what I can wear tonight."

"You girls should go shopping for outfits." Sam extracted a wad of cash from his pocket and handed some to Tracy. He saw Sharon's wide eyes. "Proceeds of last night."

"We earned all that from the gig?" Sharon exclaimed.

"Partly, but we had some ancillary sales."

"What are they, tapes of the band and stuff?"

"Extra profits, that's all." Sam flashed a half wink to Ed who was serving up. "Now, let's eat."

Frank, who had approached unnoticed by the others, shouted, "About bloody time, I'm starving!" He swigged from a can of cider and swayed defiantly.

"I've only got two servings ready to go," Ed explained. "Sam first, because this is his gaff, and Sharon, because she's new and prettier than you."

"More like you're hoping Sam will let you have a lend of her, big guy," Frank taunted, not seeing Ed's demeanour change subtly.

"I suggest you take that back. It is very rude to Sharon and to Ed," Sam said with quiet urgency.

"Why, did I hurt your little girlfriend's feelings? Or is Ed worried you'll all find out he's really a fairy like Darren?"

What was most surprising was Ed's burst of speed and agility. Within a moment, the can of cider was rolling on the floor, its contents frothing out onto the lino, and Frank was pinned to the wall, choking as Ed's vast hand tightened around his throat. Frank clawed urgently at the younger man's powerful upper arm, his face red, his eyes bulging with panic and fear as they beheld Ed's free hand balled into a fist and ready to strike him. Sam ran to calm the situation.

"Calm down, big guy, it's the booze talking," he soothed. Frank's resistance was becoming feebler, he seemed to be about to pass out. "Ed, mate, you need to stop!" The young man snapped from his angry trance, and he released his grip.

"You psycho, you could've killed me!" Frank coughed, slumping into the puddle of cider that had pooled at his feet.

"But he didn't," Sam stated, squatting to be on eye level with his drummer. "Now pull yourself together, apologise to everyone, and have some breakfast."

"He'll have none from me!" Ed protested.

"Yes, he will, he's our mate, remember? Like I said, he's still a bit drunk and didn't mean what he said. He's going to apologise, you're going to give him breakfast, and we're all going to be nice civilised friends, OK?" Sam glared at Frank with unmistakeable intent.

"Sorry, Ed, sorry, Sharon," the drummer croaked, wiping away the spittle that was trickling down his chin, "I'm still a bit drunk, yeah?"

Still squatting, Sam turned to Sharon. "Hey, gorgeous, why don't you do me a favour and go downstairs and fetch my paper? It'll be in the post box for the flat. The key's on the hall table."

Feeling like a dismissed child, Sharon dithered, but complied. Reaching the front door, she realised her shoes were in the lounge, where she had taken them off the previous night, and she would have to pass by the kitchen to retrieve them. Not wanting to go back in case Sam was annoyed, she walked barefoot down the two flights of concrete stairs to the lobby, where she retrieved the red-top tabloid. On her way back to the flat, she met Tracy who had come to find her.

"That was wild," Sharon said. "Does that sort of thing happen often?"

"Oh, it's nothing, just boys being boys," Tracy laughed. "Ed's always had a short fuse, but he's a big softie – he wouldn't have really hurt Frank. And don't be scared, he'd never harm you or me. Sam only asked you to leave because he wanted to make sure things were calm, and people are still getting to know you."

"That's good to hear."

"Sometimes I wish Frank wasn't in the band, I don't like him much," Tracy confided, "but Sam has his reasons."

"Well, he's a good drummer, I suppose."

"Yes, that will be it." Tracy switched to an excited voice. "I've just had a fun idea for our outfits this evening. Leave everything to me."

~ * ~ * ~

Pip's morning working in the newsagents was hectic. The atmosphere in the shop became humid from the breath and body heat of countless strangers, and all she could hear was the beeping of the tills and the sounds of voices; she hadn't even had her usual ten-minute coffee break.

"Finish this next customer and then take your half hour for lunch," her supervisor eventually instructed.

Pip nodded and stared at the counter, too tired to look up. Surely enough, a tabloid newspaper and a bar of chocolate appeared before her, accompanied by, "Twenty JPS as well, please." She automatically retrieved the cigarettes from the rainbow of cartons displayed on the shelves behind her and rang the prices into the till.

"That will be two pounds twelve, please," she said.

"Would you settle for a kiss instead?"

Pip looked up in surprise to see Tom grinning at her.

"Well, I'll have to see how the manager feels about it." She smiled, cocking her head to one side.

"I don't fancy snogging him," Tom laughed. He handed her a five-pound note.

"Let me get my cardi and I'll meet you out the front." Pip passed him his change and hurried to the staffroom. As promised, she emerged quickly and met Tom outside the shop, embracing him as if she could never let go. "Are you feeling better? I've been worried about you."

"What?" Tom momentarily forgot his excuse for leaving The White Hart. "Oh yeah, I'm fine now. It was probably the beer, so let's go somewhere different tonight."

"That's a nice idea," Pip said as they walked to the bakery and joined the queue. "I'm getting a sausage roll. Do you want something?"

"A pasty would be nice – and a Danish."

"You certainly are feeling better!" Pip declared. Then a thought struck her. "Oh, no! Sharon's staying tonight, and Mum was going to get in fish and chips. Would you like to come to ours?"

"I'd rather go out."

"Well, I'm sure Mum will be OK, but what about Sharon?"

"She can come with us, if she's happy being a third wheel," Tom concealed pleasure behind a veneer of annoyance.

"Thanks, you are so good."

Reaching the front of the queue, Pip bought their lunches, and they walked to the churchyard that sat just behind the high street; it was a peaceful green space where many of the local workers took their breaks.

"Thanks," Tom said when she gave him his food. "Don't forget my fiver."

"Sorry." Pip rustled in her bag and produced the money.

The half hour together passed all too soon for Pip, and she was miserable when they walked back to the newsagents. Quite by chance, Gavin was passing and spotted them having a parting kiss; he approached Tom once Pip had left.

"Can I have a word with you?"

"It's Garry, isn't it? What do you want?" Tom's disdain was an act of violence.

"Gavin. My name is Gavin."

"OK, Gavin, what do you want?"

"I was at The White Hart last night, and I know what you did. I know you left Pip and went to meet a girl and I don't think it's right."

"What are you talking about, mate? I had bellyache and went home." Tom adopted an exaggerated expression of puzzled innocence. "I don't know what you think you heard, but it wasn't me."

"I believe it was," Gavin insisted, "and Pip has a right to know."

"Look, you little ponce, what's the matter with you?" Tom switched to feigned anger. "I said you're wrong, so bugger off!"

"How do you explain leaving a few minutes after what I heard?"

"I don't have to explain anything to a little git like you. Hiding in the Gents, listening to other people's conversations and making up stories? Sounds like a poof to me," Tom sneered. "Or do you fancy Pip? Yeah, you do! Do you think my girlfriend would like a greasy runt like you? Well, just you stay away from her, or I'll kick your head in, got it?"

"Look, I just wanted to talk to you, that's all," Gavin spluttered, anger, fear, uncertainty and embarrassment uniting to bring about capitulation in the face of aggression.

"Well, we've talked, and now we know you're an eavesdropping lying little ponce who causes trouble." Tom held his fist up. "Stay away from Pip, or you'll be swallowing your teeth."

With that, he spun around and strode to his car, leaving Gavin frightened and questioning everything he had heard at the pub.

~ * ~ * ~

"What time does your friend finish work?" Tracy asked as she and Sharon walked down the high street.

"About four o'clock. She had an early start. That's why she didn't want to be out late."

"She's not very adventurous, is she? Not like you."

"Maybe," Sharon pondered. "We've been best friends for ever. She'll be bursting to know what happened last night, especially about Sam."

"I trust you'll be discreet," Tracy frowned. "Sam isn't some trophy – he likes women, not giggling schoolgirls."

The words stabbed at Sharon's insecurities.

"That's not what I meant," she gabbled, "but you're right, I won't tell Pip too much."

Tracy's smile returned, "I'm so glad you joined the band, you're a perfect fit. You look great and move well. I don't suppose you have any musical talents, do you?"

"I play the piano a bit. Mum taught me up to grade six. We had an old upright in the dining room, but Dad lost his job in '82 and we had to sell it. I still mess about in the school music room on a wet lunch time sometimes."

"Wonderful!" Tracy bubbled with excitement. "You can stand in for Darren sometimes."

"Oh, I couldn't, he's amazing!"

"It's just practice. It'd be good to have a fall back, just in case."

Sharon was extremely doubtful but said nothing. Instead, she half-sat, half-leaned against a concrete bollard and pulled a white stiletto off her foot.

"Ouch," she said, "these shoes look great, but they're hell to walk in."

"Suffering for your style. A girl after my own heart."

"I wish you'd tell me what you're planning for us to wear tonight," Sharon wheedled.

"Not yet. Stay here and rest your feet, I need to ring Hannah."

Perched on the bollard, Sharon watched her new friend go into a nearby phone box and make a call. From time to time they waved at each other. Tracy lit a cigarette, filling the cubicle with a thin haze of smoke.

At last, she emerged. "OK, Hannah will pick us up at four-fifteen and take us back to Sam's. We can stop at your friend Pip's place on the way – would she like a lift too?"

"I expect so, thanks."

"OK, well I'm off to organise outfits. Meet us outside the Post Office."

"Can I ask a favour first?" Sharon couldn't help looking embarrassed. "Would you go to the chemists and get me some more of those... things you got me last night? I'll give you the money, it's just I'm scared that one of Mum's friends will see me. She'd explode if she knew."

"Of course." Tracy seemed amused.

"I wish I could be confident and free like you."

Tracy's bubbly demeanour turned off. "Darling, it's all an act. I was tired of misery. Having to leave my home, living in that children's home where they— well, you don't want to know. If it hadn't been for Ed and Sam, I'd have given up long ago. I'm determined not to be sad, and I'll take anything and do anything not to be. You know what?"

"What?"

"It works amazingly!" Tracy laughed, her normal persona restored. With a final flourish of goodbyes and a very public kiss, she hurried away.

Sharon decided to wait for Pip in a café across from the newsagents and settled at a table near the window. When the waitress arrived to take her order, she suppressed her desire for a strawberry milkshake and instead asked for a coffee, which seemed the more mature option. Two lads were sitting nearby. They had very short-cropped blond hair, wore white t-shirts, faded torn jeans and black Doc Martens, and were arguing about football teams. One of them took a packet of cigarettes from the pocket of a black bomber jacket hanging over the back of his chair; Sharon seized her chance.

"Excuse me," she said in a sultry voice, "do you think I could have one of those?"

The man looked at her like a cat left alone with the goldfish.

"You're direct, aren't you?" he said. Nevertheless, he held the pack out and she took a cigarette, placing it between her lips and waiting patiently until the other man held out his lighter for her to use. She drew deeply, making the end glow bright red, and inhaled, relishing the tightness in her lungs, before exhaling slowly through her nostrils.

"Thank you," she said, the last of the smoke forming a wisp around her lips.

"So," said the man with the cigarettes, "what's your name?"

"You're direct, aren't you?" Sharon echoed his earlier words.

"Maybe. Come out for a drink with me tonight and you'll find out."

"Oh, that sounds lovely! Can my boyfriend come too?"

"She got you good there, Spike," laughed the man with the lighter.

"If you get tired of him, we drink in The Mitre." Spike was undaunted.

"I'll bear that in mind," Sharon said, sipping her coffee and smothering the urge to grimace. She glanced out of the window and saw Pip leaving the newsagents. "Sorry, boys, I've got to dash."

She ran into the street, yelling for Pip's attention. The two friends were soon walking along together and Sharon shared her news.

"You slept with him?" Pip exclaimed. "But you've only just met him."

"Oh, don't be such a hypocrite!" Sharon was hurt and disappointed by the lack of enthusiasm. "You're planning on sleeping with Tom. You're just jealous because I got there first."

"I've liked Tom for ages," Pip said acidly.

"I never realised what a prude you are!" Sharon stopped walking. "You just want to be married, buy a house around the corner from your mum and start having babies, don't you?"

"What's wrong with that?"

"It's boring, that's what. I want different things. I want to live."

Pip recommenced walking, taking short, angry steps; Sharon kept pace.

"OK, fair enough," Pip said, "you win. You're not a tart and I'm destined for domestic drudgery. Have you got my coat?"

"Which coat?"

"The one you borrowed last night. My long one. My only decent one."

Sharon felt a pang of guilt. "I thought you had it. It must be in the pub."

"I trusted you with it and now you've lost it."

"How is it my fault? You were there too! Just go back and get it."

"We both know it won't be there." Pip closed her eyes and took a deep breath. "Let's just go home. Tom's asked me out again this evening, and you can come if you want."

"Don't worry, I'm out with the band again tonight. I'm just coming with you to get my stuff. I've a lift organised, so you don't have to walk home."

"Thanks for letting me know you're not staying!" Pip's anger finally bubbled up. "Sod it, why don't you just go on to my house and get your stuff? Mum can let you in. Just be gone by the time I get there, OK? I'll see you at your place Monday morning as usual."

"Don't bother," Sharon growled, eleven years of friendship hanging by a frayed thread.

"What should I say to your mum if she calls?" Ice would be warmer than Pip's tone.

Sharon had a second pang of guilt, remembering her promise to her mother to be spending the day studying, but she quickly suppressed it and snapped the frayed thread of friendship in the process.

"Tell her that you're a selfish cow and I'm staying at a real mate's house," she shouted. Spotting Hannah's car parked a little way up the road, she left Pip to plod a lonely, weary walk home. Had Sharon looked back, she would have seen the tears running down her friend's pale cheeks, but she was looking forwards.

~ * ~ * ~

Pip's walk home was the longest, coldest and most miserable of her life. She felt wretched about her argument with Sharon and carried on the conversation in her head as she trudged through the streets, saying in her mind what she wished she had said at the time, swinging between anger and self-hate. She opened and closed the front door with maximum force and stomped upstairs to her room. Her eyes darted round the furniture – her bed, her bedside table, and her tiny dressing table – hoping that there would be a letter from Sharon, just a simple acknowledgement of the unbreakable bond that she had always believed existed between them. But there was nothing; the empty space where Sharon's case had been reflected the hole in her own heart. Pip shook, with anger and grief, and tears once again formed in her eyes.

Her cardigan dropped to the floor, followed by her hideous artificial uniform, which she loathed more than ever. What she wanted to do was pull back her bedcovers, put on her fluffy pyjamas, curl up, and cry herself to sleep; but Tom would be arriving to take her out before long and she needed to get ready. There was a knock at the door and her mother entered, carrying a cup of tea.

"I'm not decent!" Pip screamed as the door opened, trying to cover herself up.

"It's nothing I haven't seen before," Julia laughed. "It's just us girls."

Pip relaxed. She had been afraid that one of her brothers was the intruder and she had no wish to endure childish guffawing at her in her underwear. She flopped down to sit on the edge of her bed.

"I'm exhausted, but I've got a date with Tom again tonight," she groaned. "I should be excited, I suppose, but after the day I've had, I'd rather just go to sleep."

"Drink your tea, dear. So, you're not having dinner with us?"

"No," Pip sighed.

"You've had a falling out with Sharon, haven't you? She came by earlier to get her bag, but I've known her too long to fall for her sweet-faced tricks. I expect she'll be round here tomorrow, and everything will be back to normal."

"Not this time, Mum." Pip's face screwed up with tears. "I don't know if we can ever go back. I don't know which of us hurt the other more."

"You'll feel different in the morning."

"Don't count on it."

Chapter 4

After his altercation with Tom, Gavin paced through the town, aimlessly wandering in and out of shops but not finding a distraction for his troubled mind. As dusk drew in, he wandered home through the network of Victorian and Edwardian terraces, glancing through the living room windows at the flickering television screens and figures huddled about them. The people seemed carefree, absorbed by football scores or black and white movies. In one house, a boy stood on his head whilst watching a cartoon; in another a girl played cards with her grandmother. Were any of them plagued by self-doubt and fear? Were any of them torn between telling a friend a painful truth or letting sleeping dogs lie?

The lights glowed in the windows of St Michael's Anglican Church, which sat at the head of the road. Gavin entered through the heavy oak door and found the Reverend Johnson, a slight-framed man of about thirty-five with a thin face and short brown hair.

"Hello," said the vicar, "you're about an hour late for youth club and seventeen hours too early for Sunday Eucharist. Sit down, let's have a chat."

They sat on a pew in a quiet corner next to a tall flickering candle, and Gavin started talking. His worries and troubles poured out as a torrent of consciousness, emotional yet precise. He spoke of Pip and Tom but gave no names.

"You did the right thing, Gavin," the vicar said when the young man finished, "but I think the young lady you spoke of deserves to know the truth. That's not going to be easy for either of you."

"I know," Gavin sighed. "Thank you. I have to get home for tea now."

They strolled down the aisle, past the wooden pews and the faded hassocks, to the entrance, where they shook hands.

"Well, good night, Gavin," said Reverend Johnson. "If you run into the boyfriend again, remember what I taught you. Turn the other cheek, but if you run out of cheeks, always lead with the left."

~ * ~ * ~

"How was it with Sam last night?" Tracy asked as she put the finishing touches to Sharon's mascara.

"How was what?"

"It – you know."

"Oh, I see. It was nice, I guess." Sharon felt an extra simmer of anger towards Pip surfacing; some friend she was, not even asking what 'it' was like.

Tracy slid a large white cardboard box from beneath the bed and opened it. "Are you ready for the big outfit reveal? Ready, steady... ta da!"

Sharon stared at her costume in disbelief. A little black dress is one thing, but this was microscopic and covered with strange lacy accoutrements. It was something Sharon imagined that a miniaturised Cyndi Lauper would wear to a funeral – girls may want to have fun, but hypothermia was the more probable upshot.

"Where's the rest of it?" she asked.

"What?" Tracy asked surprised. "Oh, I see what you mean, shoes and stockings. They're still in the box. Isn't it great? I've got the exact same thing."

"But people will see us! They'll see a lot of us!"

"Welcome to the world of marketing! And don't worry about being cold, because we'll be inside most of the time."

The two girls put on their dresses and Sharon stared at her reflection in the mirror with mild horror. The hem of the skirt finished at the top of her thighs, so she was relieved the black lacy stockings turned out to be black lacy tights and the heels of the shoes were not too extreme. Feeling exposed, she reluctantly allowed Tracy to lead her to the living room.

"Very nice!" declared Sam.

Judging from his expression, Ed concurred. Another man, short, stocky, with a receding hairline at the front and a greasy grey ponytail at the back, was also in the room. He devoured the two young women with watery blue eyes.

Only Frank appeared uninterested, preferring the pages of Penthouse to two actual women.

"This is Pete," Sam gestured towards the newcomer. "He's a mate and he's driving us around in his minibus this evening, so the rest of us can drink. I've planned an itinerary of pubs and clubs to visit, so let's go."

Except for the driver, the men all wore black jeans with t-shirts sporting the band's logo, which didn't look much warmer than the dress Sharon had on; by the time Sam had ushered them outside they were all shivering. When everyone was seated in the old Leyland minibus, the bandleader pulled out a joint and a lighter.

"Compliments of Hannah," he said. "That should warm you up."

~ * ~ * ~

Pip's mood had brightened considerably by the time Tom arrived at her house, and she launched herself into his arms when she opened the front door.

"Come on in and say hello to Mum and Dad," she said, dragging him by the hand into the living room.

"Good evening, Thomas," said Julia, looking up from reading the television listings. "You both look very smart. Going somewhere nice?"

"I thought we would try The George and Dragon, Mrs Raven," Tom replied with a hint of pride.

"Call me Julia, please. Oh, it's supposed to be nice at The George and Dragon. Mavis next door said she had a lovely chicken in a basket there on her anniversary. You're a lucky girl, Pip."

"Maybe we should go too," Pip's father said, looking up from his newspaper. "It'd be nice for you having us and your brothers there. Make it a family thing."

"You'd better be joking, Dad!" Pip looked mortified.

"I most certainly am! I wouldn't take those brothers of yours anywhere civilised. You two have a lovely time. Not too lovely, though. No coming back at gone midnight again."

"OK, Dad," Pip said, full of silent love. "Come on, Tom, let's go."

"Put your coat on, it's nippy out there," her father said.

"I've got a cardi on!"

"Where's your nice coat?"

"It will be warm in the car, Dad," Pip shouted. She pulled Tom out behind her and up the street to where the Ford was parked. "Put your arm around me, please, it's freezing!"

~ * ~ * ~

As the minivan drew into the parking lot of The George and Dragon, Sharon had a surprise – Tom's distinctive Ford Escort was parked outside the pub.

"Oh, no," she groaned.

"What's wrong?" asked Tracy.

"Just my luck. Don't worry about it."

Hannah and Darren were waiting for them near the entrance to the bar. Hannah was dressed much more stylishly than at the gig, but much more appropriately for the weather than Tracy and Sharon. Darren wore the same t-shirt as the other men, but his trousers were so tight that Sharon wondered if they were painted on. Sam distributed small bundles of printed leaflets among the group.

"Right, listen up," he instructed. "Most of the pubs know we are coming. I'll buy rounds for us as we go. Think of it as a chauffeur-driven pub crawl. Hand out as many leaflets as you can, flirt with as many people as you can. I'm going to be selling the tickets and buying the drinks, so you guys will have to pair up. Darren, you stay with Hannah, Tracy, you're with Ed, and Frank, you take Sharon. OK?"

Sharon was deeply disappointed not to be with Sam but said nothing when an impatient (and cold) Frank took her hand and tugged her along behind him.

Having decided to try the chicken in a basket, Pip had begun her meal when she was distracted by a loud group of people clattering in through the door and spreading out, going from table to table.

"Isn't that your friends?" asked Tom. "You know, the band we went to see last night."

"It can't be... no, you're right – the guy at the bar is Sam." Pip hissed his name, remembering the trick he played on her.

"Yeah, and isn't that girl Sharon?"

"Yes," Pip moaned. "Oh, please don't let her come over here."

But Frank was already leading Sharon to them, oblivious to his partner's reluctance, and he laid some leaflets on the table. Frank waited for Sharon to start saying the agreed spiel, and when she didn't, he gave her a sharp dig in the ribs, making her gasp.

"Please come to our next show. Tickets are on sale this evening."

"I wish I could help, but I'm busy that day," Pip snarked. "I have to buy a new coat, you see."

Sharon's revenge was to flirt with Tom. "Maybe this handsome hunk would like to come?"

Tom sensed his girlfriend's glower. "Sorry, but I think I'm going to be busy too."

"Yes, it's a shame," Pip added, "but well done on the new look, Sharon. Not at all tarty."

"Why you little—" Sharon began, but was unceremoniously dragged to the next table by Frank who saw no point in wasting time.

A few minutes later, when they passed close to Tracy and Ed, Sharon emitted a sudden squawk and looked behind her.

"What's wrong?" asked Tracy.

"Someone just pinched my bottom."

"Well what do you expect?" Tracy was incredulous. "Put up with it, it's good for business."

Sam arrived carrying a tray of drinks and Sharon took a glass of what looked like orange juice. She gulped it down and her eyes bulged.

"Go slow!" Sam cautioned. "I put a double vodka in there to relax you, not to get you paralytic before we've left the first pub."

~ * ~ * ~

Once the band had left The George and Dragon, Pip's mood lightened, particularly after strawberry pavlova for dessert and a second glass of wine.

"That was lovely, Tom. Thank you so much for bringing me."

"That's alright," he replied sipping his Guinness, "I like to show my girl a good time."

Pip smiled; she liked being called his girl.

"It's quite posh here, isn't it?"

"I guess so. Look, Pip, I want to talk to you about something."

"What?" she asked, wide-eyed.

"This friend of yours, Gavin. I don't want you hanging around with him. Ever. Full stop. I think he's up to no good."

"Tom, I'm sure you're wrong. He's sweet and wouldn't hurt me. He rescued me last night."

"Don't exaggerate. I've seen more of the world than you, Pip and I don't want you to see him. Not in school and not out of school, OK? Or would you pick that grease-ball over me?"

"No, Tom, of course not!" Pip panicked. "I'll tell him on Monday."

"I said I don't want you talking to him. He can figure it out for himself, is that clear?"

"Yes," Pip replied, torn and confused, but mostly afraid of upsetting Tom.

"Good," he said, adopting an air of condescension. "And don't worry about the cost of dinner tonight, you can pay me for your half later."

~ * ~ * ~

By the halfway point of their pub tour, Sharon was footsore and desperate for the loo. As soon as possible, she, Hannah and Tracy went for a comfort break.

"It's going well. Sam's happy," Hannah said.

"Good, but I'm starting to flag." Sharon lifted an aching foot from a shoe and scrunched her toes.

"Me too," Tracy giggled.

"Take one of these." Hannah handed them each a small white tablet. "It'll take about half an hour to kick in, just lay off the alcohol. I'll let Sam know."

Tracy downed hers with gusto and, after a brief hesitation, Sharon followed suit before the three ladies returned to the bar.

"The next few places aren't big enough for us all to fit in," Sam told the group, "so split up and meet at The Rose and Crown in twenty minutes. Tracy and Ed, you go to The Ivy, Frank and Sharon The Mitre, Hannah and Darren The Royal Oak, and I'll go to The Grange Hotel. OK?"

As Sharon and Frank reached The Mitre, she remembered why the name sounded so familiar and stopped walking.

"Hold on, Frank," she shivered, "there are some people that I really don't want to meet in there. Let's go and find one of the others and switch."

"Grow up, Princess, we've got a job to do. You're with me, remember? I'll keep you safe."

Sharon sighed and allowed herself to be towed into the pub, feeling a strange mixture of euphoria and almost crippling anxiety; her heart was racing, she felt exhilarated and emotional. It wasn't long before they encountered her two skinhead acquaintances standing at the bar.

"So, you did decide to come!" Spike exclaimed. "And is this the boyfriend?"

"No, this is Frank. He's another member of our band," Sharon explained, feeling increasingly confused and detached.

"Hello, Frank," Spike said. "Your little friend here bummed a fag off me this afternoon and led me right up the garden path. She let me think she was gagging for it and then dropped the boyfriend bombshell."

"I think you owe these men an apology," Frank told Sharon.

"Sorry, boys, I am naughty sometimes," she said impishly, all inhibitions dropping away.

"I need to take a leak. Why don't I leave you with your mates, while I hit the bogs?" Frank said.

Startled, Sharon briefly jerked back to reality. She watched Frank disappear into the crowd with a rising panic.

"Well, well, this is a nice surprise," Spike drooled over her. His hand slid down her back and squeezed one of her buttocks.

Her flesh tingling and crawling simultaneously, Sharon was unable to distinguish what she did and didn't want. She seemed on the verge of tears.

"It's OK, Sharon," Spike laughed, "I'm just kidding you. We are harmless, I promise. Tell you what though, you look hot in that outfit. What I wouldn't give for a camera right now. Let me get you a drink – what do you want?"

"I've been drinking vodka and orange, but I don't think I'm supposed to have any more for some reason."

"One more won't hurt." Spike signalled to the bartender.

Sharon spotted Frank returning and just had time to gulp the drink down before he led her away. Five minutes later, the band was reunited in The Rose and Crown. Sharon's high was almost unbearable, and her heart was racing; she had never felt so alive. Once they finished handing out the remaining leaflets, they headed to Sam's flat.

"Have you been drinking more alcohol?" Hannah asked like a tetchy doctor.

"Yes, some friends bought me one, and I was very thirsty."

"Hmm, well no more, OK?"

They fired up the hi fi and their party began; laughter, music, and chemical bliss affected each of them in their own way. Tracy, her eyes shut and in her own world, danced alone, the low bass vibrations seeming to direct the movements of her body; she opened her eyes and smiled with a love so beautiful that it could only hurt. Sharon danced as well, alive to sensation, elation increasing until the emotion became overwhelming. She giggled uncontrollably, more and more until it turned to sobbing and she slowly sank to her knees.

"What's wrong?" Tracy asked, stooping and putting her arms around the crying girl.

"It's HIM!" Sharon screamed, pointing at a startled Frank. "He left me on my own with two scary men."

"Is that right, Frank?" Sam asked, annoyed that a pleasant evening was being spoilt.

"She was fine," Frank insisted. "I was gone a couple of minutes and I left her with two guys she knows." He looked nervously at Ed whose huge fists clenched until the knuckles were white. "Honestly, she was fine!"

"Frank didn't mean anything by it," Darren assured Sharon.

"It might be a good idea to apologise," Ed growled with all the optionality of gravity.

"Yeah, it's not nice to leave a young lady alone in a bar like that," Sam said.

"I'm sorry, Sharon," Frank muttered; he spotted Ed's glower. "No, really I am. I didn't mean for you to be scared."

"Is that good enough, Sharon?" Tracy asked, but Sharon barely responded. "Are you tired?"

Sharon nodded, her glazed eyes seeing only a dark despair beyond understanding. Tracy led her from the room.

"That went well," Sam remarked, disappointed.

"Certainly not the ending to the evening you might have hoped for," Hannah laughed. "She had too much alcohol, that's all. I'll check on her in a bit."

~ * ~ * ~

"Pip, Pip!"

The owner of the name looked up from the book she was reading, curled up on the living room sofa. In truth, she was too preoccupied to take in the words, and welcomed the distraction of her younger brother.

"What do you want, Daniel?"

"Will you play football with me?"

"It's nearly lunch time."

"Mum says it won't be lunch for an hour and that's ages!"

"I'm not very good at football, why don't you ask Matthew?"

"He's over at Simon's. Simon has computer games."

Exhausted of arguments, Pip cast her book aside, helped her little brother put his shoes on, and got herself ready to go outside.

"What are those?" Daniel pointed to Pip's flat court shoes. "You can't play football in those."

"Do you know what looking a gift horse in the mouth means?"

"No."

"It means, if you want me to play football with you, this is what you get. Otherwise, I was enjoying my book."

After a pause, Daniel decided, "They are very nice shoes. Can we go to the park?"

"No, it takes too long. Maybe next weekend. Let's just go out back."

Pip understood her brother's preference for the park. The Ravens' back garden was a long thin strip of patchy grass with thigh-high chicken wire running down either side (marking the borders to neighbouring properties) and a solid wooden fence at the rear. A small shed stood next to a gate which offered access to an alley behind.

Her thoughts still dominated by Tom and Sharon, Pip idly kicked the ball back and forth with her scampering brother. Daniel's shiny mid-brown hair bounced up and down when he ran, his mouth wide open with grinning enthusiasm, tongue lolling with concentration, but there came a point when even the boy concluded that the limitations of the little garden were making the game monotonous. Pip decided to venture their thus far limited conversation onto more risky territory.

"Did you have another little accident last night?" she asked. "I thought I heard Mummy getting up."

"Yes." Daniel briefly screwed his eyes in irritation.

"That's fine. It's just that I think that you've something on your mind that's making you worried or sad. Do you like school?"

"Mostly."

"Is there anyone at the school who isn't nice to you?"

"Maybe."

"One of the boys or girls?"

"No."

"Who then?"

"Miss Parkinson."

Pip wasn't expecting that answer. "What does she do?" she asked.

Daniel kicked the ball as hard as he could, over the wire fence and into the garden of two doors down.

"Why did you do that?" Pip sighed. If she went on tiptoe, she could just straddle the wire fence onto their neighbour's patch; she did so, crossing their lawn with a sheepish wave to the lady who lived there and receiving a sympathetic smile in return. Over the next fence; these occupants had a small dog, a Jack Russell, which repeatedly hurled itself against the lower pane of glass of the back door in a frenzy of barking. Her spherical quarry retrieved, she made the equally ungainly reverse journey only to find the Raven household's little patch of England empty, as Daniel had run inside.

Pip kicked the football alone for a few minutes, in case he returned, until she caught sight of his pale face peeping through an upstairs window. She knew to let the matter drop for the time being and mentally filed the matter under the ever-growing category of 'Something Else to Worry About'.

~ * ~ * ~

"Good morning, sleepyhead," Tracy cooed.

Sharon sat up in bed, rubbing her eyes and peering blearily around the room, which was not Sam's but Tracy's. Her hostess was standing before her in a silky red dressing gown, holding a large tray.

"I have coffee and croissants. Budge up a bit, will you?"

Confused, Sharon shuffled her bottom to one side while Tracy laid the tray down, removed her robe and climbed under the covers. Sharon, unaccustomed to sharing a bed with a woman who had so few clothes on, peeked under the sheet to check her own modesty; she was in her underwear. The movement drew Tracy's attention away from spreading butter and jam onto a pastry.

"Don't tell me you're getting all shy on me now?" she giggled. "Come on, eat up before it gets cold."

Sharon sat up and took a croissant, but its buttery flavour didn't register with her whirling mind; this was very different to sleepovers with Pip and her fleecy pyjamas.

"Um… Tracy," she ventured, "I'm a bit confused. Do you… did we… well, I can't remember, anything you see… but I need you to know that I'm not…"

Tracy was perplexed until the penny dropped.

"Strictly no hanky-panky, I promise," she laughed. "We got you undressed, and you were out like a light. Hannah slept in here too, on the floor, because she was worried about you. Come on, let's finish our breakfast and get on with the day. Everyone else was up ages ago. Sam and Hannah have gone to arrange a surprise for you."

"What is it?" Sharon shook the bed with excited little jumps.

"If I told you, it wouldn't be a surprise, would it? We need to be downstairs in about three-quarters of an hour," Tracy tantalised as she got out of bed. "I'm off to have a shower. Finish up and follow me in. Don't panic, I didn't mean you should get in the shower with me! I'll call you when I'm out, OK?" She left the room with a final snort of laughter.

Thirty minutes later, they were both dressed and watching out of the window for a sign of Hannah's car. They didn't have a long wait and they raced downstairs the moment they spied its arrival.

"Someone wants her surprise," Sam laughed. He opened a rear door and slid out a long, heavy, black case with a hinge on one side and two silver catches on the other. Sharon opened it, excited fingers slipping on the catches, to reveal a Yamaha keyboard.

"Wow!" she exclaimed.

"Tracy told us about your piano playing," Hannah said.

"It's amazing, thank you so much!" Sharon's voice cracked with emotion.

"Just promise us that you'll practise lots," Sam said. "The next gig's in a week and we thought you could give Darren a couple of breaks."

"Oh, I couldn't be as good as him!"

"No one's expecting you to be," Hannah said. "We were going to suggest just one song to start off with. Do you like Gary Numan?"

"He's OK. I liked 'Cars'."

"How about 'Are Friends Electric' from when he was Tubeway Army? Even I can play that one."

"OK," Sharon said, closing the case and standing up. "Thank you, everyone, I can't tell you how happy I am. I just wish I could show my gratitude somehow."

"Come out with us this evening," Tracy enthused. "Give us the pleasure of your company. We thought we might go to the cinema or something."

"I don't know," Sharon hesitated. "I really want to, but it's a school night, and I still haven't done my homework. In fact, I'm supposed to be home for lunch soon. Mum always does a Sunday roast."

"Go home, do your homework, and we'll pick you up at six. You can sleep here, it's close to your school," Sam said. "I have to be at work for eight, so you'll be up in plenty of time."

"Oh, I can't imagine Mum letting me stay with a boyfriend at any time. Not even if I was thirty!"

"Then tell her you're staying with me," Tracy said. "It's true, and you don't have to mention boyfriends."

"Great idea." Sam smiled. "No need for your mum to worry and I'll make sure you have something warm inside you before you go."

~ * ~ * ~

Sharon clattered into the hallway, weighed down by two bags and a large musical instrument. Her mother appeared instantly from the kitchen, enveloped by a cloud of steam from the cooking.

"There you are, young lady! I wondered when you'd get here."

"Hold on, Mum, this is heavy." Sharon leaned the keyboard case against the wall, dropped her other bags on the floor, put on a sweet smile, and turned to face her maternal parent. "What have I done?"

"Marge from next door went out to dinner last night and was very surprised to see you parading around the pub half naked. What on earth do you think you're doing?"

"Mum, it was a harmless publicity stunt, and I wasn't half naked, I was wearing a dress."

"Stunt? What kind of stunt?"

"I should have told you before, but I didn't want to jinx it. I've joined a band with two friends, Tracy and Hannah. Look, they've given me my own keyboard."

Lyn's mood changed abruptly, and she put her hands to her mouth with joy as her daughter opened the long case to show the synthesiser.

"I know it's not like your lovely old piano, Mum, but it'll help me practise. I want you to be proud of me."

"I am, Sharon darling. Oh, this is wonderful, I've so wanted you to keep up your music."

"Shall we take it up to my room and set it up?"

"Go on, then." Lyn was excited. "There is still half an hour before the roast will be done."

The keyboard was straightforward to set up and soon the two of them were trying it out, even playing one of the duets that they had practised together when Sharon was a little girl. The mother went downstairs happy, and the daughter heaved a sigh of relief.

Later that afternoon Sharon tried to study but was too distracted. She glanced at a piece of paper which listed all the gigs the band had booked, and then she looked at her new keyboard and decided what she was going to do. Throwing her pen aside, she turned the volume down on the instrument and started to play. She would just have to bodge her homework when she got to school in the morning.

Later in the afternoon, she packed her case and carried it and her school bag downstairs.

"I'm off over to Tracy's," she told her parents, who were watching television in the lounge. "She's asked me to stay over. Her place is close to the school, so I'll be there in plenty of time."

"OK, love," her mother said, distracted by the programme. "Have we got her phone number?"

"I've left it on my chest of drawers," Sharon said. The number was for the Chinese Takeaway, but she knew they would never try it. "Bye, Mum, bye, Dad. Love you!"

~ * ~ * ~

On Monday morning, Pip ate her breakfast at the kitchen table and unburdened her worries onto her mum.

"So, Tom doesn't want you to even speak to Gavin?" Julia exclaimed. "That seems a bit mean. After all, you told me Gavin got you home safe and sound on Friday night."

"I know, Mum, but Tom's my boyfriend and I don't want to upset him."

"Yes, he's your boyfriend, not your lord and master. Don't let anyone tell you who you can and can't be friends with."

"But I've liked Tom for so long and when he finally asked me out, I poisoned him by taking him to a dump like The White Hart, all because of Sharon." Pip pronounced her former friend's name like a swearword.

"Don't be too hard on Sharon. You girls have been such good friends for years, I'm sure you'll get over it."

Pip rolled her eyes and harrumphed. She was about to respond with exactly why that was never going to happen (though her heart desperately wished it would), when the doorbell rang.

"That's Tom! He's giving me a lift to school."

"That's kind of him. He's good to you, I'll say that for the lad."

Meanwhile, Gavin's morning at school was a strange one. He arrived at his usual time and scuttled upstairs to the library, where he spent a happy three-quarters of an hour planning a computer game for his ZX Spectrum, scribbling madly in an old exercise book that he kept for his programming projects. He became aware that someone was looking at him and looked up to see the librarian meet his gaze, her face beaming with approval. He smiled back and returned to his work, bemused.

The first lesson on Monday morning was double maths (many students asked themselves why such cruelty existed in the world), and he entered the classroom with his usual trepidation. It was a daily ritual for him to find someone who would grudgingly share their table with him if he arrived late; alternatively, if he was early, some poor soul, a late straggler, would realise that they had drawn the short straw and would drop their text books next to him with a loud thud and a sigh.

Today was very different. When he walked in, most people smiled at him, three girls immediately moved their files and pencil cases to make room at the table beside them, and, most remarkably of all, the same young man who a week before had directed a football onto Gavin's face, waved his arm and shouted, "Gav, Gav, I've saved you a seat, mate!"

Gavin was faced with a dilemma. The ringleader of a regime of bullying against him was now making overt and apparently sincere overtures of friendship. At any point during his time at that school until the previous Friday evening, Gavin would have run or raged, but he did neither. Maybe it was because when thirsty, truly parched, a person will drink any water, however polluted. Desperate for fear-free normality, Gavin jumped at the chance of acceptance. Almost in a trance, he took the chair that had been so ostentatiously reserved for him and unpacked his bag.

"Hi, Gav," whispered none other than Lucy Barrow, queen of the lower sixth.

As the teacher entered the room and walked to the blackboard, Lucy's slightly plumper, slightly prettier twin sister, Heather, gave him a coy lip-glossy smile, emphasising the dimples that graced her cheeks. Gavin nodded to the ladies, and then settled to work as best he could, puzzled by his new-found popularity. After the lesson, things became clearer.

"We heard what you did for Pip at The White Hart," Lucy told him. "It's nice to have a real man about the place."

"I didn't really do anything. I just walked her home."

"Don't be modest," Heather chided. "Plenty of people saw it. They were all too scared of those men, but you stood up to them."

"Yeah," agreed football boy, a little shamefaced. "It took guts, mate. Of course, I'd have stepped in, but my girlfriend held me back." This liberal interpretation of the truth earned him several knowing looks from the others.

"We're going up town at lunch, Gav. Want to come with us?" Lucy asked.

"Um – thank you."

"Great! We'll meet in the common room and go from there."

The twins left, but Gavin and the remainder of his new-found friends went to the common room, as most of them had a 'study period'.

"So, Gav, were you going to fight them?" one of the girls asked excitedly. "Do you know karate? I saw that film *Karate Kid* at the cinema yesterday. I bet you're like the guy in that."

"Sorry to disappoint you, but I really don't know how to fight," Gavin replied. "I've done a bit of boxing, but that's about it."

"You've done boxing?" asked football boy, with a mixture of incredulity and nervous realisation that his former target was not so soft as supposed. "Where did you do that?"

"Our vicar teaches it at youth group. He used to be in the army and boxed for his regiment."

"Did he fight in the Falklands?"

"No, he'd have left the army by then. He was in Northern Ireland, I know that. He said he hated the sectarian divide, so he quit and became a priest."

Gavin made his excuses and went to the library to work for a while, overwhelmed by his sudden popularity; however, when the bell for lunch rang, everyone was waiting for him in the common room.

"We are just waiting for Lucy and Heather and then we can go up town," one of them said.

Gavin nodded and glanced around the room, only to spot Sharon standing in the doorway with a look of astonishment on her face. He walked over to her.

"I'm not going to ask what's going on," she said as he approached.

"It would take too long – and it is crazy, but I'm not complaining. Look, I need you to talk to Pip about something for me."

"Sorry, but I don't want anything to do with her, Gavin."

"What's happened?"

"Like you, there's too much to explain," she replied. "Everyone here seems like little kids since I joined the band. It's a different world. I'll always be here for you, Gav, but you don't need me. Go off to town – I need to finish an assignment. Take care."

"Take care, Sharon," he murmured as she walked out of the room.

Pip was standing by the school gates as the small throng of her fellow students passed nearby, led by Lucy of course; Gavin's presence in their midst, however, was less expected, but she was pleased by the development, because it meant that she didn't need to feel guilty about having to avoid him. Gavin spotted her and broke away to approach her.

"Sorry, I can't talk to you," she called, hoping to stop him.

"I understand, but I need to tell you something. It's about Tom."

"I don't want to hear it." Her eyes implored him to leave. "I can't talk to you – I mustn't."

"OK, then know this. You're too good for him. You're too good for anyone here."

"Thank you, that's sweet. Now please go before he sees us talking. I'm sorry, Gav, but at least I know you have new friends now. Goodbye."

"See you," he replied, returning to the group and walking away with them.

Then an unidentifiable female voice carried on the breeze, "You mean she just brushed you off after what you did for her? What a prize ungrateful bitch!"

Pip knew that Gavin would be defending her, but she closed her eyes and struggled to hold her emotions.

"You hit the nail on the head, my dear," she muttered to herself as she waited for Tom.

~ * ~ * ~

An intense desire for pleasure seeking had invaded Sharon's psyche, whether the excitement was sexual, chemical, or derived from danger. She felt closer to her boyfriend than ever, as if they shared some unique spiritual plane.

They had at last been on a proper date, going for dinner at a nice pub in the countryside, about thirty miles away. The true thrill, however, had come during the journeys there and back; they travelled on a straight old Roman road, pushing Sam's motorcycle to its limits, 'topping a ton' the whole way, speeding past cars two or three at a time as if they were standing still. Her heartbeat seemed to match the stroke of the engine beneath her as she peered over her boyfriend's broad shoulders, every corner, every bump making her gasp.

Their latest gig had been their most successful and once again the band gathered at the flat. Music and hazy smoke filled the room, and everyone was mellow.

"I expect you all want your cut from the gig's takings?" Sam said, and he moved around the group passing notes out to some of the junior members.

"Thank you," Sharon murmured when a twenty fluttered towards her and she had the presence of mind to roll it up and stick it into her bra.

"Now, I'm hungry," Sam announced. "Ed, why don't we head out and get a takeaway for everyone?"

"Oh, you are good boys," Tracy purred, just on the right side of compos mentis. The two men departed as Frank wandered back into the room.

"You girls looked amazing tonight," he told Tracy and Sharon, clearly trying to ingratiate himself.

"Thanks," Sharon replied. "You sang well too. Oh, you missed Sam, he was sharing out some of the takings for the gig. We're doing really well."

"You aren't that bright after all, are you Miss A-Levels?"

"What's that supposed to mean?" Sharon's mind lifted several levels from its dreamy state.

"You think we made that much from the gigs?" Frank laughed. "We aren't that good, sweetheart. Nobody's going to pay extra to watch you two dancing around in your little skirts. If you took your kit off, we'd treble the takings and it still wouldn't make it worth Sam's while to pay you."

"Sorry, I still don't understand."

"I'm saying no more," Frank grunted. "Why don't you ask your boyfriend sometime?"

~ * ~ * ~

Once again, Daniel was snuggled up to his big sister after yet another disturbed night. She lay in the dark of the morning, stroking his head, feeling him sob.

"You almost made it through the night," Pip whispered. "Well done."

The boy shrugged. It was another case of almost but not quite.

"Daniel," she continued, "why does Miss Parkinson make you sad?"

"She gets cross with me because I can't learn my words and letters properly. I get muddled."

"Muddled? How?"

"Like *d*'s and *b*'s – they jump around. Miss Parkinson holds up her little cards, but I don't know what they say, and everyone laughs at me."

"Well, that's not very nice of them," Pip said, as softly as her mounting anger with the boy's teacher would permit, "but you can read, you've read your books to me."

"No, I just remember them."

"Well, that's very clever of you, I couldn't do that." She kissed his head.

Later that day, when her classes were over, Pip walked into the town library and spent an hour or so in the reference section, scribbling notes in a little notebook.

~ * ~ * ~

Sharon lay with her head on Sam's bare chest moving gently with his breathing and listening to his heartbeat. One of his arms lay over her, the other periodically moved in and out of her vision as he raised the lit cigarette he was holding to his lips; every so often a plume of smoke billowed around her when he exhaled.

"Sam, I'm going to spend Christmas at home," she whispered. "I love you and I want to be with you, but I owe it to them. I love them too."

"I know, I think it's good. Other than Hannah, I have no family." Sam sensed Sharon's surprise. "I'd a much older half-sister, Lucy, from my old man's first marriage and Hannah is her daughter, which makes her my niece. Mind you, her dad was worth a bob or two, so she went to all the fancy schools and universities."

"So how is Hannah related but not Darren?"

"Lucy died shortly after Hannah was born. Hannah's dad remarried and that's where Darren came from. So, you'll spend Christmas with your family, and I'll spend it with mine – and Tracy and Ed, they've got no one. Hannah's off to America in the New Year, a post doctorate something-or-other, so it'll be a nice way to say goodbye."

"She didn't tell me she was leaving." Sharon was saddened by the news. Although not close to Hannah, she respected and looked up to her.

"We'll be fine. Frank can go back to being chemist and I'll handle the rest."

Sharon turned to look up at Sam, admiring him; he smiled and proffered the cigarette for her to draw on.

"Tell me," she spoke softly, as if she feared her voice could shatter a frozen moment in time, "where does the money come from? I know bands don't make the kind of cash that you bring back." She laid her head back down, looking at the ripples in the bedclothes.

"I told you, ancillary sales – what makes you ask?"

Sharon heard Sam's voice twice, through the air and through reverberations in his chest.

"Frank said something, but I'd been wondering anyway. What are ancillary sales?"

"Do you really want to know? You can't put the genie back in the bottle."

"Yes, please tell me."

Sam sighed, as if he were about to once again take her innocence.

"People come to our gigs to buy gear, you know, pot and pills."

"You're drug dealers?"

"Yeah, not hard stuff. Well, sometimes Frank gets it to order, but most of what we sell's no worse than fags or alcohol."

"I suppose not."

"Are you OK with it, with what I do?" Sam asked.

After an agonisingly prolonged pause for thought, Sharon once again looked up at him. "I think it's just about the sexiest thing I have ever heard."

"You are my kind of girl!" Sam laughed, shaking the bed. He drew again on the cigarette and its glowing end reflected in his girlfriend's eyes as two fiery red dots.

"And," Sharon said with a dark smile, "I've an idea of how you could open up a new revenue stream…"

~ * ~ * ~

Pip waited patiently in her room, listening intently for the end of her mum's favourite television programme. As soon as she heard the music, she trotted lightly down the stairs and into the living room. Her father was rereading the sports pages of the paper and her mother was writing Christmas cards.

"I need to talk to you about something. It's about Daniel. I– I think he's dyslexic."

"Oh, Pip, that's a horrible thing to say about your little brother!" exclaimed Julia. "It's like saying he's a bit backward."

"No, it's not, Mum! I spent the afternoon in the library looking into it, and it says dyslexics are generally very clever, but their brains work differently. I tried getting him to read some letters earlier and he's struggling."

"His teacher hasn't said anything."

"Maybe so, but she makes him cry in front of the kids because he can't read properly. He told me."

"We'll talk to the school, it's their job."

"Good luck with that," Pip snorted, having lost all regard for Miss Parkinson. Now came the difficult part of the conversation. "That little private school down by the museum specialises in helping kids with dyslexia."

"We can't afford it, don't be silly!"

"I could help, I'll be earning soon," Pip offered.

"I'll find the money if I have to," her father interjected. "That's my responsibility, so you keep your money, my girl. Anyway, let's see what his school says first, OK?"

The doorbell heralded Tom's arrival and Pip hurried to be with him, leading him upstairs to her room.

"Mind you keep that door open!" Julia shouted, too late as a thud shook the house. She was about to tell Pip to open it, but her husband signalled to her.

"Leave them for quarter of an hour, then take them up a cup of tea," he advised. "That's what your mother used to do to us. Used to drive us crazy."

"How could we afford that school?" Julia moaned, flopping back on the sofa and changing the subject. "It's a struggle keeping this roof over our heads."

"I could get some more work, or a second job. Cross that bridge when we come to it, eh?"

"Yeah, I'll get a brochure for the school tomorrow." Julia looked up as creaking came from the floorboards under Pip's room and smiled wickedly. "I'd better get the kettle on."

Chapter 5

After one of the ever-rarer nights that she slept at her family home, Sharon swatted her alarm clock into submission. Turning on her shiny new stereo radio-cassette, she lay back on her pillow listening to Foreigner's 'I Want to Know What Love Is'.

"I know what love is," she said to herself, picturing Sam.

The school term had restarted a week before after a busy Christmas break filled with gigs, parties and laughter with her new friends. Sharon spent the big day with her family; her elder brother, Mark, was home for a few days too, so it was like old times (giggles, games, the Queen's speech, and too much food). She came close to telling him something of her new life and friends but settled for the official line of, 'I'm in a band'.

The telephone rang when she was dressing after her shower, and her mother's voice echoed upwards from the hallway. Thinking nothing of it, Sharon ambled down to breakfast.

"That was the school," Lyn announced, her voice tight with anger. "They want us all to come at one-thirty this afternoon to discuss your work. They aren't at all happy."

"I don't know why, I've done all my homework," Sharon sulked.

"I don't know when you've been doing it!" Lyn slammed her hand on the counter. "You're out with that band and staying at Tracy's most nights. It's going to have to stop, my girl."

"I'm sure it's a mistake!" Sharon's heart balked at the idea of spending less time with Sam. She targeted her next words carefully. "I love my music, I get that from you, so let's see what the school's got to say! I promise I'll do better."

"OK, love," Lyn relented. "I'm pleased you're getting so much pleasure from your music. Come on, have some cereal and then you can get on your way."

As she left for school, Sharon berated herself for eating breakfast, knowing that she needed to keep her weight down. With Tracy's mentoring, she had dropped a dress size since October thanks to a ready supply of cigarettes that took the edge off her appetite.

There was a quiet spot where she waited for Sam, well away from prying eyes. Sure enough, the sound of the Honda's engine soon reached her ears and the dot of a headlight grew steadily brighter until the motorcycle roared up to her. Sharon was soon riding pillion through the streets, gripping Sam's leather-jacketed torso.

~ * ~ * ~

Pip's festive season had had its ups and downs. She worked a lot of overtime at the shop and was consequently tired over Christmas, but it meant she could buy nice presents for Tom and her family. She had been given a new coat by her parents and perfume by Tom and what's more, he had taken her to his house on Boxing Day to meet his relatives.

She had written a Christmas card for Sharon but never sent it; however, her former friend hadn't sent her one either, so Pip had little regret. Her initial anger and hurt from their falling out had ebbed long ago, but new injury came from Sharon's cold body language and whispers Pip heard about herself that could only have originated from one person.

When she wasn't looking after her brother, or in the shop, or out with her boyfriend, she was working hard on her school project and counting the days to the end of her course, eager to get out into the world of business administration.

As usual that morning, she left the house in good time to walk to school. Tom couldn't give her a lift as he was away on a training course, but she was warm in her new coat and she enjoyed walking past the houses and seeing their inhabitants go about their day; she knew several of them and received some cheery greetings.

When she neared the school gates, a motorcycle roared past and stopped outside the entrance. Sharon dismounted and hugged the driver goodbye, watching him as he disappeared up the road. She glanced in Pip's direction and, to Pip's surprise, she waited for her to reach the gates.

"Hello," Sharon spoke with starched formality. "Did you have a nice Christmas?"

"It was OK, thanks. How about you?" Pip wondered where the conversation was leading.

"Good, thanks... Pip, I don't know how to say this, but I miss you sometimes. I know we'll never go back to how we were, but I'd at least like to have lunch with you like we used to. Not every day, but sometimes."

"Would you really?" Pip asked warily. "Because, I think I'd like that."

"Great. I like your new coat," Sharon remarked. "Don't worry, I won't ask to borrow it."

Pip forced a smile, but an old wound opened, and it showed on her face. Sharon spotted her mistake.

"I could give you the money for it, if you like? I've been flush lately from all the gigs we've done."

"It's OK," Pip responded with a more genuine smile. "Let's let bygones be bygones. Are you free now?"

"Definitely. You can help me prepare for the scary talking to I'm going to get this afternoon. The school want to see me with Mum and Dad."

"What have you done?"

"Let my grades slip, I guess. I only got thirty-five percent on my last Human Biology test, so I'm guessing that's lit the fuse under me."

"Oh, Sharon, you're not letting the band get in the way of your studies, are you?" Pip asked, resisting the urge to say that, if the rumours she heard were true, Human Biology should be Sharon's best subject.

"No, I've just not been getting much sleep lately. It'll get better, I don't fancy you becoming the brainy one out of the two of us!"

"That is a scary thought." Pip's smile was strained again. "Come on, let's go in."

~ * ~ * ~

After morning break, Sharon chatted casually with Fiona, one of the other girls taking Home Ec., as they waited for their lesson to begin. Fiona complained about a back injury she had suffered falling off her bike.

"It's been so painful, but I've finally got a hospital appointment, look!" Fiona plucked a small white appointment card from her bag and waved it under

Sharon's nose. "See? Not a 'doctor' but a 'mister'. Mum says that means he's a consultant, and you can't get higher than that."

"Well, I'm glad you're getting it sorted at last," Sharon feigned sincerity. "You've been through so much."

"Thanks, Sharon, no one else seems interested."

During the class, Sharon had a flash of inspiration and realised how to neutralise the fallout that she would experience when her parents arrived at the school later that afternoon. It would take careful timing, but she was sure it would work. She was sitting beside Fiona, so slowly, cautiously, Sharon reached her hand into the girl's bag, pulled out the appointment card unobserved, and slid it into her own pocket.

When the class finished, Sharon ran to the library and scanned the room looking for someone, anyone, she knew. Fortunately, Gavin was there.

"Have you got some scissors I can borrow for a few minutes?" she whispered.

"I have a new modelling knife," he replied, rummaging in his coat pocket.

"Perfect." She almost snatched it from his grasp. She hastened to a corner study cubicle and started to scrape away at the appointment card in the area where Fiona's name was written in blue biro. Before long, all traces of the letters had disappeared, and Sharon wrote her own name in the space. It would certainly stand casual inspection.

She returned the knife to Gavin and then hared to the Head of Sixth Form's office, tapping politely on the door. The exertion of running had the added benefit of helping her to appear emotional, so all she had to do was feign a little teary-eyed sobbing.

"Why, Sharon, you aren't due until half-past one, and it is only ten-to," the teacher said when Sharon entered.

"I need to speak with you, to confide in you before my parents get here," Sharon explained in a small voice.

"What's the matter, my dear?" Mrs Wood cooed, swept along with the drama and emotion of the moment. "There is a tissue in the box on the bookshelf."

"Oh, Mrs Wood," Sharon croaked as she extracted a tissue and dabbed her eyes, "I need to talk to you, I've been so worried, and I simply cannot tell my parents."

"Go on."

"It's a bit personal. Private, if you will— since my boyfriend and I— you know…"

"Yes, yes I do dear."

"Well, I've been to see the doctor and I've got an appointment with a specialist next week, and then it should all be over." Sharon waved the appointment card.

"Oh, my pet!" cried Mrs Wood, hurrying around her desk to put her arm around Sharon. "You have done the right thing in coming to see me."

"Please, can you see why my parents mustn't know?" Sharon asked through magnificent sobs.

"Why yes, dear, but you really should think about telling them. I'm sure they would be a huge support."

"No, think of the shame!" Sharon wailed.

"Of course, of course. We'll handle things delicately. Don't worry about your school work, the drop off is completely understandable in the light of your news. I knew a bright, sensible girl like you would have a good explanation. Now, why don't you toddle off to the cloakroom and get yourself together, so your parents don't see you've been crying."

"Oh, thank you, Mrs Wood, I— we all— are so blessed to have you to watch over us, to guide us."

Sharon humbly exited the office, offering a brave smile to her Head of Sixth as she closed the door behind her.

"Well, that's just made her day, the nosy old cow," she said to herself as she went to wait for her mother and father at the school gates.

Sharon couldn't have hoped for the meeting to go better. Mrs Wood sung her praises to her parents, saying how talented and clever she was, what a bright future she had, how there were no worries about the poor marks of late, but that Sharon should probably take things easy for a couple of weeks.

"What was that all about, then?" asked Lyn as they walked to the Cortina. "Your dad's lost two hours of work for a complete waste of time. Sorry I doubted you, though."

"That's alright, Mum. I think I might stay at Tracy's for a couple of nights, if that's OK?"

"I guess so, it doesn't look like there is anything to worry about."

Sharon kissed her parents goodbye at the school gates and was at her leisure to carry out the second half of her plans for the day. She walked back around the school building to the playing fields, her shoes slipping on the damp grass as she climbed the gentle incline to the little-used cricket pavilion, which was the hangout of those fourth and fifth-year pupils who thought themselves rebels. The usual suspects were there, a mixture of boys and girls dividing their time between smoking cigarettes and overt snogging. Sharon noted the appreciative glances from the males and the jealous disdain of the females as she strolled into their midst.

She crooked a finger at one of the group leaders and beckoned him to follow, which he readily did, like an enthusiastic beagle. Once out of sight, she opened her bag to show him four joints that Frank had prepared for her; the leader gazed at them with greedy eyes and Sharon easily negotiated a price.

"You can take them now and pay me tomorrow," she said. "I'll have more then, and I'll give you a percentage cut on what you sell." She waited until he grasped his illicit treasure with both hands. "One thing you need to remember – whatever happens, my name never gets mentioned. The people I'm with wouldn't like that. I watched one of them choke a man with his bare hands a few weeks back, and he'd snap yours like a twig. Mess with me, and you'll be meeting him."

Machismo briefly flared up in the boy's young face, but then he realised just how serious she was, so he simply nodded. Sharon smiled.

"This is going to be the start of a beautiful friendship," she said.

~ * ~ * ~

Pip could hear her parents bickering again. They rarely argued but excelled at minor spats with ascending levels of mutual incredulity. It frustrated her that, despite her being the one who spotted Daniel's dyslexia, she was kept out of the conversations and decision making. She crept down the stairs and into the kitchen, completely unnoticed.

"Alright," Julia sighed, "we can afford the first term's fees, but what do we do after that?"

"If we can find it this time, we can find it again."

"Where from? Unless you're planning to win the pools or rob a bank, it's not likely to turn up."

"Well, what do you suggest?"

"Second mortgage," Julia stated. "Pay it off a bit at a time."

"I suppose so…"

"We've got enough for the first term and we'll have the mortgage before the next one is due. What's worrying me is the costs of the uniforms and everything else. It's very expensive – hundreds."

"I'll pay," Pip interrupted. Both parents turned to her in surprise.

"No, love," said her dad.

"Why not? It's just sitting in my bank account."

"Have you really got that much?" her mother asked.

"Yes. I've saved it up. Please take it, you can pay me back when you've got the money. Honestly, I'm grown up now and I want to help, I want to help Daniel."

The parents exchanged tempted glances.

"You're a good girl, Pip," they said in unison.

~ * ~ * ~

Sam and Frank had developed a grand plan and they gathered the group together for dinner in a Chinese restaurant to tell them about it.

"I have bad news and good news," Sam announced. "The bad news is that Darren has quit the band. No hard feelings, he just wants to pursue his own music. He's found a mate and they're moving up to London to make it big. It's no surprise, I don't think he found it easy being a queer in these parts."

"That's exciting for him," Tracy bubbled, genuinely pleased for their friend. Sharon and Ed concurred.

"I'm glad you said that, because here's the good news," Sam grinned. "Darren's inspired me and thanks to Frank's contacts, we can take this operation up to London. We've a real chance of making something of the band, not just playing in the local dives around here, and of shifting higher value product. We could make serious dough."

With little to stay for, Ed and Tracy were thrilled by the possibility, but Sharon's heart was breaking. She still had a year of sixth form and her entire life was in the town – but Sam *was* her life, her reason for breathing, so it was unthinkable to stay without him.

"When do you want to go?" she asked, desperately hoping the answer would be far in the future.

"Next week," Sam replied, oblivious to her suffering. "Frank's got a gaff organised and I'm already working my fortnight's notice at the workshop."

"I can't believe you've planned this and not told me," she hissed, leaning close to Sam. "Is this your way of dumping me?"

"No, love, I just didn't want to worry you until it was definite."

"Quitting your job already seems definite!"

"I told you, toolmakers are in demand, I can always get work." Sam placed a comforting arm around Sharon. "I don't want to do this without my girl by my side, are you coming or what?"

That was the first time that he had called her his girl. How quickly anger can ebb and infatuation flow into the space it leaves. How could she not want to be with this man? Why care about A-levels when she could make it big in London? Briefly, the image of her parents' faces when she told them flashed into her mind, but she planned to go to university soon anyway, so her departure was brought forward a bit, that's all.

"Try and stop me," she replied, leaning forward for a very public kiss. Sharon felt only excitement. There was no going back, no second thoughts, this was it, this is what she wanted more than anything else in the world; it was a magnificent high, as if perched on a clifftop with only blue skies and calm seas ahead of her.

However, after the meal was eaten, washed down with plenty of alcohol, and plans discussed, Sam became serious.

"This is all great, but we need money. Money for the move, money for new product, money for promotion. I've most of the cash but everyone's going to have to chip in. I reckon five hundred quid each is fair. That's a fraction of what I'm putting up."

Sharon's heart sank. Five hundred pounds might as well be five thousand, or five million.

"Are you OK?" Tracy asked. "Why so glum, sweetie?"

"I haven't got that kind of money."

"Me neither, nor Ed, but don't worry, we will find a way."

"Thank you," Sharon's terror of being left behind abated as an idea planted itself in her mind. She smiled to herself – she knew what she had to do.

~ * ~ * ~

Pip felt awful. Her limbs ached, her throat was burning sore, her nose ran, and she had an annoying tickle in her chest. She grabbed a handful of tissues and went downstairs to be fussed over by her mother with hot lemon tea and toast dripping with honey. A flask of chicken soup and two soft ham rolls were stuffed into her bag, and she was forced to cover her neck and chest with a thick scarf before leaving for school; she protested but was secretly comforted by the attention.

As Pip neared the school gates, Sharon was once again waiting.

"Are you OK? You don't look well," she asked, taking an unconscious step back.

"Just a bit of a cold. I'll be fine," Pip croaked.

"Are you free for lunch today?" Sharon asked. "I need to talk to you, but I've got to get an essay done."

"Sounds good. I'll meet you in the common room."

Despite Mrs Wood's gullibility, Sharon thought it prudent to turn work in punctually, no matter how substandard. She scribbled her essay out in the library and then ran to her lesson. The morning seemed to last a hundred hours, subjects that she had once taken seriously now seemed irrelevant to her, but at last she was in the common room, where she found Pip drinking a cup of soup.

"That looks nice."

"Do you want some?" Pip snuffled. "If you can find a cup, you're welcome to a share."

Sharon scouted around the small kitchenette that was provided to the sixth-formers and found a chipped mug, which Pip filled with soup from her thermos; she also gladly parted with one of her ham rolls. They chatted idly about gossip and family, and once again relaxed in each other's company. Sharon was looking to broach the subject she wanted to discuss but could find no appropriate opening, until Pip herself brought the subject up.

"So, what did you want to talk to me about?"

"It's about the band," Sharon began slowly, choosing to ignore the cold expression on her friend's face. "We've had the most amazing news."

"That's nice for you," Pip managed to say civilly.

"Well, we've been offered a big chance and we need to go to London for a bit."

"What's that got to do with me?"

Sharon decided to be direct. "I need to borrow five hundred pounds and you're the only person who has that much who I can ask." She stared in nervous expectation.

"You cow!" Pip eventually growled.

"What?" Sharon reacted, genuinely perplexed.

"You cow, you manipulative cow!" Pip grabbed her thermos and stuffed it into her bag. "I'm not staying for this."

"What? Why?"

"I must be so stupid," Pip rebuked herself, fighting back tears, "I thought you really wanted to be my friend again."

"I did! I do!"

"No, I don't think so. You pretended you want to be mates again to get me to stump up my hard-earned cash, while you blow it on God knows what. I've heard the rumours, Sharon, and I see right through you. Bad news, I don't have the money, and I wouldn't give you a penny of it if I had. Sod off, Sharon. I mean it, just sod right off!"

"Well sod you too!" Sharon's shock turned to fury. "I should have known better than to try to be your friend."

"I can do without friends like you!" Pip's ferocity made her throat sting. She grabbed her coat and stormed from the room.

Sharon watched her leave, her eyes blazing with anger. However, after a few moments, anger turned to laughter. Plan A had failed, so on to Plan B and she fancied that dear Philippa would approve of Plan B even less.

Gavin was in the opposite corner of the room and witnessed the argument. Indeed, everyone had watched the spectacle, mouths gaping as they witnessed the oldest, dearest friendship in the school violently die with no hope of resuscitation. Pip had stormed out of one door and Sharon through another a few seconds later. Opposite directions, different intent.

"So, Princess Slag and Queen Bitch are off each other's Christmas list," one person commented.

"Which is which?" asked another.

"That's not very nice," Gavin defended his friends.

"It's true, though. Have you seen Sharon at her gigs, flashing the flesh? And why are you defending Pip Raven? She wasn't very nice to you."

He forbore from pointing out that she was nice when everyone else present had not been; it was cowardice on his part, fearful of upsetting his fragile new friendships.

"I don't mind about Pip," he said instead. "She had her reasons."

"That's nice, Gav. Defending her again."

It seemed that he couldn't stop being a hero.

~ * ~ * ~

Sharon had in mind a scheme to solve her liquidity issues which should provide both a solid amount of cash and the possibility of revenge. The concept was simple but needed assistance to implement – people not connected to her or the band. She went in search of accomplices, and struck gold at the first attempt, locating Spike and his seemingly constant companion in The Mitre; this time she bought the drinks.

"So, what do you boys do for a living?" she asked.

"Pretty much sod all," Spike replied, lighting a cigarette. "Rick here did a bit of roof-tiling in the past."

"You've always got some cash to flash, though," Sharon falsified nubile admiration.

"I have my ways." Spike touched a fingertip to the side of his nose.

"In that case, I have a little venture that might be right up your alley. Are you boys interested?"

"Could be," sniffed Rick. "I'll never say no to making a quid or two, as long as I don't actually have to work for it." That joke seemed to require a long laugh from all three of them.

"I need a fourth person, preferably a woman," Sharon told them.

"My girlfriend might be up for it."

"So, we split the proceeds four ways, then?" Spike said.

"No," Sharon replied, "I take a third, you split the rest however you like. It's my idea. I can find other people, but you can't find another plan."

Spike and Rick went into a very indiscreet huddle but took very little time deciding; once they had all shaken hands to seal the deal, she outlined her plan.

~ * ~ * ~

The remaining piece of Sharon's jigsaw was in her father's garage. She found him out there on Saturday morning, contentedly polishing the Cortina with such effort that it was almost too bright to look at in the pale sunlight.

"Hello, darling," he smiled when he saw her. "Come to help?"

"No," Sharon grinned, her arms folded just like her mother would, "I wouldn't want to steal your fun. You've done a great job with the wheel arch. I can't see the difference."

Bob was delighted that his daughter should be so interested. "Well, when you've got rust bubbles, you need to act quick. It's horrible, corrupts everything around it, so you cut it out, fill the gap, smooth the whole area down and paint it, double quick."

"Is this the paint?" Sharon asked, picking up a gold aerosol from the neatly arranged shelves in the garage.

"That's the one, but I don't need it today."

"OK. I'm going in to make a cuppa, do you want one?"

"That would hit the spot just right," Bob smiled. "It's nice to have you here for a change, you're always out with your band."

Sharon was momentarily struck with doubt; she almost ran to her father, to ask him to hold her, to keep her, to stop her. Almost. Instead she said, "Well, I'm off again soon, but I'll bring your tea first."

If Bob had been a little less trusting and a little more observant, he would have seen his daughter conceal the spray can under her jumper before she left.

~ * ~ * ~

On Saturday afternoon, Sharon met Rick and Spike in the town centre. Rick introduced his girlfriend, Sophie, who was an attractive mass of heavy makeup and wavy fair hair.

From hearing Pip talk about her Saturday job, Sharon knew that the newsagent had busy mornings and hectic lunch times, but that custom soon tailed off. By about two-fifteen in the afternoon, only one member of staff would be on checkout while others took breaks or went home; at this point, the tills would be crammed full of cash until they were emptied down to a residual float at approximately a quarter to three.

The team watched from the café opposite and moved efficiently as soon as the shop was empty. Poor Pip had the misfortune of being on duty, so Sharon remained out of sight while Sophie entered alone and began asking complicated questions, cunningly drawing the unwitting sales assistant to a corner of the store; Pip's back was kept to the checkout, while Sophie kept clear of the antiquated surveillance camera.

Rick entered, moving covertly through the racks of products to a lookout position near the staff-room, where he could intercept any shop staff who might emerge. At the same time, Spike blinded the only security camera with a burst of paint from Sharon's spray can.

Each of the team held their breath when Sharon darted in through the open doors, quietly opened the tills, and extracted the cash. She was wearing a long blue shirt, close enough in colour to the staff uniforms that a casual observer would assume she was an employee. Poor Pip had no hope of hearing the activity over the noise from the street, and Sophie distracted her with constant inane questions until well after Sharon had scampered out of the doors, followed closely by Rick and Spike.

Cool as a cucumber, Sophie thanked Pip for her help and strolled out, leaving the sales assistant none the wiser. A few minutes later, the shift supervisor arrived to empty the tills and realised what had happened. Of course, no culprit was ever identified, but a tearful Pip was fired on the spot for leaving the checkout unattended and was told that she was lucky that she wasn't a suspect.

~ * ~ * ~

Her share from the theft, plus the cannabis distribution proceeds, made Sharon more than the requisite five hundred pounds. However, she had another problem – how to break the news of her leaving to her parents. In her mind's eye, she could see her father's face and hear her mother's words, so she decided to take the easy route: go to London and write to them from there. She stayed at Sam's so often that they wouldn't realise for days that she was gone. Problem solved.

The band planned to leave for London the following Tuesday. Sharon told her mother that she would be staying with Tracy for a few days and advised Mrs Wood that she had a follow-up hospital appointment.

However, on the Monday, the boy who had been distributing pot on Sharon's behalf sought her out; it seemed one of the fourth years had been caught smoking a joint and the school had instigated a full search of all pupils, including bags and coats. Sharon took the remaining joints from the panicked boy and thought quickly about her next move.

Bitterness and anger made Sharon Wells sink to her lowest point of wickedness in her nearly seventeen years, for she walked unnoticed behind Pip's chair in the common room and stashed the joints into the bottom of her former friend's schoolbag. Then, she hurried to see Mrs Wood, who was as usual in her office.

"May I have a word?" Sharon asked.

"Of course, my dear, is it about tomorrow?" the teacher asked, brimming with empathy.

"No, it's about my dear friend Philippa Raven, well…"

"Yes, dear, do go on."

"It's just that lately, she has changed so much and has fallen in with some very unsavoury types. I think she might be… smoking stuff, not tobacco, if you understand me. Oh, I need your advice on how to help her."

"Leave the matter with me." Mrs Wood moved from behind her desk to pat her troubled student's arm reassuringly. "There is no need to fret, I shall investigate the matter personally. You really shouldn't be having to worry about other, selfish, people when you have your own difficult journey ahead of you."

"But no one must know I told you. People might call me names, or worse."

"This is just between you and me, I assure you."

Sharon's spiteful victory over her former best friend was complete, marked with a grateful hug of reassurance from the gullible Head of Sixth. She spent the remainder of her last day at the school without the slightest remorse, and left unseen, long before the final bell had rung, waving a final goodbye to her academic career with a triumphant V-sign.

Pip's distress at being hauled into Mrs Wood's office was matched only by her bewilderment when the joints were discovered in her bag. Her tearful protestations of innocence were brushed aside as a mixture of deceit and denial, and she was forced to wait in the school secretary's office, shaking with nerves and misery, until her parents arrived, pale-faced and wracked with worry.

Mr Raven wanted to believe his daughter's story, but couldn't, mainly because Julia and Mrs Wood insisted she must be a duplicitous drug user. It was too painful for Pip to bear, seated between her parents and facing Mrs Wood behind the desk; her distress manifested itself physically, with shallow breathing and a raised heartbeat pushing her to the verge of being in a dead faint. She clung onto her father's arm to avoid slumping off her chair and implored them to believe her in ragged whispers.

"You are clearly genuinely upset, Philippa," Mrs Wood said, thoroughly unconvinced by her pupil's display, "and you do have a good record, so I'll recommend to the headmaster that the police need not be involved. However, expulsion is inevitable."

Pip sobbed from the depths of her gut and begged her to reconsider, "But my course; my exams; my project."

"Very well," Mrs Wood relented, very slightly, "you may still submit your project and sit your exams – in isolation, naturally."

"Naturally," Julia echoed, glaring at her daughter. "That is most generous of you."

"Thank you, but I must also tell you that the careers master felt compelled to advise Wilsons Packaging about the matter and the offer of a secretarial training place has been retracted. They're a family firm, you know."

"Oh, no!" Pip cried. "Please no, it's not true, I wouldn't do it! Please, won't someone believe me?"

"I am getting weary of this, Philippa," Mrs Wood snapped. "You're getting off far too lightly in many people's opinion. You need to face up to what you have done and get yourself sorted out. Please don't test my patience any further."

Defeated, dejected and all but destroyed, Pip walked out of the office to her father's car and travelled home in oppressive silence. She spent the evening mute, hearing lectures from her mother while her father was thinking how his little girl had been corrupted by a terrible world. At length, Julia ran out of things to say, so Pip refused all offers of food and went to bed to weep into her pillow.

After a long sleepless night, she lay shut in her room and dreading the world outside her door. She heard life – her father leaving for work and her mother getting the boys ready for school – but she saw only bleak desolation. Her future was not an undiscovered country but a bleak and unforgiving wall.

And while all this was happening, Pip's old friend Sharon was sitting behind Sam on his motorcycle, arms tight around him, riding towards London and adventure.

Chapter 6

Gavin was chatting with a group of fellow sixth-formers when Heather burst into the common room, desperate to distribute the juicy gossip that had just come her way.

"Pip Raven's been expelled," she whispered as loudly as a shout. "Drugs. Pot. I always knew it. You could tell by looking at her."

"There has to be a mistake." Gavin was incredulous.

"No, there's more. You know Joanne Barns? Well, her mum works in the newsagents with Pip, or I should say used to work, because Pip was fired for stealing. Caught with her druggy hand in the till!"

"Not Pip," Gavin insisted. "Something doesn't add up. Where did you hear about the drugs?"

"Well, it's going around school that she was expelled, but Mary Thompson saw Sharon Wells on Monday afternoon, and she said it was because Pip had four joints in her bag. Sharon's bound to know, isn't she?"

Gavin frowned, but said nothing. He instinctively trusted the school's judgement, but it sounded wrong. With Pip not speaking to him because of Tom, he had to hope the truth would come out another way.

~ * ~ * ~

By Friday, Pip was past confusion, past anger and was perpetually numb. She lay in bed until ten o'clock in the morning, tired from yet another sleepless night and unable to motivate herself to get up. Everywhere she went, accusing eyes seemed to stare at her, even in her own home.

Her brothers were at school and her father at work, so the house was silent save for the murmur of her mother's voice as she spoke on the telephone. Pip was sure that the person at the other end of the line was her grandmother and her heart broke some more. She had cried, begged and pleaded with her parents, but they merely looked at her with worried eyes and mumbled platitudes, for she had no convincing explanation for her possession of drugs; crueller still, her siblings seemed to be being shielded from her, as if she was infectious.

Her father now treated her with silent sadness, looking at her with eyes that could no longer see the many colours of gladness that they once did when she was with him. Her mother was tight-lipped, a pressure cooker with no release valve, watching her daughter's every movement for signs of degeneracy.

Eventually, she found the will to get up and plod downstairs for some breakfast, though by then it was closer to lunch. As she passed the living room door, her mother's voice fell silent; Pip paused for a moment, wanting to go in and beg for a hug, for a sign of forgiveness or understanding, but instead she went into the kitchen. She wasn't hungry, she hadn't been for days, but she still had the last remnants of her cold, so she opened the refrigerator door and removed a carton of orange juice and poured some into a tall glass.

"I wish you'd eat something, young lady," Julia said from the doorway.

Pip mutely tore a banana from a bunch in the wooden fruit bowl beside the fridge and ate it pointedly.

"It's good to see you up, at least," her mother continued. "Well, if you're not at school and you're not at work, you can give me a hand around the house. I don't suppose you have anywhere else to be."

"I do actually. Tom is back from his course, so I thought I'd walk up to see him in his lunch break." Pip finished the banana and threw the skin into the kitchen bin.

"Well, run the vacuum around the place before you leave," Julia instructed. "And you can help make dinner when you're back. You'll be coming straight home?"

"No, Mum, I thought I'd visit my dealer and shoot up," Pip snapped. "That's what you mean, isn't it? You think I'm an addict, desperate to get high or something, I can see it in your face. You even think I might be serious now, don't you?"

"What do you expect me to think?"

"I expect you to believe your own daughter." Pip acidly started to roll up the sleeves of her cardigan. "Look, see? No needle marks."

Julia peered at her daughter's arms.

"Good grief, Mother!" Pip screamed. "They found pot, not heroin. You smoke pot."

"Well, I wouldn't know that, young lady," Julia shouted back, "and I rather wonder how you do!"

"Everybody knows! Why not ask Sharon?"

"Oh, you haven't got her into it too, have you?"

"You are unbelievable!"

By some indefinable synchronicity, the two women fell silent, minds racing. Pip sought to diffuse the situation by changing the subject onto someone they both loved.

"If the weather improves, I thought I might take Daniel up to the park after he finishes school. He's been wanting to go for ages."

Julia's body language stiffened – and then, slowly, terribly, she put two and two together, to come up with seven.

"Pip, the money for Daniel – did you steal it? Did you use dirty drug money to pay for your brother's uniform?"

Pip stared in sheer disbelief and anger that made her shake from head to toe.

"I don't have to listen to this," she said through a clenched jaw, persecuted pain evident in every syllable. She stormed to the front door, stomped into her shoes and left the house.

"Put your coat on!" Julia called, too late to be heard before the door slammed shut. She stood, frozen in time for several seconds before a deep sob forced itself up in a convulsion of heartbreak. There was no option but to sit on a chair at the kitchen table, cover her eyes and let the tears flow.

Pip was less than twenty paces from her house before she realised that she had no coat, no handbag, no purse, no money and two hours to wait until Tom would be on his break. Looking up at the wintry sky above, she did entertain the idea of returning for her coat but couldn't face the prospect of continuing the confrontation. By the time that she reached the town, she couldn't feel her hands because of the cold, even though she had pulled the ends of her sleeves over them; the misty moisture swirling in the air permeated her clothes and flattened her hair.

Seeking warmth, she went into the launderette and sat on the plastic bench, watching other people's washing spin around in the big yellow tumble driers. A well-built lady with short hair and a ruddy complexion emerged from a small room at the back of the premises; she was wearing a blue nylon tabard, the uniform of the establishment.

"Are you using any of these machines?" she asked.

"No," Pip replied quietly, "I came in here because it was cold."

"I'm sorry, luv, but paying customers only in here." The woman pointed to a sign pasted on to the wall which said much to that effect. "We get tramps and all sorts in here, otherwise."

"Oh, I didn't know. Sorry," Pip responded flatly, getting up to leave.

"Don't forget your coat," the lady mothered.

"Oh, I didn't bring one." Pip was distant, unable to connect to anything. "That's why I came in, I think I forgot it. I'll be fine."

"You will not! You'll catch your death out there and you're already peaky. Come with me." The woman led Pip into a room at the back of the shop and hauled a cardboard box from under a table; it had 'Lost Property' written on the side in permanent marker. "Look through here. People leave all sorts in this place – some of that stuff has been in there for years."

Pip complied, picking up items and looking at them with blank, uncomprehending eyes. The woman watched her for a few moments, and then poured out a mug of tea from a chipped brown teapot that sat beside the stainless-steel sink.

"Tell you what, you sit and drink this and I'll find something for you. I made the pot fresh about ten minutes ago, so it should be perfect."

Pip obeyed, holding the warm cup in both hands and sipping the tea. Tendrils of heat worked their way through her veins, and she began to wake up.

"Thank you," she said, "you are very kind."

"I'd like to think someone would do the same for one of my kids." The lady held up a long blue mac in her hands. "This should keep most of you dry. It's been in here for ages, so no one's going to miss it." She rummaged once more at the bottom of the box, pulling out an umbrella. "And take this in case the rain gets worse."

"Thank you." Pip was confused by the generosity of a stranger. "I can bring them back tomorrow, or did you want some money for them?"

"They didn't cost me anything," said the woman with a dismissive wave of the hand, "and no one else seems to want them, so I suggest you keep them. They're only cluttering up the place."

"Thank you," Pip repeated, finishing her tea, "I suppose I'd better be going."

"I suppose you had, dear."

Pip made her way to the door but hesitated on the threshold. She turned back to face the woman, the kind stranger who had shown more warmth to her than any friend or relative had in the last few days.

"Is there something else you would like?" asked the woman.

"Please..." Pip faltered, "I wondered if I might..."

"Yes, luv?"

"Please may I have a hug before I go?"

~ * ~ * ~

Tom was irritated to see Pip standing humbly outside his work, particularly as her hair was messy and she was wearing an 'old lady' coat two sizes too big for her; she looked ridiculous, he thought, and was showing him up.

"What are you doing here?"

"I've missed you," Pip replied, putting her arms around him and pressing her damp head to his chest, getting a little smear of machine oil from his overalls on the side of her temple. However, after a few moments, she realised he was not returning the embrace and she pulled back. "Is everything OK?"

"The thing is, Philippa—" Tom began, reaching the highest echelons of pompousness.

"Philippa? No one calls me Philippa unless I'm in trouble."

"Well, aren't you? I came back from a trip to find people telling me you're a thief and a druggie."

"It's not true! You must know it's not true!"

"Maybe, but my mother says there is no smoke without fire. I'm sorry, Philippa, but I've my family's good name to think of."

"What are you saying?" She knew the answer. Her arms dropped to her sides; she was losing her remaining anchor of hope and was once again adrift.

"I'm breaking up with you, Philippa. Sorry and all that, you're a nice girl but I can't be seen about with you. Goodbye."

Tom joined the queue for the pasty van, not glancing back for a second. Pip stared after him, vainly hoping for a change of heart, but he was resolute in his unkind rejection; she started her lonely walk home, just as the heavens opened with a deluge of rain.

~ * ~ * ~

Pip had a troubled night, tossing and turning, replaying her conversation with Tom again and again in her mind; more than once she cried herself into a fitful sleep, from which she would jump awake after just a few minutes. Finally, at about six o'clock on Saturday morning, sheer exhaustion, combined with the warmth of the central heating coming on, meant that she sank into a deep, dreamless blackness, from which she didn't emerge until almost midday.

It was the sound of voices that woke her; she lay in dread of the visitors below and their disapproval. Eventually, her parched throat forced her to get up, put on her dressing gown, and creep downstairs for a drink, hoping that the callers would be in the living room. As Pip entered the kitchen, she saw her grandmother sitting at the table and her mother leaning against the counter; they were deep in conversation but broke off as soon as they realised she was there, serving to justify her paranoia.

"Hello, Gran." Pip kissed the old lady's cheek. "Sorry to interrupt, I just came to get some juice."

"I'll get it for you," Julia said, opening the refrigerator door. "Your grandmother wants to talk to you."

With resigned dread, Pip sat on the chair facing the only adult she knew who was shorter than her. Gran's wrinkled round face had a kindly smile and bright grey-blue sparkling eyes.

"Your grandad and I thought we'd better come over and see you, Pip. We've been hearing all sorts of nonsense, so we thought we'd get to the bottom of things. He's in the living room with your dad watching Grandstand or something. I just hope he doesn't nod off and end up all crotchety for the drive home. Now what's this all about?"

"Drugs. Money going missing," Julia stated, deeply distressed. She stamped Pip's orange juice onto the table. "I don't know what to do, I'm at my wits' end."

"That's enough, darling, I want to talk to my Pipsqueak." Gran took Pip's trembling fingers between her own soft hands and skewered the girl with an unbreakable stare. "Tell me, Pip, did you have anything to do with the money going missing?"

"No, I promise."

"And what do you know about these drugs they found in your bag?"

"Nothing, Gran, I don't know how they got there, truly I don't."

The elderly woman stared into Pip's eyes for a silent eternity, before she broke the gaze and addressed her own daughter.

"You silly fool, Julia! How I raised a twit like you, and you raised a girl like Pip, I will never know. Don't you know your own daughter? Of course she had nothing to do with any of it."

"But, Mum," Pip's mother responded in exasperation, "the drugs were found in her bag."

"That's as maybe, but Pip here says she doesn't know how they got there, and I know she is telling the truth. For heaven's sake, she's never been able to lie! Not since she was five years old and I asked her who licked the cake mixture off my wooden spoon and she tried to blame the cat. She is as transparent as she's always been."

"Thanks, Gran," Pip whispered, a tear trickling down her numb cheek.

"You are welcome, my darling," cooed her grandmother, producing a scented hankie from her sleeve and handing it to Pip. "Now, my girl, pull yourself together, and get yourself upstairs and into the shower. Pack a bag and come home with me and your grandad. I think you should get away from this place for a while, and you can lend me a hand looking after him."

Pip nodded, dabbed her eyes, returned the handkerchief and hastened upstairs. When she returned, suitcase in hand, her grandfather met her in the hallway and hugged her as if there wasn't a care in the world for either of them.

"If you decide to stay for longer, your dad will bring some more of your things over next weekend," Julia offered as she walked them to the car. Then she noticed her daughter's coat. "Why are you taking that tatty old thing? Where is your nice new one we bought you?"

"I think I need to wear this one for a while. This one means something to me."

"Well," Julia tutted, "it's your decision."

Pip hugged her family goodbye and was about to get into her grandfather's car when she heard her name being called. Gavin was running towards her.

"Hello, Pip," he panted, "I know I'm not supposed to speak to you..."

"It's fine. Tom and I have broken up."

"Oh, I'm sorry. His loss, though."

"At least someone thinks so," she smiled.

"I just wanted you to know that I heard the rumours and I don't believe a word of them."

"Thank you, that means a lot."

"Are you going away?"

"Yes, to stay with my gran and grandad for a while. It will be a relief to get away from this place."

"I was going to put this through the door," he gave her an envelope. "It's just a card saying I'm thinking of you."

"Thank you, Gav. You're a real friend. I'm sorry I let Tom stop me from being one to you."

"Water under the bridge, I assure you. Goodbye, Pip."

"Goodbye," she replied, getting into the car. She continued to wave as the car drove away until Gavin was long out of sight.

It took a little under an hour for Pip's grandfather to drive to their home. It was a tiny two-bedroomed bungalow in the middle of a small terrace of identical properties that sat on a raised bank near the centre of the village. He parked his aging Chrysler Sunbeam in the nearby garage block and insisted on carrying his granddaughter's suitcase indoors. The hallway carried the familiar aroma from Pip's childhood of lavender mingled with boiled cabbage.

Pip almost cried when she walked into the second bedroom, which her grandmother had already lovingly prepared for her; a little fluffy pink blanket was laid over the bedspread, on the pillow was a cushion with a crocheted cover featuring the letter 'P', a Poinsettia plant (still ablaze in scarlet glory) sat upon the dresser, and a tub of home-made shortbread was placed on the bedside table.

Several pictures hung on the walls, chocolate box images of old cottages and hayfields, and a needle-point of a bible verse, 'And now these three remain: faith, hope and love. But the greatest of these is love'. Pip smiled, for she was now in a place where she felt surrounded by love.

The window looked out onto her grandfather's immaculate garden, where he could be seen, sleeves rolled up, striding purposefully to his tiny shed, though Pip had no idea what horticultural activity he would be planning on doing on such a winter's day.

"Thank you, Gran, it looks lovely."

"I'm glad you're happy, my darling. I can't tell you what a boon it will be for me to have you here. Now, what do you say we put the kettle on?"

Two delicate china cups with roses decorating their sides were placed on matching saucers, alongside an old brown mug, which had a chip on the handle.

"That's for your grandad," said the old lady. "He'll be wanting his in the shed, and he's not getting my best crockery out there. Now, I've got some lardy cake in a tin somewhere, we can have a bit of that. You still like it, don't you?"

Pip took the mug and a plate of cake out to her grandfather, who was listening to the radio in his shed while he cleaned out some old flower pots; when she returned, Gran bade her to come into the living room, where they sat at the dining table by the window overlooking the church, the pub, and the little Post Office stores that served the village.

"Now, my girl, I need to ask you something. Have you been praying?"

Pip looked evasively about the room. "No, Gran, well, I suppose I did in a way, but a fat lot of good it did me."

"God is not like your personal fairy godmother," Gran explained, "He doesn't answer wishes, but He can be your staff and your comfort in times of hardship. Bad things happen, but that doesn't mean He isn't listening and hurting right beside you. Now, promise me you'll have a good pray tonight. Promise?"

"OK."

"Good girl. Now, I've got a nice bit of beef in for our lunch tomorrow, so you get up good and early with me and we can do the veg and get things all nice and ready before church. Then in the afternoon, we can go for a walk around the village and I'll introduce you to some of my friends."

"Um, I had wondered about maybe having a sleep-in tomorrow," Pip ventured. She was, however, met with a steely-eyed look.

"You need to be keeping busy, my girl. I know you've been through a hard time, but there is no use moping about it. Keep active."

~ * ~ * ~

Pip awoke early on Sunday morning. With more energy than she had had in a long time, she jumped from bed, pulled on her dressing gown and hurried to the bathroom; when she returned, a cup of tea was waiting for her on her bedside table.

She enjoyed sitting with her gran at the tiny kitchen table, peeling potatoes, cutting Brussels sprouts, and slicing swedes. Then, they walked arm in arm to the church, leaving Grandad asleep at home, as his wife of fifty-seven years was worried about his angina flaring up.

Pip had respected her grandmother's wishes and had said some token prayers before bed the previous evening, but in much the same way as most people read the instruction manual for a new television. However, in church, she found herself swept along by the service; every word seemed to speak directly to her, "I will fear no evil: for thou art with me". Accustomed only to mumbled prayers at lacklustre school assemblies, the proceedings were alien, but peaceful and she lost herself in the moment.

When the congregation gathered in the foyer for coffee and biscuits, chatting about village affairs, the anonymity was liberating, and several people struck up conversation with Pip totally unaware that back home she was a social pariah.

"Thanks for coming, Pip," Gran said as they pottered up the hill to the bungalow. "I don't want you to feel you have to come again, I just wanted you to give it a try."

"I might," Pip replied, "I found it peaceful, beautiful. I've been so down lately, like I'm in a dark tunnel, but I forgot for a while."

"You've been through a bad experience, and if people tell you to snap out of it, they don't know what they're talking about. I've been on this planet nigh on eighty years, so I know you can't rush these things. Keep yourself busy, but let yourself have a little cry now and then, and then come and talk to your old gran, OK?"

"OK, I promise."

"Good girl. Let's get home so that I can show you how to make a decent Yorkshire pudding."

~ * ~ * ~

On Wednesday morning, Pip walked down to the village shop to buy food and groceries. It was a time capsule from the 1930s, with two long wooden counters and the goods stacked on shelves behind; the customer would read from their shopping list, and the shopkeeper would reach down the items, ringing the prices into the old mechanical till. The owner, Mr Elstree, was a tall, balding man with a long grey face and thin half-moon spectacles. He always wore his flat-cap on his head, and a long brown shopkeeper's coat. There seemed to be nothing he didn't carry in stock: shoes, spades, candles, local cheeses, fresh vegetables from his garden, reels of film, stationery, lightbulbs of all types, items of haberdashery – you name it, he had it somewhere in his storeroom.

"On your grandmother's account, I assume?" asked Mr Elstree rhetorically, taking a small ledger book from his shelf and entering the details of the sale.

Pip made her way home along the narrow lane, pulling her grandmother's tartan shopping trolley behind her, and stopping on the grass verge from time to time to allow a car to pass. One vehicle, an old Land Rover, drew to a halt and a lady wearing a thick military-green jersey, jodhpurs and long riding boots climbed out. She was in her mid-thirties, with curly fair hair tied in a ponytail, and bright blue eyes set in a round, slightly weather-beaten face.

"It's Pip, isn't it?" she asked in a cut-glass accent. "I'm Lucinda, we met at church. Your grandmother cornered me the other day and asked if I knew of any jobs going. Well, I didn't at the time, but things have changed a bit. I run some stables on the edge of the village and I need someone who can help around the office. The whole system is a complete mess, I'm afraid, and I don't have time to get on top of it. Invoicing, keep the books, order the feed, you know the sort of thing. Frightfully dull, really."

"I don't think that's boring," Pip told her, "I love organising things and getting everything straight."

"Do you indeed? Look, Pip, I'll be straight with you. It seems I'm going to be popping out another sprog in a few months." Lucinda patted her tummy. "I've got my hands full with the business and my four existing little perishers, so, would you be interested in working for me in the office and helping mind the kids from time to time?"

"I would, but I don't know anything about horses."

"Unnecessary for the job, I assure you, other than the obvious, of course – four legs, food in one end, shovel up what comes out of the other – and I'll teach anything else that you need to know."

"There is another thing," Pip faltered. "I have to tell you I was fired from my old job because some money went missing when I was on duty. And I've been expelled from school because they think I take drugs. They're not true, but I couldn't expect you to take the risk. Sorry."

"I know," Lucinda replied. "I've known your gran for nearly twenty years and she's the most honest person I've ever met, present company excepted I suspect, and she told me all about it and what she thinks of the people who say it's true. You could've tried to hide it, but you were honest, and I like that. Still want the job? I can't pay much, forty quid a week and you can have lunch with the family if you're a glutton for punishment. What do you say?"

"I say, yes please! Thank you so much."

"Wonderful. You can start Monday." Lucinda suddenly stopped short as an idea struck her. "I say, you're not any good at netball, are you?"

"Um, well I played a little bit at school," Pip replied, taken aback by the turn in the conversation.

"Excellent. Look, some of the younger womenfolk around here have started a little team, just for fun. We play in the school hall on Mondays, and we need a recruit. Are you up for it?"

"I can give it a try."

"Marvellous! Pip, you really are a godsend. I must go now, but one more thing: you'll need wellies to walk through the yard, so bring some old shoes to change into, which you can keep in the office."

Pip assured her that she would and immediately headed back to the shop to buy Wellington boots, making a mental note to ask that sports kit be added to the stuff her dad would be bringing over at the weekend.

~ * ~ * ~

"I know Sharon said she was going to be at Tracy's for a few nights, but this is getting ridiculous," Lyn grumbled, staring into her coffee cup.

"She's a sensible girl," Bob replied, sipping his own drink. "Why don't you call her?"

"I did. Last night. She must've made a mistake, because it was that Chinese restaurant near the cinema. I'm worried."

"Look, she must be going to school or they would have rung up creating a fuss, wouldn't they?" Bob reasoned. "They dragged us in over nothing a couple of weeks back, so they're bound to let us know if she's disappeared."

"Don't say disappeared. Don't tempt fate."

Bob nodded, cross with himself; he was as worried as Lyn, maybe even more so. Already late leaving for work, he had no will to go, too miserable, missing his little girl and wishing that she might spend more time at home with them. There was a clatter from the letterbox in the hallway. He stiffly rose to his feet and walked to collect the post, while his wife continued to gaze at her coffee in contemplation.

A pathetic, whining, strangled sound brought Lyn to her senses. It wasn't a scream, it wasn't a cry, but it was terrifying; she ran into the hall. Bob stood before her, face white, shaking, staring at her as his mouth moved but no sound came. His trembling fingers held out a postcard. She knew what it was going to say before she read it.

'Dear Mum and Dad. Gone to London with the band for our big break. See you when I'm rich! Try not to worry, lots of love, Sharon'

The postmark was smudged – maybe it said 'Tower Hamlets'? Probably not.

Lyn managed to reach Bob's arms before her legs gave way and he held her as they both sobbed.

~ * ~ * ~

Mrs Wood sat, ashen-faced and replaced the telephone handset. Numb shock crept like ice through her veins and she struggled for breath. She walked out of her office and through the school corridors at a moderated pace, fighting the urge to run.

Through the narrow vertical pane of glass set into a pale wooden classroom door, she could see a lesson in progress; the teacher, a woman in her late twenties, was standing in front of a whiteboard trying to impress the ramifications of the English Civil War on a group of disinterested thirteen-year-olds. Mrs Wood knocked and entered.

"I wonder if I might disturb you for a moment, Miss Harris?"

Sue Harris told the class to do some quiet reading (an act of optimism, she knew) and joined the Head of Sixth in the corridor.

"You are Sharon Wells' form teacher, aren't you?" Mrs Wood didn't trust her own memory.

"Yes, why? Is there a problem? I believe you told me she was in hospital."

"I did, but it seems I may have been misled. Her mother just called in a very distressed state and told me she's received a card from Sharon saying that she's in London. Naturally, I checked with the hospital, but they had no record of her. The consultant whose name I had been given is a spinal specialist, not a gynaecologist or obstetrician."

"Why did you think she would be seeing an obstetrician?"

"Why would any young girl?"

"Goodness! Did Sharon give any reason for leaving and going to London?"

"Her mother thinks it may have something to do with a rock band. The police are involved, but there's little they can do – she is over sixteen. Sue, can you remind me if Sharon had any specific social group?"

"Well, she's quite popular, but she was close to Pip Raven, and I've seen her with Gavin Knight many times."

"Well, young Philippa won't be much help," Wood remarked with a sharp tang of disapproval.

A stand-in teacher was summoned to cover the class, and the two women hurried to the sixth form common room. The general buzz of conversation died off when the students realised the teachers had entered; several of them suddenly feigned industrious study but were fooling no one. Heather and members of her entourage straightened up when they realised Wood and Harris were approaching.

"Heather, you know Sharon Wells, don't you?" Sue Harris asked, her tone unusually blunt.

"Sort of. We aren't best friends or anything. Gavin knows her best. He'll be back in a minute."

Surely enough, just as she finished speaking, the young man appeared through the door.

"Gavin," began Mrs Wood, "we need to try and reach Sharon Wells. Do you know where she is?"

"No. I spoke to her last week briefly, but she keeps herself to herself lately."

"Oh, Sharon's in with that bunch of fourth and fifth years that hang around up by the cricket pavilion," one of Heather's friends chipped in. "I saw her up there a few weeks ago. You know the ones - the headmaster had a barney at them because they were smoking wacky-baccy."

This information started a new niggling worry at the back of Mrs Wood's mind, but she pressed on with the more urgent matter in hand.

"I understand that she is in a band, is that correct?"

"Yes, it's called Black Metal Armour," Gavin replied. "I don't know much else about them. I think that's why she and Pip fell out."

"She's fallen out with Pip?" Miss Harris asked. "I'm amazed – they were always so close."

"Yeah, they were, but they fell out when Sharon dumped her on her own after one of her band's gigs," Heather's friend once again contributed. "And then a few weeks back I heard Sharon ask Pip to borrow a load of money and Pip told her to sod off, pardon my language."

"Really?" Heather interjected. "If she's not her mate, how did she know that Pip was chucked out for having four joints in her bag?"

"Four?" Mrs Wood asked; the nagging doubt in her mind was now a probability which settled on her like a clammy blanket, for that information was only known to a select few.

"I know Pip was scared stiff by the idea of drugs," Gavin stated. "She pretended she wasn't, but she freaked out after she saw Sharon smoking pot at the gig."

"That's true," Heather confirmed with a dismissive wrinkle of her nose. "Pip always was a goody two-shoes."

The two teachers departed and returned to Barbara Wood's office.

"I think the school was hasty expelling Philippa," Sue stated bluntly. "I found it hard to believe at the time. I know that every student found with drugs is going to protest their innocence, but it rings true for her."

Mrs Wood was in turmoil. It seemed she was responsible both for a terribly cruel miscarriage of justice and for unwittingly aiding Sharon's disappearance; her career was over.

"Yes, Sue," she said in as business-like a voice that she could muster. "We need to speak to the Head now, and then I need to call Miss Raven to eat humble pie, as she may be able to help find Sharon."

The conversation with the headmaster was the first of three excruciatingly painful ones for Mrs Wood; he lost no time in laying blame at her door. The second was on the telephone with Julia Raven; a justified, but nonetheless upsetting, tirade of expletives erupted down the telephone line. Then came the third painful conversation.

"No thank you," Pip was polite but icy, "I don't think I would like to return to the school. I think there will be too many funny looks and wagging tongues. I'd like to sit my exams, like you said I could."

Mrs Wood assured her that the school would help in any way that it could. The only assistance that Pip could give regarding Sharon was to say that the band leader was called Sam and that he worked in a unit on the industrial estate; she added that Ed and a Tracy were also in the group.

Armed with this information, the teachers drove to the industrial estate, navigating its warren of roads until they found a unit that fitted Pip's description of it. However, their investigation ended when the manager said he knew Sam, but since he left, they hadn't been able to find his personnel card.

The situation was bleak.

"Oh, Sharon," Mrs Wood sighed to herself, "what have you got yourself into, my dear?"

Chapter 7

Every ring on the doorbell brought cruel hope to Bob and Lyn. They always dashed to answer in irrational optimism, only to have their hopes dashed by a perfectly pleasant person standing on the threshold who wasn't their daughter. The milkman took to an elaborate knocking to avoid seeing such heartbreak every time he called to collect his money.

The chimes sounded once again, and once again their hearts ruled their head; on this occasion, the disappointment was a young man who introduced himself as Gavin, a friend of Sharon's.

"I'd like to help," he told them, sitting in their living room with a cup of tea balanced on his knee. "Sharon was very kind to me in the past. She and Pip both were."

"Ah, poor Pip," Lyn sighed. "I'd give anything to have Sharon back, but the first thing I'd do is give her a piece of my mind."

"It's not the first thing you'd do," Bob corrected her, "but I wish she still had young Philippa as her best friend – now we know about the boyfriend and motorbikes and whatever else."

"And drugs," Lyn spat. "How did we not notice? Are we bad parents?"

"Sharon always said nice things about you," Gavin assured her.

"Then why?"

"I don't know." Gavin was at a loss. "Have the police been able to help at all?"

Lyn shook her head and shrugged, fumbling in the sleeve of her sweater for a crumpled tissue. She gave a single sniff.

"They've been bloody useless, that's what," Bob growled.

"Be fair, love, they explained she can leave home if she wants." Lyn turned to Gavin as if pleading a case before a judge. "She might be fine, mightn't she?

She might be having a lovely time with her friends, and we're worrying about nothing like a couple of sillies."

"Maybe," Gavin smothered his incredulity.

"It's the not knowing, you see. I'd just like to know, to make sure she's eating properly."

Gavin nodded and they all sat quietly, each in their own thoughts for a minute or so.

"It's the not knowing," Lyn whispered.

"Well, I'm taking action!" Bob slammed his hand on the arm of his chair. "I've done a leaflet with her picture on saying she's missing and giving our number. My boss has said he'll run off as many as I want for as long as I want on his duplicating machine. So, I'm off to London this weekend and I'm going to ask everyone I see to watch out for her."

"I keep telling him it's daft," Lyn moaned. "London's huge, isn't it?"

"Yes, it is rather large."

"I don't care!" Bob was almost feverish. "If my girl's there with some bike-riding fly-by-night, then it's my duty as her father to find her and bring her home to her mum."

"Please, you'll make yourself ill," Lyn pleaded. She was torn between worrying about her husband, and a desperate need for his plan to work.

"My mind's made up," Bob insisted.

"I'll come with you," Gavin pledged, "every week until you want to stop."

"Don't be silly, lad, you've got exams and stuff, that's your future. No point in another one messing up their lives."

"Mr Wells, I'll be on the London train every week whether you like it or not," Gavin said, "so you might as well let me help."

~ * ~ * ~

Julia Raven was nervous. She stood in the kitchen, arms folded, watching her sons having a kickabout in the narrow garden. The ball arced towards her and slammed against the window; it was Matthew's misjudged strike, but Daniel retrieved the errant football and was consequently the main recipient of the maternal frown.

There was a scratching at the front door, a key in the lock, and Pip walked in, smelling of fresh air.

"Hello, darling," Julia faltered. She ached to be close to her daughter again but was hurt that Pip chose to remain with her grandparents now the "unfortunate misunderstanding" was resolved.

"Hi." Pip's hug for her mother was reflex, not desire. "Where's Dad?"

"Working overtime, but he'll be home for lunch. Want a cuppa?"

"Thanks." Pip was distracted by her brothers in the garden. "By the way, what are all those boxes in the hall?"

"It's your stuff," Julia replied, wishing that she had put them out of sight, "from your room. Well, Matthew's room now."

"What do you mean, my stuff? You just went through my things and dumped them in boxes?"

"No, I packed everything up carefully, my girl, and I'll ask you to drop that tone with me," Julia snapped. "You've made your choice, you're living with Gran and Grandad, you've got a job there, so you're not coming back, are you? It wasn't fair to have the boys sharing and your room going empty."

"But all the handles on my bedroom furniture had little pink flowers on. Matthew won't like that," Pip tried and failed to be funny. She saw her mother's point of view but was irked by the fait accompli.

"I'm not an idiot, Philippa, I can go down to Johnsons Hardware and get a handful of knobs."

Pip half smiled at the unintended innuendo but wasn't in the mood to laugh.

"I've got nowhere to store the boxes," she said. "There's no room at Gran's."

"Do you think I'm an idiot?" Julia sighed. "Sort through the boxes after lunch. Take what you want, we'll put the rest in the attic. Dad can drive you back, so you don't have to carry stuff on the bus."

"Yeah, OK," Pip said. It felt a very final decision, and she was emotional. "Matthew looks fed up. Why don't I take Daniel to the park? I promised him ages ago and never got around to it."

"I'll come too."

"Why? Do you still not trust me with him?"

"No, you twit," Lyn laughed. "I want to spend time with you while you are here."

The three of them strolled up the road together, and into the public gardens; the first sights and scents of spring were there to greet them with sticky buds and drowsy bees. Daniel ran around the network of paths, never out of sight, dashing back every so often to give his big sister a hug.

"It's not ever going to be the same, is it?" Julia said when the two women were walking alone. "Us, I mean, how you feel about your dad and me."

"I don't know. I'd like it to be, but you didn't trust me."

"What else were we to think? The evidence was overwhelming."

"Except that you never believed it was possible that I was telling the truth. Not for one minute. In fact, you seemed to be looking for a reason for me to fail."

"No!" Julia exclaimed, dismayed.

"Ever since I gave you that money."

"Philippa, did it ever occur to you that we were angry with ourselves? Can you imagine how humiliating it is to need your teenage daughter to pay for her brother's school uniform? I hope you're never in that position when you have kids."

"So, it was easier to believe I was a thief or a drug dealer? You must know I don't care about things or money. All I've ever wanted is to be like you, to settle down and have babies. I'm not like the others who wanted to go to university and have careers, it's alien to me."

"But you're not like me, are you?" Julia said. "That wasn't what I wanted, but I didn't have a choice in the matter. It's what you did in those days. Husband, house, kids, grandkids, grave. That's it, that's what we looked forward to. I wanted a nicer house, two cars, a proper holiday and a real social life. I could never live in that village you're so happy in, I even find this place too boring. This is your dad's town, I grew up near London."

"You should still have believed me," Pip stabbed her words, an accusation to the heart.

"I should have done but I didn't, because you, Pip, you have always been too good to be bloody true! You went to bed on time without complaining, you slept through the night, you ate what was in front of you, you helped with your brothers, you worked hard at school, you came home when we told you to. When Matthew turned up, I didn't know what hit me. Talk about a pain in the backside! And then, just as I was getting my life back, along came Daniel and I was back to square one. So, yes, maybe I wanted to find a chink in your perfect armour, my dear."

"What, so I'm supposed to apologise for doing what I was told?" Pip was unable to process her mother's apparent displeasure.

"No, no, it's not like that at all," Julia realised she had gone too far. "It's just that we're very different people."

"OK, Mum, let's drop it, shall we? Have a nice walk," Pip was hurt, angry, and most of all confused.

Julia had a small plastic bag containing the stale remnants of a forgotten loaf of bread. They walked to the duck pond and threw the dry white crumbs to the small group of mallards bobbing on the surface of the murky water. Habituated to such delicacies, the birds swam towards them and squabbled among themselves.

"Where's the little one?" Daniel anxiously counted the birds.

"What little one?" Pip asked.

"There's normally eight, but there's only seven. The little one is missing. It never got to be as big as the rest, so we need to make sure it gets lots of food to make it strong."

The two women racked their brains to remember the details of the birds. Julia had been up there with Daniel only a week or so before – maybe she did recall a smaller, more fragile one, but she couldn't be sure.

"Hang on." Daniel squatted at the very edge of the pond peering closely. He stood straight again and announced, "The little one is there after all! He's just got bigger, so I didn't recognise him."

"That's good," said Pip.

"There's still one missing though."

"Maybe he's found a lady duck and they flew off together to get married?"

"I doubt it," Daniel dismissed his sister's romantic world view.

"Well, I think you're very clever to know how many ducks there are."

The bread finished, they dusted off their hands and circumnavigated the pond, following the little paved path that marked its outline. The mallards tailed them, suspecting them of still having food concealed about their persons. Whereas the humans had the disadvantage of being obliged to follow the perimeter, the birds were able to move in straight lines across the water, segmenting the pond and heading them off at regular intervals, quacking loudly for more bread until eventually, the ducks accepted that the Ravens had nothing more to offer and swam away.

They found the remains of the eighth bird at the far end of the pond, behind some tall rushes. Probably mauled by some nocturnal predator, only its head was intact, the eyes still and lifeless, the beak slightly parted; the body had been ruthlessly torn open, its innards now little more than a pale smear on the concrete. Pip stared, burning the image into her mind before she realised that her brother was similarly transfixed. Julia pulled Daniel round by his shoulders to stop him looking.

"What happened to it, Mummy?" the boy asked.

"Nature red in tooth and claw," Julia answered, almost in a dream. "An animal probably wanted to eat it, dear."

"What sort of animal?"

"A cat I expect."

"Would a cat do that to me?"

"No, dear, pussycats don't eat little boys."

"Do you think the duck's mummy and daddy are sad?"

"I think all mummies and daddies are sad when they lose their babies," Julia sighed. "Come on, let's go home for lunch. I expect Daddy's back by now."

Daniel once again ran ahead and waited impatiently by the park gates.

"Mum, I'm not dead by a duck pond," Pip remarked. "I'm just living in another place. You know I'm safe."

"But that's what I'm grateful for," Julia replied, "I couldn't stop thinking about Lyn and Bob Wells."

~ * ~ * ~

The train rumbled fitfully into the station, teasing the passengers into thinking it was coming to a stop and then rolling on just a little bit more. Bob reached through the window of the carriage door, turned the handle and jumped onto the platform before they juddered to a final halt. Gavin, tired from hours of travel since the early morning, followed more cautiously.

They followed the herd of Saturday morning shoppers to the exit. Diesel fumes billowed around them like the satanic chlorine gas at Ypres, depositing grime on the stone and glass of the grand Victorian station and clogging people's airways with black smut. Both the small-town men were disorientated by the hustle and bustle about them, but they pressed on and found themselves in the broad, echoing entrance hall.

"Where now?" asked Gavin.

Bob dithered at his first hurdle. Leadership means at least appearing to have a plan, so he marched into a dusty newsagent at the edge of the foyer and purchased an A-Z; he pored through the pages for a location that he recognised.

"Trafalgar Square," he answered a good few minutes after the original question was posed.

The Tube map was clear, concise and ingenious, yet baffled Bob. Fortunately, Gavin devised the route easily and they descended into the depths of the underground with the determination of Hercules.

What Bob expected at Trafalgar Square was not clear to Gavin, but they stood together in the traffic and chaos, holding bundles of leaflets bearing Sharon's image, the air around them swirling with exhaust fumes. Flocks of pigeons were regularly startled into flight by mischievous children running amongst them on the pavement, adding to the chaos.

Sharon's father went up to person after person, trying to speak to them, begging them to look at the girl in the picture, but they all, man, woman and child, were unable or unwilling to help; some just barged him out of the way, others gave him strange looks, some were tourists thinking he was an entertainer, but only a very few men and women (old-school salt-of-the-Earth Londoners all) gave him the time of day.

Their advice was simple. Give up. And if he wouldn't give up, Bob should try elsewhere. Sites in the vicinity of Kings Cross Station, Bow, Soho, China Town, Lambeth, and Peckham were all suggested, but these were exotic places to the desperate stranger and the names dropped from his confused mind as soon as they were said. Sometimes he would hold out the A-Z, hoping for a person to point on a map, and sometimes he would try to write down what they had just said with an old pencil he kept in his pocket, but most of the time the words were lost in the constant rumble of traffic.

Gavin also tried to approach people, but he lacked Bob's paternal drive and allowed embarrassment to hinder him. Most people who took a flyer did so automatically, assuming he was handing out promotional leaflets for a show or event; every so often, a familiar looking crumpled piece of discarded paper would tumble past him in the breeze.

One unkind young man, showing off to a group of his friends, ran to Bob, snatched a handful of flyers and threw them in the air, shouting and mocking; he would never know how close he came to being beaten beyond recognition by Sharon's father, but a grieving parent has no place in their heart for such petty revenge. At length, Bob surrendered to the inevitable. He sank pathetically on the steps outside the National Gallery and Gavin sat next to him.

"This was a mistake," the older man admitted. "There has to be somewhere we can go to make a better start, but where?"

Gavin realised that they needed a starting point, somewhere to tick off the list. It would have been ridiculous to have expected to come to London and find Sharon on the first attempt at the first place they looked, but they seemed to have picked the worst place possible to begin. There was no hope in Bob's illegible pencil-written notes, scrawled on the A-Z. Gavin needed to come up with a specific spot, but not somewhere famous like Piccadilly Circus which would have the same problem as Trafalgar Square. No, they needed a more domestic location, somewhere central.

His parents watched very little television, but Gavin's father did enjoy a series about an Old Bailey barrister, a hack who always defended lost causes and generally somehow won. Sometimes, Gavin watched with him, and now, sitting in fumes and feathers miles away from home, a street name came to his mind.

"Gloucester Road," he said. "We should go there. It's on the tube line."

"Why?" Bob asked, his hopes raised just a little. "Did someone suggest it?"

"Um, I have heard it mentioned."

"Well come on, lad, let's go!"

When they arrived, they found fewer tourists and more people willing to stop and talk. Several elderly ladies walking to the shops solemnly promised to look out for Sharon. A clergyman took some leaflets and said he would pin them up on notice boards at his nearby church. Several cab drivers who were waiting for business promised to hand some flyers out to their colleagues at the taxi ranks. A newsagent stuck Sharon's picture in his window even before they had left the shop.

Both Bob and Gavin knew these people weren't going to be directly able to help, but they at least felt listened to, that people in that great city had hearts and recognised that Sharon and the pain of her disappearance were real. That was enough to raise the men's spirits and their strength.

"Maybe we should find a place to get a drink and a bite to eat," Bob suggested.

They entered a tall grey brutalist hotel that stretched vertiginously overhead. It was strange that such a modern building had a bar and bistro modelled on a traditional English pub, but neither of the weary men were going to question the décor (in fact, it reminded them of home). They each ate a substantial meal, washed down with several drinks. Reenergised, they walked through the hotel's main lobby where Gavin paused beside a wall of lift doors.

"Let's go to the top to see if there's a view."

Bob was about to object but decided to give his young friend the benefit of the doubt. If a free view was all the boy asked for his help and support, it was very little indeed. They rode the elevator to the top floor and walked down a long corridor, past many identical anonymous doors, towards an area of natural light. They passed through some opaque fire escape doors and were presented with a large plate-glass window with an astounding view over the City; both men felt giddy and took a few moments before they dared edge closer.

London was before them, undulating over the ground below, countless buildings stretching into the distance in all directions; it was alive, a breathing organism made up of millions of individuals. There was order in chaos, beauty beside brutality, patches of green and blocks of grey.

"Where I grew up, there wasn't a place that you could stand where you couldn't see out... but here..." Bob was awestruck.

"It's going to take forever to find her," Gavin resigned himself.

"But she's out there somewhere," Bob whispered. "My Sharon is out there. When I look out of here, I see everywhere, so I must be looking at the place where she is right now."

Gavin studied the A-Z, looking for landmarks. He pointed, "I think I can see Harrods, so that must be Knightsbridge."

"Worth looking there, do you think?"

"I don't think so, do you?"

"Nah," Bob snorted. "That's where rich people live. I think rich people live around here too. No, they've taken our Sharon somewhere where people don't have Bentleys. But we've got no better ideas. When we get home tonight, we'll divide up the map and do a different bit each week."

"Well, I've nothing better to do, so no rush."

"Yeah, we've got the rest of our lives, son," Bob said, patting the young man on the back.

~ * ~ * ~

As the year moved on, Pip became ever more content living with her grandparents. She did miss her family, particularly Daniel, but they spoke often on the phone and exchanged letters. Lyn Wells corresponded regularly with her, and she also wrote to Gavin, not minding the brevity of his infrequent replies, as she knew he studied all hours so that he may travel to London at the weekends. Pip did worry about Sharon, ardently hoping for her safe return and mourning their lost friendship, but she had no desire to see her; she would not (could not) dare expose herself to Sharon's hurt and betrayal again.

She enjoyed her walk to the stables in the mornings, breathing crisp country air and watching nature wake up; she got to know several of the dog owners in the village, who would be out with their animals for their morning constitutionals, and she seemed to merit the devoted adoration of a black Labrador and a border collie, both of whom followed her at any given opportunity.

However, her relationship with the horses at her job was less close. She adored the sight of them, she thought they were majestic and magnificent, she loved their whinnies and neighs and the sound of hooves on the concrete of the stable yard, and she saw in their eyes their loving, gentle nature. Unfortunately, she was also irrationally and irredeemably terrified of them. Lucinda tried to combat Pip's fears by offering free lessons on the small, docile pony that was used for nervous children. The first and last session was curtailed after only a few minutes because the even-tempered steed became so weary of Pip's screaming that he refused to move until she dismounted – if getting a foot stuck in a stirrup whilst trying to escape and ending up on your backside in the mud can be called dismounting.

Equine unfamiliarity aside, Pip enjoyed her work, and soon had the office operating at new levels of efficiency. She negotiated with suppliers and chased delinquent invoices relentlessly, handled customers with natural courtesy, and kept meticulous records in large ledgers. As time passed, an increasingly pregnant Lucinda felt comfortable leaving Pip in charge much of the time.

Netball was a fun way to relax. She was far from the fittest or most able member of the team but was at least the youngest by some margin. No one took the games seriously, which was a good thing because Pip hadn't the foggiest idea what she was supposed to be doing, other than throwing the ball towards the disturbingly tall girl in Goal Attack.

Pip had always been a reader, mainly of *Mills and Boon* romances, but she ran out of her own books soon after arrival. Her grandparents had a small set of shelves in the hallway and another in the lounge, upon which were a dictionary, several gardening guides, a Bible, and a selection of old novels; she became caught up in the worlds of *Pride and Prejudice*, *Jane Eyre*, *David Copperfield*, and she lost count of how many times she read *Far from the Madding Crowd*, fascinated by Bathsheba but was, oh, so in love with Gabriel Oak. Every fortnight, a large old grey truck would rumble into the village and park outside the church; it was the mobile library, and Philippa Raven became their most loyal patron.

She savoured spending time with her gran, who taught her so many things that she never believed could be interesting. She sewed, and even made a tiny costume for Daniel's Action Man doll, which she posted to him with a little letter and a small bar of chocolate (her heart sang when she received his handwritten reply, for he had come on leaps and bounds at his new school), and she learned to cook, not fancy dishes but robust, satisfying dinners and puddings.

But her greatest love was being with her grandfather, learning how he gardened, helping him tend their tiny bit of England. Not that he would let her near his vegetable patch or his lawn very often, for they were his domain, his contribution to his family, but he taught her to tend the heart of the little garden, the roses.

Both her grandparents adored roses and now she did too; she had an almost spiritual affinity with the plants and they thrived in her care. Where to prune, how to cut, and how to judge the shape of the plant came to her naturally; but she listened and learned nevertheless, and she mentally stored away Grandad's precious wisdom about fertiliser and watering, about types of soil and drainage, and about light and shade.

"Now you see, my lovely," he said when they were in the potting shed preparing a small indoor rose to have in her room, "you'll find lots of books on roses, and I'm sure they're all very fine, but you've got to listen to the plant. Sometimes you'll get a wayward shoot, or a bad branch, or a bit of blight, and you need to chop it away to stop it spreading. But sometimes doing that might upset the balance and you'd either have to chop it right back and start again, which is a shame because you'll miss the bloom, or say, 'the rest of this plant is lovely and I'm going to live with this bad branch and try to make it better, and if I can't, well the whole thing is still pleasing while it lasts, because the shape is right'. Do you see?"

"I think so, Grandad. Look at the whole plant and only cut away what's bad if it might kill the rest of it, but most importantly, make sure it is balanced."

"Quite right, my little Rosepip, but don't forget that balanced doesn't necessarily mean symmetrical but means pleasing to the eye – well, that's what it means in my garden anyway. See the good, see the whole, that's what's important."

And then Pip saw his hand shaking as he tried to prune, and she understood why he was teaching her, why it was so important to him that she understand – it was his legacy to her.

~ * ~ * ~

The London train trip became a painful duty for Gavin. Every weekend, the same grinding hours there and back, the same fading of optimism from Bob's eyes. The journey was in two parts; the branch line that lumbered from their town to a mainline station, and the intercity express that sprinted to London. They were on their homeward leg, late in the evening, sitting in the loud, dirty open carriage. Bob was asleep, exhausted, his mouth hanging open, his head lolling side to side with the movement of the train; on his lap was the battered A-Z and a stubby pencil.

Gavin tried not to think about the day. It had been a harrowing one, trying some sordid district with strip clubs and mysterious doorways guarded by huge men. One person misunderstood when Gavin said he was looking for a girl and offered him the services of an emaciated, pale young woman of indeterminate age. He had wanted to help, wanted to rescue her, but what could he do? Only be haunted by her memory.

His stomach rumbled. He and Bob had long since given up on buying food in London, other than crisps or a chocolate bar; it was too expensive, and the train fares were crippling. They brought sandwiches from home and lasted as best they could until they returned. He had a tube of mints in his pocket, so he absentmindedly popped a sweet into his mouth while he idly gazed around the carriage. A young man sitting a short distance away looked familiar; his hair was different, but Gavin was sure he recognised him. Taking care not to disturb Bob, he moved along the aisle.

"Excuse me, but are you in a band called Black Metal Armour?"

"Not any more, I'm pleased to say," the young man snorted.

"But you were in the band?"

"Yes. Why? It's just a third-rate soft-rock joke. Not proper music."

"It was keyboard you played wasn't it?" Gavin decided to add a little flattery, "I thought you were really good, you held the whole thing together."

"Yeah? Thanks. Not that the others thought that way, they replaced me with the bandleader's girl. She could just manage chopsticks without going cross-eyed. She couldn't sing, couldn't play, danced alright, and even I could appreciate that she helped draw a crowd, if you know what I mean?"

"Do you know where they went?"

"The band? No. Why, have they disappeared?"

"Yes, they went to London. I'm Gavin by the way."

"Pleased to meet you, I'm Darren. Gone to London, you say? Well, they never said anything to me about it. I'm kind of related to the bloke whose band it is, but we've not been in touch lately. I live in Hammersmith now, I'm just coming home for the night to see my folks – well, Mum really, Dad'll be up The Legion, ignoring his embarrassing son."

"Why embarrassing?"

"When you've been a sheet metal worker all your life, it's a disappointment when your only boy turns out to be a – what did he call me last time? – 'deviant, fairy, nancy-boy poof'. Well, I told him that was quite enough tautology for my liking and left before he'd finished looking up tautology in the dictionary."

"I'm sorry."

"Oh, he's alright really, just a bit of a temper. Nothing physical, he just rants. He was born in different times, and I have got an acid tongue which winds him up. I— I think he's trying to understand, so I've got to give him points for that."

"Is Sam a relative, then?" Gavin guided the conversation back on course.

"Oh, you know him? Well, kind of. He's my half-sister Hannah's half-uncle, if that makes sense?"

"What about Hannah, is she in touch with him?"

"I doubt it. She's overseas – what's with all these questions?"

"You know Sharon, Sam's girlfriend?" Gavin decided to come clean. "She never told her family she was going to London, and she hasn't left word except for one vague postcard. I'm a friend of hers and that man over there is her dad. We've been looking for her every weekend for months, handing out leaflets and asking people in the street if they've seen her."

"Bloody hell! Well, now I understand the reason for all the questions. Where have you been looking?"

Gavin fetched the A-Z from Bob's lap and showed it to Darren; some roads had been shaded out and notes written all over the pages, marking where they had searched.

"Well, that's completely wrong," Darren commented. "Half of these are too expensive, and the other half don't have the right kinds of venues. Sam may be a lot of things, but he's not a pimp."

"I didn't think of that," Gavin groaned, slapping his forehead. "We've been following the people, not the band. We should be looking for places where they might perform, not where they might live. I'm such a fool!"

"Well, I can help you narrow it down a bit more. They won't be in respectable places playing weddings and the like."

"Why not?"

"Because they're drug dealers," Darren whispered. "They don't make their money from music, but from what Sam calls ancillary sales. Mind you, they're idiots if they try it up there, they'll be eaten alive – seriously, they could get themselves killed."

"Then we need to find her all the quicker." Gavin looked over his shoulder at Sharon's sleeping father.

"I'll help you," Darren offered. "I don't know London well, but I know it a lot better than you. You must look like a right pair of country yokels, marching around talking to random people."

Chapter 8

It was Philippa Raven's seventeenth birthday and she was travelling with her grandparents to meet her family for lunch at a country pub near the midpoint between their two houses. The aging Chrysler swayed along the road under Grandad's expert guidance; the drivers in the queue of cars behind might have believed it was safe to do more than thirty-five, but they were probably all boy racers.

"How can you read back there, Pip?" Gran asked. "You'll make yourself car sick."

"It's poetry, so I read a bit and then close my eyes and listen to it again in my head."

"Mercy me! You and your books. Who are you reading, then? Mr Wordsworth?"

"No, William Blake."

"Go on, read some," Grandad requested.

"Here's one you might like, it's about a rose," Pip said, with a naughty half smile.

"'*O Rose thou art sick.*
The invisible worm,
That flies in the night
In the howling storm:
Has found out thy bed
Of crimson joy:
And his dark secret love
Does thy life destroy'."

"Bit of a funny sounding rose," remarked her grandfather.

"It sounded a bit rude to me," Gran commented.

"I think it's meant to," Pip giggled.

"Well, I'm not sure I think any the better of Mr Blake for it. Anything a bit more wholesome?"

"Um… OK, try this:

'Tyger Tyger, burning bright,
In the forests of the night;
What immortal hand or eye,
Could frame thy fearful symmetry?'"

Before Pip could proceed to the next verse, her grandmother complained, "Well, that one doesn't even rhyme properly!"

"Yes, it's not like The Owl and the Pussycat, is it?" Grandad added, making it increasingly difficult for Pip to politely contain her mirth.

"Shall we stop teasing her?" Gran asked.

"Well," said the grandfather, "let's try this:

'They are not long, the weeping and the laughter,
Love and desire and hate;
I think they have no portion in us after
We pass the gate.
They are not long, the days of wine and roses,
Out of a misty dream
Our path emerges for a while, then closes
Within a dream'."

"That's beautiful," Pip said.

"Downson was popular when I was at school and I had to learn it by heart," Grandad recalled. "There was a Latin bit too, but I forget it, though the translation was, *'the shortness of life prevents us from entertaining far-off hopes'."*

"Well that's a lovely thought on my birthday!"

"Let's give Pip her present now, shall we?" the old man suggested.

With a contented chuckle, Gran passed a small box to her granddaughter.

"Shouldn't I wait till we're with Mum and Dad?" Pip asked.

"No, let's just keep this one between us."

The box contained a small golden heart-shaped locket on a matching chain. It had ornate Art Nouveau swirls etched into the surface.

"Oh, it's beautiful, thank you so much! I think it's the loveliest thing I've ever seen."

"It belonged to one of my aunts," Gran said proudly. "She gave it to me when I was a girl because she was entering a nunnery and wasn't allowed fine things. She was a lovely lady, lived to a ripe old age, very happy, and I think she'd want you to have it."

"You haven't opened it yet," said Grandad.

Pip fiddled with the miniature clasp and finally swung the lid open on its tiny hinge. Clipped in place were several trimmed and pressed rose petals.

"Now you'll be able to smell our roses wherever you go."

"But why would I ever want to go away from the garden?"

"You will, one day my little Rosepip," he chuckled.

~ * ~ * ~

Later that afternoon, back at home in the village, Pip and her grandfather walked to the village hall where the local flower and produce fair was in full swing. They worked their way around the exhibits, examining them closely, sniffing the blooms, checking out the competition, and watching closely as the judges assessed an entry made by a 'Miss P Raven'.

Awaiting the results, they sat in the humid refreshments tent, sipping tea and enjoying slices of home-made coffee and walnut cake, until distorted words over the antiquated loudspeakers summoned them to hear the outcome of the competition; they held hands as they heard the pronouncement.

"Third place!" Pip exclaimed as they walked home. She was holding a rolled-up certificate and a small silver trophy.

"You were robbed," huffed her grandfather. "It should have been first for you."

"No, it shouldn't, Grandad. I am so happy with third, I've never won anything before. Come on, let's hurry back to tell Gran."

They quickened their pace, chatting happily for the hundred or so yards from the hall to the bungalow, but the old man started to slow and grew paler.

"I need to stop here for a few minutes, Rosepip," he wheezed, "just to get my breath back."

"Are you OK, Grandad?"

"Actually, I'm not feeling quite right."

"Let's get you home. Can you walk if you lean on me?"

Pip took his surprisingly light weight on her shoulder and they slowly progressed home, where Gran instantly started to fuss over her husband. He was packed off to bed and the doctor summoned.

"It's worse this time," the doctor said. "He'll need bed rest for a few days. Let's try to keep him out of hospital for as long as possible."

"What did he mean 'for as long as possible'?" Pip asked when the doctor had gone.

"Your grandad might have to have a procedure or something," Gran explained. "Let's wait and see. So long as he doesn't have to go into one of those homes, he'd hate that – I'd like to live in one, but he and I were always chalk and cheese. He's ever so upset he's spoilt your birthday."

"He couldn't if he tried. Thank you again for my lovely locket."

"Happy birthday, darling girl." Gran kissed Pip's cheek. "I think I'll go and sit with him for a little while now, just until he falls asleep."

~ * ~ * ~

"So, young Gavin, how's your studies coming on?" Bob sat with Gavin and Darren on a metal bench under a scrawny silver birch set back from the road and the relentless rumbling vehicles. They ate chips from polystyrene trays, vainly trying to warm themselves from the chill of the late-autumn winds that cut along the Thames.

"Alright, thanks," Gavin replied, not in the mood to think about his mountain of schoolwork.

"He's a bit of a maths boffin, you know," Bob told Darren.

"Yeah, you've mentioned that."

"Have I? Sorry, my mind's a bit distracted."

Having finished their food, they walked to an overflowing waste-bin and added their disposable trays to the pile.

Bob belched and bumped his fist to his ribs. "Pardon me." He took a half-used tube of antacids from his pocket and popped two tablets into his mouth.

"Where are we?" Gavin asked, staring at the A-Z.

"Um, well we're south of the river now," Darren replied, sounding more knowledgeable than he was, "so, down there is Peckham and that way to the Elephant and Castle. But the place we are headed is about five minutes this way."

"You are good lads, the both of you." Bob walked between his two associates and patted them on their backs with workworn hands. The pats turned to gentle pushes – he was eager to be back on the hunt.

Some minutes later, the footsore men entered a pub which stood at the meeting point of three terraced streets. During lunch hour, the establishment was patronised by working men labouring on nearby building sites, but their numbers had thinned and there was little demand on the landlord's time. Gavin and Darren both held nervously back, but Bob strode confidently to the bar, ordered three pints of bitter, beckoned to the boys to join him, and struck up conversation with the man behind the counter; the landlord, Richard, was in his late fifties, balding, and his check shirt strained across his ample belly.

After establishing a good rapport, Bob started his now horribly familiar explanation about searching for his daughter and the band that she was in. However, instead of the normal disappointment of mumbled platitudes, the barman frowned and scratched his head, trying to remember something. He stepped to an archway behind the bar and called out in a deep chesty voice, "Angelique! Get down here, will you, love? I need your memory."

A tall black woman joined her husband at the bar. She wore a vibrant green dress and her hair was cut short, accentuating her cheekbones.

"Yes, Richard?" she said, with a smile that could change anyone's day for the better.

"That band, the one your cousin's boy was in. You remember, we didn't like the look of them and told them not to come back after their first gig."

"I remember. Young women showing themselves like they have no shame, oh and don't get me started on that caterwaul of a noise they called music."

"Yeah, love. What were they called?"

"As if I could forget! Black Metal Armour. We should have known from the name that they would be awful, but I wanted to give young Lloyd and his friends a chance." Angelique gazed suspiciously upon the three patrons on the other side of the bar. "Why? Who wants to know?"

Richard explained that one of the girls in the band had gone missing from her home and that Bob was her father. The change in Angelique's demeanour was instantaneous and before the three visitors knew what was happening to them, they had been ushered upstairs to the kitchen, and were being plied with food and tea.

"Now you wait here," she instructed, "and I will go and fetch young Lloyd. His family live not far from here."

Bob could barely sip his tea, such was his excitement. Every second that his hostess was gone felt like an hour, but she returned at last, accompanied by a young man who seemed eager to help. Lloyd was medium height and like Darren, his hair was styled into a sharp wedge; he wore tight jeans, a tan bomber jacket and immaculate trainers.

"I don't know how much I can help." His accent was London with hints of his Caribbean heritage. "I was never actually in the band, but their drummer got in touch and asked me to stand in for a few gigs. He heard about me from my cousin Jay-Jay."

Angelique frowned. "A cousin on his father's side. He's trouble, that one, not like Lloyd here."

"Anyway, they weren't my style," Lloyd continued. "All cheesy rock ballads, but I'm more Stevie Wonder."

"What do you play?" asked Darren, to Bob's silent irritation.

"A bit of everything. Keyboard mainly, but drums, guitar, and some sax. I'm really a cellist, studying music theory at university. Then I'm out of here."

"I play keyboard," Darren told him, "maybe we could meet up?"

"Please!" Bob interjected desperately. "Please let Lloyd tell his story. What happened with the band?"

"OK, so I played a couple of gigs with them," Lloyd explained, "but then I realised that they were into some heavy stuff. The music's just a front for them, they're selling drugs, hard stuff."

"Which would explain why they know Jay-Jay," Angelique interrupted with undisguised venom. She closed her eyes and nodded an apology to Bob, who seemed near to tears.

"I told them I wasn't interested," Lloyd said. "I've too much to lose getting mixed up in that stuff, including my life if my ma ever found out. There were two girls, your Sharon and another one called Tracy. Then there was Frank the drummer, but he seemed to be using too much of their product to be any use; Sam, who thinks he's a tough guy, on lead guitar; and Ed, who is a tough guy, on bass."

"So, your cousin Jay-Jay must know where they are!" Bob exclaimed, euphoric at the very sound of Sharon's name. He jumped to his feet, but Lloyd motioned for him to calm down.

"It's not that simple. That was when I knew them, but I still heard things after. There was some bad business, they got into debt with some nasty people;

even Jay-Jay is scared of them. Well that Frank guy pulled a fast one, disappeared but—" Lloyd paused because what he was about to say was beyond belief.

"Go on," Gavin urged.

"He sold one of the girls. Tracy, I think, because Sharon was Sam's girl."

A haunting silence fell as everyone absorbed the words.

"You can't sell people!" Bob spluttered.

"You can where I live! You have no idea what it's like," Lloyd replied with such emphasis that no one dared dissent. "Anyway, Ed decided to be a hero and get her back. He did a good job too, because he's doing time for GBH or something."

"And that poor young woman?" asked Angelique, not wanting to know the answer.

"I don't know for sure. Some people reckoned a few girls got away, but she never went back to her friends. I know that because Sam was asking around for another female singer. It was stupid, because the band was dead. I think he's just straight dealing now, probably helped by your daughter, Bob. Sorry."

"How do you know all this for sure?" Darren felt he was in a gangster movie.

"Jay-Jay told me, and he had no reason to lie."

"Do you know where they live?" Gavin asked.

"I know where they were," Lloyd replied. "North of the river, Bow way, but they won't be there now. If they've got any sense, they'll be out of London."

"So, they could be anywhere?" Bob asked, his carpet of hope torn from beneath him.

"Yeah, and I hope for their sakes that they stay far away."

"If I could talk to your cousin," Bob suggested feverishly, "I could – I don't know – I have some money, would that help?"

"Not really, sorry. Jay-Jay ain't looking for them, and the people who are wouldn't be interested."

"But who are these people actually after?" Gavin asked. "You said Frank disappeared. Is it him or Sharon and Sam that they want?"

"Not Sharon," Lloyd replied, "except she'll know where her man is. Frank's too much of a smack-head to stay ahead of them for long, so if they want him, they'll have him. No, Sam's the main man, he's the one they want."

"Could we go to where they lived?" Bob asked, fading. "Maybe they left a forwarding address." He knew the question was stupid and didn't expect an answer. Angelique laid a compassionate hand on his shoulder and glanced at her husband who was standing in the doorway, listening to the conversation.

"I think you blokes should go home and rest," Richard said. "You can't do more than you have done. Come on, my car's out back, I'll drive you to the station."

Lloyd wrote down his home number in case any of them wanted to contact him. Like automata, the three stunned visitors thanked him and Angelique.

As they rode silently towards the station, Darren was saddened, Gavin was crestfallen, but Bob was crushed; there was an abyss in his gut and it was pulling in all that he was.

~ * ~ * ~

Pip ran down the shallow steps outside her grandparents' home to her father's waiting car.

"Hello, Dad," she said with a smile and a kiss, "this is a bit of an adventure isn't it?"

"Is it? I wouldn't have thought visiting relatives was that exciting."

"It is when I've not seen you for ages. Plus, I just spent ages trying to explain to Gran and Grandad how to use their new remote-control telly," Pip laughed. "Honestly, they keep saying 'Where's the wire?'"

"Yeah, I suppose they are a bit behind the times on that, but it's five years since we got ours. Not very long." Five years ago Pip was his little girl, now she was a woman, blooming and independent; a hard truth to acknowledge. "Well, not very long when you get to my age. How's Grandad?"

"He seems a lot better. I really think he's turned a corner these last couple of months."

"Good. Have you thought about your plans for Christmas?"

"I thought I might stay here, and we could all come over to yours for the day." Pip sensed her answer saddened her father. "It's just that I'd have to sleep on the sofa and there's not much privacy. Oh, I do miss you though, Dad. It's hard to decide."

"You could sleep in your old room. We still have the bunk bed – the boys can muck in together."

"That's not very fair on Matthew." Pip closed her eyes and made her decision. "I'll be fine on the sofa. I'm being silly."

"Your mum will be pleased."

"For about five minutes," Pip snorted. "I don't know why, but she has to make comments about everything."

"Your mother's someone who deals with guilt badly. She has a good heart and hates herself for believing those lies about you, but she'll always be reminded whenever she sees you, so she gets defensive and a bit ratty."

"So, this is how it's going to be from now on?"

"Probably, sorry. It's like today, she'll never come to your Uncle Ted's if your Aunty Jane's there."

Ted was the older brother of Pip's father. The families had been close; Ted and Jane's eldest child, Charlotte, was eighteen months older than Pip and the two girls had a good friendship. They saw each other regularly, until a falling out between their mothers about five years beforehand. Striving to maintain their relationship, the two brothers tried to meet at least every six months. Neither was talkative, so their get-togethers were short affairs, but had deep significance. Now it was Pip's father's turn to make the biannual pilgrimage; he had invited his daughter to join him, partly so she could see Charlotte, but mainly because he wanted to see Pip himself.

Their relatives lived on a development of about thirty council houses on the edge of a small town. Near the entrance to the estate was an old railway station which had been closed down and left to rot since the 1960s. Abandoned and unloved, its Victorian red bricks were crumbling, and its windows broken. As girls, Charlotte and Pip would sneak in there, standing on the platform and screaming when the express trains hurtled past in a nightmare of sound and turbulence that sucked the breath from their lungs and dishevelled their hair and clothes.

A few of the houses on the estate had been bought by their occupants under 'Right to Buy', often distinguished from those around them by new front doors; for their owners, it was a mark of pride, an outward sign that they were achieving what their parents had not, though others considered it bragging. Ted and Jane's house sported new double-glazed windows and a shimmering red door with a brass knocker.

Aunt Jane gave Pip a genuinely warm greeting, and Charlotte made a huge fuss of seeing her. It was dry, and the early December sunshine took the chill off the day, so the fathers sat in the garden, smoking and discussing the state of the world, while the two cousins went for a walk.

Charlotte was in many ways the opposite of Pip. She was taller, broader of frame, with long straight hair and cute dimples when she smiled. She was training to be a nurse at the local hospital and still lived at home, planning to move to a larger town and get a place of her own when she qualified.

They stopped outside the old railway station, its dirty windows and peeling paint testament to its ongoing neglect; however, a tatty 'FOR SALE' sign now had a fresh sticker pasted over its wrinkled weather-beaten surface, reading 'SOLD'. The rustic peace was interrupted by the rumble of the approaching express train, which became a roar, and then an air-battering howl, before the sounds reversed and calm was once again gradually restored.

"It looks smaller than I remember," Pip remarked. "Less creepy too."

"Let's go in," Charlotte suggested. "The old gap in the fence is still there."

"Oh, I don't know, Charli. We aren't kids anymore."

"Don't be such a goody-two-shoes, it gets on my nerves! Live dangerously, come on!"

It was exciting to sneak through the gap once again and stand on the platform under the old green veranda. They whistled and laughed at the echoes as they had done years before. There was a wrought-iron bench beside the entrance to the obsolete ticket office, and the two women sat on it, watching a robin hop daringly amongst the weeds between the rails.

"I wouldn't have thought you would be worried about a bit of trespass," Charlotte observed. "You were expelled from school, from what I hear."

"It was a mistake. The school apologised."

"If you say so."

"I do. And so does the school. You must believe me."

"OK, I believe you! Anyway, why do you care so much about what I think?"

"We are family."

"Oh, please don't start singing Sister Sledge!" Charlotte groaned and they both laughed.

A ginger cat jumped from the low roof onto a rusted old porter's trolley and then down again to the platform, scaring the robin away.

"Adorable!" Charlotte made noises to attract the cat's attention. "Here, puss, here, here, puss-puss-puss." The animal padded closer, sniffing her hand before letting her scoop it up in her arms. "It's number sixteen's cat, but I think he prefers me."

"Who can blame him?" Pip asked, tickling the beast under the chin.

The cat extricated itself from Charlotte's grasp and made its way onto Pip's lap.

"You're getting cat hairs all over me!" Pip tried to hand the tom back to her cousin, but it wriggled uncontrollably and used claws to assert its preferences. She stood up, giving the creature no option but to desist, and brushed the hairs from her black pencil skirt. The cat, resigned to the circumstances, returned to the nurse's tender care.

"I don't know why you got all dressed up to come here," Charlotte grumbled.

"I wanted to look nice. I don't have much cause to these days, and you always look good whatever you wear."

Mollified, Charlotte asked, "Any boys on the scene?"

"No chance in our village. How about you?"

"I'm too tired to bother with men, but I have hopes."

"I have missed you, Charli," Pip sighed. "Why did we leave it so long?"

"Families are difficult. It's hard when things are like they are with our mums."

"What is going on between them? I've been trying to find out for years and no one will tell me."

"Search me," Charlotte shrugged. "Mum insists that the last civilised conversation they had was about the kids. All she said was that your younger brother doesn't take after our side of the family, and your mum went nuts and called her all the names under the sun."

"I think she might have had – what's it called? – post natal depression," Pip mused. "I read about it in a magazine a while back. She's not been the same since Daniel was born."

"Both our mums are a bit loco, if you ask me," Charlotte laughed. "Come on, let's go home before our dads eat all the lunch."

~ * ~ * ~

The festive season was going to be unthinkably hard for Lyn. The terrible thought of waking up on Christmas morning knowing her daughter's room was empty crippled her, and not seeing Sharon's face when she opened her presents or hearing her giggle at terrible cracker jokes was unbearable. Moreover, Lyn had to watch Bob, her rock, being eroded by the relentless pain of his little girl's disappearance. The futility of his search diminished him; once proud and strong, he seemed physically smaller. However, Mark would be visiting for Christmas, so a pretence of celebration must be made, a cruel game of charades that they all would play.

In the early afternoon, Lyn trudged miserably to the bus stop, going to buy presents and greetings cards, because she had no choice. The town centre was busy, the shop windows glowed gold in the grey afternoon, their richly coloured seasonal displays suggesting that the products contained therein would be the ideal way of marking the birth of a man who shunned all worldly goods. Lyn regarded them numbly, wondering if Mark would like a new jacket. She entered the bank, chequebook in hand, queuing patiently until a till became available.

"I'd like to withdraw some money, please," she said to the long-faced woman on the other side of the glass, sliding a cheque for fifty pounds made out to 'Cash' through the till.

The bank teller tapped away on a small computer keyboard and frowned.

"It says Insufficient Funds, Mrs Wells."

"Really? I must be getting confused about Bob's payday. It's normally earlier at this time of year. Can I transfer seventy-five from the deposit account, please?"

With a look of forbearance, the woman slid a transfer slip through the gap and Lyn entered the details of the two accounts from memory. After she returned it, there was more tapping.

"That account has a zero balance."

"There must be a mistake, there should be over seven hundred pounds in there!" Lyn was shocked.

"I'm sorry, Mrs Wells, but all funds were withdrawn by your husband earlier today. He was here only about an hour ago, I served him myself."

"Then why did you let me go through this bloody charade?" Lyn shouted, close to tears. Not waiting for an answer, she hurried from her humiliation into the street, looking around her as if the world was new and strange. As quickly as possible, she walked the three miles to her husband's place of employment and went into the office, a prefabricated hut with condensation trickling down its windows.

"Hello, Lyn," said the owner, "we don't see you down here very often. Is Bob alright?"

"I was about to ask you that," she replied. "He might not be after I speak to him."

"But he went home after lunch. I said it was OK, because he looked a bit peaky, to be honest."

Lyn didn't understand what was happening. She mumbled her thanks and left, walking through the muddy yard to the gates. On the opposite side of the road was a garage which sold second-hand cars; it took her a few moments before she recognised her husband's prized Cortina sitting on the forecourt with a price sticker in the window. Within seconds, she was speaking to an amiable salesman in a sheepskin coat.

"Where did you get that car?" she asked, pointing to Bob's former pride and joy. "It's my husband's."

"Sorry, love, he sold it to us this morning. Wanted cash, there and then."

Lyn reeled. What was going on? Why would he want all that cash? There was an explanation, but Bob wasn't that stupid, was he? Maybe Gavin could answer the question. She hurried a hundred yards up the road to a phone box, taking ten pence from her purse as she went.

Gavin had just arrived home from school when the telephone rang. He answered in weary expectation of having to take a message for one of his parents, but instead, Lyn's worried voice poured out her fears. His thoughts simmered with a hundred possibilities which soon reduced to one. Gavin hung up and scrabbled in a drawer for the railway timetable; a fumbled check of the tables told him he had very little time. Mrs Knight glanced through the window and spied her son sprinting down the road as if chased by the devil himself.

Gavin ran, ran until his lungs might burst, and then ran some more. A storm was brewing, the clouds were dark, and a divine wind blew on his back, driving him towards his destination. He had never been good at middle-distance running (or short-distance or long-distance, for that matter), but he might have set a school record by the time he arrived at the station. The train for the London connection had just arrived at the platform. Rasping for breath, he pushed his way past the travellers, looking for a familiar face – then he spotted Bob and grabbed the man's elbow.

"Please don't do this, Bob, please talk to me," he panted. Sharon's father went to pull away, so Gavin blocked his path, resolute. "Tell me, explain it to me. If you do, there's another train in an hour and I'll be on it with you."

The guard was walking the length of the train, ensuring its doors were securely shut. Bob tried one last stab to get on, but Gavin blocked him again, just as the guard blew his whistle and the engine groaned with exertion.

"What have you done, boy?" Bob snarled, eyes wide with frustration. The gathering gale blew dust and debris around them.

"Please tell me what you are planning to do," Gavin persisted.

The older man relented, and they sat on a bench at the far end of the platform, far away from prying ears. The seat was recessed into an alcove, which afforded some respite from the elements.

"I ought to punch your lights out. Teach you a thing or two about minding your elders," Bob threatened, but he couldn't be angry with his one true ally. "Sorry, Gavin, I'm just a bit upset." He fiddled with a blue carrier bag which bulged irregularly in his hands. Bob leaned closer to Gavin and whispered over the wind, "I've got over two grand in here. I've got Lloyd's address and I'm going to make him take me to this Jay-Jay person. I reckon he's got an idea where my Sharon is."

"Lloyd said there was no point," Gavin pointed out. "Why would he lie? Even if you talked to Jay-Jay, he might want more money, or he could lie and make up a place and you'd have lost everything and know nothing."

Bob sat stunned, digesting the simple dismantling of a plan that he had devised through countless sleepless nights.

"Anyway," Gavin pressed his point, "Lloyd said that Jay-Jay is dangerous, and you heard what Angelique said about him."

"I can handle myself," Bob muttered, "I've been around." But he was already defeated. The winds around them calmed a little. He looked at the bag clutched in his hands. "This is all I've got for a lifetime of hard work. I've grafted since I was a lad, bought my house, done it up, made it nice for Lyn and the kids, but this bag is all I could manage. And it wouldn't even buy the time of day from Mr Jay-Jay, would it? I'd sell the house tomorrow and give it all away if it meant I had my Sharon back, but I've lost her, haven't I?"

"Shall we get home before the rain starts?" Gavin patted the man's arm.

As they walked back along the platform, the winds returned, battering their faces and deafening their ears, so Gavin didn't hear his companion say, "I'm not feeling so good," and didn't realise he was no longer beside him for several paces.

Bob leaned against a support pillar with one hand, struggling. He waved his free hand at Gavin to stay back, fear and confusion in his wide eyes; then he vomited, his back arched, and he collapsed to the ground, legs scrabbling, arms flailing.

Sometimes, birth can be a violent, disturbing process, and so can death. Gavin tried to help, his cries for assistance lost in the storm, but slowly Bob's movements abated, his chest stilled, and the heart attack completed its terrible devastation. The blue carrier bag that Sharon's father had clasped so tightly had torn open, and his sightless eyes beheld his life savings blown away down the track.

Chapter 9

Robert Wells' funeral service was the first of the New Year. Christmas had not existed for many people connected to the man, forced to wait until government and undertakers would allow him to be laid to rest.

Lyn sat in the centre of the front pew of St Michael's Church, surrounded by family. Mark was beside her on her right, but she left a space on her left for the absent Sharon. She wore the dress Bob liked and the nice shoes which made her feet hurt, and she was composed. Motionless, she listened to the vicar without hearing the words; she was a perfect statue, an unwilling memorial to her truelove who was supposed to have grown old with her.

She was numb, but not without emotions. There was unimaginable sadness and emptiness, of course, but anger as well – anger that Bob had not looked after himself better, and anger that their son had borrowed to pay for his own father's funeral because she had little income and no savings left.

There were several friends and former colleagues of the dead man squeezed onto the unfamiliar seating, mainly men of a similar age, grim-faced and dwelling on their own mortality. Gavin was there, flanked by his solemn parents, who were comforting him through the nightmares and morbid thoughts of futility. He felt guilty for not being able to help Bob, and for lying to Lyn that her husband had passed away peacefully when in truth his spirit had been betrayed by a monstrous contortion of biology.

Also present, alone at the back of the church, was Philippa Raven. She felt more of an observer than a participant, unable to connect the man she knew to the long wooden box at the far end of the aisle. Pip remembered the time that she and Sharon had tried skateboarding in the park, how she had fallen and hit her head, and how Bob had so tenderly carried her to his home and cleaned her cuts and given her a paternal kiss on her brow.

Unexpectedly, Darren and Lloyd had also made the long journey from London to pay their respects. They intended to keep themselves to themselves, but Gavin introduced them to Lyn, who insisted that they come back to the house for the wake.

Lyn's limited budget meant that she had only been able to provide basic fare for her guests. She had been up for nights, baking cakes and sausage rolls, preparing salads, and cooking joints of meat to carefully carve into delicate slices. Pip had not been able to stay for the food, needing to catch the bus, so she had a hug with Lyn at the church and slipped away unnoticed by anyone else, but the rest of the attendees packed into the widow's house and ate all before them.

When most people had departed, Lyn begged the two London boys to tell her everything about their lives. Their shared appreciation of music delighted her; when she discovered Lloyd was classically trained, she begged him to tell her of the places he had played and the pieces he had performed. When the evening drew on, Darren and Lloyd knew their purpose for the day was ending and they left; it was time for the mother and son to be alone, silent and still together.

~ * ~ * ~

The first warmth of early spring was at last reaching the unheated office at the stables, and bright sunlight streamed through the windows after a night of heavy rain. Pip had spent much of the morning calculating a feed order and was pleased for the interruption when she heard a car pull to a stop outside. She peeped out of the dusty window to see a Renault slithering to a halt on the damp surface.

A young man got out, tall, broad-shouldered with neat dark hair and a military air. Pip felt her mouth dry and her heartbeat quicken – he had to be the most attractive man that she had ever seen. Convinced that she was blushing, she pulled on her Wellingtons and squelched out to greet him.

"Hello, how may I help you?"

The man looked at her and seemed to do a double-take, fascinated by the small brunette approaching him.

"I'd like to arrange for some riding lessons."

"We have a good range of horses for various abilities here. Have you done much riding?"

"No, but the lessons aren't for me, they're for my daughter, Bobbie. She hasn't ridden before either. She is six."

"How lovely." Pip desperately tried not to sound disappointed that he was a family man. "Well, we have some very friendly ponies and excellent instructors. If you'd care to wait here a moment, I will fetch a leaflet outlining the costs."

He watched her tramping back to the office, transfixed.

"Is this your place, then?" he asked when she returned.

"Goodness, no! I just work in the office. Lucinda's the owner, but she's had a baby and is taking some time off."

"So, you're the one in charge?"

"Maybe of the office, but not the horses." Pip coyly brushed a loose coil of her dark hair behind her ear. "Are these lessons a birthday present for your daughter?"

"No, that will be a menagerie of Care Bears, I believe. No, the lessons are for Daddy time. Her mother and I have separated."

"Sorry to hear that," Pip lied. "It must be hard for you."

"Serving in the navy I got used to being away. And I have to say, you don't look old enough to be running a place like this." He inwardly winced at his clumsy compliment, but it found receptive ears.

"I'm old enough," she replied with unconscious sultriness. "Are you still in the navy?"

"For the next few weeks." He saluted. "Lieutenant Theodore Dickson at your service, ma'am. But people call me Theo."

She laughed and returned the salute, "General dogsbody Philippa Raven, sir! But everyone calls me Pip."

"A general, eh? I think that makes you my superior officer, so, tell me, how do you feel about fraternising with the junior ranks?"

"How do I feel about doing what with who?"

"Would you like to come out for a drink with me tomorrow night?"

~ * ~ * ~

Darren and his flatmate Will had invited Lloyd over to their home in Hammersmith, to try out some new ideas on the keyboards. The evening passed quickly for the three men, absorbed in their mutual obsession for music.

"It's getting late," Will remarked, chewing on a cold slice of pizza, "do you want to crash here?"

Lloyd didn't respond to the offer, but merely gazed off into space.

"Lloyd? Earth to Lloyd!" Will tried again.

"Sorry, guys, I was miles away," Lloyd replied with a jump.

"Do you want to crash here?" Will enquired, as if for the first time.

"Yeah, thanks. Look, I need to talk to you, Darren, about Bob's daughter."

"Sharon?"

"Yeah. I saw Jay-Jay yesterday and he said there's word a band is going around up north with the same idea as Sam's."

"It was a stupid idea then and it's a stupid idea now," Darren remarked. "Making a few quid selling pot to middle-class kids is one thing but thinking you're a drug baron going to make it big is something else. Why does your cousin think it's them, are they still playing the same crap music?"

"I wouldn't know," Lloyd laughed.

"Did Jay-Jay say where up north?"

"No. It'll probably come to nothing. I hope so, anyway."

"What would Jay-Jay's friends do if they found them?" Darren asked.

"How should I know? It's not my world!" Lloyd was annoyed to be considered an expert. "Let's just hope they don't find them."

"If I was Sam and Sharon, I'd try to make sure I had the money to pay them," Will observed. "By fair means or foul, it's their only chance."

~ * ~ * ~

"What made you decide to leave the navy, Theo?" Pip asked as they sipped their drinks in a quiet corner of the pub.

"My ex, Claire, or rather my sense of duty to her," he replied. "She found the whole Falklands thing very stressful. It wasn't a barrel of laughs at my end either, so I'm leaving the Senior Service to join civvy street. Paperwork – soul destroying after being out there making a difference, but the pension is good, and it has the small advantage of not being shot at with Exocet missiles."

"I think that's a huge advantage," Pip giggled.

"It'll certainly be nice to see Bobbie more often." Theo became wistful. "Not as regularly as I'd like, though. Claire finds it confusing. She'd got used to my absences. She's a funny thing – she left me but got upset when I told her I was coming for a drink with you."

Pip thought back to the kiss she had shared with Theo when they had met a few minutes earlier. It had been her first romantic touch since Tom, over a year beforehand, and it had thrilled her with promise. The pressure of Theo's lips upon hers had been exquisite, eclipsing anything she had experienced before, but news of Claire's reaction affected her feelings.

"Tell me about Bobbie," she said.

"We just call her Bobbie, but her real name is Roberta. Would you like to see a picture?" Theo took a small photograph from his wallet. The child in the picture was a mass of smiles and golden curls, posing confidently with the seaside in the background. Pip idly turned over the photo and read some pale-blue handwriting. 'Bob: Summer '85. Lyme Regis'. The name 'Bob' stabbed into her heart.

"You miss her a lot, don't you?"

"Oh, yes. I'd just got used to seeing her every day. She grows up so fast."

"Theo," Pip spoke slowly, choosing each word with precision, "I won't be a wedge in your relationship. If there's the slightest chance of getting back together, you owe it to Claire, to yourself, and especially to Bobbie, to try."

"What are you saying?"

"You are the most handsome man I have ever seen in real life, and I'm in danger of falling for you, but I think you'll get back together with Claire. A few months ago, I went to the funeral of a good man who died of heartbreak because he lost his daughter. You owe it to yourself to try, for Bobbie's sake — if you and Claire still break up, then at least I won't have made things worse. Anyway, I still have some growing up to do myself."

"I hate to say it, but you're right," Theo sighed. "But you don't need to grow up, Pip, you're the most sensible, kind person I know. And damned attractive too – if the men back on the ship knew I'd let a bit of prize totty like you get away, I'd never hear the last of it."

"Prize totty?" she laughed. "Charming! I suppose I have to take what compliments I can get, but I hope you don't call Claire that."

"I'll make a note of it," Theo made light, but he was in anguish. "God, I hate this! Can you and I at least keep in touch, as friends?"

"I'd like that. Maybe a drink here sometimes. And I like letters. I could write to you, about books I've read, or how my roses are doing. And you could tell me about Bobbie. Only ever as friends. Any sentiment, anything from either of us that you couldn't show Claire gets burned and we never hear from each other again. Deal?"

"Deal," he replied, suppressing his passion.

They finished their drinks and parted from one another with a chaste kiss to the cheek, yet even that briefest of physical encounters was almost too sweet to end. When they were that close, the electricity between them was undeniable and separating was like parting two magnets. Pip dared not look back as she hurried to the bungalow, unsure if she was relieved or disappointed to hear the Renault accelerating up the lane.

She slept fitfully, replaying her conversation with Theo, wondering if she could stand to just be friends with him. The degree of attraction that she felt disturbed her; Pip had had crushes before (pop stars like Adam Ant or all of Duran Duran), and there had been boys like Tom, but this was something different.

Her mind lied to her heart about Tom. She believed he dumped her because of her many faults: had she been a better girlfriend, more attractive and less demanding, then he might have stuck with her and weathered the storm. The events at the school had crushed her self-regard – she believed a flaw in her personality made the falsehoods believable, even to her own family. Only the kindest people, Gavin and her grandparents, had trusted her word because they could overlook her failings.

Had she pushed Theo away because she thought herself undeserving? No, because what Pip lacked in self-confidence, she made up for in hope; she needed to love again, and to be loved in return, and so would always be ready to offer her heart to someone and chance it being broken.

Telling Theo to go back to Claire stemmed from her own moral code and her wish to see Bobbie happy. She did it instinctively, willingly, without regret and with grace.

Yet giving up on him, albeit after only half a date, was a greater sacrifice than she could express, because her soul believed he might be the love of her life, and from the look in his eyes, the feeling was mutual. If they were both strong, if they were both true to a purer love, then their friendship might be beautiful, but they must keep to their rules and not open the floodgates to the primeval attraction that existed between them.

Any passing stranger who met Pip would only see a confident young woman, witty and charming, kind and unselfish, and they wouldn't know that inside she was broken by lies, by betrayal, and by her own goodness.

~ * ~ * ~

Gavin sat at the breakfast table, reading revision notes with uncharacteristic desperation whilst spooning cereal down his gullet. He looked at his watch, swore mildly, dropped his spoon into the bowl with a clatter, and hurried to put on his jacket.

"Slow down, Gavin, Dad can drop you off at school," his mother counselled. She had been watching him eat with sympathetic indigestion.

"I'll be fine," Gavin replied, "the walk will clear my head." He patted his pocket to confirm the presence of pens, pencils and his precious calculator. Followed by a chorus of "Good luck" from his parents, he was out of the door.

Mrs Knight sighed, "He's going to mess up this exam, I know it."

"Not necessarily," her husband soothed. "He's been revising steadily for weeks."

"Has he?"

"Well, what else?"

"I found a ticket to London dated two days ago in his jacket when I was hanging it up. He's lied to us! He's obsessed with finding that girl Sharon. I thought when poor Bob Wells died it would be the end of it, but no, Gavin has to go chasing after her."

"Yes, but why London? She's almost certainly not there – maybe he went for another reason?"

"I cannot imagine what, and why keep it a secret?"

"You are right, of course." Mr Knight had his argument skewered by logic. "We'll have to hope Gavin's too sensible to throw his chances away. There is little enough that we can do about it and he'll be his own harshest critic if he doesn't get the grades."

~ * ~ * ~

Pip paused digging the flower bed and wiped her brow with the back of her wrist. She took the glass of home-made lemonade that her grandmother was holding out and gulped it down, savouring the cool sharpness as it restored her energy.

"Where's Grandad?" she asked. "I wanted to show him how this rose is coming on."

"Oh, you're worse than he is." Gran examined the flower in question. "It looks fine to me. Old Mrs Nelson's got problems with her honeysuckle, so your grandad's gone down to look at it."

"Old Mrs Nelson? She's younger than you, Gran," Pip chuckled.

"You're only as old as you feel."

"In that case, I'm ninety-two!" Pip brushed her dirty hands on the legs of her tatty gardening jeans. "I think I'll wander over and lend a hand."

"And maybe have a slice of her coffee cake? You're as transparent as your grandfather."

Despite her motives having been rumbled, Pip walked through the centre of the village and up the hill opposite towards the churchyard. Late spring was at its finest, with blossoms to please the eye and birdsong to serenade the ear. A bee took an interest in her, buzzing about her head as she made her way along the lane, darting up and down and weaving side to side but always returning to escort her.

She found her grandfather sitting, looking very confused, on the step that led into Mrs Nelson's garden. The lady of the house was there, trying to persuade him to have a glass of water.

"Is everything OK?" Pip asked.

"Yes," replied her grandad.

"No," insisted Mrs Nelson, "he took a tumble just now."

"What happened?"

"Neither of us rightly knows," Mrs Nelson replied. "He'd just come down from the ladder, and I asked if he'd like a slice of cake, and he said yes, so I went to get it, and the next thing I knew, he was lying on the grass, flat as a pancake."

"I must have caught my foot in something," Grandad scratched his head and frowned, "because all I knew was that I was standing up one minute and the next thing I'm on the ground. Back in the war, I jumped out of aeroplanes and landed just fine, but now I can't even seem to stand up without falling over."

"You didn't hit your head, did you?" Pip asked.

"Nope, I've only hurt my pride."

"Come on, let's get you home." Pip helped him up and let him lean on her.

After a slow walk to the bungalow, Grandad decided to have a lie down, but asked if someone might bring him a cup of tea. Pip washed the dirt from her hands at the sink and filled the kettle, but before she could turn it on, a loud thump came from the master bedroom. She and Gran arrived at the door together, and found her grandfather lying on the soft brown carpet, unconscious and not responding to their calls.

After an interminable wait for an ambulance, they travelled with him to hospital to receive some very sombre news; the old man had suffered a series of strokes and would be very unlikely to make a recovery. He would fade away over the next several weeks, and all they could do was keep him comfortable; it was improbable that he would regain consciousness.

Pip's father picked them up and drove them home for a numb evening of planning how they were going to be able to visit Grandad. Family were contacted, and arrangements made for regular lifts to enable Gran to go, but unfortunately the elderly lady's own health was the biggest obstacle, as the travel quickly wore her out. However, Pip found that the bus service facilitated a daily evening visit, and she took it upon herself to make the trip every day after work until it was no longer necessary.

Every day, she sat beside the old man who lay on the cusp between earthly sleep and eternal rest and told him how the garden was doing and how Gran was keeping, and every few days, she brought a fresh rose from the garden to put in a glass of water beside his bed.

And then, one blissfully warm evening, with the golden-red sun burning into the horizon, she walked onto the ward and his bed was empty; he had passed away whilst she was on the long dusty bus journey to visit him.

In a dazed mixture of shock and relief, she made her way to the quiet hospital chapel and sat on one of its pale-wood chairs, staring at the simple altar. In her hands was the small cardboard box in which she had transported a single white rose, and she opened it to examine the bloom, one of the finest the garden had produced. Then, through her fog of grief, she felt her grandfather's steady, reassuring hand upon her shoulder, and through it a vow of gentleness and unconditional love. A single tear ran down her cheek and dropped onto the ivory petals as she raised her hand to touch his, but of course it found only the soft cotton of her blouse.

Silently, reverently she walked to the altar and laid the rose to rest on top of the crisp white linen cover, directly above the embroidered crimson cross, and left to take the bus home to her grandmother.

~ * ~ * ~

"I'm not happy about this, Gavin!" Mrs Knight was trying to keep her temper.

"Why?" he asked. "My exams are long finished and I've got a few weeks spare before—"

"Before what?" she snapped. "You haven't applied to a single university, so I don't know what you think you're going to do. But it's you going to London all the time I'm worried about. How are you affording it?"

"I've got the cash from the job I had last year."

"No, darling, that's supposed to be to help with your living expenses at university."

"I'll get a grant, won't I?"

"It's little enough."

"OK, you win, Mum. I'll ask the pub if they can give me some more work. Maybe they have another cellar that needs clearing out."

"Please, Gavin, stop it! You can't keep going on with Bob's search, it's stupid to keep going to dangerous places and asking people if they know where Sharon's gone. Face it, she has moved up north and nobody's going to tell you more than that. This summer is your last chance to have some freedom in your life, don't squander it. And if you want to be a friend to Bob, visit his widow rather than chasing rainbows."

"You're right," Gavin eventually admitted, struggling not to cry. "If you must know, I keep getting there and chickening out from talking to anybody that might really know anything. I just hang around hoping I'll fluke a lead. I've been a fool, haven't I?"

"No, you've tried to be kind, but just give yourself a break. Enjoy yourself for a few weeks."

Gavin outwardly agreed but was inwardly appalled to do so. How could he stop the guilt he felt? How could he stop the image of Bob's staring dead eyes from flashing into his mind? How could he let that good man's death be for nothing? Everyone else was giving up, so Gavin knew it was down to him to find some overlooked clue that would bring Sharon home; he just needed to find courage.

~ * ~ * ~

Pip struggled to contain the guttural sob lodged in her chest as she clutched her grandmother's soft hand in her own. The warm summer breeze dried her tears before they reached the end of her cheeks, and the heady summer scents in the churchyard were overwhelming.

"Oh, Grandad," she whispered hoarsely, as the wooden coffin was slowly lowered into the shadows of the grave. Pip struggled with the impulse to demand he was lifted back up, to open the lid and free him, for surely it was a terrible mistake, surely her strongest rock couldn't be being snatched away from her so cruelly. Or rather, snatched from them, for the elderly lady by her side was battling her own wish to climb into the hole and lay down with the love of her life.

All Grandad's friends and family stood close by, ashen faced and clinging to one another in their wretchedness. The soothing recitation by the vicar seemed to pass through Pip, ancient words forgotten almost as soon as she numbly heard them, but her mother's jagged breath and strangled whimper drilled into her memory for ever.

As roses from his garden and handfuls of earth were cast into eternity with Grandad, so the service tapered to its conclusion, and Pip noticed for the first time how many people had attended the funeral. Gran clapped her hands and all faces turned to look at her.

"There's food and drink down at the church hall. Please join us there to remember Jim."

With her granddaughter's support, the old lady walked a few paces, but then stopped and looked back at the grave. She held out her hand as she would when she waved to her husband from the kitchen window while he pottered in the garden.

"Sleep well, my darling, I'll come and see you tomorrow." With a tremble of her lip she pulled Pip close. "He could never settle anywhere new. Bravest man I ever knew though, not scared of anything, least of all dying. He knew where he was going, and who would be waiting for him. And I'll see him again soon enough."

"Don't talk like that, Gran," Pip pleaded as they resumed walking. "You're not going anywhere."

"Not yet, but none of us lives forever. Your grandad and I had a lovely life together, and the most wonderful granddaughter – I don't know what I'd have done without you these last weeks, my dear."

After all the guests and the mourners had gone, Pip and her grandmother settled on the little bench beside the front door of their bungalow to bask in the warm summer evening. Both knew that the other's eyes were trained across the valley to the churchyard where they had stood and wept earlier that day.

"At least I can keep an eye on him from here," Gran sighed. "A piece of me is lying there with him already."

"Grandad was such a big part of my life," Pip said. "One of my earliest memories is going for a walk with him. He cut a length of reed with his old penknife and made me a whistle."

"I remember! You went around tooting that thing for hours, it was a relief when it broke. He was such an active man, he hated getting old. A wonderful provider too, we'll be pulling up fresh veg until Christmas, I reckon. He was still fussing about his winter leeks the morning he went into hospital."

"You two were the only ones who believed me about the drugs. Grandad said he'd whack anyone who believed the rumours with his walking stick. I hate going back home - I know how people in the town see me, even now."

"Pipsqueak, I don't think people look at you how you think they do. You've been depressed for a while now, and I don't mean down-in-the-doldrums."

"No, Gran, I'm happy when I'm here! I love living with you and Grand—" Pip corrected herself with a little choke, "with you."

"No, my darling, you feel safe here, but you need to be out in the world, making real friends. I think you should be thinking about moving on."

"But I need to look after you!" Pip pleaded, close to tears.

"Fiddlesticks and stuff-and-nonsense! I'll be on my own sooner or later. I've got a few years in me yet, and you're not wasting your life fussing over me, my girl. You've better things to do."

"What about the roses? What about the garden?"

"I can look after them, and there are gardeners around here who can do the rest."

"What would I do?" Pip felt her world crumbling.

"Get out in the world and have friends your own age. Meet a boy, get married and have babies. You're a pretty girl, you know."

"I have friends – I have work and netball and Theo."

"That job won't take you much further, and a netball team made up of mothers ten years older than you is not a proper social circle. Your friend Mr Dickson sounds a nice fellow and going for drinks with him and writing letters is fine, but he's a family man with his own life and it's no future for you. One day you and I are going to part in this lifetime, and I'll want to know you're settled and happy. My mind is made up, you should make plans to move on. I see the look on your face, so don't panic, there's no rush – we might even have Christmas together."

"Sharon went out in the world," Pip reflected as she gazed across the valley, "and look at the misery she left behind."

~ * ~ * ~

Mr and Mrs Knight sat in their car, sweltering in the summer heat and waiting with bated breath as Gavin emerged from the school brandishing an envelope. He hurried to them and climbed into the back of the vehicle.

"Well?" asked both parents in unison.

"I haven't opened them yet, I wanted to wait for you."

Mother and father twisted around anxiously as Gavin tore the envelope open and read his exam results.

"It's more than I deserve." His disappointment was palpable as he handed his mother the piece of paper.

"You've done really well," she enthused, "I didn't know what to expect, but these grades are good."

"Maybe, Mum – I need to think about things."

By the end of the day, Gavin had been showered with hollow congratulations. Even Miss Harris, who had replaced Mrs Wood as the school's Head of Sixth, called him to say well done and that he still had time to apply for university entry that year. He joined his family eating a celebratory dinner but was isolated from their smiles and laughter. He felt a fraud – Bob was dead, Sharon was still lost, and he had failed them both.

"I'm not going to university, it doesn't feel right," he announced.

His father frowned, setting down his knife and fork with a clack. "Gavin, you can't waste a year lolling around. You need to start building your life. Don't let things drag you down."

"Don't let things drag him down?" Mrs Knight was incredulous. "Good grief, only seven months ago Gavin saw a man he knew die right in front of him, and you say that?"

"In the war—"

"Oh, that bloody war! It's all you men ever talk about. This is different."

Husband stared at wife, but he saw the truth in her words and nodded.

"It's fine, Dad," Gavin said. "I just don't think I'm meant to go away, not yet. But I went to see Mr Simms of Simms and Bartlett, and he's agreed to take me on as a trainee accountant. If I work hard and pass the exams, I could qualify in three years."

"Well, that's good, Simms and Bartlett is an excellent firm, but working all day and then coming home and studying isn't easy."

"It's what I want." Gavin was immovable, unwilling to countenance anything that would distract him from his main objective, wherever she may be.

Chapter 10

Gavin was excited about his first day at work. He rose early, put on his new suit, and overcame his nerves sufficiently to eat breakfast. His mother met him in the hallway, examining him with proud, dewy eyes as she straightened his tie and brushed the shoulders and lapels of his jacket with the soft palms of her hands.

"You look very smart." She planted a maternal kiss on his cheek. "Now go and make your mark in the world. Here is a good luck present from me and your dad."

She handed him a brown faux-leather attaché case and Gavin flicked the brass catches open to look inside, freeing the scent of the soft suede lining. He thanked his mother, placed his calculator and lunchbox inside, secured the catches with a satisfying 'click-click', and left the house, still rubbing the side of his face with tissue to remove any remnants of lipstick.

When he had realised that his new job required a car, Gavin used his savings to buy a cheap eight-year-old Morris Marina; its blue paintwork looked faultless, glittering in the morning sunshine, though under Gavin's stewardship the condition would deteriorate rapidly.

Twenty minutes later, he parked outside Simms and Bartlett's offices. Mr Simms himself showed Gavin around, introducing all the members of staff. Gavin was to share a small office with Mrs Rogers, a genial lady, whose red hair was moulded into a once fashionable beehive; she was to be his supervisor and trainer, and it quickly became clear that she was one of the most valued and experienced members of staff.

Gavin's desk sported a dark-brown push-button telephone, and a large desk calculator. In the drawer he found paper, coloured pens, and a pot of liquid paper (his greatest ally). His first task was to sort through a shoebox containing all the receipts accumulated by a local farmer over the last year, ordering them by date and then writing the details of each purchase on an analysis sheet. For a young man who loved numbers, it was manna from heaven. When adding up the totals for each row and column on a page, he clicked away at his desk-calculator, the paper reel at the back whirring as he did so. However, Mrs Rogers was able to do her additions in her head, never touching an adding machine; she caught him watching her and smiled.

"It's easier than it looks. Just practise, and you'll be as good as me before you know it."

Mrs Rogers went home at four, so Gavin nearly always had the last hour and a half of his working day unsupervised. A trainee secretary called Mel, who was about his age, decided that she would take her afternoon breaks with him, so at ten-past four every day she appeared with two cups of tea and they chatted about their lives and interests.

Gavin was at last in a place where he could put recent history behind him and look to the future, yet thoughts of Bob and Sharon were never far from his mind.

~ * ~ * ~

Pip plodded home from the stables, struggling to understand why she was so tired. Yes, she had worked a long day, but she had been sitting at a desk most of the time; the bookings were no busier than usual for September, though there had been a feed order to prepare, and two visitors wanting a tour of the facilities. The climb up the lane to her grandmother's house seemed steeper than usual, and the scratchy sore throat that had been annoying her all day felt ever more like she had swallowed a razor blade. She sneezed, then coughed and then swore; frequent colds were a hazard of working in a place with the owner's small children running around.

Pip heard a vehicle approaching from behind her and stepped onto the grass verge of the narrow lane to let it pass. She didn't realise her foot jammed in a small furrow until her leg twisted in an unnatural way and she experienced a sudden pop followed by severe pain in her left knee. Pip fell backwards and screamed in agony, which only made her throat sorer. The pain was too great when she tried standing, and she dropped back again. A glance at her legs showed that her knees were no longer the perfectly matching pair that they had been just minutes earlier; instead, the left one was misshapen, and the kneecap was now at the side of the joint.

The car was long gone, and she was alone again with no help in sight. Again, she got up, this time putting all her weight on her right leg, and managed an agonising sequence of hops, clinging to the verge.

"Are you alright, Pip, my dear?" a voice asked. A familiar face from church, a semi-retired architect called Mr Trevallyan, was striding along the lane in his familiar tweeds.

"It's my leg," she whimpered. "Please help me. It hurts so much."

They managed to make progress, Pip resting her weight on him, and before too long they were at the bungalow. Gran immediately fussed, sitting her granddaughter in a comfy chair and making a hot cup of sweet tea. The doctor was summoned and said that Pip had a badly dislocated knee cap; he performed a reduction to manipulate it back into place, and then put her leg in a splint, with strict instructions to rest for several days and keep the foot elevated.

Pip was in for a period of being looked after by her Gran, rather than the other way around.

~ * ~ * ~

At five past four, after Mrs Rogers had left for the afternoon, Mel appeared in Gavin's office bearing paperwork and a plate of chocolate cake.

"It's Shirley's birthday," she placed the papers in his in-tray and handed him the plate, "I thought you'd like a bit."

"I would, thanks."

"How are things with you?" she asked, leaning on his desk and toying with a strand of her mid-brown hair.

"OK, thanks. I've started my correspondence course. It's very interesting."

"I'd hate it," Mel wrinkled her nose. "I don't like studying. What I do like is the cinema, but nobody wants to go with me."

"Really?" Gavin was surprised. "You must have loads of friends."

"I do, but I don't want to go to the cinema with them," she dangled a clue.

"That's a shame."

"You aren't very good at hints, are you?"

"Um, I didn't know I had been hinted to."

"Ask me to the cinema this evening, and I'll explain it to you," she laughed.

~ * ~ * ~

Pip was delighted to be once again moving around the bungalow without making a fuss and to at last make a light breakfast to her own liking, rather than the delicious yet enormous offerings prepared by her grandmother.

"It's so good to see you back on your feet again without that silly splint," Gran declared. The rubber soles of her slippers squeaked as she shuffled into the kitchen. "How's the knee this morning?"

"Still tender," Pip replied. "I'm paranoid it'll happen again."

"Did you do your physio exercises last night?"

"Yes."

"And again, this morning?"

"Give me a chance, I still haven't finished my breakfast!"

"Well you'd better hurry up and do them, Lucinda will be here to pick you up soon."

"I really should start walking again, now I'm out of the splint." Pip tested the ground. While she was grateful to her boss for collecting her and dropping her home every day, she missed her privacy and the peaceful stroll to work through the lanes, even in the bad weather. Sometimes, she craved solitude.

"The doctor said it could take six weeks, remember? Those ligaments need to heal."

"I think that more applied to sports – no netball for a while."

"Well, I think you should learn to drive, Pipsqueak. I know Grandad started teaching you, but the best laid plans of mice and men…"

"I just couldn't get the hang of using the clutch. Poor Grandad was quietly going spare, but he never complained, bless him. I suppose I can afford some lessons, but I'd still have to buy a car."

"Nonsense, you can use the Sunbeam, and I'll pick up where you left off and teach you to drive."

"You, Gran? But you don't have a licence."

"But I do!" Gran had a mischievously triumphant smile. "I learned during the war. I just didn't like driving, and your Grandad hated being a passenger, so I never bothered. I taught your Aunty Sybil, though."

"Aunty Sybil is older than mum!" Pip exclaimed. "When was that?"

"Oh, it must have been about 1971, I remember young Wayne was about ten and Cecily was maybe seven. Those two little monkeys were sliding all over the back seat and shouting at their mum to go faster. Ah, happy days."

There was a ring at the doorbell announcing Lucinda's arrival.

"I'd better go," Pip said, slurping a last mouthful of tea.

"Have a lovely day – and buy a Highway Code from the shop in your lunch, I think we'll both need it. Oh, and don't forget your exercises!"

~ * ~ * ~

"Really?" Mel chuckled as she and Gavin queued for the cinema. "You're taking me to see *Highlander*?"

"My sister saw it with her husband last week and they really liked it."

Mel scanned the movie posters in the lobby, "I suppose you could have done worse, at least it isn't *Day of the Dead*. Yuck!"

The queue shuffled forward, and a kiosk became free.

"Two for Screen One, please," Gavin pushed money under the Perspex divider. With the weariness of the put-upon, the young lady on the other side gracelessly tore two green tickets from the roll in front of her and slid them to her customer.

"Shall I buy the popcorn and sweets?" Mel asked as they passed the colourful display of confectionery staffed by an acne-riddled youth who was slowly realising that he was as far as he was going to get in the film business.

"Um, I think I'm supposed to buy that too," Gavin replied. "My father says a gentleman always pays for the evening when escorting a lady."

"Oh, you're priceless!" she marvelled, gripping his arm. "And so is your dad."

They made their purchases and went into the large auditorium, finding their seats in the semi-gloom.

"Oh dear," said Gavin. "We seem to be on the smoking side. Do you want to switch?"

"It won't make any odds by the end of the film. Unless you have asthma or something?"

"If you're happy, I'm happy."

"Priceless," Mel whispered with a giggle as the lights dimmed, and the adverts and trailers began.

A little later, as the sparks from sword fights flashed across the screen,

Gavin became very aware of Mel's face inching closer to his; in the darkness her eyes caught the light of the projection beams overhead. Before he knew it, her moist lips were pressed against his own, and he was torn between excitement and fear at this new experience.

Mel drew back. "Haven't you ever kissed a girl before?"

"No, was I doing it wrong?"

"No, you seem to be a fast learner."

They kissed again, melting into one another, until Mel sensed herself being manoeuvred into a peculiar position.

"Are you trying to watch the film over the top of my head?"

"Um," was all Gavin could say.

"Blimey, you definitely learn fast! From beginner to pro in ten minutes. But it's fine, we can watch the film."

"No, I think I'll wait to rent the video," he whispered, and this time closed his eyes when he kissed her.

~ * ~ * ~

Dreading the inevitable and no longer able to use her knee as a convincing excuse, Pip walked through the garden to the block of garages at the rear of the bungalows for her first driving lesson under her grandmother's tutelage. At several points, she wondered if a horticultural emergency may present itself and allow her to escape, but all the plants decided to be stubbornly healthy. Clutching a pair of L-plates in one hand, Pip opened the garage door with the other, and was astonished to not see a silver Chrysler Sunbeam, but a dark-brown Mini.

"It's an automatic," Gran chortled. "I switched it for the Sunbeam last week. Ron down at the garage said that Mrs Isaacs needed something bigger for the kids, so we did a deal. I've got the log book back in the house for you to put your name in when we get home."

"My name? But this is your car!"

"Nope, it's yours," the old lady said firmly, "I've talked to your mum and all your aunts and uncles, and they agree that it should be yours after everything you did looking after your grandad. And before you say anything, we know that's not why you did it, but you need to accept that good things can happen to you, my girl. Come on, let's get those L-plates on."

~ * ~ * ~

Gavin heard Karen and her husband telling the family about the holiday they had booked but he was too preoccupied to listen. Suddenly he realised everyone was looking at him, expecting an answer to a question he had not heard.

"Skiing, Gavin," Karen repeated with a condescending tut. "There's an extra place on the trip. Do you want to come?"

"Um, I'm not sure that I should take time off work and my studies, thanks all the same."

"That's very diligent," said their father, "but a holiday might do you good."

"I don't want to take any chances."

"Well, I'm sure you are being very wise." Mr Knight's thin lips sported the hint of a smile. "On another subject, a funny thing happened this morning. I bumped into Penny from over the road, and she was telling me about her trip to the cinema to see a film about Scotland, I believe."

"Oh, yes?" Gavin had a growing sense of foreboding.

"Yes indeed, and she said there was a young couple a few rows in front of her who had very little interest in Caledonian history. You may wonder why she thought that I might be interested in these tidings – would you care to hazard a guess as to the identity of the amorous young man, who was enjoying the company of a pretty girl?"

Gavin saw his mother and sister, mouths agape, trying to comprehend the conversation.

"Were you snogging a girl in the cinema?" Karen asked, clearly basking in her brother's discomfort.

"I might," he faltered, blushing bright red, "have… a girlfriend."

Uproar consumed the table. What was her name? How old was she? How did they meet? Why hadn't he said anything?

It was Gavin's brother-in-law who eventually interceded to rescue him.

"Good on you, Gav, she's a lucky girl."

"Lucky?" snorted Karen. "Don't mock the afflicted. She probably needs glasses."

~ * ~ * ~

Summer passed, the leaves died and dropped, and autumn arrived. It was cold, the constant east wind giving little respite from its Siberian nature, and people hurried from place to place, not stopping to chat or to window shop, eager to reach their destinations and blessed warmth.

Lyn left the supermarket with three plastic carrier bags stuffed with groceries and started her weary walk home. The uneven distribution of her shopping made her back hurt, and she constantly shifted her load between hands, hoping to ease her discomfort. A fine grey misty rain swirled about her, matting her hair and making her coat heavier. She had worked consecutive shifts, the first to make ends meet, the second to help pay back Mark for the funeral; it was precious little, but she was getting there slowly.

Finally, she was home, but it was cold, dark and, worst of all, empty. Exhausted, Lyn peeled off her coat and put the kettle on, unpacking her shopping while the water came to the boil. A ring at the bell elicited a few swearwords and she tramped through the hallway to irritably haul open the front door.

"Mrs Wells?" asked one of the two police officers standing before her.

Chapter 11

Lyn regarded the uniformed man and woman in mute terror. Her vision shrank, and speech was impossible. There was only one explanation for their presence, and it made her want to slam the door and erase their existence – they had to be bearers of some final, mortal news of her Sharon. With an effort of will that came from having to hear what she must, Lyn nodded and stepped back to allow the officers inside.

"Is there somewhere we could all sit down, Mrs Wells?" asked the female officer.

"Of course," Lyn replied, as gently as the first kiss she had ever given her daughter. She led them into the living room. "Would you like some tea?"

"No thank you," replied the man. "I am Sergeant Trent, and this is WPC Cooper. We need to discuss your daughter, Sharon."

"I thought you might." Lyn sat on the sofa and lit a cigarette with trembling fingers.

"You reported Sharon missing early last year, is that correct?" asked WPC Cooper. "Do you have a recent photograph of her?"

"The one on the mantlepiece," Lyn said, pointing to a silver-framed picture of Sharon. "It was taken in summer '84 after her O-levels. I wish we'd taken more, but you don't think of these things until it's too late."

"May I borrow this photo for a little while?"

"Yes. I have copies upstairs." Lyn was frustrated that they were delaying the inevitable news. "She's dead, isn't she?"

"Mrs Wells," the sergeant spoke slowly, "our colleagues at Greater Manchester Police have been in touch to say they recovered the body of an unidentified female from a crime scene. They are in the process of determining her identity, but she had items on her person that belonged to your daughter."

"It's her, then."

"It's too early to say, Mrs Wells. We need the picture as part of the identification process."

"What happened to her?"

"We don't have details as to the cause of death. Once a formal identification has been made, the family would then be appraised, at the discretion of the investigating force. But I emphasise, we cannot draw any conclusions at this stage."

"Well, if a picture's going to be of use to you, her face must be alright," Lyn reasoned bitterly, "which is something, at least."

"Sharon's a very pretty girl," the WPC said as she removed the photograph from the frame. "May I confirm some other details about her? How tall is Sharon?"

"Um, five foot seven."

"Any distinguishing features? Birthmarks or scars, maybe?"

"No. Well, yes. She had a small red mark on her left cheek when she was born. It faded as she got older and you couldn't see it at all when she wore foundation; she called it her 'little rose'. Everyone else forgot it was there, but I could still see it – a mother notices."

"That's helpful, thank you. We'll pass that on to Greater Manchester."

"What were they?" Lyn asked.

"I'm sorry?" asked the sergeant.

"What were the things they found?"

"The deceased's bag contained a purse. Sharon's library card and a video rental shop membership card were inside."

"Well, that's it then." Lyn drew on her cigarette and exhaled.

"Nothing is certain, Mrs Wells. Could you describe Sharon's purse?"

"Um, well it is blue, made of material like denim and it had little pink flowers embroidered on. It was a sixteenth birthday present from her friend Philippa. I never saw inside it."

"That's very helpful," the sergeant assured her as he jotted down the details in his notebook. "We'll let you know what Greater Manchester have to say when we've wired them the photograph. We should have more information by tomorrow. Do you have someone who could stay with you, maybe a friend or a relative?"

Lyn shrugged, not caring.

"Please can you go now?" she whispered, struggling to retain her composure. "I need to be on my own."

~ * ~ * ~

As Gavin arrived home from work, his mother met him at the door, ashen-faced.

"Come in, dear. Lyn Wells has just been on the phone with some bad news. The police have found the body of a young woman they think is Sharon."

"Oh no!" Gavin cried hoarsely, dropping his briefcase and clinging to his mother.

"Poor girl, and poor, poor Lyn." Mrs Knight stroked her son's precious head.

"And poor Bob. Are they certain it is her?" Gavin asked.

"The police have to check from a photograph, but she had Sharon's purse."

"OK," Gavin sighed and straightened up, "I think I'll go over and check on Lyn. Is Mark coming down to be with her?"

"I didn't think to ask."

"Did— did they say what happened to Sharon?"

"No, and don't jump to conclusions. Let the police do their job. Have some dinner before you go to Lyn's."

Gavin was too weary to argue. "OK, I'm just going to call Mel and cancel seeing her this evening."

Mrs Knight went through to the kitchen, to strain and mash the potatoes for their meal. She could hear her son raising his voice as he spoke on the telephone. "I'm sorry you're disappointed, Mel, but someone has died!" echoed into the room. Gavin slammed down the receiver, swore and stalked into the kitchen.

"Don't take it out on her, son," his mother said. "Mel didn't know Sharon, and you have rather obsessed over her. I'm not saying you're wrong but try to make allowances."

"Why should I? She's being selfish!"

"Maybe, but maybe she doesn't know how to deal with it or you. Mel's a nice girl."

"So, what are you saying I should do?"

"Be gentle, always."

~ * ~ * ~

Lyn's cup of tea was cold. She didn't know how long that she and Gavin sat alone together in her kitchen, as silent as the grave, thinking about her daughter but unable to speak her name. Earlier, she had telephoned Pip and Darren with the news from the police and both had been distressed and were sincere in their kind wishes, insisting she mustn't give up hope, but their voices betrayed their secret conclusions, which were the same as her own.

"They telephoned just before you got here," Lyn blurted out, making Gavin jump. "The police, asking if they could come tomorrow and collect something with Sharon's fingerprints on."

"Did they?" Gavin strove to gather his thoughts. "I suppose it helps with identification."

"I told them they could take what they like... they can take the whole bloody lot!" Lyn snarled her words, like a vixen protecting her cubs.

Gavin nodded, at a loss for anything soothing to say. "Is Mark coming down?"

"Yes, the day after tomorrow, Saturday. Pip Raven said she'd drop over then too."

"That's nice of her. Forgive me if I don't come that day? I've errands to run, and I'm behind on my coursework."

"Of course." Lyn's world was slowly shrinking to a tiny dot, a single point in an ocean of black. She felt no human contact. "You are very kind... everyone is so very kind."

Gavin glanced at his watch. "It's almost midnight. I have work in the morning."

Lyn heard him and realised the yawning dark abyss between them, because for her there was no tomorrow, the sun could not rise, it was sucked into the black hole of her grief. Tomorrow, she would know for sure – there would be no sliver of doubt – tomorrow, her daughter would be dead, like Bob was dead.

But when would tomorrow begin? When the clock's hands moved a few degrees further and twelve tinny chimes marked the hour? Or at the impossible, unthinkable dawn, when she would rise and wait for the police? Maybe, for her, tomorrow didn't have to come. Maybe she could sleep and not wake up to hell on earth; maybe she could sleep a permanent, pain-free sleep, courtesy of the contents of the plastic pill bottle in her bathroom cabinet; maybe she could rest eternally with Bob and Sharon.

Lyn synthetically smiled at Gavin. "You must be tired, dear, go home. You've done enough."

Something in her words and her countenance evoked an unspeaking voice in Gavin's head, warning him of the tragic portent that lay behind them.

"It's getting late to be dragging across town," he lied. "May I sleep on your couch?" Gavin saw Lyn panic, lest she be thwarted. As he had done at the railway station with her husband, he blocked her path to destruction. "I'm sure Mark would be glad if I did."

A dagger of truth killed death. Lyn found her beacon in the dark realm – she must exist for her son. This time her smile was real, though heartbreak still lurked behind.

"Of course, Gavin. But there's no need for you to doss on this old couch. Give me a few minutes to make up Mark's bed for you."

"Thank you, Lyn."

"No, Gavin," she said, "it's me who should be thanking you. And I always will."

~ * ~ * ~

An excited bundle of blonde curls, blue eyes and childish giggles burst through the door of the compact office at the stables and skidded to a halt beside the old wooden desk where her new best-grown-up-friend was working. Bobbie eyed her quarry with sudden shyness, finger hooked into the side of her mouth.

"Hello, are you here for your lesson?" Pip asked. The curls wobbled as the head beneath them nodded. A slightly crumpled piece of paper was held out. Pip took the picture with the utmost solemnity and studied the pencil and crayon upon it. "I like this, it's very good. It's Polo isn't it? He's your favourite, I know. I bet if I looked in your pocket, I'd find some treats."

The finger came from the mouth with a pop. "Yes, some mints."

"Oh, I like mints. Maybe I'll steal one," Pip teased.

"No! They're for Polo, not for you," the girl giggled.

"But these are," Theo strode into the room and dropped a small tube of caramel-filled chocolates onto the desk. "We stopped off to fortify ourselves for the horse riding with crisps and sweets, and Bobbie told me that we had to bring something for you."

"Well, thank you, Bobbie," Pip smiled. "Shall we be naughty and have one now?" She peeled open the paper, rolled back the gold metal foil and offered a chocolate. When small fingers had popped the top one into their owner's mouth, Pip followed suit. "Yum. Do you think Daddy should have one?"

Just as Pip held out the tube to Theo, Lucinda walked in. "Capital!" she declared, taking a chocolate. "Just what I needed. Now, young Roberta, are you ready for your lesson?" Her pupil nodded her head and the curls shook again. "But you're not, are you? For you have no hat upon your head. Come along, let's get you ready." She ushered her charge away and Theo and Pip were alone.

"I think I'll have that chocolate," he said, taking the confectionery from the tube which Pip still held outstretched. "Bobbie's got rather taken with you these last few months, you know."

"I'm lucky. She's adorable."

"Yes, I don't know where she gets it from. Certainly not Claire," Theo remarked.

"You shouldn't say that," Pip admonished. "Not about Bobbie's mum. She's part of her. Are things that bad between you?"

"No, quite the opposite, we are quite reconciled," he replied, "I thought I'd said as much in my last letter."

"Sorry, you did. I had some bad news last night and things are a bit jumbled. You remember my friend that I told you about? The one who ran away? Well, the police have found a body."

"Oh, Pip! I'm so sorry. That's awful! And so soon after your grandfather too. If you want to talk to someone who might understand, I'm here."

"Thanks. It means a lot," she told him. "I have so few friends. I find it difficult to trust people."

"You've said that before, in your letters. Why do you feel like that? It doesn't strike me as your nature."

"It isn't," Pip hesitated. "Or rather, it wasn't. My best friend betrayed me, not in a school-kid way, I'm not overstating it. Well, everyone believed the worst of me. My parents, the school, my employers. I was fired before I started a job, expelled, and practically disowned. Only my grandparents and one boy from school believed me. Everyone else said they were sorry when the truth came to light, but the damage was done – they obviously believed I could do such things."

"What were you accused of doing?"

"Drug dealing," she said, bracing herself for him to demonstrate the tell-tale signs of 'there's no smoke without fire'. Theo stood dumbfounded for several seconds before he burst into uncontrolled laughter. "Stop it!" Pip protested but the guffawing was too infectious, and she started giggling. They laughed for minutes, wild and abandoned, as if exorcizing the demons of their private pain. Eventually, they regained their composure and they stood, red-faced, dabbing their eyes.

"They're idiots! You could be standing there brandishing a kilo of heroin and a machine gun, and I'd still assume you were holding them for a friend." Theo gazed at her with a look in his eyes that she both loved and dreaded. "I wish we could have met before. Eight years ago. When I wasn't…"

"I really don't think you'd have liked me back then."

"Why not?"

"Because I was ten."

"Ah, yes. You are so much more mature than Claire that I forget you're still in the bloom of youth."

"Bloom of youth?" Pip aped with disbelief. "You are twenty-seven, that's hardly old."

"Pip, will you meet me at the pub tonight?" Theo entreated. "You may have news about your friend. I'd like to be there for you."

"I don't want to give you the wrong idea." Pip was tempted, but loathsome common sense prevailed.

"Don't worry. I'm not a fool," Theo said, wishing he was. "I know how we stand, how we must stand. I know you're leaving the village soon, you've written about your job search, but your friendship is too important to lose. We understand each other. Please, just a drink in the bar."

"OK."

~ * ~ * ~

Lyn spent the morning and most of the afternoon sitting in her living room, staring out of the window. She had called the supermarket, told them her news and been smothered with sympathy. One workmate, Jo, stopped off with some flowers on the way home after the morning shift and offered to sit with her; not knowing why, Lyn accepted. Fortunately, Jo was content to sit quietly, making the occasional cup of tea. They both saw the police car draw up outside and the same two officers climb out and walk to the door. Jo let them in.

"Mrs Wells," the sergeant said in measured tones, "we've heard from Greater Manchester Police and I wanted to speak to you in person."

"Go on," Lyn said.

"It has been confirmed that the young woman who was found deceased is not your daughter, Sharon."

It took a long time for the import of the statement to register.

"Not my Sharon?" Lyn asked, slowly, not believing she was saying the words. The policeman shook his head.

"Oh, that's wonderful!" Jo exclaimed.

Lyn sat in stony silence before she broke down. "It's still some mother's daughter," she sobbed. "Someone's hurting. What right have I to be happy?"

"If she's not Lyn's Sharon, who is she?" Jo asked, stroking her crying friend's back.

"No name's been released, but we understand that the deceased has been identified as a pickpocket known to Derbyshire Constabulary. It seemed that she had recently moved to Greater Manchester where she wouldn't be recognised and was working shoppers in the Arndale Centre."

"Mrs Wells," WPC Cooper interjected, "most pickpockets don't keep their stolen property very long. It is extremely likely that the purse was taken in the last few days. Sharon was probably in central Manchester earlier this week."

"I don't know how to feel." Lyn was sideswiped. In the space of minutes, she had gone from grieving a dead daughter to firm evidence that Sharon was probably alive and well. "Am I further forward or back to square one?"

~ * ~ * ~

Gavin's reaction to the news about Sharon was mixed. Elation was followed by emptiness and frustration; he was somehow disappointed that it wasn't over, that he must summon the strength to search again.

Mel was spending the evening at his house; she had rented the video of *Highlander* from the local convenience store, a funny reference to their first date, but Gavin was too distracted to engage. Mel didn't mind about the film because she hoped the evening would turn romantic, but that was also not happening. She kicked off her shoes and snuggled closer to him on the couch.

"What's the matter?" Mel kissed Gavin and received little response. "You should be happy. Instead you're moping around and ignoring me. Your friend's OK, that's good."

"Yeah," he muttered, "I know, but—"

"But what? Why can't you have your mind on the here and now? I'm here, and this is now. Are you even listening to what I am saying?"

"Sorry, look I need to make a phone call. You go ahead and watch the film." Gavin hurried from the room.

Fuming, Mel wriggled her feet back into her shoes, ejected the video, and marched into the hallway.

"I'm going," she growled. "I'm willing to overlook this evening because you've had some big news, but you promised to take me car hunting tomorrow. Pick me up at midday, do you understand?"

Gavin paused, halfway through dialling a number. He seemed startled by her behaviour.

"Um, sure," he said, "noon tomorrow. Car hunting."

~ * ~ * ~

Tucked into the little snug near the fireplace at the pub, Pip and Theo chatted happily about anything other than how they really felt. The fire flickered and spat, filling the room with a savoury scent, but they were both oblivious to it, their attention fixed upon each other.

"So, it wasn't your friend they found?" Theo whistled. "That's incredible."

"Yes, it was a pickpocket. She'd obviously taken Sharon's purse at some point. It was one that I gave her for her birthday nearly two years ago. Maybe I still mean something to her after all, if she chose to keep it."

"That sounded like more than just friends who've lost touch," Theo frowned, making a connection. "Pip, is she the friend who betrayed you?"

"Yes," Pip replied, feeling disloyal.

"Well, blow me down, Miss Raven, but I think you may qualify for sainthood."

"I can't forget about what she did, but I couldn't wish anything bad for Sharon. I'm going to visit her mum tomorrow, and it's a good excuse to see my

~ 166 ~

family. Gran is insisting that I drive over. My test is next week, so I suppose I need all the experience that I can get."

"And then I suppose you'll be off to pastures new?" Theo stared at the flames in the grate, hurting.

"Not if I can avoid it. Gran seems to have forgotten that she wants me to leave, so maybe I can stay a bit longer."

"I don't know if that's good or bad," Theo murmured.

"Why would you say that?"

"Because the more I see you the more I—"

"Don't say it," she begged, frightened the dam in her heart might give way, "I feel the same, but we had a deal."

"You are right." Theo stood up, knowing that if he stayed a minute longer, he would finish the sentence that she had interrupted. "We had a deal and I couldn't stand to lose having you in my life."

"Give my love to Bobbie," Pip said, gazing into the fire as Theo walked away.

~ * ~ * ~

When Darren imparted Lyn's news about Sharon, Lloyd's reaction was close to anger.

"What a waste of time and emotion," he grumbled. "Honestly, that girl's messing up all our lives, and I barely knew her."

"Yeah, she always was a pain," Darren agreed, lazing on his scruffy couch. "One night she drank booze after pills, despite Hannah telling her not to. Man, she got so out of her head that we almost took her to hospital. Sharon never apologised, but I was pretty far gone, so couldn't care less – you know what it's like."

"Nope," Lloyd replied, "not my scene."

"What, not even a bit of grass? You of all people must have done."

"Why me of all people?" Lloyd flared. "Jamaican? Because I'm Jamaican I must be high on ganja? I didn't expect that from you, mate."

"I'm sorry. It's just that— you're a musician."

"Yeah, and I'm also in a gospel choir but that don't make me a preacher!" Lloyd immediately knew he overreacted. "Sorry, I'm a bit on edge because I left my bag on the tube this morning."

"That's bad," Will sympathised as he entered the room. "Was there anything valuable in it?"

"Not really. Some uni work, some sheet music and a small music stand. No address or anything."

"Well, keep an eye on the paper. People put stuff like that in lost-and-found hoping for a reward."

Darren, who had been lost in thought, suddenly exclaimed, "Somebody kiss me!" He didn't notice Will's willingness to oblige. "Do either of you two know anyone in Manchester?"

"I've got an aunt who lives in Stockport," Will replied, mildly bewildered. "She's nice – sends presents on my birthday."

"We could put a lost-and-found notice in the paper for Sharon's purse and put your aunt's phone number on it, Will. If Sharon rings, your aunt can organise a meeting in a safe place and we'll go instead. Gavin too – he's bound to be up for it after all his trips up here lately. What do you guys think?"

"It's a long shot," Lloyd said, "but it could work. I'd be willing to try for Lyn's sake."

~ * ~ * ~

"I need to get petrol, Gran," Pip said as they drove through the outskirts of her home town. "Is that OK or do you need to get to Mum and Dad's?"

"I'll be fine, stop fussing!"

After she replenished the tank of her little car, Pip entered the shop, where she picked up two bags of jelly babies as small gifts for her brothers – Matthew would be unimpressed, which gave her considerable big-sister satisfaction. The queue snaked away from the counter and she waited patiently, lost in her thoughts. She barely registered a man wearing a dark blue suit stop short when he saw her.

"Pip?"

"Tom," she replied, cursing her luck.

"You're looking good," he smarmed. "I heard that business with the school was sorted out – I knew it would be."

"Did you? I gained quite the opposite impression when we last spoke."

"Don't be like that, we can still be friends, can't we? I said you look nice."
He sounded a little too much like he was trying to pick her up at a bad disco.

"You look smart too." Pip tried to be conciliatory. "Is that a new suit? Not at work today?"

"I am actually," he boasted, "I've moved into sales. Great money and a company car. I picked up my new Ford Orion this week."

"Well, I'm pleased you're doing well." She tried to mean it.

"What do you say we go out for a drink sometime?" he suggested. "We could pick up where we left off."

"Actually, I can't think of much that I wouldn't rather do," Pip replied a little too loudly by any measure of discretion. "You see, I've got used to having drinks with men who don't have to ask their mummy's permission first."

"Cow," Tom muttered as he walked out of the garage to the sound of sniggers from some of the other members of the queue. Pip allowed herself to smile. She was still smirking when parking outside her family's home but began to feel bad about what she had done; it was not in her nature to wish to see anybody, even Tom, publicly belittled.

She and her grandmother ambled to the house where they were greeted on the doorstep by hugs and kisses. Daniel was happy to see his big sister, and was pleased with his sweets, but he was not as effusive as he once might have been, and Pip feared he was beginning to forget her.

Having made sure Gran was comfortably ensconced with their family, Pip promised to be back for lunch and started walking to Lyn's house, still limping slightly. She had barely got a hundred yards when the sound of stomping running broke into her solitude. Daniel ran up to her.

"Mum said I can go with you if you're happy to have me," he said, eyes wide in childish entreaty.

"That sounds nice," Pip replied, elated that he wished to be with her.

"Thank you for your letters," Daniel was still panting from running, "I'm sorry I don't write back very often."

"That's OK, I don't expect you to."

"Mummy reads me the stories you put in them. She says they make her laugh and make her cry."

Pip had taken to writing little fairy tales or funny anecdotes in her correspondence with her little brother. They were just silly ideas that came to her when she walked to work or cooked a meal.

"I'm glad you enjoy them," she laughed, tousling his hair. "Come on, let's get a move on."

At first, Lyn was surprised and irked that Pip brought Daniel. It had been so long since a young child had been in her house that it felt alien, but his innocent smile and childish fascination broke through a wall around her heart in a way that no adult could. It was not long before the boy was enjoying a glass of milk and enough chocolate digestives to spoil his lunch, and Lyn was the most surprised of the three of them when she suggested that they go into the back garden and kick around Mark's old football.

For late autumn, it was a very mild day and the sky was a crystal blue. Lyn's heart pumped blood around her veins with renewed vigour, the pale sunlight on her skin rejuvenated her, and she joined the little boy's laughter when a still less than fully mobile Pip slipped up, landing on her bottom with a squeaked "oh!"

Later, when she was alone and ready for bed, Lyn thought back to those events in the garden.

"It's been a good day today, Bob," she said as she turned out the light.

~ * ~ * ~

Gavin was excited by Darren's plan to find Sharon, so it was torture to be car hunting with Mel. Showroom after showroom, car after car, statistic after statistic – it was an annoying blur. Mel, however, may well have said that the only annoying thing was Gavin himself.

"I like this," she said, settling into the driver's seat of a Ford Fiesta.

"It's expensive," Gavin grumbled, looking at the sticker in the windscreen.

"Be glad you're not the one paying for it, then," Mel retorted. "Stop being grumpy and get us a coffee. There's a machine at reception."

Gavin walked away, muttering about the whole experience.

"Can I help you, madam?" A salesman appeared, crouching beside Mel. She felt sure he was looking at her legs and chest but let the matter pass.

"Yes, please. Which model is this one?"

"It is the Ghia, madam, the luxury model. Only four years old and a negligible mileage. My name is Tom, by the way. May I ask if the gentleman who was with you just now is also buying the car, or is it just for yourself?"

"No, he's got his own car. It's an old banger, but he doesn't seem to mind. It's a waste of time bringing him, but you know – boyfriends."

"He's your boyfriend? Lucky chap." Tom engaged flirt mode.

"Yeah, right," Mel agreed. "Not that you'd know. He's got other things on his mind."

"That," said Tom, "is a criminal waste. Perhaps you'd care to go on a test drive while he waits?"

~ * ~ * ~

"Sorry to be so long on the phone, Gran," Pip apologised as she hurried into the kitchen, "I hope you didn't let your dinner get cold."

"I popped the plates to warm." Gran opened the bottom door of the cooker and used a tea towel as a makeshift oven glove to remove two dishes of macaroni cheese. "So, were your mum and dad pleased that you passed your test first time? I bet they were."

"Dad was, but Mum was just being Mum, if you know what I mean?" Pip blew on her food to cool it, disturbing the cloud of steam that was billowing above the plate.

"I do, but you shouldn't say it." Gran popped a forkful of dinner into her mouth.

"How can you eat it when it's so hot?" Pip tested a sample of her own meal with the tip of her tongue and resumed blowing.

"It's called having children. You learn to eat what you can, when you can, hot or cold – normally cold."

"When did you get to be so clever, Gran?"

"Years of practice, my girl. And you'll be even cleverer, just you wait and see. Now, as you're in the mood to listen to my pearls of wisdom, it's time for us to talk about your future again."

"Oh."

"We discussed it last year, do you remember? We said maybe one more Christmas together, and then you're off into the big wide world."

"I remember," Pip muttered glowering at her macaroni, "but I hoped you had forgotten."

"Two things never forget: elephants and me," Gran chuckled. "Lucinda's youngest will be starting nursery soon. She'd go bankrupt before firing someone, but she'd be relieved if you moved on. The local paper came today, so have a look through the situations vacant, eh?"

"OK, Gran."

That night Pip wrote to Theo with mixed news, that she had passed her driving test, but that her time in the village was coming to an end.

~ * ~ * ~

Gavin, Lloyd and Darren lurked near the window of a clothes shop in central Manchester, taking it in turns to monitor the street, while the others feigned interest in the assorted garments on display. On the opposite side of the road stood Will, looking cold and miserable; he had drawn the short straw because he was the only member of the party whom Sharon wouldn't recognise.

"I still can't believe she replied!" Gavin struggled to contain his excitement.

"Well, we aren't sure it is her, are we?" Lloyd pointed out. "We're relying on Will's aunt and the old girl seemed gaga to me."

"Yeah, but she said the caller described the purse perfectly and said her name was Sharon," Gavin insisted.

"Yeah, but the old bird might have told her all Sharon's details and then forgot." Lloyd was tired and irritated to be taking time off from his dissertation. "We might've blown our train fare on a wild goose chase."

"What's the point of arguing?" Darren interrupted. "We'll know soon enough. The important thing is that we don't desert Will. It's not going to take whoever shows up long to figure out he doesn't have the purse – then they'll either go or hit him first and then go."

"We might not even recognise her," Lloyd sulked.

"Keep your eyes on the prize," Darren whispered.

"Is that her?" Gavin asked, peering through the window as a young woman with long wavy copper-brown hair approached Will.

"It could be. Why else would she be talking to him?" Darren replied.

"OK, let's go!" Gavin decided, and the three young men dashed out. The woman was already walking away, but the hunters gave pursuit until Will shouted at them to stop.

"She was only asking for directions to the railway station," he explained when they broke off the chase.

"Why did you talk to her for so long?" Lloyd asked, exasperated.

"Because it's the only place I know how to get to," Will said, "I wasn't going to waste that. Anyway, why are you all standing here, shouldn't you be hiding?"

It was impossible for them to argue with that, and they turned around to head back to the café. As one, they stopped in astonishment, looking at an equally (and more rightfully) amazed Sharon. She looked well, dressed in a ski jacket, pale tight jeans, and trainers; her hair was still its natural honey blonde and she seemed to be making no effort to conceal her identity.

Sharon froze, mouth open, trying to understand how three people she knew from entirely different circumstances could be standing in front of her, miles away from their respective homes. Her immobility was only temporary, however, and she recovered her wits more quickly than the boys; like an athlete, she ran down the busy pavement, weaving among the shoppers.

"Stop her!" shouted Gavin, breaking into a sprint. It occurred to him as he dodged the other pedestrians that they should have decided beforehand what they were going to do with Sharon if they did catch her.

She was fast, but the boys were faster, and they slowly closed the gap until Sharon was a mere ten paces from being overhauled, but just as the young men sensed victory, she unexpectedly got into the back of a burgundy Jaguar, which screeched away as they approached. They saw her face at the rear window mouthing, "I'm sorry."

"Damn!" Gavin exclaimed. "We were so close. We're never going to get a chance like that again. What bloody bad tossing luck!"

"Actually, mate, I think we might have just been lucky," Lloyd said. "Did you see those two geezers in the front? There could have been ten of us and we wouldn't have stood a chance."

"What do we do now?" Gavin asked.

"We go home," Lloyd answered. "We stop searching. We've seen Sharon. She looked fine to me and she ran when she could have asked us for help. It's over. We know she's OK and she definitely doesn't want to be found."

"Yeah, it's done," Darren agreed. "Let's get on with our own lives."

"Some friends you are, just giving up," Gavin snapped.

"Yeah, but that's just it, isn't it?" Darren said. "None of us are her friends, not even you. Lloyd and I didn't even like her, we did this for Lyn. But you can't kidnap her, it's not what she wants. You saw her, she's OK, Gavin. It's over."

"It's not over for me," Gavin muttered.

Chapter 12

Christmas came and went. Pip spent the day with her grandmother, and they cooked a meal for her family, who came to join them. She was quiet for most of the time, preoccupied with her search for a new job and only joining in with the festivities as a duty to be observed. Her parents appeared to bicker a good deal, or rather, in Pip's opinion, her mother bickered at her father who absorbed the acid remarks like a patient sponge; the worst barbs were reserved for occasions when Daniel was seeking his dad's attention, to help assemble a tiny trainset or extract a toy from its packaging. Someday, Pip planned to confront her mum about her behaviour, but this was not the occasion.

Any hopes that she had of finding a job within easy travelling distance of the little bungalow had faded away by the end of February, and she knew that she must look further afield. Fortunately, her regular correspondence with Charlotte led to several possible leads in the more sizeable town where her cousin now lived.

Meanwhile, Gavin continued searching for Sharon. He constructed elaborate ideas in his mind as to what she was doing and who the mysterious men in the car were. He even subscribed to The Manchester Evening News, poring over its articles in the hope of spotting a clue. Consequently, as his A-levels had before, his accountancy studies suffered, but he enjoyed his job and his work was more than satisfactory.

The long-suffering Mel became distant, making plans that didn't involve him (which he barely noticed), and Gavin more than once cancelled a date, deciding to follow some spurious, almost imaginary, lead in his quest for Sharon.

~ * ~ * ~

During her morning at work, Pip received an unexpected telephone call from Bobbie's mother. It seemed Claire and Theo had a long-standing engagement that evening, and their regular baby-sitter had let them down. Bobbie had wondered if her friend from the stables would be willing to take over.

At the agreed time, Pip parked her Mini on the pebbled driveway outside the Dicksons' eighteenth-century thatched cottage, scrunched her way to the entrance, and pulled the old black bell-chime. Though the March evenings were getting lighter, the heavy overhead rain clouds oppressed the Earth below with a wintry grey and there was a chill in the air that merited a heavy coat to be worn by anyone going outside. Golden light from the windows bathed her, and she caught the comforting scent of the smoke from the chimney as a gust of wind briefly twisted and teased it down to greet her.

Claire opened the door. She was statuesque, even more so in her high heels, wearing a long peach chiffon dress which enhanced every contour of her perfect figure; her golden, loosely permed hair was held back by a sparkling headband and her perfume hung in the air like a sophisticated promise of things to come. Pip, who wore a black jumper and her tartan trousers, felt tiny and inadequate next to the vision of perfection who invited her in.

Bobbie was nestled on the settee, already wearing her yellow pyjamas and cuddling a vivid-blue Care Bear. Obviously having been told not to get up or run around, she squiggled on the sofa with glee when her friend from the stables came in. Theo descended the stairs, wearing a dinner suit and looking like James Bond, and he ushered Claire through the door with unseemly haste, barely giving her time to tell Pip about Bobbie's bedtime.

The two young ladies enjoyed a pleasant evening. Firstly, Pip was introduced to the Care Bears, of whom there were several, then they played Snakes and Ladders, then they had ice cream, and then they watched some telly until a small head slowly laid its weight on the baby-sitter's tartan thigh and sleepy breathing began. Pip gently stroked the golden curls with one hand and used the other to reach for the remote control and turn off the television.

"I was watching that," Bobbie complained with a murmur and a sigh.

"I don't think you were. I think you were asleep."

"No, I wasn't," the little girl protested.

"Well, it's five minutes past when you're supposed to be in bed, and I don't want to be in trouble with your daddy and mummy. Shall I carry you up?"

"Yes, please."

"Oh, you are a big grown-up girl," Pip grunted when she stood up, encumbered with a Bobbie. For a moment, she feared her knee would give in, but all was well, and she creaked up the stairs with a face-full of curls and two small arms tightly wrapped around her neck. The girl's room was not hard to distinguish, the pink walls and mountain of cuddly toys being something of a giveaway. The bed, festooned with Care Bears, had a white-painted ornate headboard and a large downy pillow upon which Pip deposited the golden curls.

"Hm," said the baby-sitter, "I think you should have cleaned your teeth first. Do you think you can manage to do that?"

"Too tired," the head beneath the curls proclaimed.

"Be sure to give them an extra-good clean in the morning," Pip instructed. "Good night, Bobbie."

"No, tell me a story. Please."

After a knowing look at her charge, Pip scanned the bookshelves. "What shall I read?"

"No, tell me one of your stories, like you write for Daddy. He says that you write funny things that make him smile."

Pip racked her brains for an idea. "Once upon a time, there was a little old lady called Mrs Nestyhead."

"That's a funny name."

"I think so, and so did everyone else. Mrs Nestyhead lived in a little house in the countryside, far away from all the people who laughed at her silly name – isn't that sad? Well, Mrs Nestyhead had very wild, messy, black hair. She never brushed it, because she never saw anyone, and it was all tangled and itchy. One day, she went for a walk and a pigeon landed on her head and thought it was in a comfy nest. Well, Mrs Nestyhead didn't want to scare the poor bird away, because she knew it was about to lay an egg, so the pigeon stayed. But it wasn't so bad, because its toes scratched her itchy head. One day, the egg hatched, and a baby bird was born. It grew up and flew away and so did its mummy, but then, next year, they both came back and they both laid eggs – then there were four pigeons! Well, this went on and on and on, until Mrs Nestyhead couldn't stand up because having so many birds on her head was very heavy, so she had to sit in a chair all the time until the eggs hatched."

"Didn't she get hungry?" Bobbie asked.

"No, because the daddy pigeons brought her worms and spiders to eat. Yuck!"

"Yuck."

"Well, when all the pigeons had gone for the year, Mrs Nestyhead had to go into the town to buy some flour to make cakes. So, she walked into the shops but – oh, disaster! – she didn't spot that someone had dug a deep narrow hole, like a well, in the street and not covered it over. Poor Mrs Nestyhead fell in, and no one had a rope long enough to reach her. Just as everyone had given up hope of rescuing her, a pigeon flew over and saw what had happened. 'Coo Coo,' it called to its friends and all the pigeons who had ever lived on her head came along and they all flew down into the hole and together they picked her up by her hair and lifted her out. Everybody cheered as the birds carried Mrs Nestyhead around the town, high above their heads, before putting her down on a comfy bench in the park. Well, everyone thought this looked great fun, so they all grew their hair like Mrs Nestyhead and they all let the pigeons live there and they all went for exciting flights with their feathery friends. And that town is now called Nestytown and no one laughs at Mrs Nestyhead any more. The end."

Bobbie's gentle breathing didn't say whether she enjoyed the story, but it did indicate that its objective of inducing sleep had been achieved.

~ * ~ * ~

It was a little before a quarter to five in the afternoon, when Mel entered Gavin's office at the accountants.

"Guess what," she said with an impish grin.

"Um… sorry, I've no idea," Gavin looked up from his work, befuddled.

"I just quit!"

"Why?"

"I've got a new job. Receptionist at that garage where I bought my car."

"Well, I don't know what to say. It's a shock but it's up to you."

"It's a shock is it?" Mel reacted strongly. "I'm surprised you can spare the time to be shocked, what with your obsession with that Sharon. I'd assumed you'd lost any interest in a woman who is actually here."

"Look, I'm confused. Sorry if I've been thoughtless, but we love each other, don't we?"

"Do we? I'm sorry, Gav, but I think— well, maybe we should just be friends."

That last word burned like acid. "Is… is there someone else?" Gavin stuttered.

"No… well," Mel evaded, "I've been out for drinks with someone, but that's all. One of the salesmen at my new job." She tailed off, feeling wretched for making Gavin so sad. "If you could've just let the Sharon thing go, even a little bit. I've tried to understand, and I think you did a good thing trying to help, but there is no such thing as a knight-errant any more. I can't go on waiting for you to accept that Sharon's gone. Sorry. I hope you find someone who deserves you, because you can be fun to be with when you aren't thinking about her, it's just that I can't compete any longer."

She left the office, leaving Gavin in a fog of confusion, hurt, and misery.

"It's not a competition," he said, long after she had departed. He replayed the conversation in his mind, interspersed with flashbacks to the happier days, but the truth was there had been no truly happy days since the storm at the railway station when he had helplessly watched Bob die. Mel was right. Sharon's father had bequeathed him a mania.

~ * ~ * ~

Now down to part-time at the stables, Pip supplemented her income by regularly babysitting Bobbie. However, the arrangement came with complications. Theo's attitude was contradictory – his letters remained warm and affectionate, but he was coolly formal, verging on brusque, when with his family. Claire, meanwhile, delighted in her own status and always made sure Pip was completely aware of their differences in terms of looks, relationship and wealth; hints would regularly be dropped about a photo shoot, or a gift from Theo, or a foreign holiday, and they served to undermine the baby-sitter's already fragile self-regard.

There was no such awkwardness between Pip and Bobbie, however, and they grew ever closer. Maybe endlessly repeating Mrs Nestyhead was tiring, but Pip never wearied of the delight that it brought to her young charge. The two of them became so close that Pip felt a creeping guilt that her inevitable departure for pastures new might be painful for Bobbie – and for herself. If she did find a job near Charlotte, it wouldn't be practical to travel back regularly, but there might be the chance for an occasional visit, and she would make sure to write often.

It wasn't clear what Claire did in the daytime, she never mentioned a job, but Pip ended up becoming a regular at the school gate, collecting Bobbie and taking her home, often with a secret stop-off for a milkshake and a biscuit at a nearby café. From netball, Pip was already friendly with several of the mums waiting who like Claire wanted a private education for their children.

One afternoon, Pip was chatting to her usual associates when they were joined by a mother whose twins had just joined reception class. The newcomer was made welcome and the conversation flowed comfortably until the distant bell rang and a chaos of children began to pour out of the sombre building. Bobbie immediately homed in on Pip and ran full-pelt until she smashed into her, flinging her arms around her and nestling her golden curls against her soft chest.

"I've missed you so much," the little girl exclaimed.

"Me too," Pip laughed, kissing the curls.

"She's lovely," said the mother of the twins. "She must get the fair hair and curls from her dad."

"Oh, no, from her mum," Pip smiled. "I'm just the baby-sitter."

"Oh," the woman's smile froze into that of a benevolent shop mannequin.

Pip paid no heed and led Bobbie away by the hand, listening to the exciting stories of the school day – but she could hear the woman saying to the group, "I don't think I'd stand to have a child of mine so pleased to see the hired help."

~ * ~ * ~

The Reverend Johnson was tidying the vestry when he heard the click, creak and thump of the heavy old church door being opened and closed. He popped his head out from the little room and saw a familiar figure.

"Hello, Gavin, what brings you to see me?" he asked.

"Some advice, if possible."

Several minutes later, two steaming mugs of tea in their hands, they settled into two threadbare old easy chairs beside the Mother's Union notice board.

"So, what's the story?" asked the vicar.

"I think I've made a mistake staying around here."

"Aren't you enjoying your job?"

"I am – or I was. Work all day and study in the evenings suited me fine at first, but then I met Mel."

"Your girlfriend?"

"Ex-girlfriend, she dumped me last week. I'm a fool! I never considered myself much of a catch, but then this incredible girl turns up and somehow, I alienate her. Mel said I'm obsessed with finding Sharon Wells, and I think she's right. Now I realise how lonely I am here. Everyone at work is nice, but Mel and I were the only two under twenty-five, and now she's quit."

"Giving up her job as well as breaking up with you?" remarked Reverend Johnson. "Mel may have more going on in her life than you realise."

"My parents said that too," Gavin sighed. "The thing is, after Sharon's dad died, I wanted to stay here, to support her mum, but even she seems happier now. Why can't I let Sharon go? I think I need to get away. Maybe I'll go to uni – a fresh start."

"It makes sense."

"So, you think I should go?"

"I have no views either way, but I can see why you'd want a clean slate."

"But I'd be letting Mr Simms down," Gavin moaned.

"A few months in a job can change a person's outlook on life, so he'll understand."

"I miss Mel so much," Gavin fought back tears. "Everywhere I turn, I see something that makes me think of her. I just want to go. Now."

"I see," the reverend rubbed his chin thoughtfully. "In that case, I may have a solution."

~ * ~ * ~

"How did the interview go?" Gran asked as her smartly-dressed granddaughter walked through the front door.

"Well, I think," Pip replied, gratefully accepting a mug of tea from her grandmother. "It's an amazing company – all glitzy and modern with fountains in the entrance, glass doors and a huge lobby. There's a restaurant and even a gym. I was met by a lady from HR and she showed me around and then I had an interview with five people. It was scary, but I think I did OK."

"I'm sure of it," Gran stated.

"They said they'd let people know if they've got jobs late this afternoon. There are a few different positions that I might be right for." Pip was interrupted by the ringing of the telephone, and she exchanged an excited glance with her grandmother before tentatively lifting the receiver. "Hello? Yes, this is her speaking. Yes. OK, well thank you. Yes, that's great, thank you." She hung up.

"Well?" enquired Gran.

"I got it! I can't believe it! Part of the secretarial team supporting the legal department, with training to become a legal secretary or PA. I start in two weeks."

"That's wonderful!" Gran hugged Pip tightly. "You are such a clever girl. Now, what are your living arrangements going to be? It's far too far to commute from here."

"Yes, but Charlotte's looking for a flatmate. I rang her when I heard I got the interview and she's quite excited to share with me."

"Your cousin Charlotte? Oh yes, she's very sweet," the old lady gave her granddaughter an extra-tight squeeze.

"What will I do without you, Gran?" Pip whispered.

"Just make sure you come and visit regularly."

"Of course!" Pip promised. "I have to make sure my roses are being looked after properly."

~ * ~ * ~

Gavin was unsurprised by his parents' elation when he told them he planned to go to university in the autumn, but his decision to immediately leave Simms and Bartlett caught them out.

"But why leave your current job now?" Mrs Knight sensed her son had more to tell.

"Because Reverend Johnson has put me in touch with an organisation that arranges for gap-year students to work abroad. They have some openings at a soccer camp in Tennessee that's just about to start, so I need to hurry."

"Oh, Gav, is that wise?" his mother asked. "You've hardly been away from home by yourself before, and now you're jetting off to America?"

"To teach soccer?" Mr Knight interjected with a note of even greater surprise than his wife.

"I know how to play, Dad, I'm just no good at it. Look, it is an opportunity to try something new, and I've made my mind up."

"Well," his father responded, struggling to process the information, "if the adage 'Those who can, do; those who can't, teach' is correct, you should make a fabulous soccer coach, but surely being able to kick the ball in the approximate direction that you wish it to go is a prerequisite of the job?"

Gavin burst into laughter. "Reverend Johnson put me up to that. It's really a maths camp. Kids go there in their holidays for extra tutoring and schools send gifted pupils there for courses during the term."

"That's a relief," Mr Knight chuckled. "Well, it seems your mind is made up and you've everything in hand. It's a good idea to put all the nasty business behind you and start afresh. New adventures await."

~ * ~ * ~

Poor Darren didn't look himself. His hair was slicked down with gel, he was wearing a dark grey suit, and his neck was constricted by a starchy white shirt and sombre tie. He sat behind a shiny black grand piano in the high-ceilinged, plush-carpeted lounge bar of a swanky West-End hotel. Another little piece of his rebel soul died when he commenced playing Moonlight Sonata for the third time that evening, and for the umpteenth time since he had taken the job a week before. To make matters worse, his two best friends were watching his humiliation.

"Poor sod," Lloyd said, "he looks like a miniature undertaker."

"Poor us, more like," Will grumbled, jealously nursing half a pint of lager. "He gets free drinks. Have you seen the prices in here?"

"Yeah, but I'm going to make the most of the evening and have some grub, to celebrate being offered a place for my PhD."

"Oh, yeah, Darren mentioned something about that. Manchester University isn't it?"

"Yeah, I liked the look of the place when we went up there. It's still got a city vibe but is miles away from all this."

Two middle-aged men conspicuously entered the room in a state of mild inebriation. They were portly, limited of hair and wearing expensive suits; hanging on their arms were two beautiful young women, who gazed at their dates with doe-eyed fascination. The group's raucousness intruded into the ambience of the lounge, but the bar staff had no intention of quietening them, for they sensed large gratuities coming their way.

The taller woman, a blonde in Achilles-destroying heels, looked puppy-eyed at her consort and gently pressed her palm to his chest. "Olly darling," she teased her words out, "I need to powder my nose. Will you get me a little drinkie while I'm gone?"

"Of course, gorgeous," the man drooled, removing a large wad of money from his pocket and peeling off the top note. "You may need this for any expenses."

Taking the money, she giggled outrageously, strummed his arm and gave him a coy semi-smile from beneath her perfect platinum waves. Many eyes followed her departure, none more lecherous than her generous benefactor.

"Actually, I could do with a slash myself," Olly declared, ostensibly to his male companion, but possibly for the benefit of the room. "How about you, Ted?"

"I'm right behind you."

"You'd better not be, ya dirty bugger!"

Ted turned to his own female escort and said, "Order some champagne for us all, love. Tell them to put it on the tab and not to give us any of that cheap stuff they keep behind the bar."

His companion, a dark-haired Asian woman in a scarlet dress with matching heels, smiled a million-pound smile. She had no trouble attracting the barman's attention while her two companions sauntered off in search of the Gents.

Lloyd was in a state of animation, waving frantically at Darren and rushing over to the piano.

"That girl at the bar is Tracy," he hissed.

"Maybe you're right," Darren peered indiscreetly. "Come on, let's talk to her before her friends come back."

Tracy was briefly elated to be reunited with her former bandmates, but told them, "I can't talk to you now, I'm working. My client will be back shortly."

"Tracy, you don't have to sell yourself to that slime-ball," Darren told her, "we'll get you out of here."

"Sell myself!" she repeated with a mixture of disbelief and laughter. "Oh, that is so sweet. But don't worry, you don't have to defend what little is left of my honour – I'm an escort, not a hooker. In a few hours, he'll be fast asleep, and I'll be on my way home four-hundred richer, plus incidentals. If he gets too touchy-touchy it will require a little visit to Tiffany's before he gets to see me again. He's a regular, from Chippenham; comes here on business for a couple of nights once a month." She saw her old friends stare at her, mouths agape. "Honestly, I'm fine. Look, I've got a flat just off Sloane Square for goodness sake. Oh, hell, they're coming back."

"We have so many questions," Lloyd said.

"Wait in the foyer," she whispered. "I'll make an excuse and meet you there." Her demeanour and voice changed instantly as her clients returned. "Ted and Olly, you naughty boys left me all on my little own for far too long!"

Lloyd and Darren waited in the lobby for over five minutes, listening to inane chatter and raucous laughter from the bar until Tracy made her excuses and she joined them.

"Well, you've done well for yourself," Darren observed.

"Yes, I landed on my feet and not on my back." Tracy sounded teasing but there was no mistaking the intent of her cutting words.

"We'd heard rumours that bad things happened," Lloyd said. "We've been looking for you, well for Sharon, because her family was so worried."

"Sorry, I don't know where she is," Tracy told them. "It all got very messy. Frank and Sam ran up a load of debt and Frank panicked. He said he needed my help with something and took me to a disgusting old house and left me; he'd done a deal with the guy who ran the place. They made dirty movies and I was his new star, whether I liked it or not. There were at least five other girls. It was horrible. They put me in a room with an old mattress and a video camera, gave me a costume and told me to get changed."

"That's terrible!" Darren exclaimed, shocked.

"I thought that was my destiny, but the next thing I knew there was a huge noise somewhere in the building. I could hear fighting and then Ed's voice shouting my name. The boss-man came in, covered in blood – he looked like he wanted to kill me, so I ran. I could hear the man chasing me, but I got outside before he caught up. There was Ed, wrestling with a policeman. I couldn't help him, so I kept running until I was sure no one was behind me."

"Then what did you do?" Lloyd asked.

"Well, I wasn't going back to the house, Frank might be there, so wandered around for ages. Shock I suppose. Then I remembered an ad for escorts I'd seen in an upmarket magazine. I was worried that it was a cover for a brothel, but it wasn't."

"Do you know any more about the others?"

"Well, I visit Ed in prison every week. He might be out on parole soon, and he can live at my flat. I did go back to the house where we all lived, once I was sure things would have calmed down, but the others had long gone and there was no sign of my stuff or Ed's."

"Why is Ed in prison when he helped get you girls out? I'd have thought they'd give him a medal."

"You know he doesn't have an off-switch." Tracy replied. "He sees a red mist and will attack anyone and everyone he doesn't care about. Hitting policemen is always going to put you away."

"Tell him I think he's a top bloke," Lloyd said.

The sound of Ted and Olly lamenting Tracy's absence was becoming ever louder. She took a business card from her purse and handed it to Darren.

"This is the escort agency. Call and leave your number if you need me. I have to go now."

With a final dazzling smile, she returned to her clients, a vision of scarlet sensuality.

~ * ~ * ~

Pip had finished packing her things for the move to Charlotte's flat and her new life. All her clothes and possessions were in three suitcases now wedged in the back of the Mini, a leather Filofax was on the passenger seat (a parting gift from Lucinda), and three potted miniature rose plants were carefully stowed in the boot. She was building up the courage to depart when the postman arrived, bearing a package addressed to her. Inside was a book and a letter from Theo.

'*My dear friend, Pip,*

A note to wish you well for your move. I hope your new job and home will be all you hope for and more.

Bobbie keeps telling us your Mrs Nestyhead story and we all laugh at it. You have such a talent for bringing ideas to life and I do hope that you will still have time to write – we both enjoy your letters very much. I know that Bobbie is going to miss you terribly, and we are having a great deal of trouble persuading her to even consider another baby-sitter, though you are so much more than that – you are true friends. I hope that you know that I feel the same about our friendship.

In mind of this, I have enclosed a small gift, which I hope you will accept from Bobbie and me with our love. It is 84 Charing Cross Road. I first read it some years ago when I picked it up in an airport and read it from cover to cover on my flight – twice. I hear they are making a film of it. It is about two great friends who write letters over a far greater distance than you will be from us.

I expect you know that Bobbie is less keen on her riding lessons since you left, but she still likes to make sure Polo is well.

Have a safe trip,

Theo

(and Bobbie)'

"Isn't that nice?" said Gran. "It looks like you're going to be missed by lots of people."

"Oh, Gran," Pip started to sniffle, "I'm going to miss you most of all."

"Brave heart, my girl," said the old lady, just about marshalling her own emotion. "On to new adventures."

~ * ~ * ~

It was well before the appointed hour of ten o'clock when Pip arrived for her first day at her new job. She steered her little Mini through the huge car park, observing that the vehicles became progressively less grand the further she drove away from the entrance to the offices. For her interview, she had used a visitor's space but now that she was a lowly junior employee she must park amongst her ilk. She found an empty space next to a battered red Renault with a black front wing – the appropriate corporate reward for her station in life.

The tall office building, a shining cathedral to commerce, seemed miles away, and it took several minutes for her to reach the large glass revolving doors; they turned endlessly, meaning anyone entering could not simply turn back but must complete an entire circle if they wished to leave. The foyer buzzed with activity as smartly dressed men and women walked around with serious intent or clustered together to discuss urgent matters of business. Both immaculate receptionists, seated behind their tall white desk, were deeply involved with visitors, but Pip patiently waited until a dazzling smile of flawless lipstick greeted her. The smile faded when the newcomer explained that she was a new member of staff.

"No need for you to be here," the woman snapped, "just go to security for your pass and get to work."

Deflated, Pip approached a smaller desk, behind which stood a blue-shirted giant of a man who was at least civil to her. He found her name on a list and handed her a laminated staff card with her photograph staring out.

"Right," he said, "if you'll adopt the position, all I need to do is frisk you for weapons and then you can go up to work."

"What?"

"It's a joke! Off you go."

Pip forced herself to smile. "Sorry, where am I supposed to go? All I know is the legal department."

"There is a company map on the wall by the lifts," the guard told her. Then he sighed as if doing the greatest favour imaginable. "Second floor."

Reaching the correct floor proved to be only a minor part of Pip's quest, because the open plan office was huge, stretching away in all directions almost as far as she could see. She asked a passing man, who looked about her own age, if he could direct her to the legal department and he pointed into the distance. As she made her way through the desks, serenaded by typewriters clicking and phones ringing, not one person made eye contact or returned her smile, though one woman did tut at her when Pip briefly obstructed her path.

At last, she reached a quieter corner, where a small team of women sat at two rows of desks, facing each other. The supervisor, tall, with close-cropped pale-brown hair, sat at a large workstation, placed so she could look down the rows of her staff. Sick with nerves, Pip breathed deeply to calm herself and approached.

"Is this the legal secretarial team?" she asked, trying not to shake. "I have been told to ask for Glenda."

"Well, you've found her," the woman snapped, assaying her visitor with cold eyes. "You are?"

"Um, Pip Raven, I am your new trainee."

"Pip?" Glenda echoed. "What kind of name is that?"

"Sorry, it's short for Philippa, but no one calls me that... unless I'm in trouble."

"Well, Philippa, you're not supposed to be here until ten and it has barely gone half-nine."

"Should I go away and come back?"

"No, you're here now, so you might as well make yourself useful." Glenda picked up a piece of lined paper with handwriting scrawled over it. "You can start by typing this up. Your desk's at the end on the left."

Without so much as a welcome, Pip moved to the far end of a row of five desks. There was an electronic typewriter, a yellow pushbutton telephone to its right and a lamp on the left; her foot knocked against her metal wastepaper bin as she sat down, making the faintest of sounds but nevertheless drawing a glare from Glenda.

The handwriting was almost illegible, as if a spider had got ink on its feet and decided to dance an Irish jig across the surface of the paper, but eventually Pip managed to discern the words and create a presentable document. Glenda received the work as if it were infused with the plague and proceeded to loudly criticise it while her new junior stood beside her, cringing with embarrassment.

"Some of this grammar is dreadful," the woman stated for all the room to hear, "your margins are all wrong and you have used the wrong paper."

"I'm sorry," Pip apologised, "I used the paper in my desk drawer, like everyone else was doing, and I just copied what was written, I didn't realise I was supposed to correct grammar."

"Do it right," Glenda instructed, handing it back. "I suppose this paper will have to do for the time being. If you're the sort to make so many mistakes, it's probably better not to use the good stuff."

A few minutes later, Pip returned with a revised document.

"What a good thing it is that you're a lawyer," Glenda mocked, "changing the meaning of bits of it as you see fit."

"I was just correcting the grammar, like you asked," Pip defended herself, but the look on her supervisor's face chilled her.

"I didn't ask you to change the meaning! I'll have to show this to the departmental manager. You've certainly got off on the wrong foot with me, my girl. Just see that you come back with a better attitude this afternoon."

The office started to empty as people left for lunch. No one made conversation with her, or asked Pip to join them. Soon, she was left alone with her peanut butter sandwiches and no idea of where to go to eat them, so she remained where she was and read the book that Theo had given her, wishing she was back at the stables.

Two of her colleagues returned about ten minutes before the break ended but ignored their new workmate when she attempted to be friendly. Pip tried again when their conversation ended and one of them had started to touch up her makeup with the aid of a small hand mirror.

"Look, no offence," the woman responded, "but we don't tend to get too close to the juniors in here. Glenda doesn't like it. Anyway, I've got to take dictation with Mr Simpkins now." She flicked the case for her mirror closed, straightened her top (which Pip thought needed several buttons doing up), picked up her notebook and pen, and made her way to a line of office doors close by.

"Who's he?" Pip asked, but the other woman flicked through a magazine and blanked her.

Glenda returned to her desk. "Lunch is over," she barked. "We don't pay you to make chitchat, Philippa. Retype that awful letter you did earlier - most disappointing from someone supposed to have experience. I'd been led to believe you were going to be a help. When you've done it, we'll see what your audiotyping skills are like."

"I'll do my best, but I am a bit rusty. I haven't done any audiotyping since my course."

"I am not your nursemaid! I'm sure you'll get back in the swing of it soon enough. You'd better, because I don't like complainers on my team, do I, girls?" Glenda sought and received the other secretaries' agreement. "See? Now, get on with it and don't mess up again. Probation means what it says."

Pip sensed hostile looks as she returned to her desk and felt a prickle of tears in her eyes.

Oh, what have I done? she thought to herself. *I can't mess this up, everyone's expecting big things of me.*

She began typing. Oh, how she missed the little garden at her grandmother's house, oh how she just wanted to be out there with her non-judgemental roses.

Chapter 13

At the end of a long, tiring week at work, Pip arrived home, looking forward to an evening in with her cousin.

"How was work?" Charlotte's voice drifted from her bedroom.

"Awful," Pip sighed. "My supervisor still finds fault in everything I do, blames me for her mistakes, and forgets to tell me about new work assignments. She seems to like giving me an ear-bashing."

"Well, at least you didn't have some strange old bloke telling you he had to have his temperature taken rectally."

"Is that unusual in a hospital?"

"It is when it turns out that he's not a patient," Charlotte snorted with laughter.

"Seriously?" Pip screeched, wide-eyed. "You didn't do it, did you?"

"I might have done if the ward sister hadn't told me who he was. I'm new on the ward, but everyone else knew that he's a regular visitor who wanders in from geriatrics – they had a good laugh at my expense."

"I bet," Pip giggled. Then she sighed. "I don't feel like cooking. What do you say to a takeaway?"

"Fish and chips is all we've got nearby, but I'm game if you are."

"OK, but let's stop at the off-licence and get a bottle of wine too, shall we?"

"I knew you'd be the perfect flatmate, Pip. Oh, by the way, your friend Lyn rang earlier. She wanted you to know that a friend of yours is going overseas. Garry, or something."

"Gavin?"

"Yes, that's it. America, I think."

"Jetting off overseas and I've never been further than the Isle of Wight! Happy travels, Gav, wherever you are."

~ * ~ * ~

Disorientated by the changing time zones but exhilarated by the adventure ahead, Gavin lugged his suitcases through the terminal building of the airport. The cavernous foyer was crowded with people streaming in different directions and it was hard to know where to go, but in the distance the artificial lights were overpowered by bright sunshine streaming through the towering glass entrance, a beacon to his way out. Gavin pressed through the throng, his eyes and mind fixed on reaching the doors. A young man with brown eyes, a golden tan and shiny mid-brown hair blocked his path; he wore a bright orange shirt and faded denim jeans.

"Hello, traveller," the young man said with a broad smile and perfect white teeth. "Please accept this flower as a welcome to our town." He held out what appeared to be a miniature sunflower from a small bunch which he was carrying. Gavin accepted it with bemusement. "You seem to be in a hurry, friend, rushing everywhere, and for what? Don't you long for the warmth and peace of the sunshine all year round?"

"Well, I suppose so," Gavin replied, "but I'm from England, so sunshine's a bit of a novelty."

"That is very funny," the man laughed appreciatively. "Tell me, friend, what is your name?"

"Gavin."

"Welcome, Gavin. I want you to know that you have friends in this town. We are here or down at the park every day and we want to help travellers like yourself find where they are in this world."

Feeling trapped, Gavin looked around the foyer. To his immense relief, he spotted a white cardboard sign bearing his name being held up by a young woman standing near the entrance.

"I'm sorry, but I have to go now," he said and made his escape, noticing for the first time that the mysterious young man was barefoot.

"Go in peace, friend. Be blessed."

Gavin hurried away to the woman holding the card. About his own age, she had a pale complexion, slightly sunburned, and her cascade of dark curls bobbed when she moved her head. She was so immersed in scanning the crowd that she almost failed to see her target arrive.

"Gavin?" she asked. "Hi, I'm Tori."

Gavin dropped a suitcase and enthusiastically went to shake her hand; both were surprised that he also handed Tori a small battered sunflower, which he had been grasping along with the luggage handle.

"Um, thank you," she said, "it's very nice... is it for me?"

"No – well, yes – well, I suppose so. Sorry. A man gave it to me back there and I forgot that I still had it."

Tori momentarily seemed simultaneously interested and distracted by this news, looking at the people moving about the airport. Distributing Gavin's luggage between themselves, they exited the terminal and walked to a car park, where they loaded the cases into the back of an aging Buick station wagon.

"You could fit my entire car inside here," Gavin remarked, peering inside.

"Yeah, it is kind of big. It's not mine, it's Miss Lucille's. She's the lady that runs our boarding house."

Gavin nodded, remembering the information that he had been sent by the Maths Camp. Mentors lived on-site with the children, while tutors like him (who were there to assist individual students with their work, rather than to teach) were put up in local bed and breakfast accommodation and bussed to the campus.

Once in the car, he had to suppress a smile when he noticed his companion perched on top of two cushions to see over the steering wheel. Tori sensed his silent mirth and flashed a brilliant smile.

"Miss Lucille doesn't like people to move the seat about too much."

They drove past the entrance to the terminal where steady streams of people were going in and out of the building. The young man who had given out flowers was standing with a group of similarly dressed youths and seemed to look straight at them as they passed. Gavin waved awkwardly, and Tori also gestured acknowledgement.

"It's about a twenty-minute drive to Miss Lucille's," she said, staring straight ahead. "Maybe a bit less if the freeway stays clear."

The bright midday sun had warmed the car well past the point of comfort so, after a few minutes of travel, Gavin started to wriggle out of his jacket. Tori observed his struggles sympathetically.

"It does get pretty hot here. I'm a Boston girl, so it was a shock to me too, but it's not so bad once you're used to it. Miss Lucille must own the only car in the state with no aircon, but you can crack the window open if you like."

Gavin did as she suggested and moved his head to allow the cool thin stream of air to play over his perspiring brow. He was worried that his new landlady sounded like a forbidding woman and he began to wonder what he had signed up for.

"Miss Lucille sounds a bit stern," he remarked.

"She's a sweetheart, don't worry, but she likes things just so, if you know what I mean? I remember when I moved in and she said to me 'Miss Victoria, we ladies sleep on the second floor and the gentlemen sleep on the third, and I see no reason why you should need to be up there, nor why they should need to linger when they're passing by. We have a lovely living room if you wish to socialise' – how adorably old-fashioned is that?"

"So, are you a tutor at the Maths Camp too?"

"Yup. I was due to be studying at Berkeley starting last fall, but we had some family problems, so I deferred a year and came down here. I've got it all planned out: Berkeley, M.I.T. then NASA. I want to work on the Space Shuttle. How about you?"

"I had a friend who went missing and I helped her parents look for her, but I'm off to university this autumn, just like you."

Tori appeared to study him closely, as if his words were significant. Her lack of attention to driving was disconcerting for her passenger, but fortunately her fascination was fleeting and the road ahead soon once again enjoyed her full attention. Before long, the Buick swung lazily into a wide cement driveway outside a large whitewashed house. In the shade of the building's broad veranda, a tall grey-haired African-American woman was seated on a small bench; as the car slowed to a halt, she walked to greet them.

"Welcome to my home. I'm Miss Lucille."

Gavin returned her warm greeting rather formally, shaking her hand and eliciting a broad smile before she led him inside for a tour. The house had a large, comfortably furnished living room at the front and a sizeable kitchen-diner to the rear, at one end of which was a long wooden table that easily sat twelve adults. Breakfast and dinner, Miss Lucille explained, would be eaten there every morning and evening; lunch would be provided by the Math Camp. Downstairs was a basement with laundry facilities, and a small games room, which had a battered pool table as its main attraction.

After lugging his cases upstairs to his functional but comfortable bedroom beneath the eaves, Gavin spent a few minutes in his bathroom, washing away the sweat and grime of the journey. He put on a fresh shirt and buttoned it up while admiring the view of the neighbourhood through his window, framed by handmade mauve floral curtains. From the landing outside the faint rattle of bone china preceded a gentle tapping at the door; Tori entered, balancing a tray which bore a cup and saucer, a small jug of milk and a bowl of sugar.

"Miss Lucille thought that you may care for a cup of English tea," she explained, laying the tray on a small table under the window. "I think she went to the store to get it just for you the day she heard you were coming."

"Thank you," he said, taking the tea, "but I thought young ladies weren't allowed up to this floor?"

"Normally no, but today Miss Lucille sent me to see if you like crumpet." Tori became indignant when Gavin almost spat out his mouthful of tea, his eyes watering with suppressed laugher. "What's so funny? She got them special for you, because English people like crumpet, don't they?"

"I'm sorry," he struggled to say soberly, "I didn't mean to laugh, but it has a double meaning in Britain."

"Really," she goggled, "what?"

"It also means a pretty girl."

"Gavin, you surprise me!" Tori gave Gavin's arm a playful swat. "I can see we are going to have to keep an eye on you. Now, would you like one of those disgusting looking cake-things that I saw downstairs?"

"I am quite hungry, so yes please."

"Good, well finish your tea and come down." Tori moved to the door and looked coyly back. "You can tell me how you feel about the other type of crumpet another time."

~ * ~ * ~

"Charli!" Pip called, putting down the phone in the living room. There was no response, so she hastened to her cousin's bedroom and knocked on the door.

"What do you want?" a muffled voice replied. "You know I'm on late shifts."

"Oh, Charli!" Pip burst through the door, half sobbing. "Mum's just called. My gran's in hospital. She had a fall last night in the garden and lay there until the milkman found her this morning."

"I'm sorry to hear that." Charlotte sat up in bed and tried to sound sympathetic, rubbing her sleep-deprived eyes. "Did they say what's wrong?"

"Something about a broken hip and exposure."

"Those can be very serious at her age."

"I'm going there right now," Pip said. "Please can you call my work at about ten to nine and let them know I won't be in because of a family emergency?"

"Sure," Charlotte replied, lying back down as a clear indication that she should now be left alone, "I hope she's OK."

~ * ~ * ~

Pip arrived at the hospital just after nine-fifteen. She trotted urgently through the corridors, wanting to sprint but worried about colliding with someone. Her parents were already waiting outside the X-Ray department.

"How's Gran?" Pip asked, hugging her mother.

"Not too good," Julia replied. "She may have fractured the other hip too – that's why we are waiting here. And she has a temperature."

The heavy double doors to the department opened and a bed was pushed out by two orderlies; lying in it was Gran, looking even tinier than usual, her skin wan and her eyes dull. But she smiled when she saw her Pipsqueak and held out a hand; Pip pressed the fingers to her cheek and warmed their tips with her kisses and tears.

"What's all this fuss about a silly old woman who can't stay standing up?" Gran croaked as the orderlies resumed pushing her along the corridor. "And shouldn't you be at work, my lovely?"

"Not to worry, Gran, they know I won't be in today."

"I'll go up to the ward with her and get her settled," Julia said. "Pip, go with your dad for a coffee and I'll come and find you when I know what's what."

Pip was about to protest, but her father shook his head and guided her towards the cafeteria.

"Gran needs to take things slowly," he said, "and I need to bring you up to date on some things too. Have you had breakfast?"

They joined a queue holding plastic trays and bought matching plastic eggs on plastic toast, along with warm drinks that may have been tea but could have been anything. Pip found that she was hungry and cleared her plate while her father talked.

"Your Gran's been fading for a while now. When you were looking after her, you probably were managing her symptoms without realising it – she's a crafty old crow. She called us about a month after you left and told us she wants to go into a home. I think she's lonely and missing your grandad."

"But I'd have gone back." Pip was consumed with guilt. "I'd have looked after her."

"She wouldn't have let you, and if she had, I'd have had something to say about it. We wondered if she could live with us, but we can't afford to move, and she wouldn't cope with our stairs or your brothers. The daft old bird called us last week to say that she'd written to the council saying they could have the bungalow when they had a place for her at the home."

"But the garden!" Pip exclaimed, causing other diners to look at her. "Grandad's roses… my roses."

"Someone else will have to enjoy them now, that's all. Gran's going to be in here for some time – she'll be having surgery, pinning the bone or something, and then she'll need to go somewhere she'll be looked after properly."

"What can I do?"

"Nothing. It's lovely that you're here today, but this is a job for your mum and me. We'll go to the bungalow this weekend and start packing things up. I've a mate with a lock-up and he can store her stuff in there for a bit. Let someone have Gran's place and it might free up a bigger house for a family."

"You always find the positive," Pip smiled.

"And you are the positive," he smiled back. "Now, finish your eggs and I'll get another round of toast and some marmalade."

Pip spent the remainder of the day waiting, chatting about trivialities with her parents, and occasionally speaking with her grandmother when the old woman woke up. She left mid-afternoon and arrived home in the early evening to find her cousin about to leave for work.

"How's your gran?" Charlotte asked.

"Not great, but they think she'll be alright," Pip replied, wandering into the kitchen to look for some food. "Was work OK about me not being in? Did you speak to Glenda? I bet she was grumpy, she always is, and she's had a particular downer on me this week."

The lack of response led Pip to look through the archway into their sitting room. Charlotte was looking guilty.

"Oh, Pip," she said, "I fell back to sleep and completely forgot about it."

~ * ~ * ~

Miss Lucille liked to summon her guests to meals by banging on a faux antique gong, a parting gift from one of her first tenants, and its reverberations still hung in the air.

"Fancy a walk after dinner?" Tori asked when she met Gavin on the stairs. Two weeks had passed since he had arrived at the guest house and they had taken to spending quite a bit of time together, doing puzzles or playing pool in the basement with their housemates, so her suggestion was not a surprise. "I want to see what's out back. Miss Lucille told me she owns a whole stretch of the land behind this place. She lets some folk from her church keep horses there, but there's an old barn and stuff. Come on, let's explore. It's so hot, it might be a bit cooler outside this evening."

Gavin agreed and after a T-bone steak followed by cherry pie, they set off down a track that ran between Miss Lucille's home and the house next door. Tori was right; once outside, the oppressive heat was mitigated by a gentle breeze and the walk transpired to be a wonderful suggestion.

"The house looks so suburban," Gavin remarked as the track led through an expanse of dry grassy meadows. "It's crazy to think all this land is here."

"Well, your room is at the front of the house," Tori pointed out, "and the trees at the back of the yard hide a lot of the view from the kitchen. It doesn't look it from the road, but we're on the edge of town."

"You're right," Gavin nodded, "I never look in that direction, so I've never thought about what's behind."

They walked along the dusty track running between weathered wooden fences, content in making small talk and telling stories of home. At length, they came to a square with a large barn in one corner, a rusting tractor in another and three little-used roads just like the one they had approached on. The horses in one of the fields trotted to the fence to greet them and Tori took some sugar lumps from the breast pocket of her red-check shirt and held them out on her upturned palm.

"I stole them when Miss Lucille was setting out the coffee," she sniggered while the horses took turns to sample the treats. "Does that make me a thief?"

"Hmm. I don't think she'd mind, but maybe I should be on the safe side and call the sheriff, to give you a chance to come clean."

Tori laughed, rubbing her hands together and removing the trace evidence of sugar. She petted the horses, but Gavin hung back, watching.

"Don't you like horses?"

"I like them, but I'm not at ease around them," he replied. "I've always been like that with most animals."

"He's frightened of you," she whispered loudly to an affectionate rowan. "You're too scary!" Tori stepped away from the fence and suddenly darted up to give Gavin a quick kiss on the lips. "Boston girls are very forward. Maybe you should be more scared of me."

He reacted by pulling her back to him and returning the kiss.

"I'm going to have to go to Boston," he murmured when they stopped for breath.

"No need," she laughed, "you have the cream of the crop right here. Come on, let's look in the barn."

The old building was gloomy inside, even with one of the large creaking doors pushed half-open, and the air was heavy with dust. Beams of evening sunlight burst through the cracks between the vertical wood planks of the western wall making the corners of the barn seem even darker. Slowly their eyes adapted to the shadows, and they began to make out the hay loft and rusting scythes and rotting pitchforks propped up against its support pillars. A scratching, scurrying sound came from the shade.

"What's that noise?" Tori asked, feeling she had wandered into the plot of a low budget slasher movie.

"I don't know," Gavin replied. "Raccoons, maybe. Or rats."

"Yuck!" Tori shuddered.

"What were you saying earlier about liking animals?" Gavin laughed.

"It's hardly the same. Horses weren't responsible for spreading the plague."

"Yeah, well, the rats are welcome to this place," Gavin grunted. "I don't think a human's been in here for years. Mind you, the roof looks OK and it's dry enough, so it could be used."

"Yes, it's perfect," Tori said vaguely.

"Perfect for what?"

"Oh, I don't know. Perfect for being an empty old barn where no one ever goes. Perfect for being the place where we kiss for the third time."

"Third time?"

"Yes, twice out there and once in here."

"Did the first one count?"

"For the love of—" Tori exclaimed. "Are all Englishmen so exasperating?"

"No," Gavin replied, an impish smile playing at the corners of his mouth, "you have the cream of the crop." And with those words he pressed his lips to hers once again.

~ * ~ * ~

After the scorching, humid day, Gavin's attic bedroom had retained a good deal of heat. Even the oscillating efforts of an electric fan did little more than stir the warmth, rather than provide cooling respite. He lay awake, perspiration forming on his bare skin, staring into the shadows, his mind buzzing too much for sleep through a mixture of excitement and confusion. After Mel had left him, Gavin believed he could never love anyone else, but now this incredible American girl had burst into his life. With Tori, he felt an animalistic draw, that she needed him and wanted him in a way Mel never had.

The luminous dial of his travel alarm clock said he had to be up for work in five hours, but he remained annoyingly awake. Gavin was debating creeping downstairs for a glass of milk when, in the darkness, there was a faint squeak and a creak as the door gently opened and closed. Tori moved silently across the room and sat at the edge of his bed.

"What are you doing here?" Gavin whispered urgently. "If Miss Lucille finds you here, she'll be upset."

"She won't hear, I waited until I was sure she was asleep," Tori replied in similarly hushed tones. "It feels a bit naughty, doesn't it?"

"Very," Gavin agreed. Somehow in the darkness he could see her eyes sparkling, alive with the thrill of taboo.

"Well, if we're being naughty," Tori pulled her nightshirt over her head, "let's be very naughty."

"Are you sure?" Gavin gasped, fearing his beating heart might burst through his ribcage.

"Very," she replied, crawling towards him, "I told you, Boston girls are very forward."

Gavin forgot to breathe when her soft flesh met his. All other senses faded away – there was no heat, no dark, no silence, only Tori, moving, caressing, drawing him into her very soul with hurried panted kisses.

Later, still basking in an afterglow, Gavin lay in the grey dawn, scarcely believing that Tori was there. Her head rested gently on his chest and he half-kissed, half-inhaled her hair.

"Are you still awake?" she asked.

"I don't want to go to sleep, in case I wake up and it's just a dream."

"It's real," she promised looking up at his face and examining his pale features in the half-light. "I'm real."

"Pinch me anyway."

Tori obliged, eliciting an "Ouch". She laid her head back down.

"Help me to calm down. Tell me a story. Tell me about your friend," she said quietly. "The one who went missing."

"Why?"

"Please. It's important to me, it sounded so sad."

"No one knows exactly what happened," Gavin sighed. "Sharon and Pip were my only two friends in the world and they'd been best friends forever. Then, one day, everything seemed to change. Sharon got heavily involved with a band and they all ran off to London to seek fame and fortune. After they vanished, it turned out that she'd been dealing drugs and framing Pip for it."

"Bitch," Tori snorted.

"I suppose so. Pip might agree. Anyway, Sharon's dad went looking for her as often as he could. I'd go with him every weekend, but sometimes he'd go alone – finish work, catch the late train, walk the streets of London, and then catch the first one home in the morning. It made him ill, but he still insisted on going."

"I can understand why he'd do that for his daughter. You were a good friend to go with him."

"I tried to be, but one day he collapsed at the train station – all I could do was hold his hand and watch him die."

"Poor baby." Tori squeezed Gavin tightly as she felt his chest involuntarily spasm with emotion.

"After that, I kept looking for Sharon, for her dad's sake. The whole thing dominated my life and I messed up my exams and lost my girlfriend. I realised that I had to get away, so here I am."

"In a way, I'm glad of it," Tori said, "because it brought you to me."

They lay quietly for a few more minutes, sleep dragging at their minds.

"Is what's happening between us just a fling, or does it mean more?" Gavin asked. "I'm going back to England in a couple of months. I don't know if I can cope with losing someone again."

"Try not to worry," she murmured. "Let's have a summer of love we'll always treasure. If it goes well, lots of people manage long distance relationships. When we've finished college, who knows? Maybe I move to England or you come and live in the US."

"OK." Gavin allowed himself to hope.

"Let's get some sleep," Tori sighed. "I've got to sneak back downstairs in two hours."

~ * ~ * ~

On Saturday, Pip visited her grandmother in hospital and then went to her parents' home. Her mother was in the kitchen, putting a cake in the oven.

"How was your gran?" Julia asked.

"Much better – itching to get out of hospital," Pip replied, rubbing her temples and blinking her tired eyes.

"Dad and me will take her personals to her new place on Monday. It's a lovely spot with a pretty garden."

"Yeah," Pip said absently, as she began rummaging in her handbag. Her search seemingly unfruitful, she opened a kitchen cupboard and peered in, wrinkling her nose in concentration.

"There was a letter for you." Lyn retrieved an envelope from behind the toaster. Pip took it and pushed it absent-mindedly into her still open bag.

"I'll read it later. I've got a banging headache and terrible cramps," she moaned. "Have you got any painkillers?"

"Not if there aren't any in the cupboard."

"I've still got to drive home, so I'll nip over to the corner shop and get some. Need anything?"

"We need more milk, thanks," Julia replied.

Pip walked into the living room where her younger brother was sitting cross-legged in front of the television, transfixed by the computer game he was playing.

"Do you want to come with me for a walk, Daniel?" she asked.

The boy barely registered her presence but managed a "No", so Pip wandered back to the kitchen, suppressing her disappointment.

"He loves that Commodore thingy that you got him," she remarked. "It must have cost a bit."

"What's that supposed to mean?" Julia flared up. "He shouldn't have things because we owe you money? If you must know, someone gave it to him as a present."

Broadsided by her mother's reaction and fuddled by the throbbing in her head, Pip struggled to understand what she had said wrong. She felt it easiest to apologise.

"Sorry, Mum… it's this headache."

Wondering who Daniel's generous benefactor was, she let the matter drop and walked to the corner shop. It was a muggy day with no breeze, which didn't help her headache, but soon she was the relieved owner of a packet of painkillers and the temporary custodian of two pints of milk. She walked back through the park, opening the blister pack and swallowing two capsules as she went. A couple on a bench in the shade of a beech tree caught her eye, and she recognised Tom at once; the woman he was with was clearly crying.

"I've got to go to work now, Mel," Tom said, standing up. "I'm sure you'll figure something out." He spotted Pip and gave her a smirk and a wink as he sauntered smugly away.

"Are you OK?" Pip asked the crying woman.

"Not really," Mel replied. Her words carried the salt of her tears.

"I know what Tom's like," Pip told her. "He can be… unkind."

"Yes, well his fiancée doesn't think so, not that I knew about her until five minutes ago," Mel spat. She pulled up a sigh from her core and seemed to resolve something within herself. She stood. "Thanks for stopping, you've been very kind. What's your name?"

"Everyone calls me Pip."

"Not Pip Raven? Do you know Gavin Knight?"

"Yes, but I've not seen him in a long time. Why?"

"He used to talk about you, said you were nice. We went out for a while, but I was stupid enough to dump him for that poor excuse for a man."

Mel's accusing finger jabbed angrily towards the far end of the park and the space once occupied by Tom's car. She left and walked, lonely, up the snaking path that passed the duck pond. Pip sat on the bench, appreciating the shade afforded to her by the tree. She realised she was still holding the packet of painkillers, so she put them in her bag and then drew out the mystery envelope that her mother had given her. Several seconds elapsed before she recognised the handwriting – it was unmistakeably Sharon's. She urgently tore the envelope open and read the letter inside.

'*Dear Pip,*

A few weeks back, I saw some people that I used to know and one of them was Gavin. I don't know how or why they were there, but please let them know that I am fine and want to be left alone.

Pip, I want to say sorry from the bottom of my heart for what I did to you. I hope you didn't get into too much trouble. I was angry with you, but I can't remember why. Every day I regret how things finished between us and I wish I could turn the clock back. I lost that little purse you gave me for my sixteenth and it was all I had to remind me of you. When someone put an advert in the paper saying they'd found it, I wanted to believe it was true, but it was a trap. If you knew about it, then I am glad because it means you forgive me. But I already know you forgive me because you're the best person I've ever known.

I promise I'm fine. Please let Mum and Dad know and give them my love. I miss them too, but my new life is one that I can't go back on. You wouldn't approve of how I make my living these days, dear Pip. Sam, the band, everything I ran away from is history and I am not in any danger. I promise.

I wonder what you are all doing these days. Is Gavin a boffin at university? Are you now a top secretary and married to Tom with babies? I want to believe you're both happy.

Please don't try to get in touch. Forget me and enjoy your life. But somewhere out there, I'll be thinking of you, darling Pip.

Love,

Sharon'

Pip read and reread the letter several times before she hurried to see Lyn.

~ * ~ * ~

The barbeque sizzled and spat, filling Miss Lucille's back yard with a wonderful smoky aroma. In addition to her normal residents, she was playing host to her church choir as they rehearsed for their summer concert. The pastor himself had taken on the role of chef and stood before the hot grill moving burgers and chicken pieces about to ensure they were evenly cooked, and occasionally sipping from a cool glass of home-made lemonade.

When Gavin reached the front of the queue, the preacher surveyed him paternally before piling his plate with burgers and drumsticks. "We need to get some meat on your bones, son," he boomed when Gavin protested that it was too much.

Beside a trestle table draped with a meticulously laundered white cloth stood Miss Lucille, ensuring that people were taking liberal helpings of side-dishes from the large bowls she had set out. A huge spoonful of potato salad, dripping with mayonnaise specked with herbs, was dolloped onto Gavin's plate, alongside a corncob steeped in butter, and a warm American biscuit.

"You've been here for well over a month now, so you'll know I like to see folks eat well," she said when she saw his expression.

Most of the house's residents had gone back inside as the conversation was dominated by church chitchat, but Gavin spied Tori sitting alone at the far side of the yard on the sturdiest part of an upturned wheelbarrow; she had her plate balanced on her knees and was delicately nibbling a chicken wing. He joined her and attempted to sit down on a nearby inverted metal bucket which creaked under his weight – the stifled mirth on his girlfriend's face told him he looked ridiculous.

"Come and sit next to me, good looking." Tori scooted across on the back of the barrow. Then she saw his plate. "Hey, how come you have all that food and I only got a couple of little wings?"

"They think I needed feeding up," Gavin explained, nestling beside her.

"So, what am I? The already fatted calf?"

"Please have some of mine, there's too much for me," Gavin implored, sliding food off his plate and onto hers.

When they finished their meal, they once again ambled up the side track towards the old barn, holding hands and enjoying the singing of the choir serenading them in the dusty eventide.

"What would you have done if you had found your friend?" Tori asked suddenly.

"Which friend?"

"The one who ran off to London. Sharon. What would you have done if you'd found her?"

"We did at one point, but she saw us and ran off. I realised then that I hadn't considered it. I always thought it was a fool's errand, but Bob's belief was contagious."

"But you went on looking even after he died," Tori pointed out. "Why would you do that? Did her mum ask you to?"

"No, quite the opposite in fact, she wanted me to stop. Before Bob died, I remember her saying that he was looking for a selfish needle in a haystack – but I think she secretly believed he'd find her. Much later, after Bob had passed, the police discovered a body they thought was Sharon and I think Lyn was on the point of suicide."

"How awful!"

"When the news came that it wasn't Sharon's body, Lyn suddenly changed and let it go."

"And yet you didn't?"

"And yet I didn't," Gavin echoed pensively. "Maybe I did believe I'd find her."

"Even though you didn't know what to do with her if you did?" Tori pressed.

"I guess I'd have said to come home, that her family missed her and were grey with worry."

"And if she wouldn't come? What if she stayed with the band, like they had some mystical hold over her?" Tori pressed further, shaking with emotion.

"What could I do? Frogmarch her home?" Gavin stopped dead and glowered at her, but his temper abated when he saw the painful conflict in Tori's features. "What's this all about? Why are you so damn interested about a girl you've never met?"

"Paul," she whispered, beginning to cry.

"Who?"

"Paul," she repeated louder, the sum of human misery etched onto her face. "My brother. He ran off last year and joined a cult."

"Bloody hell!" Gavin exhaled a long breath and then pointed to a nearby tree stump. "Let's sit here and you can start from the beginning."

"Paul worked at Math Camp last year, just like us." Tori pulled her knees up to her chest and focussed her gaze on a strand of dry grass that she had plucked, twisting it between her fingers. "He got mixed up with a group of kids from some crazy commune that calls itself the Seeds of the Sun. You must have seen them around in their orange shirts, handing out flowers and creeping everybody out."

"Yes, I have," Gavin nodded. "As a matter of fact, I met one at the airport the day I arrived."

"I remember. It was Paul. I saw him when we were driving out and you waved to him. Well, about a week before he was due to fly home to Boston, Paul wrote saying that he'd renounced all worldly possessions and had joined the freaks at the commune."

"I assume those weren't his exact words," Gavin observed dryly.

"No," Tori replied with a humourless dark laugh. "That's Dad paraphrasing. My parents flew straight down to reason with him, but Paul really had renounced everything – they couldn't threaten him, and they couldn't bribe him. They tried dragging him off, but my brother's really fit and easily got away, so they came home without him."

"That sucks."

"I'll say! Paul's been brainwashed by those sickos and no one will do anything."

"What could they have done?"

"He's not in his right mind! They'll let him just throw his life away. Well, I won't!" Tori stood up and paced about for a few moments, agitation manifest in her movements. She humbled herself. "I lied to you. I'm not going to Berkeley, I'm not going to MIT and I'll never get to NASA. I'm going to community college and I've a job lined up waitressing at a diner to pay tuition. I've used my college fund to hire some expert deprogrammers, ex-CIA types who specialise in people brainwashed by cults. I read about them in the paper. They're expensive, but I have to get my brother back."

"How will you get Paul to them?"

Tori agonised. "I trust you, so please don't let me down and tell someone what I'm about to tell you."

"I promise."

"I've bought a van, it's parked up at the Camp, and we're going to snatch him when he's walking back to the commune from the airport next week."

"That's courageous," Gavin said, more impressed than alarmed.

"It's the right thing to do," Tori insisted fiercely. "I have to save him. It's just—"

"Just what?"

"Just that Paul's very fit, so it'll take both the guys I've hired just to get him in the van. I'm the lure, because Paul will trust me and follow me. So, I'll have to be in the street and…"

"And you need someone to drive the van?"

"Yes – just a couple of blocks, then I can take over," Tori said, daring to hope. "I'll drop you off in town, so you won't know where we take him. I didn't want you mixed up in this, but I need help in this one small bit. Will you?"

Gavin held her hands, meeting her eyes with steady certainty.

"Your problems are my problems. Your fights are mine," he promised.

~ * ~ * ~

Charlotte fumbled around the kitchen making a strong coffee. She was presently working late shifts at the hospital, but staff shortages meant she was woken up mid-morning with a phone call asking her to come back in urgently. There was at least the consolation of a little extra money, which she began to spend in her mind while she finished getting ready.

She was surprised to glance out of the window and see Pip's car still parked outside – her cousin should have been at work hours ago – but gave it no further thought until she left for her shift and discovered Pip sitting on the cold concrete floor at the bottom of the stairwell in obvious pain. It took mere seconds to see that the problem was a dislocated knee.

"I'm so glad you're here, Charli," Pip groaned through clenched teeth. "I've been trying to get back up to the flat, but it's agony."

"I'm not surprised. We are going to need to get you into casualty."

"No, can't you fix it?" Pip begged. "I'm already late for work."

"I'm hardly qualified! You need a doctor."

"Please, you know how to do it don't you?" Pip implored, desperate. "Please, Charli, I'll get fired otherwise. You know Glenda's got it in for me. She didn't believe me when I missed that day because of Gran."

"I've only ever seen it done, so hold still." Being reminded, however innocently, of her oversight may have influenced the brutal aspect of Charlotte's nature. Pip's scream echoed up and down the staircase, but she was at least able to move her leg. "You need an expert to look at that, so get your GP to refer you. Have you got some painkillers?"

"Yeah, in my bag. Thanks, Charli."

With her cousin's help, Pip limped to her car, expressing her gratitude at regular intervals. She drove to work as quickly as possible, but (of course) by the time she arrived there were no nearby parking spaces available. It was a long, slow hobble up to, into, and through the building to her desk. Glenda looked up sharply and observed Pip's painful progress across the office with detached sadism; naturally, she waited until Pip was seated before she barked, "Come and see me, please, Philippa."

Rather than their usual indifference, the other members of the typing pool watched in mute sympathy as their young colleague hauled herself up and limped to her summoner's workstation – "Chin up," one of them whispered as Pip passed.

"Did you think you could turn up late and just slip into the office unnoticed?" Glenda asked. "You're extremely tardy and lack the basic manners to come and see me."

"I'm sorry," Pip replied, desperate to placate her overseer, "I was going to come and speak to you, honestly. I'm very sorry I am late – I slipped on the stairs outside my flat and dislocated my knee."

"Did you have to go to the hospital?"

"No."

"A doctor?"

"No. My cousin is a nurse and she helped me. You can check with her, if you like?"

"Hardly an independent medical opinion, is it? Really, Philippa, you are going to have to do better than that. Being late and making up excuses is bad enough, but feigning a limp is just being silly, and getting your relatives to back you up is disgraceful."

"I'm not pretending!"

"I don't wish to discuss it further. This isn't the first problem we've had with your attendance, is it? I shall bring the matter to Mr Simpkins' attention." Glenda coldly relished her power. "It's no use gaping at me like a stranded pilchard, young lady, get back to work."

Pip returned to her duties, Damocles' sword dangling mere millimetres above her head. The remainder of her morning passed in agonised anticipation; every telephone call, every door opening, every whispered conversation might be connected to her. Eventually, she was told that she would be seeing the Head of Department the following week, meaning nearly seven days of fear lay ahead – she simply had to keep her job at all costs.

~ * ~ * ~

Gavin sat in the driving seat of Tori's battered van watching a small group of orange-shirted young men and women approach from a distance. He strained to see if he could recognise the man who had greeted him at the airport.

"There's Paul!" Tori pointed with excitement.

She opened the door, jumped down from the van and jogged lightly across the road to intercept her brother who was evidently pleased to see her. Their long embrace made Gavin briefly homesick for his own sister, Karen. Tori obviously successfully engaged Paul in conversation because he soon turned to the other members of the group and clearly suggested that they go on without him. They left with a chorus of "Be blessed".

Maintaining a steady stream of affectionate chitchat with her brother until the others were out of sight, Tori casually led him towards the van. As they passed, the side door slid open and the two burly deprogrammers darted out of the vehicle, grabbed Paul, forced an old hessian sack over the struggling young man's head, and dragged him into the vehicle. Tori crawled in beside them, trying to calm her terrified brother, who blindly writhed and screamed. As soon as the door scraped closed, Gavin pulled away into the deserted road and drove to a secluded spot behind an old hardware store where he got out. Tori moved behind the steering wheel and lowered the window to kiss him goodbye.

"I'll see you back at Miss Lucille's in a few days," she promised. "Thank you for everything. Love you."

As the van drove away in a cloud of dust, Gavin watched until they were out of sight.

"I love you too," he whispered.

~ * ~ * ~

Mr Simpkins was a gaunt faced greying man in his late fifties and his long Roman nose had protruding nostril hairs stained yellow with nicotine. His brown suit had been expensive eight years ago, but now it was shabby. Once a young man full of promise, he was now a sad, pompous figure, overlooked for promotion and sidelined into his present position.

He stood at his window, appreciating the view from his office. The sunlight danced on the multicoloured patchwork of cars in the company car park below, and the hills beyond the business estate were verdant and inviting, but Simpkins dragged his thoughts back within the monotonous confines of the brown brick walls when Pip tentatively knocked on the door for her appointment.

"Ah, Philippa," he said brightly. "Close the door behind you, please. I hear you've had a problem last week. A little late, perhaps?"

"Yes, Mr Simpkins," Pip replied, relieved that her boss wasn't hostile. "I fell down some steps and dislocated my knee. I'm never normally late, sir." Her heart was heavy with anxiety at the prospect of what might come of the meeting – would she be disciplined or, worse still, fired?

"Then you must sit down, my dear."

Simpkins gestured towards a long burgundy leather couch which ran along one wall of his office and Pip perched nervously on one end, only to find Mr Simpkins come and sit beside her. He was uncomfortably close, placing his arm behind her on the back of the couch and leaning towards her with a compassionate leer. Pip arched back over the armrest, striving not to be repulsed by his bad breath. For a while, Simpkins quietly assessed her, the silence interrupted only by a faint whistling from his nostril and the occasional squeak from the leather cushions.

"You know," the manager said airily, leaning closer, "Glenda believes that you merely affected your alleged injury, that you were late and made up a story that cannot possibly be independently verified. I wonder if that isn't a little harsh, though – you don't strike me as an untruthful girl, Philippa."

"Thank you, sir," Pip replied, grateful for his understanding, "I'd injured it before, some time ago."

"Ah, so you would know the symptoms," he observed. "Which knee is it?"

"The left," she told him, before suppressing a startled gulp when he placed his hand on her leg. She was numb with shock – was this normal? As ever, she wore a modest business appropriate skirt, but when she had sat down on the sofa, the hem had risen several inches and exposed both her kneecaps; now his bony touch had pushed the dark material upwards even further.

Simpkins sensed her confusion. "Stay calm, my dear, I am very experienced in these things. Now, is this where it hurt?" He dug his thumb firmly into a tender spot, causing Pip to jump and squeak with pain. Tutting soothingly, he began to massage her leg. "Is that nice, does that help?"

"Um. I suppose so," she replied, perfectly certain that it was not helpful and not nice. His hand began to work its way up her leg. "Please stop that, Mr Simpkins."

"Oh, don't be a tease," he admonished. "You know it's in your best interest to be nice. I've had my eye on you for a while and I can help, I can protect you from Glenda."

Pip remained silent, struggling to make sense of the situation, questioning what she must have done to invite her boss' attentions. She twisted her body away from him as far as she could but wedged as she was in the corner of the seating, it was to little avail. Simpkins sensed her discomfort and pressed his advantage.

"You'll catch more flies with honey," he advised.

Just as his mouth approached, lips parted, Pip found inner strength and stood up.

"Thank you all the same, Mr Simpkins, but I wouldn't want any special treatment."

The manager leaned back and frowned, his expression that of an exasperated parent, or a psychiatrist disappointed with a patient's lack of progress.

"Very well, Philippa," he said, all pretence at compassion gone. "You've made your attitude very clear and I must say I'm disappointed. I'd hoped you'd prove to be the type of mature person we want in this company but must say that I'm having my doubts. All I can say is that Glenda and I are of the shared opinion that one more mess-up, one more unauthorised absence or instance of bad timekeeping, and we will be forced to reconsider your position."

"I understand," Pip nodded, willing modulation into her voice.

"Very well." Simpkins dismissed her with a wave of disgust. "You may leave now."

Pip departed quickly, still trying to comprehend what had just come to pass. With the door to Simpkins' office closed behind her, she straightened and smoothed her skirt, took a deep breath and returned to her work, partly relieved she wasn't formally disciplined, but also terrified of messing up again – all Pip knew was that she couldn't afford to lose her job.

~ * ~ * ~

Tori had not once turned up to dinner for five days and Miss Lucille's irritation was becoming evident.

"She's wasting good food," she grumbled. "Lord knows there are many poor souls who would be grateful for a fine meal like this. What has got a hold of that girl? Out all night, hardly here, and then I get a call from the Camp asking how she is and saying she had called in sick. Do you know where she is going to, Gavin? I know she's your special friend."

"No, ma'am," he replied, relieved that the question was one of location rather than activity.

"She must love those horses down at the back paddock," Miss Lucille remarked. "Folks next door say she's off to see them at all hours."

A suspicion formed in Gavin's mind and after dinner he took a familiar walk, down the lane between the fields. It seemed a longer trek without company, but eventually the old barn loomed into sight. He crept towards the building and detected the sound of voices from inside, one of them raised yet pitiful. Gavin couldn't make out any words, so, not wanting to disturb either of the huge doors, he pressed his face to a crack between two wooden slats.

It was darker inside the barn and it took several moments for Gavin to discern what was happening. What he eventually beheld made him back away, dry mouthed and uncertain of how to proceed. The sound of tyres on gravel reached his ears as Miss Lucille's aged Buick rolled to a halt in the courtyard behind him, loose chipping rattling in the wheel arches. The car door opened, and its owner climbed stiffly out, her wise eyes locked with Gavin's.

"Is Tori in there?" she asked, gesturing to the barn.

"I think so," he replied, hoarse with nerves and shock. "How did you know?"

"You and young Miss Victoria have been like two cats on a hot roof this last week. When we were at dinner, I could see you thinking where she might be. I went upstairs and watched you walking along this road. It doesn't take much to put two and two together, not when you've been alive as long as I have."

"Something you said earlier made me realise where she was."

"What is going on in my barn, exactly?"

"Tori's got the best of intentions," Gavin babbled. "Her brother, Paul, was brainwashed by a cult, and Tori's used her college fund to hire some professional deprogrammers. I helped grab Paul a few days back, but she didn't want me to know where they took him. Now I realise why."

"So, she mixed you up in her little plan, did she?" Miss Lucille whispered. "You helped grab him? Don't you know that kidnapping is a felony, son?"

"Surely the cult kidnapped him first?" Gavin was just realising the terrible implications of his actions.

"I sure hope you're right!" Miss Lucille marched to the barn and dragged open one of the tall doors; four startled faces turned to face them.

The van and a Ford pick-up truck were parked inside by the left wall. Tori was seated opposite on a pile of old sacks, hugging her knees to her chest. Even in the relative dark of the building, glistening trails on her cheeks stood testament to her tears.

In the centre of the barn stood the two deprogrammers. Tall and muscular, their clothes were sweat-stained. Between them, tied to a chair, was Paul, stripped to the waist, his face dirty, swollen and bleeding; tears had cut pale little rivulets through the grime smeared under his eyes.

"What exactly is happening here?" Miss Lucille demanded to know.

"Easy, lady, we are professionals engaged by his family trying to help this boy," one of the men replied.

"He looks like he's had quite enough help," Miss Lucille stated acidly. "I have never seen the like."

"He's been brainwashed. This is what you need to do, believe me."

"I most certainly will not believe you! Now, you boys can either get in that truck of yours and drive away and not come back, or I return to my house, call the police, and tell them there are kidnappers trespassing in my barn. The only reason I've not done that already is because of young Tori over there."

The second man tapped his partner's arm and the two exchanged glances. Without saying another word, they walked to their vehicle and climbed in.

"No!" Tori jumped up and raced towards the Ford like a scalded cat. "No, please, you have to cure Paul. You've not finished!" The engine roared into life and the truck drove out of the barn with the young woman pathetically hanging on to its wing mirror and running alongside. "You've got all my money!" Tori tripped and crumpled to the ground, sobbing as the car accelerated away in a shower of stones. It was only then that she noticed Gavin. "Traitor!"

"No! But he may have saved you and your brother," countered Miss Lucille. She untied Paul, cradling the young man's head, not caring that a brown-red smear of dirty congealed blood now stained the white cotton fabric of her skirt. She signalled Gavin to assist her and between them they helped Paul to the Buick, followed by a distraught Tori.

Back at the house, they laid Paul on the couch in Miss Lucille's private sitting room and the elderly woman tenderly cleaned his wounds. Exhaustion meant he was asleep before she finished, so she covered him with a handmade quilt and instructed Gavin and a recalcitrant Tori to join her in the kitchen.

"Let's start at the beginning," Miss Lucille said. "What is this about a cult?"

Tori remained silent, so Gavin explained. "They are called Seeds of the Sun. You must have seen them in the town and at the airport?"

"I surely have, but they are no cult!" Miss Lucille's incredulity unintentionally mocked the two teenagers. "Why, they painted my porch for me a few years back. They're eccentric, but harmless."

"They brainwashed Paul!" Tori snapped.

"Why do you think your brother's brainwashed?" Miss Lucille asked. "Because he's made choices you don't understand? What he believes may seem naïve and silly to you and maybe me, but he believes it. The Seeds of the Sun are a harmless, old-fashioned commune – people come and go from there all the time. They just teach that you should love one another."

"But he renounced all his worldly goods," Tori said.

"Good for him!" Miss Lucille laughed. "There's plenty of folk who should do the same. It's hardly a new idea. My preacher talks about it quite often too – am I in a cult?"

"No," muttered Tori, "but—"

"But nothing," Miss Lucille interrupted. "There are wicked cults out there, of course, but not Seeds of the Sun. People these days are so darned keen on saying people are brainwashed just because they disagree with them. What is brainwashing anyway? I spent the first thirty years of my life giving up my seat on the bus to white folk like you, even when I was pregnant with my two boys – was I brainwashed, were my boys brainwashed when they grew up and went off to fight in some God-forsaken place on the other side of the world for a country that treated their mama like that?"

"Some people might think so," Tori sulked.

"Then some people are dumber than I thought! But then some people are dumb enough to think they can sneak up my stairs in the middle of the night and think that I don't know about it. Listen, you can't un-brainwash someone by brainwashing them into being what you expect of them – that's just coercion. Instead, you help them by engaging with them, talking to them, reasoning with them, listening to them and, most importantly, loving them. No inducements and certainly no threats."

"When did you get to be such an expert?"

"When you're my age, you've seen it all," Miss Lucille said with a wry chuckle. "But Paul is healthy and happy – no one forced him to go to the commune and nobody's making him stay. It's his home and you've got to take him back there."

"No! I have to save him!" Tori's head snapped up, her eyes wide.

"He'd probably say the same about you, but he wouldn't resort to sleep deprivation and beatings to persuade you."

"Miss Lucille is right," Gavin added, gently touching Tori's hand, "you have to take Paul back. It's his choice."

She snatched her hand away, glowering at him, but said nothing.

"Have you really spent all your college fund on hiring those two men?" Miss Lucille asked.

"Yes," Tori sniffed.

"And do your mother and father know of this?"

"No."

"Then, when you and I have taken Paul back tomorrow, you must fly home to Boston and tell them the truth. You know it's the right thing to do. Now, let's go and sit with your brother and be there when he wakes."

Gavin realised he was no longer needed or welcome, so he climbed the stairs to his room and tried to calm down. Eventually, he fell asleep but jumped awake in the dawn when a landing floorboard creaked. He instinctively knew it was Tori and his heart leapt, but the handle didn't turn, and she didn't come in. Instead, a slip of paper was pushed under the door and Gavin put on his glasses to read the note with a sinking heart.

'I'll never forgive you. Now I'm going back to Boston with no brother and no money. Goodbye Judas.'

For a moment he wanted to follow her and beg forgiveness, but stopped for two reasons: firstly, Tori needed someone to blame and he knew it had to be him; secondly, he felt used and deceived. Instead, Gavin went back to bed and lay miserably awake.

At a little after six-thirty, the front door opened and voices, Paul's, Tori's and Miss Lucille's, carried up through his open window, so he silently looked out. Tori was loading her luggage into the car and glanced up at his window; Gavin knew she couldn't see him, that she didn't want to, but it seemed a goodbye.

He lived his remaining weeks at Miss Lucille's with numbed emotions as he nursed a second broken heart.

Chapter 14

In the pale morning light, the hands of Pip's alarm clock pointed obstinately to ten past five. A knot gnawed in her stomach – never in her life had she felt such dread all day every day, not even at the height of false accusations that had ruined her life before. The constant fear of making the slightest slip in her work eroded her spirit and deadened her eyes; even a simple typing error might lead to her being fired, and unnatural vigilance took a terrible toll on her state of mind.

Giving up on sleep, she got out of bed and drew back the curtains to watch the world outside begin to wake up. A house martin swooped down from the eaves of the building, making its carefree salutation to the start of a summer's day. Another joined it and the two rose and fell through the air in an innocent ancient dance to the glory of creation.

On her windowsill sat her three indoor rose plants, nestled in sturdy terracotta pots which had been brightly daubed in glutinous colours by Pip and Daniel one afternoon. She meticulously examined the shiny green leaves, savoured the tiny pink blooms, and used a small spray bottle to refresh them and ensure the soil was not too dry. This would be one of the few points in the day when she could lose herself in a world free of judgement, where her love shared would be returned with colour and scent. It was during these times that Pip communed with something so transcendent, so peaceful and wise and deep, that she knew it could easily conquer death in the blink of an immortal eye and sing a song older than the universe itself.

Content in her work, Pip lost track of time, but reality called her back when a small red van trundled to a halt in the street outside. The postman climbed out and rummaged in the rear of the vehicle for a large pile of letters and bills to be delivered to the occupants of the flats. Pipped donned her dressing gown and slipped her feet into her shoes to trip lightly down the stairs to meet him.

"Good morning. Anything for flat eight?" she asked.

His smile creased his tanned stubbled face as he searched through the post.

"It's nice to speak to someone at this time in the morning for a change," he remarked, handing her some envelopes.

She thanked him and hurried back upstairs, sorting the letters as she went. In the kitchen, she laid Charlotte's pile, mainly bills, on the counter. Pip instantly recognised Theo's handwriting on the solitary item addressed to her. She opened the envelope with glee but froze on reading the opening lines.

'*My Dearest Pip,*

I love you. There, I have said it and we both know what that means. It means this is the last time one of us shall write to the other. I am sorry, my love, my true love, but it must be so, even though it will break my heart and Bobbie's too.

This is because of Claire, but it is not her fault. You know that she is a good mother and she has been very loyal to me. I still love her for what we were and what she does. When I was serving in the South Atlantic, the only thing that got me through the day was the thought of her. She and I may have both changed, but we both want to make things work, and I know that is what you would want too, because you are unselfish.

Claire has said nothing, but I can see she is jealous of you – she cannot make me laugh or cry like your letters can. A few nights ago, Bobbie had a nightmare and cried out, but she didn't want either of us, she asked for you. I saw the hurt in Claire's eyes.

Claire's parents have a place in Jersey and we have decided to move there. We have put our house on the market and received an offer already. We're buying a little bolthole in Richmond, for when we come back to visit my family, but we head off to Jersey soon to find a school for Bobbie.

There, my dear sweet Pip, I have laid all before you and you must see how things stand. Can you ever forgive me? I hope and believe that you will.

I know that you will burn this letter, but please carry its sentiment and love with you always I beg of you. I was going to say not to reply, but I know there is no need. If I did get a letter from you, I would think that you had not received this one, and I would have to find the strength to write again.

I wish you all the happiness and love imaginable.

Love,

Theo'

The words engraved themselves onto the copper plate of her memory; a thousand times, Pip would be able to perfectly reproduce them at will. Her heart broke from a cruel blow when the rest of her life was so difficult, but she also felt it was just and maybe noble. Mechanically, she turned on the gas hob and placed a corner of the letter into the pale blue flame. Soon it was gone, just memories and a few ashes clustered around the drain in the sink; a dash from the cold tap and they too were lost forever.

Charlotte stumbled in, bleary with sleep and scrunching her tousled hair.

"Can I smell burning?" she asked.

"Maybe," Pip shrugged. She was distant, imagining Jersey.

"Are you alright?" Charlotte was uncharacteristically empathetic and doubly so for just after six in the morning.

"Of course." Pip flashed an artificial smile, "What are you doing up? You're off today, aren't you? Did I wake you?"

"No, it's my bloody body clock! It's messed up with working mixed shifts. I think I'll head into town for a bit of retail therapy later."

"Is that your medical advice?" Pip laughed.

"It is," Charlotte preened, "and it is the kind of advice you could do with taking, my girl. Tell you what, why don't I catch the bus up to your offices and we can meet for lunch?"

"I could do with seeing a friendly face," Pip sighed.

~ * ~ * ~

Time slowly crumbles all defences if they are not maintained. Weeks of emotional loneliness without Theo and crippling self-recrimination ground away at Pip's resolve. Only duty to her cousin and unwillingness to let her family down made her function, a heartbroken robot who went to work because she must and because she hoped for some miracle to change her circumstances.

Yet another day had to begin, but she curled up beneath her bedclothes and wished she didn't need money to survive. Her remaining financial reserves had been devoured by an unexpected car repair and a large utility bill. If she could find some encouragement, it would help, but Charlotte was no help and Gran was too poorly to be burdened. To make matters worse, Pip had somehow annoyed her mother over the phone the previous evening but had no idea what she had done wrong. The loss of Theo's letters hurt like a knife between the ribs – she had been a fool to believe she wouldn't fall in love with him, and now she was suffering.

She swore, rolled out of bed, and stumbled bleary-eyed to the bathroom where she found a naked man brazenly cleaning his teeth with her toothbrush.

"Hi, Pip," he splattered, grinning sheepishly as peppermint foam oozed from the corners of his mouth. He waved her toothbrush. "Charli said you wouldn't mind."

Pip sighed and turned her back. Charlotte's boyfriend was tall, and his large frame and dense body hair gave the impression he wore an oversized gorilla costume.

"Couldn't you at least wear some pants, Adam?" she asked, too weary to care if he did and too depressed to protest his presumptuous use of her toothbrush.

"You look tired." Adam pointedly ignored her question. He spat and rinsed his mouth from the tap. "Were Charli and me a bit too loud last night?"

Pip snorted, unwilling to give him the satisfaction of a 'yes'. She sensed him move behind her and jumped when he placed his damp hands on her upper arms – his grip was uncomfortably tight, and the heat of his palms oozed through the cotton of her nightshirt. She squirmed from the unwanted touch.

"You could always come and join us, you know," Adam continued, "Charli wouldn't mind."

"That shows how little you know about women!" Pip spun round and moved past without making eye contact. She slammed the bathroom door, bolted it, and threw away her toothbrush.

It was bad enough that Adam was at the flat all the time, but Pip also had to work with him because he was a security guard at her offices. He had chatted up Charlotte when she met Pip for lunch a few weeks before.

She squeezed some toothpaste onto her fingertip and ran it around the inside of her mouth as a makeshift toothbrush. After she showered, she remained in the bathroom until she heard Adam say goodbye to his girlfriend and the front door slam.

Twenty minutes later, Pip was dressed and sitting in her car, ready to go to work. Just as she turned the ignition key, a loud banging on the roof startled her. A glance around revealed the cause of the noise was Adam who bent down so his face was separated from hers by the thin pane of glass in the door; she wound down the window.

"What do you want?"

"I've missed my bus, or it's late. Either way, can you give me a lift to work?"

Pip briefly agonised before leaning across the interior of the Mini to unlock the passenger door. Adam sauntered around and climbed in, making the car wobble. He bulged over the sides of the seat and Pip's hand brushed against his outer thigh when she moved the gearstick; thankfully, the car was an automatic, so she would at least not be further inconvenienced until they arrived at work.

They drove in silence for a while, passing slowly through the grey streets, in a worm of traffic that expanded and contracted through junctions and traffic lights. Pip stopped at a zebra crossing to allow an elderly shopper to cross.

"What do you make of the takeover?" Adam asked.

"What takeover?" Pip felt bad that she sounded irritated, for the question was genuine and unencumbered by Adam's usual innuendo; yet his very voice tormented her like fingernails down a blackboard.

"Haven't you heard? Some big organisation is taking us over. Loads of investment and new opportunities for everyone." Adam bore an unnoticed cruel half-smile. "Well, almost everyone."

"Not much hope for me," Pip sighed. "I'm just hanging on, hoping to keep my job, which is looking shakier every day. That's probably why no one told me."

"That bad is it?"

"Worse. No one speaks to me. My supervisor won't give me a good reference, so I can't look for another job and I daren't get fired – how could I pay my share of the rent?"

"The way things are going, I'll be chipping in soon enough."

Pip was stunned. Had Adam discussed moving in with her cousin? Charlotte certainly hadn't said anything about it. The idea of him being a permanent fixture was appalling, but she said nothing.

"Of course," Adam continued, "you're your own worst enemy. Try being a bit friendlier. I can always put a good word in for you."

"Not being rude, but I'm not sure what good that would do." Pip strived to not sound hostile. "It's just that you're in security and I'm in legal – when do you have any contact with the people I work with?"

"Tell you what, I'll wager that things will get better at your coffee break this morning." He was cruelly enigmatic. "If I'm right, you'll know it was down to me. OK?"

"OK," she replied, thoroughly sceptical.

At a little after half past ten that morning, Pip sipped her mid-morning cup of tea and worked diligently through her break.

"Philippa, come over here," Glenda summoned from her sedentary position before adding an uncustomary, "please." Pip picked up a notebook and pen and walked with trepidation to her supervisor. Glenda waved a document Pip had typed earlier. "Well, young lady, your work's improving. Maybe you're starting to show the potential to be a half-decent legal secretary."

"Thank you." Pip was astonished.

"If you can stop your little shenanigans, we may start to get along – keep up the good work."

Pip once again mumbled gratitude and returned to her own desk in silent disbelief. She was ecstatic to be praised in earshot of her colleagues, but the good news tempered when she realised that Adam had predicted it.

"Well done, Pip," said Nicola, her closest working neighbour.

Half an hour later, Pip took some files to the top floor, where the board and their secretarial staff were based. To her surprise, there was tangible emotion in the air. That morning the entire team had been told that they were being reassigned to different roles to enable the new owners to bring in their own PA's. This news caused yet another knot of fear to the pit of Pip's stomach as her own position once again looked precarious. She returned to the lift and pressed the button for her floor.

"Hold the doors, please!" Pip waited for two men to board the elevator with her. She experienced a brief thrill when she recognised one of the men from his photograph in the entrance lobby; he was Mr Sanders, the Chief Executive. The other gentleman smiled at her genially. Pip fancied that his suit would cost her a year's salary. Mr Sanders pressed the button for the ground floor and the doors whirred shut.

"Are you satisfied with the developments, Mr Reeves?" the Chief Executive asked, oblivious to Pip.

"Yes, I believe my clients will be pleased. Once everything's in place, it's going to open new opportunities to all the staff here." Reeves gave Pip a grandfatherly wink. "Does that excite you, young lady?"

Sanders was annoyed that Mr Reeves should address a menial, but nevertheless said, "Yes, new opportunities, Miss…" He tailed off, not knowing her name.

"Raven," Pip informed them, calming her heartbeat. "Yes, sir, they sound very exciting."

Their joint descent stopped when they reached Pip's floor and she exited, relieved that she had not embarrassed herself before two such important people. Her nerves did, however, necessitate a brief stop-off on her way back to her desk. Meticulously clean and climate controlled, the staff restrooms were quiet chambers, with subtle overhead lighting. As Pip washed her hands, Nicola emerged from one of the stalls and they exchanged smiles in the flawless mirror.

"Pip," Nicola whispered, looking around nervously, "don't be too confident that Glenda's warming to you. Don't trust her."

"I have to, or I might go mad. I need this job."

"Then try to get into Simpkins' good books, he'd protect you. That's what most of us do."

"But he… he tried it on with me. Did he try it on with you too?"

"He knows my Wayne would punch his head in if he tried anything too much," Nicola giggled. "Simpkins tries his luck, but he's generally happy with a quick grope."

"And you let him?" Pip was aghast.

"It's not nice, but it's not the worst either." Nicola was matter-of-fact, prickling from Pip's moral shock. "It's water off a duck's back. Suck it up. This place is amazing; the perks, the pay and the pension are worth the occasional fumbling of a dirty old man. Anyway, he loses interest pretty quickly and moves on to the next lucky girl. And look on the bright side – he'll be dead long before us."

Pip returned to her desk, working diligently and accurately, trying to organise her jumbled thoughts. New opportunities – she had to hope. But Simpkins? Yuck.

She was so absorbed she only became aware that it was lunch time because a phone was constantly ringing, and she realised that she was alone in the office. A small plastic carrier bag tucked into her drawer contained the peanut butter sandwiches she had made that morning. She was about to start eating when she was overcome by memories of life in the village with her grandparents – Pip ached to see natural colours: trees, grass, sky, clouds, rain, anything not man-made.

She briefly considered eating in her car, but she was parked so far from the building that she would waste too much of her break just getting there and back. Sitting with other staff members was out – they were even less welcoming of late. In fact, that Mr Reeves had been the only kind face she had seen all day, except for Nicola whose motives were unclear. Then a thought struck Pip and she took her lunch to the fire escape stairwell.

The concrete dust covering the surface of the unforgiving steps softened the clack from her flat soled shoes as she descended the several flights to the ground floor. Nevertheless, the echoes resounded up and down the tall shaft, increasing the eerie isolation. At the bottom, a pair of glazed double doors offered a clear view to the distant hills and trees beyond the estate. She removed her sandwiches, laid the carrier bag on the second to bottom step and sat on it, trying to avoid getting her black skirt dusty. There she ate, at last free from observation and scrutiny.

But Pip was not unobserved, for CCTV cameras were discreetly located in the stairwell. In the darkened security office, Adam closely monitored her movements; he kissed his finger and ran it down the screen, tracing the outline of the solitary young woman as she sat and gazed out of the building.

~ * ~ * ~

The next day, Pip again ate her sandwiches in her little oasis of peace at the bottom of the stairwell. She winced when she heard a door open and close somewhere above her and the sound of booted feet on the steps coming ever closer, ever louder until Adam appeared. Pip sighed with relief.

"Hello, Mr Magician, I am glad it's you. I was scared stiff."

"Mr Magician? Oh, you mean my making you less of a – what's the word? – pariah."

"Yes, how did you do that?"

"A magician never reveals his secrets." He tapped the side of his nose with a fingertip. "So, are you sticking to our deal?"

"What deal?"

"To be nicer to me. Friendlier. Charlie would like that."

"I thought I was being. I'll try harder." Pip knew her efforts had been minimal.

"Good. In that case, budge over and give me a sandwich. Don't worry about sharing your little bag to sit on, I don't mind a bit of dust on my arse."

With mixed emotions, Pip made room for Adam to sit beside her. Company was nice, but a large amount of his body seemed pressed against her – were he not happily dating Charlotte, it might have been worrying.

~ * ~ * ~

The next day dawned, remorselessly. Pip dragged herself from her bed, picked up her new toothbrush, and padded to the bathroom. Charlotte and Adam could be heard messing about and giggling in the kitchen, so at least the exhibitionist gorilla wouldn't be flaunting himself.

Showered and dried, Pip returned to her room and opened a drawer to look for clean underwear. She was not one for flimsy lingerie, preferring practical cotton briefs to lacy things, but she did like colours and she had a peculiar private system of specific pairs for specific days of the week. Today was supposed to be blue, but they were not to be found; feeling that the day was already going wrong, she pulled on a white pair. It was too warm to be wearing tights, so she donned a comfortable long skirt and a cotton blouse and went to make breakfast.

Charlotte and Adam were still in the kitchen, looking flushed; she seemed embarrassed, but he looked triumphant. Pip ignored his smug smile and started to make peanut butter sandwiches.

"That's twice what you normally make," Charlotte remarked.

"Sometimes I share them." Pip glanced nervously glance at Adam. Why did she not mention their lunch time meets to her cousin? She decided she should. "Your boyfriend steals them, actually."

"Yeah, that sounds like him," Charlotte snorted. "Two lunches, eh, big boy? No wonder you've got so much energy."

Like the cat that got the cream, Adam kissed his girlfriend goodbye and strutted from the room to go to work. Pip stooped to look in the washing machine.

"Have any of my knickers got caught up with your stuff?" her voice echoed in the metallic tub.

"I'm surprised you wear any, you little tart!"

"What?" Pip asked, stung and confused.

"I see you flirting with Adam. Get your own boyfriend, if anyone wants you."

"I don't know what you're—"

"Sharing your sarnies with him, giving him lifts, laughing at his bad jokes, shouting out about your knickers?"

"I was just trying to be nice. I honestly don't fancy him."

"Not good enough for you, Princess?"

"Look, Charli, I'm sorry," Pip's temper frayed, but she couldn't afford another falling out with someone. "It's a misunderstanding. I'll be more careful."

"Just see that you are."

Bemused and disconcerted, Pip hastily left for work and jumped in her car. She closed her eyes in despair when she heard the thump-thump on the roof; Adam wanted a lift.

"I don't know if it's a good idea," Pip glanced back at the flats and was relieved Charlotte wasn't at the kitchen window.

"It'll be fine. Come on, open up," Adam insisted.

She had no choice but to let him in. Pip took the opportunity to tell Adam that they needed to be more considerate of Charlotte's feelings, but he scoffed, insisting it was a fuss over nothing and that he would deal with it.

Once at work, the morning passed peacefully, and even included another public congratulation from Glenda for a job well done. Her spirits raised, Pip focussed on her work, unaware of the CCTV camera in her office slowly turning to point directly at her desk.

She took lunch earlier than usual and went to her quiet place at the bottom of the stairs, yet somehow Adam again intruded on her solitude. She preferred isolation, accepting her pariah status, letting her mind drift among happy memories of the village and of Bobbie and Theo, but Pip tried not to mind Adam's seemingly inevitable intrusion and shared her sandwiches, fervently wishing that he wouldn't sit so close.

~ * ~ * ~

Thank heavens for Fridays, because two days of freedom beckoned. Pip endured yet another lunch time of Adam's unwanted trespass into her personal space, her 'exclusion zone'. It was a hot day, even in the relative cool of the deserted stairwell, and he stank of sweat. She didn't want to offend him so, rather than complain, she reminded him of Charlotte's feelings.

"Put up with it," he grunted, not moving a millimetre, "unless you want me to drop you in it for being in a restricted area."

"How can a fire escape be a restricted area?"

"It's for emergencies only. So, unless we keep up these little meetings, you'll be in trouble. My magic works both ways, you know."

"I could tell Charli," Pip half-warned in a small voice.

"You know what she thinks about you," Adam gloated, standing up and brushing crumbs from his trousers. "She'd chuck you out. It's her name on the lease, remember. I think I'll chat with your supervisor, to remind you why you need me."

"No, please don't!"

"Too late, but it won't be too bad. You'll be here Monday?"

"Oh, very well."

Pip stayed frozen until the stomp of boots had faded and the sound of a door closing reverberated before she hurried to her desk, desperate to be there before Glenda. To her relief, Nicola was the only person in the department.

"Oh, good," Nicola said. "Your phone's been ringing nonstop, so I answered it. It was the home, about your grandmother. I wrote the number on your pad. It's a lucky thing Glenda wasn't here, or she'd roast you alive for having personal calls."

The care home had grim news: her grandmother was in hospital after a fall, they had failed to reach her parents and she was the next person on the list. Pip agonised over the right course of action. She knew she must go to Gran, but asking Glenda for emergency leave would be futile, dismissed as insubordination or fantasy, and she couldn't just go, or she'd be fired. Only one course of action remained. With Nicola's advice echoing in her head and nauseating her, Pip knocked on Mr Simpkins' office door; his face was cold when he saw who entered the room.

"Philippa, what do you want?"

"I wanted to apologise for the other day, sir," she said coyly, suppressing the screaming in her head. "I behaved like a silly girl. It's just I'm so... innocent, but I know you're a kind man who wouldn't rush me."

"That's quite alright, my dear." Simpkins' visage softened. "It takes time to understand the ways of the corporate world."

"Yes, sir. May I make an appointment to meet with you, to discuss how I might get on?" Pip permitted the slightest movement of one thigh against another, which spoke more words than a thousand volumes and made her hate herself a thousand times more. How she missed her job at the stables.

"There's no time like the present." Simpkins stood up, his leering eyes absorbing her essence.

"Oh, but I have to leave now, sir." Pip sounded disappointed. "My grandmother's in hospital and needs me urgently. Is that alright?"

"Monday morning, at eleven?"

"Monday, sir."

"And, Pip, you dress so much beyond your years. You should share the bloom of your youth with others. Do wear something more... appropriate for our meeting."

Pip nodded, wanting to scream and run. Fighting the urge to retch, she left, just as Glenda returned.

"Where do you think you are going?" the supervisor barked.

"Mr Simpkins said it was alright," Pip replied, almost at the lift. "It's an emergency."

Powerless and simmering, Glenda watched her leave.

Pip's mental state was reflected in her driving. Normally cautious, she pushed herself and the car hard, desperate to get to the hospital and her grandmother's bedside. The Mini was not fast, but slower vehicles tortured her, and she pressed past with uncharacteristic daring. Periodically, her mind turned to Monday and Mr Simpkins, nauseating her.

Once at the hospital, she ran to Casualty, her loose shoes flapping against the soles of her feet and her lungs burning. A man from the care home greeted her and led her to a cubicle where Pip's distress turned to stunned confusion – the patient in the bed was not her grandmother.

Cold, cruel shock overshadowed any relief.

The care home was apologetic; the woman had a similar name to Gran and the mistake was understandable, but they couldn't know the terrible cost of their error. A numb hopelessness spread through Pip and fogged her thoughts.

Automatically, she drove to her childhood home and rang on the doorbell. Daniel answered and tolerated a hug before rejoining a schoolfriend in the living room where they were playing computer games. Julia waved from the kitchen. She was speaking animatedly on the telephone, so Pip lurked in the lounge doorway and watched chunky multicoloured computer sprites dance around the television screen at the schoolboys' behest.

Daniel yelled triumphantly as the game announced a winner and he jumped around the room, pulling grotesque faces and grunting like a monkey. His friend joined in, roaring like a lion and following the ape around the room; they jumped from sofa to floor to table to chair and back again in a bestial loop. Julia, her call finished, stood beside her daughter and tutted good-naturedly at the animal antics.

"Did I ever do that?" Pip asked.

"You did your fair share of daft things, but you'd grown out of it by their age," Julia laughed.

"Boys are weird – I can't imagine Dad ever behaving like Daniel."

Julia's mood switched abruptly; she viciously grabbed Pip by the elbow, dragging her into the hallway.

"What is that supposed to mean?"

"What's what supposed to mean?"

"You know perfectly well," Julia hissed. "Been listening to nasty little rumours?"

"What? No!" Pip reeled from yet another incomprehensible outburst from her mother.

"I'm sick and tired of your insinuations." Julia sounded more animal-like than anything her younger son had achieved a few minutes before.

"Mum, I don't understand, I need—"

"No, Pip, I don't want to know."

"Tell you what, just forget it, Mum. Go and play with the boys, you might learn to grow up!"

As was her nature, Pip immediately regretted her words, but they came at the end of an intolerable day in a sequence of intolerable days and she had no residual capacity to be peacemaker. Instead, she marched out, slamming the door behind her, and sobbed alone.

Chapter 15

"**D**o wear something more… appropriate for our meeting."

The words echoed in Pip's dreams and shouted at her when she woke on Saturday morning. She owned no clothes that Simpkins would deem appropriate because she was never invited anywhere that merited them – parties, clubs, friends, socialising were all notions rather than reality. She had not minded missing out on a typical youth (Gran called her an 'old soul'), but it might have been nice to be asked.

Pip spent the day wandering the shops and did manage to find a few items which didn't make her skin crawl too much – a lilac strappy top, a rather nice flared navy miniskirt with creamy swirls, and some high heels in which she managed to walk without excess wobbling.

Where Saturday was a stressful fluster of unwilling actions, so Sunday was slow and terrible, like being pursued to the centre of a labyrinth by some lumbering monster, where there was no choice but to wait at the centre for the beast to arrive and devour you.

The weather was hot and the sun relentless. To escape Adam's unwelcome presence in the sweltering flat, Pip went out and walked along the streets, moving between shady spots to escape being scorched by the unforgiving rays. Children ran on the parched yellow grass, laughing and full of joy for the day.

Pip replayed her conversation with her mother, trying to understand her unintentional transgression. She had gone to the house hoping to stay the night and ask advice on escaping Mr Simpkins. Instead of support, she found anger – would she ever feel welcome there again?

The next day would be Monday and she saw no alternative to meeting Simpkins. Maybe, like Nicola said, it wouldn't be so bad, but such things were against her nature, against the very core of her womanhood. However, it was inevitable. There was no upward appeal – Glenda's dossier of alleged poor performance meant Pip would seem to be protecting herself by accusing an innocent man. If she quit immediately, she would get no job references, Glenda had made that abundantly clear.

Pip realised she had arrived at a small triangle of public gardens, a pleasant patch of grass and a bench where one might wait for a bus in welcoming surroundings. Six rosebushes stood evenly spaced along the verge, but their white blooms were withering, their limp warped petals starting to decay.

"Someone's not been watering you, have they?" she said to them.

There was a garage a short distance up the road, so she bought a large bottle of still water; she permitted herself a few gulps as she walked back to the parched plants, before she poured out the remainder, sharing it evenly between the little trees. Under the last rosebush was the remains of a blackbird, stiff and disfigured; ants swarmed around it and over it and inside it, stripping it of its dignity. Revolted but impotent to stop the inevitable, Pip walked away, back to the flat, back to her own destiny.

~ * ~ * ~

Early Monday morning, Pip crept into the bathroom. Adam's and Charlotte's snoring was audible through the wall, alternating one deep, one light, but unclear which came from whom. Fearful of disturbing the sleepers, Pip willed the drumming droplets of tepid water to quiet themselves as they fell from the spluttering showerhead into the porcelain bathtub. Her small razor moved with melancholic determination, under her arms and down her legs, oblivious to its guide's self-loathing for making such meticulous preparations.

Hair still wet and shins shiny from their close shave, she tiptoed into the kitchen to make her lunch and a strong black coffee. She carried the drink and her bag of sandwiches (purposely only enough for her) back to her room as quietly as possible, but a floorboard creaked under her foot and she froze; the snoring cycle stopped, but soon resumed.

Praying that the sound of her hair drier wouldn't disturb the slumbering lovers next door, she teased her locks, adding volume; the recent spell of hot weather meant that her room had barely cooled overnight, so the heat from the drier was uncomfortable on her skin.

Pip was no longer the girl who meticulously studied the trends in fashion magazines, but she was still stylish. Her thick raven hair was longer, now covering the nape of her neck, and her cheeks less plump, making her dark eyes larger and more innocent.

She applied makeup more heavily than usual, much like she had for Sharon long ago, and put on the skirt, strappy top and high heels. Pip examined herself in the mirror, twisting, checking all angles; the outfit was not indecent in any way, but she felt exposed and infantilised. Yet the young woman in the mirror had an ironic smile – she may not have much 'up top', as her mum used to remark, but she had always been pleased with her legs. "If you've got it, flaunt it," Sharon used to say, but Pip remained sceptical.

Her judgmental sarcasm from years before about her former friend's clothes returned to haunt her – 'not at all tarty'. This skirt was barely an inch longer than Sharon's had been and the top no less revealing. She went to put on the locket her grandparents had given her, realised her fingers trembled, and paused; unable to forgive herself for what she planned to do, Pip banished all thoughts of family and dropped the necklace into her handbag, instead wearing a chain she had bought in a charity shop when she was fourteen. It hung loosely to just above her collar bone, and she felt its cheapness completed her look.

Where was that teenage girl who bought the chain, then on the verge of womanhood? Was she really going to work looking like this? Admittedly she was dressed like many other girls in the office, including Nicola, but now Pip knew why, and braced herself to join their sad contingent just to hang on to a desperately needed job. Picking up her handbag and sandwiches, she crept to the front door of the flat.

"What the hell do you think you look like?" Charlotte's voice cut into the morning. Pip slowly turned to face her bed-tousled cousin.

"I look like a girl going to work, Charli," she sighed, as if the question was tiresome.

"Got a job in Tartsville, then? Or working your way up the greasy corporate pole the only way you know how?"

The words, so true, burned Pip to her very core.

"Please don't, Charli," she begged, "I don't know how much more I can take. There is a bloke at work that I want to… I need to… to make a good impression on. Please, I feel cheap enough as it is."

"Sorry, Pip, I don't know why I say some things. You look nice." Charlotte was uncharacteristically compromising, mainly because she wanted to go back to sleep. She returned to her room and Adam sat up in bed, just as Pip called a last goodbye.

"What was that all about?" he asked.

"Oh, it's Pip, done up tarty and showing some flesh." Charlotte climbed back into bed. "She's so holier than thou, but happy to dress like a tramp to get the attention of some mystery bloke at work."

Adam's heart quickened; he got up, pushing Charlotte aside as an inconvenience.

"Where are you going?" she asked.

"To the bog, where do you think?" he snapped, pleased he made her flinch.

However, Adam didn't go straight to the bathroom, but instead hurried to the kitchen and looked down into the car park. His quarry was crossing the tarmac to her Mini, and he was beyond excited that she should dress like that… for him.

~ * ~ * ~

The clock ticked ever closer to the dreaded eleven o'clock appointment. It was a quarter to the hour.

"Miss Raven, we don't pay you to daydream!" Glenda had been vile to Pip all morning, sniping at every action that the girl made.

Startled, Pip recommenced typing, but her nerves got the better of her and she started to walk to the Ladies.

"Where are you going now?" Glenda snapped. "Your appointment with Mr Simpkins isn't for another fifteen minutes."

"I need to spend a penny." Pip was tight-jawed from embarrassment and discomfort, and even Glenda couldn't doubt her sincerity.

In the toilets, Pip sat in the clean white stall and suppressed the urge to cry. At the basins, she stared at herself in the mirror. Eleven o'clock was nigh, the bell tolled, and it tolled for her. She wanted to walk away, just quit, get in her little car and go home. But where? No job meant no money to pay the rent and Charlotte wouldn't keep her. Her parents weren't an option and Gran couldn't help. Her choice was between zero self-respect with a degraded future, and very little self-respect with no future at all. No one wanted her, she was trapped… and her time was up. She sensed knowing looks from her colleagues as she walked to Simpkins' office, but she didn't realise they were expressions of commiseration and sympathy.

"Oh, excellent attire, Miss Raven," Simpkins complimented her when she walked in.

~ * ~ * ~

Back in the toilets, Pip washed her hands again and again, and stared in the shining mirror.

"You idiot!" she berated her reflection. "How could you be so stupid?"

She replayed the events in her mind. Sitting on the chair in front of Simpkins' desk while he closed the door, sensing him behind her like a slavering predator, jumping when his fingers touched her shoulder. They were like jaundiced twigs, scraping over her skin towards her neck, inducing an involuntary shrug and a squirm. She was prepared for the hand that slid down to her chest beneath her top, but not for the caress of her neck – that was the touch of a lover.

"Please," she whispered through clenched teeth.

"Please what?" Simpkins basked in her helplessness.

"Stop!" Pip stood up. "I'm sorry, but I think it best that I just resign."

"No, I don't think you will want to do that," Simpkins scoffed, his eyes narrowing as if assessing an exhibit. "Such an expensive mistake. You've clearly failed to read your contract of employment. If you leave this department within two years, voluntarily or dismissed, you must repay your training fees, and they are substantial. Even your word-processing course ran to several hundred pounds."

"I'm sure that can't be right," Pip protested. "That's for bigwigs, not people like me."

"I don't think your brief time as junior secretary equates to my thirty-five years in law. No, my dear, you're not going anywhere. You must return to your desk where you'll dangle upon Glenda's thread until you return with an improved attitude."

Alone in the lavatories, Pip fought back her tears and touched up her lipstick. She still harboured one hope of salvation. She had originally planned to eat lunch at her desk, unable to face the idea of seeing Adam in the stairwell, but now she had no choice – her remaining hope was that his magician's skills might help her.

It was forty-five minutes to lunch and she needed to get back to work. All eyes in the office seemed to watch her lonely return, and when she reached to her desk there was a note resting on her typewriter.

'*Now everyone knows what a little tramp you are.*'

The words hit like a punch. Paranoia pressed down on her and she glanced nervously around the office. Who had left the note?

Pip managed to work until her break without crying, but only just. She descended the fire escape to wait, sitting on her usual step and aching to be anywhere else. High above, a door opened and closed; Adam's lumbering footsteps resounded about her as he neared. She looked up, trying to smile as he sat beside her, closer than he had ever done before, oppressing the very air she breathed with his own exhalations. He grunted but said nothing, sitting like a boorish squire with rights to all he surveyed.

"I'm so glad you've come," Pip said, "I need some of your magic."

"You look nice," Adam leered. "You should dress like that more often."

"Thank you." Pip mentally cringed, wondering why he had not asked what magic she was asking for. She handed him her sandwiches and prepared to beg for help, but he tossed the food away to land on the dirty floor. What was that about? Now they would both be hungry.

"We didn't come here to eat, did we?" he said.

"Well, I've had to give up on the idea," her voice was dry as sandpaper. Adam's hand moved onto her knee. Pip would have moved her leg, but she was pressed against the wall, so she pushed the clammy paw away instead. "Let's not be silly."

"We both know why you're here, dressed like that." Adam moved his face closer, lips parted.

The stairwell had become airless in the oppressive heat of the summer day. Pip stood up, partly to breathe, partly to talk about her problem, but mainly to give the unambiguous message that she wanted no further advances. Adam, his bestial eyes fixed upon their prize, also stood and stepped towards her, backing her to the wall. Pip placed her hands on his broad chest and pushed, feeling thick body hair beneath his shirt's thin blue fabric.

"Please stop, Adam. I'm not sure what I've done to make you think I'm interested, but I'm not. Sorry. Please think about Charli." She turned her face away from his.

"I'd rather think about you – I usually do." He oiled his face closer.

"No!" Pip shouted, hoping to jolt him to his senses. She stepped smartly past him and began to ascend the stairs.

"Enough games," Adam snarled. He would not be denied his prey and grasped her wrist with his huge hand, arresting her progress with a jolt and forcing her to turn around.

"Bloody hell, Adam, that hurts!" she scratched at his grip with her free hand. "This isn't funny, let me go!"

"I'm not laughing, and you're not going anywhere."

"I'll scream."

Adam leaned back and screeched at the top of his lungs, the horrendous sound filling the echo chamber. He cocked his head, mocking Pip, to see if anybody came.

"I doubt that you could top that," he sneered.

"Adam, please stop this. Please, I'm sure you're a good person. Just let me go." By now, Pip was terrified and tugging futilely to free herself.

"You don't get it, do you? Dress like a slapper, get treated like a slapper."

"How I dress is my business. I'm no slapper, certainly not for the likes of you, so get off me!"

Surely that would be enough for him to desist? But no. He began to pull her to him; she was now on a direct eye level with him and trying not to topple off the steps.

"This is happening, Pip. Get used to it." Adam was factual but angry. How dare she tease him, dress like that for him, and then withhold herself? She was his and he would have her whenever and however he wanted.

Squeezing and twisting her wrist without compassion or remorse, Adam used his free hand to sharply cuff Pip about the head; there was an audible thud when his palm met her scalp, ruffling her dark hair and almost knocking her off the step. He drew his hand back once more and glared at her.

"Behave yourself, or there's more where that came from," he threatened, sadistically crushing her wrist even more. With satisfaction, he saw her cease to struggle and her body lost rigidity. He was breaking the stupid filly and she would be his for the taking, just like her cousin.

Many people do not understand rage. They think of it on a scale of anger, finishing at rage. But rage stands alone. Anger is evil because intellect can overrule it, kindness must temper it, and goodness may thwart it. Parents get cross with children, but never feel rage. Rage is a pure, unstoppable, awe-inspiring force of nature, without wicked sentiment. Storms rage; they have no mind, no thought, they simply are, and they are terrifying. The tempest rages and then is gone, divine in magnitude and ephemeral by nature.

So, Adam was right that he was breaking something in Pip, but it was not her will. It was the dam within her, behind which was years of meek acceptance of misfortune, cruelty, betrayal, misery, crushing loneliness, and, now, twisted abuse. She was someone who sought only to love and be loved, but now, her rage was birthed, ripped from deep within, raw, passionate, and unstoppable.

With the speed of Mercury and the might of Mars, Pip's free hand was a blur until the base of her palm made exquisite splattering contact with Adam's nose. The security guard couldn't have known that his victim's grandfather was an ex-Para who ensured his little Rosepip was prepared for the cruelty of the world.

Adam no longer knew what do with her; shocked and pained, he jolted back a few inches, his hands moving to his blooded face. Pip didn't wait any longer; from her vantage point, she aimed a perfectly weighted kick to his solar plexus. What air that remained in his lungs rushed out in a long wheeze; his shirt was torn, and his hairy torso scratched by her heel. He collapsed against the banister, gasping.

Pip stood above him and glowered, a victorious gladiator prepared to finish the kill; but her heart softened and the raging storm within abated on seeing his pain. Believing him vanquished, she started to walk upstairs.

"Bitch!" Adam spluttered. "I'll kill you!"

Pip rolled her eyes and retraced her steps, a divine fire in her eyes.

"No, you won't."

Her good knee jolted upwards, finding its tenderest target. Adam's bellow of agony echoed up and down the stairwell, like his mocking scream a few minutes earlier (but louder, Pip fancied). He sank to the ground.

"My grandfather gave me some advice once," Pip told the moaning guard. "If a man won't see reason, turn him into a farmer by giving him a lovely couple of acres. Now, stay away from me and my cousin!"

Pip ran off, leaving a groaning Adam to listen to the echo of her shoes.

~ * ~ * ~

For the third time in as many hours, Pip went into the Ladies, this time to wash the blood spatters from her hand and lower arm. She brushed cement dust from her skirt and examined her reflection in the mirror. With great satisfaction, she noted that there wasn't even the sign of a bruise, although there was a sore red mark on her wrist.

Feeling better than she had done in a long while, she returned to her desk and started to type. Lost in her work, her fingers flew over the keyboard. Adrenalin pumped through her system and she felt invincible... for a while. Nagging doubts entered her mind. Maybe she should report what happened? Yes, because Adam tried to force himself on her, and things could have gone very differently. He might attack her again, or he might try it with another girl. Why hadn't she thought of that before? Triumph slowly turned to trauma. She remembered fear and degradation which might haunt her dreams for a lifetime. Tears formed.

"Are you OK, Pip?" Nicola asked.

"Not really."

"Was Simpkins that bad?"

"It's not him. It's—" Pip was interrupted mid-sentence.

"You have really done it now!" shouted Glenda, who had just put down the phone. "I don't care what you say, you are out of here, you little— and don't think you can hide behind Mr Simpkins, because a short skirt won't get you out of this one."

Pip was almost manhandled by her supervisor into the manager's office. He sat behind his desk, looking grave.

"Philippa," Simpkins began, pompously for a man who not long ago was abusing his authority over her, "we've had a serious accusation made against you by a respected member of our security team. He challenged you in a restricted area and you assaulted him without warning. Is this correct?"

"No, he tried to attack me, to force himself on me."

"But you were in a restricted area?"

"It's a fire escape."

"But restricted."

"Surely that is beside the point? He tried to make me— to force me to— you know?"

"I think you need to be more specific." Simpkins seemed to be enjoying the conversation.

"He attacked me. Look, my wrist is red."

"Giving yourself Chinese burns won't do any good," Glenda interrupted, "and this charade is pointless. Mr Simpkins, she needs to go and go now."

"I didn't do anything wrong!" Pip exclaimed. "It's his word against mine."

"I'd take his any day," Glenda's expression was between contempt and triumph. "He is my son after all."

A whole bag of pennies dropped into place.

"If you go now with no fuss," Mr Simpkins offered, "we won't refer the matter to the police and your employment record will state that you resigned. No disciplinary record. And we may consider not asking you to repay all your fees."

"It's me who should be going to the police. Right now," Pip insisted.

"And tell them what?" asked Simpkins. "You haven't a mark on you to speak of, you admit to being in a restricted area, and the guard in question has an impeccable record. According to Glenda's meticulous records, you've a history of insubordination, and my own opinion is that you are fanciful. They'll laugh at you, and rightly so."

"But—" Pip began.

"Look, I am tired of this. Any chance of a good reference is now off the table and I am feeling increasingly disinclined to forbear reporting you to the authorities. Glenda, Miss Raven has fifteen minutes to be out of the building. Please see that she is escorted from the premises."

Pip managed to whisper a goodbye to Nicola before she left the building, flanked by two uniformed men more than a foot taller than she was and three times as broad. She left her once dream job behind her. Only that morning she had degraded herself before Simpkins in the hope of keeping it, and now she was even worse off. No job, no money, no prospects, no reference, no hope; but maybe she did still have a little self-respect.

~ * ~ * ~

Mr Reeves' driver stopped the Daimler at the entrance to the car park to allow a pretty girl driving an old Mini to pull out into the traffic; she gave a little thankyou wave but seemed distracted. The Daimler purred to the main entrance, and Reeves alighted, met by Mr Sanders who led him to a tedious board meeting.

An hour or so later, the two men were the only remaining occupants of the boardroom. Cigar smoke filled the air and it swirled around Sanders as he moved to the drinks bar and prepared two scotches.

"That meeting went well, I thought."

"Indeed," Reeves concurred.

"But I'm still not the man to run things?"

"My dear man, you are keeping your salary, car, and secretary, you're getting a charming new office, and you'll have fewer onerous duties. What is not to like?"

Sanders sulked as they sipped their drinks. A blonde secretary entered and sashayed across the room to pass a folder to him.

"I wouldn't trouble you with this normally," he said when he had scanned the file's contents, "but you insisted you be consulted on all personnel decisions. Well, a girl in the legal secretarial team was fired today after she assaulted a security guard in a restricted zone."

"Consultation normally takes place before a decision," Reeves rumbled, displeased by a fait accompli. "Where did this incident take place?"

"Fire escape E."

"How can a fire escape be a restricted zone?" Reeves asked.

"That's beside the point." Sanders had no answer. "She assaulted him, so was summarily dismissed."

"Who was this Amazon, this warrior of the fairer sex who mercilessly attacked your dedicated protector?"

Sanders examined the folder.

"Miss Philippa Raven. Nineteen years old."

"Surely not the same petite Miss Raven whom you and I met in the lift?"

Sanders eyed the passport photo of Pip. "Yes."

"And what of the poor weakling that she attacked? He seems a curious selection for your security force. What are his credentials?"

"Um…" Sanders hesitated while looking at a second piece of paper from the file, "six foot four, dropped out of military training on undisclosed grounds some years back, black belt in karate, been with us for five years without incident."

"What was Miss Raven's side of the story?"

"She claimed he attempted to force himself on her, but not a mark on her. The guard has an impeccable record."

"They often do. Were there no CCTV pictures of the incident?"

"No, there was a technical hitch."

"How very inconvenient."

"Anyway, I was only advised of the sacking after Simpkins had done it."

"Ah, Simpkins. He seems a good man. Excellent legal mind, just not a good corporate climber," Reeves mused. "What's the extent of the guard's injuries?"

"I only have vague notes, but suspected broken nose, maybe a fractured rib, and bruises and abrasions."

"I am getting to like Miss Raven." Reeves clapped his hands.

"There was debate as to whether it was a police matter, but Simpkins thought not."

"He's right, unless you want newspaper stories about one of your security personnel being disabled by a small teenage girl defending her honour? For that's exactly how they'll describe her, probably beside a very attractive picture of Miss Raven."

"And what about reclaiming her training fees?"

"I don't understand."

Sanders passed a copy of Pip's contract of employment.

"This isn't the standard contract." Reeves frowned. "It is entirely unenforceable in law, you understand?"

"It's drawn up by the legal team and is beyond me."

"I think I'll have to investigate Simpkins rather more closely. And I think it prudent to change the rules regarding the guards, and this one in particular." Reeves pointed to Adam's records. "I don't care what reason you use, I want him to be placed with another member of the department at all times."

"And Philippa Raven? Your clients won't want any scandal."

"Least said, soonest mended," Reeves sighed with regret.

~ * ~ * ~

Pip arrived home, dying to change clothes. She hurried straight to her room and stopped short – everything of hers was gone. All that remained was the furniture that came with the flat. Her curtains flapped in the open window – had they been robbed?

"Hello, slut!" Charlotte said from the doorway.

"What are you doing back?" Pip asked. "Aren't you on late shift?"

"I came home after I was called down to casualty to patch up Adam."

"Look, Charli, he's bad news. He—"

"Save it, he told me all about it."

"What?"

"All about you trying it on with him and getting upset when he said no. Kneeing him in the goolies and hitting him in the face with something. You wanted to impress someone at work, you told me – well, I didn't think you meant my bloody boyfriend!"

"It wasn't like that!"

"I want you out, liar!" Charlotte screamed, red-faced with anger. "Your stuff's in bin bags in the living room. Except your clothes, they're in the rubbish skip – nice girl stuff doesn't suit slappers. You're disgusting. I know you offered yourself to some old man for favours."

The assertion rocked Pip – it was one thing having rumours and innuendo at work, but for them to come home into her own family was unthinkable.

"Charli, I—"

"Shut up! You don't get it. I want you out. Get your scummy stuff and leave! I swear, if you don't get going right now, I'll ring my dad and have him tell your father what a slut his little girl is, just like her mum. Believe me, Dad would love to stick one to your stuck-up family."

"What do you mean, stuck-up?" Pip knew of hidden animosity that existed between their families, but she and Charli had been friends, hadn't they?

Her thought process took too long.

"Right, that's it!" Charlotte marched to the living room, picked up the telephone receiver and held her finger over the dial.

That was threat enough. Defeated, Pip dragged the bin bags to the Mini and then checked the skip to see if she could salvage any of her clothes; she found a coat, a skirt and two winter jumpers which hadn't landed in the worst part of the putrid garbage, but the stench, made worse by the summer heat, made her gag and stop searching. Everything else was ruined anyway.

Most unkind of all, her beloved rose bushes lay below the still open window of her former bedroom, their painted pots smashed. She wrapped their roots in the skirts and jumpers that she had salvaged and carried them to her car. The earth clumped about their bases was from Grandad's garden; oh, how he must be looking down with such sad disappointment.

She needed a place to go and liked the idea of being close to her grandmother. There was a cheap B&B near the care home and enough in her bank account to stay there for a few days. Two hours later, she sat on the edge of the creaking bed in a sweltering, sparsely furnished, attic bedroom with bubbling linoleum on the floor, staring at three bin bags, her rosebushes, and some clothes that needed a wash.

~ * ~ * ~

Memories of the day flashed through Pip's mind; Simpkins' foul touch, Adam's terrifying lust, Glenda's triumphant sneer, and Charlotte's unstemmed fury. Self-loathing overwhelmed Pip, as it had before when the world seemed against her. She rued her actions, for fleeing her manager's molestation and for hurting and humiliating her cousin's deviant boyfriend. The other secretaries put up with Simpkins and maybe she had given the wrong signals to Adam. Glenda might not have found fault with a better secretary, and Charli would have let a better flatmate stay. Instead, because she lost self-control, she was completely alone.

Pip lost perspective of the truth. Crippled by shame, she had an urge to pray, to find peace and solace, but felt unworthy. Yet a distant intangible notion formed that she would find someone who needed her and who would be there for her.

Her tummy rumbled, and Pip realised she hadn't eaten since the previous night. The B&B only served dinner if booked before breakfast, so there was no hope of a meal. She needed to conserve money, but she also had to eat, so resigned herself to going back out. At that time of the evening hardly any stores would still be open, so she drove to one of the few places that might still be, the little corner shop near the park, where she and Sharon went as children.

The cars of nearby residents filled all the spaces in the roads near the shop, so Pip was obliged to park several streets away and walk, only to arrive after it had closed. That was the end of her hopes for dinner – both the fish and chip shop and the Chinese takeaway closed on Mondays, and she was too ashamed to go to her parents, even if she had believed she was welcome. Walking back, full of despair, and wondering if the garage sold anything more than crisps and chocolate, she bumped into Lyn who was tramping home with three carrier bags of shopping.

"Are you off to a party?" Lyn asked, looking at Pip's clothes. "You look a bit tasty. The boys won't be able to keep their hands off you."

"Would you like a lift home?" Pip asked, inwardly screaming at Lyn's innocent remarks.

"No need, I'm nearly there. The place is a mess, so I won't ask you over, but come by in a couple of days and see how my redecorating's coming on."

"I will," Pip promised, grateful to be welcome somewhere. She looked longingly at the carrier bags of shopping. "Cheeky question. Have you got anything in there I can eat? I'll pay."

"Of course, darling, but keep your money. There's some sausage rolls and a bit of fruit in this one. Take it, save me carrying it back."

And so, Lyn's simple act of unthinking kindness was a beacon of good at the end of Pip's darkest day.

~ * ~ * ~

The next day brought new priorities for Pip. She needed a job (hard to find without a reference) and money for clothes and other essentials. Several personal items had been ruined by a broken bottle of perfume inside one of the bin bags and she needed to get replacements. At least the book from Theo and Bobbie had survived intact.

She had handwashed her underwear in the sink in her room and hung them over the towel rail to dry overnight. Pip had considered attempting the same with the skirt and jumpers salvaged from the bins, but it wasn't realistic; anyway, the sweaters were too heavy for summer, and the skirt had been torn by one of her rosebushes, which were presently thrust in the unsatisfactory sanctuary of the wastepaper bin. So, she again wore the hated clothes until she could buy more.

As the money in her bank account was needed for food, she had to turn her sole asset into ready cash, but first she needed Gran's blessing.

"Goodness, Pip, what are you wearing?" the old woman asked when Pip arrived at the home. "It's not your usual style, but you look lovely."

"It's all I have left to wear," Pip spluttered.

"That's a bit odd – why?"

"Because Charlotte thought I'd tried it on with her boyfriend, but I hadn't," Pip shuddered. "Anyway, she chucked all my clothes in a rubbish bin and threw me out."

"Well, she was always a bit funny," Gran observed. "Not that I know that side of your family very well, but they all seem a bit snooty."

"That's what they think about us," Pip laughed, but without finding it funny.

"So, home at your mum's?"

"No, I don't think she'd have me. I'm staying… somewhere near."

"So long as you're happy."

"I'm not happy, Gran," Pip started to cry. "I did a terrible thing, terrible. Let you down, let Grandad down. I… I let a man… touch me… you know… to keep my job, so I could get on, but it all went wrong when I changed my mind. Later, Charli's boyfriend tried to… force himself on me and I hit him and hurt him. I was fired because it was his word against mine and I'd broken company rules by being on the stairs. I've no job, no future and I've behaved like a tart. I've lost your good opinion and I can't bear that. I'm so sorry!"

Gran took a little while to digest the outburst and extract the important points from the confusion.

"Pipsqueak, you're priceless! Standing up to an ungentlemanly oaf and giving him a hiding? Your Grandfather would be bursting with pride."

"What about letting the old man—"

Gran interrupted, sparing her granddaughter.

"Did I ever tell you about your Great Aunt Peg? No? She was a bonny girl – your grandad's sister – married a good man, Norman, had a couple of little boys. Well, Norman was killed at Dunkirk, oh it was so sad. Poor Peg was in a terrible way. Sent the boys to Norman's mother in Warwick, as I recall, so she could take a job. Anyway, she fell in with some spiv – you know what a spiv is?"

"A black-market dealer."

"Good girl. Well, he was a nasty piece of work, got Peg into all kinds of debt – the tallyman was always knocking on their door. We only found out about this later, but this spiv would bring men over to her house and expect her to entertain them, if you get my drift? Your grandfather came home on leave and found out. Oh, he was magnificent! Marched straight over to hers, a good few miles, and beat the living daylights out of the fella. Made such a ruckus that a policeman turned up."

"Was Grandad in trouble?"

"Goodness, no. The policeman held the spiv down so your grandad could hit him a bit more. Then Peg stayed with us for a bit before she moved to her mum's and met a nice chap – a greengrocer. Now, what Peg did was wrong, but she thought she had no choice and was more sinned against than sinning. It was that man and those he brought that were the bad'uns. So, Pipsqueak, don't let one mistake define you. Wipe the slate clean and start again."

"You mean a fresh start?"

"Yes. 'Sometimes you need to go backwards to go forwards', your grandad would say. If he were here now, he'd punch that horrid man that touched you, but it seems you're quite capable of doing that for yourself."

Pip kissed Gran on the cheek.

"Thanks," she said, "you always make me feel better. But there's something else. I need your permission to sell my car, for the money."

"Oh, Pip, what a shame. Maybe I can give you something?"

"No, Gran. Thanks, but I need to do this." Pip knew full well that the old lady had nothing but a few pounds a week.

"If I still had the bungalow, you could come and live with me again."

"I think it would have hurt too much. It's a happy place, and I'm not ready to be happy, if that makes sense?"

"It does," Gran burst with empathy. "You need to embrace your pain for a while. Don't worry about the Mini, it's yours – and it would be a poor gift if it came with strings attached. Sell it and get yourself on an even keel."

After a cuddle and obligatory pray with Gran, Pip took her Mini to a garage which had not long before displayed a much-loved Cortina on its forecourt, and then almost skipped to the shops to buy a change of clothes.

~ * ~ * ~

The next day, the owner of the guesthouse cornered Pip as she was leaving to go job hunting. It seemed the bin in Pip's room contained three rosebushes, and the chambermaid wasn't prepared to deal with things that belong in the garden. Pip must make alternative arrangements for the plant or they would be treated as refuse.

The summer sky had threatened rain all morning, and now the promise was fulfilled with a deluge of large splattering drops and distant thunder. It seemed ironic that the long spell of hot dry weather should break just when Pip had sold her car. Fortunately, she had brought her coat, one of the few items rescued from the skip, and wrestled with the fastener as she left the guesthouse.

"That's a bit big for you," the landlady observed.

"This coat has special memories for me; the kindness of a stranger who had no reason to help me other than that I was cold and wet and looked sad," Pip explained.

Even with the coat, she was soaked by the time she reached the bus stop, so she saved the fare and walked to town. She trekked from business to business, shop to shop, asking if they had any jobs. Some people were put off by her soggy, bedraggled state (her oversized unfashionable coat didn't help), while those who overlooked her appearance required references. It looked hopeless.

Pip realised she was outside the launderette. Inside, the lady who had been so kind to her years ago was emptying a machine into a pink plastic washing basket, wearing what looked like the same blue nylon tabard. Almost without realising it, Pip pushed open the door and stepped inside. The lady smiled.

"Hello. Did you want to use a machine?"

"No, thanks. I'm here because, well you won't remember, but I came in here once and you gave me a cup of tea and this coat. My name's Pip, well Philippa, but everyone calls me Pip."

Recognition dawned after a brief pause.

"Yes, I remember! You're not much drier this time. What have you been up to, then?"

"I went away to live with my gran for a bit. Then I moved in with my cousin, but it didn't work out. Now I'm back here."

"It's always nice to come home."

"Sometimes. Um, cheeky question: do you have any jobs going?" Pip ventured.

"No, luv, well, not out front. A few years ago, maybe, but now there's only three of us, and two are part-time. I can offer you piece-work doing ironing, if you like, but it's hot in this weather. Interested?"

"Yes, please, anything," Pip smiled.

"And there's always people coming in asking if we know someone to do charring, you know, cleaning their house and the like. They leave cards pinned over there," she gestured to a large cork notice board fixed to one of the walls; it was covered with small pieces of paper, some selling cars or general miscellany, and some asking for gardeners or help with housekeeping.

"Thank you," Pip enthused. At last, things were looking up. "Do you need any ironing done now?"

"Blimey, you're keen. Come out back and I'll stick the kettle on and show you the ropes. I like your style, Pip. Not many like you left. I'm Bren, by the way."

~ * ~ * ~

Later that afternoon, the Reverend Johnson listened patiently to Lyn talk about Bob and how she missed him. It was a regular conversation, gradually helping her to work through thoughts and emotions, but she had so opened her heart that he felt unable to help himself to a biscuit from the plate on her living room table; to have done so would be insensitive, crass even, as if her words didn't merit concentration, but he had missed lunch because of an urgent hospital call and was hungry. When Lyn finished speaking, he could at last give inward thanks and reach towards the delicious goodies. Alas, a ring on the doorbell interrupted him – Lyn instantly jumped up to answer its summons, and the clergyman didn't wish to greet a potential newcomer with his mouth full. His hostess returned with Pip in her wake.

"Goodness me, Philippa," the vicar exclaimed, "I can't remember the last time I saw you!"

"I moved away, but I'm back," Pip explained, not wanting to remind him in front of Lyn that Bob's funeral was their last encounter.

"Lovely. Are you back at home?"

"No, I'm in a B&B, but I can't afford it much longer," Pip replied. "Do you know anyone with a room to rent? I've found work, so I can pay."

"I'll ask around," Rev. Johnson promised, "but if all else fails, Rebecca and I would be delighted for you to be our guest at the vicarage until you're sorted."

"Would you like to live with me for a while?" Lyn interjected, thinking of Sharon and Pip running around the house when they were little girls. "You could help me redecorate. It can only be until I find a buyer, I'm moving up near Mark."

"Are you sure you wouldn't mind?" Pip was full of hope.

"Oh, I need it," Lyn assured, "it would be a blessing."

"Then I suggest we celebrate with a custard cream," declared the vicar, finally getting his biscuit.

Chapter 16

Gavin's return trip to Britain was tiring but uneventful. His parents met him at the airport, but their hopes for him to have returned with renewed optimism were soon disappointed once he had given an edited account of his time at the Maths Camp and Miss Lucille's.

"It taught me one thing," Gavin finished. "That Sharon and Paul both made the same decision in different ways, and they both left hurt and devastation behind them."

"From what we know, Paul may be pursuing a more noble course," Mr Knight observed.

"Lyn Wells called us," Gavin's mother said. "Did you know Sharon sent a letter to your friend Pip Raven?"

"Yes, Lyn wrote to me," Gavin replied. "I'm not sure what I feel. Betrayed, I think. That's the closest that I can come to describing it. Bob convinced me Sharon must have been coerced in some way and that she needed rescuing. I certainly don't believe that now."

"I think people can act of their own accord and also have their head turned," Mr Knight said. "When I was seventeen, I tried to elope to Gretna Green with the fishmonger's daughter." He became aware that his wife and son were both sitting open-mouthed at this rather overdue news. "Yes, I know that sounds like a joke. I could find Gretna on a map of the British Isles and I knew where we lived, but I was less clear on the best method of travel. We also thought we could get there and be wed on one pound six shillings, which transpired to be optimistic."

"You've never mentioned this! What was her name?" asked Gavin's mother.

"Gertrude… Please stop laughing."

Mother and son needed several minutes to recover before they could comply.

"Did you get to Gretna?" Gavin asked, dabbing his eyes with his sleeve.

"We got twelve miles from home when Gertrude's bicycle got a flat tyre and we missed the train. Our fathers caught up with us before we got any further."

Mrs Knight snorted and was lost in convulsions of contagious giggles for another few minutes.

"What happened to her?" she eventually managed to ask.

"Well, Gertrude blamed me for embarrassing her and refused to see me again. She was married the next year to a trainee carpenter from the next town. I believe she had several children and a good life, but we didn't keep in touch."

"That's really rather touching and sad."

"I thought so too," Mr Knight concurred. After a pause, he added wistfully, "I did hear through the grapevine that he dropped a hammer on her foot and she lost a toe to sepsis. Not that I ever saw her feet, well you didn't in those days, but they always struck me as rather dainty— Why are you two laughing again?"

"Dad," Gavin eventually managed to say, "if you'd told that story three months ago, I might never have needed to go to America."

~ * ~ * ~

Once she had moved in, Pip developed a new routine. She rose at six every morning, tended her rose plants (which she had painstakingly replanted in three pots purchased cheaply on a market stall), and breakfasted with Lyn, who was delighted to again have company at the kitchen table. At seven o'clock, she caught the bus and worked from seven-thirty until noon at the launderette, followed by a quick lunch with Bren. Then she cleaned houses until five, at which point she returned for dinner with Lyn, and then decorated until bedtime. Lyn was as generous as she could afford to be and more, accepting only a token rent and a contribution towards food, though the help with redecorating was worth more than money.

Pip earned less than her former salary, but she was infinitely richer in terms of peace of mind. No one cared what she wore, though she still took pride in her appearance – jeans, shirt, and trainers were her standard uniform (beautifully ironed of course). Her schedule, though arduous, provided variety and most of the houses she cleaned were owned by people who relished company; afternoons were liberally sprinkled with tea breaks and cake with an interesting slice of the client's life story.

From time to time, Pip visited Reverend Johnson, but was too ashamed to speak directly of her trauma. The clergyman pieced together the truth, knowing well how betrayed and abused people who are naturally trusting often find fault and blame in themselves. Their gentle unjudgmental conversations soothed Pip, and she took to sitting alone in the quiet side-chapel in anonymous contemplation, detached from corporeal limitations. For the first time in a long time, she found peace – it was too soon for happiness, but calm contentment was at her core.

However, Pip was still painfully estranged from her family. Determined to get to the bottom of the matter, late one afternoon she trekked to her father's place of work and waited outside for him to finish. He was exhausted, but his spirits soared as soon as he sighted his daughter leaning against his car; he would have been content for their hug to have lasted the rest of eternity, but reluctantly accepted that she wanted to talk, and he knew what the topic must be.

"Are you coming home for a visit?" he asked.

"No, Dad, I want to speak to you alone," Pip replied. "How's your day been?"

"Same as every day for the last twenty-five years," he laughed, waving to a couple of departing workmates, "but that's not why you're here, is it? It's about the falling-out with your mum."

"I don't understand what happened. I came for help and wasn't given a chance to explain. Something bad happened to me at work. I can't tell you, I'm too ashamed."

"I gathered as much. After you went to see your gran the other day, she rang and spoke to me. Told me you sold your car and a bit about what happened at that company, but only after I promised not to do anything, nor to tell your mum."

"How can you stand to talk to me? I let you down," Pip whimpered.

"Philippa, my lovely, you're as daft as a brush sometimes. Let's say no more about it. Unless you'd like me to give someone a hiding? I've a length of copper piping back in the workshop."

"Tempting, but no thanks, Dad."

"All things heal with time, my girl. Your Uncle Ted called me last night, and had some ungentlemanly things to say about you, courtesy of young Charlotte. I don't think we'll be getting together any time soon, but I expect one day we'll let bygones be bygones."

"Oh, no," Pip groaned, "I never thought about that. My mistakes have come between you and Uncle Ted."

"Enough of that talk, you've nothing to blame yourself for. What you're here to talk about is this business with your mother," Mr Raven pointed out. "Come on, get in the car. Where are you living?"

"Lyn Wells' house." Pip saw the hurt in her father's eyes. "What did I do wrong with Mum?"

"You touched a nerve. It's how she is."

"All I said was I couldn't imagine you were like Daniel when you were a boy, and Mum went crazy."

"Ah, well I can see why." Mr Raven shook his head and winced as he started the car. "I suppose I'd better start from the beginning. Do you remember when you were ten and Mum went away for a month or so?"

"Yeah, Aunty Sybil was poorly, and Mum was helping."

"No, Pip. Your mother left me."

"No, that's not possible!"

"Sorry, it is. She took up with an old boyfriend of hers from Watford. They'd lost touch for years, when suddenly he cropped up at Ted and Jane's anniversary bash. Small world. Anyway, he left his wife and your mum left us and they set up home together. Your gran said it wouldn't last, and she was right, as usual."

"But Mum left us? You and me and Matthew?"

"She planned on having you kids come and live with her, but as I say, it was doomed. It was some last fling, trying to hold on to youth, I suppose."

"And you just took her back?" Pip asked, emotions eddying in her mind; anger, sympathy, pity, self-pity, and sadness renewed.

There was a long pause before her father replied.

"Do you know, I'd never been in a house with an indoor privy before I met your mother? When I was a boy, we had a shed at the bottom of our garden to do our business – horrible it was, dark and full of big spiders. There was one tap in the whole house, and that was the kitchen sink, but we were clean, mind you."

"What's that got to do with it?"

"I'm getting there, have patience. Now, where was I? When I was about nineteen, my mate heard about this great deal going on a motorbike that he was after – a bloke in Watford was selling it. It was a fixer-upper, it didn't run, so he needed a van to get it back. Muggins here had access to a work truck, so I drove him to the place, a nice council house, much nicer than where I was from. I was stuck waiting for my mate to look the bike over, when I noticed how nice the front garden next door was. And standing in it, talking to a friend of hers, was the most beautiful girl I had ever seen."

"Was that Mum?"

"It was. I got busy, turned on the ol' Raven charm. Of course, I gave the big 'I am' and the next thing I knew I was sitting in her living room drinking tea out of nice little cups and saucers with roses on. Very fancy. My mate didn't buy the bike, but I drove to Watford every weekend for six months before I plucked up the nerve to ask your mum to marry me."

"I didn't know that story."

"I remember the first time she came down this way to our house. We had no fancy cups, no heating, no indoor facilities, but she was a true lady and mucked in with the rest of us. I knew it was hard for her, so I promised her that day that she'd never want for anything. After we wed, we rented a flat, I passed my trade exams, grafted two jobs, and she worked every shift she could at BHS, until you came along. We got a car, bought our own house – the first people in either of our families to – and we felt we were going places. But then things got tough – inflation and recession, and kids aren't cheap!"

"Sorry," Pip three-quarters joked.

"You're worth it. But I slowly saw the light go out in your mum's eyes. This wasn't just our first house, it was also our last house, you see. We got left behind. I'd come so much further and had no disappointments, but she did. I'd let her down."

"No, you didn't!" Pip protested. "And it's not an excuse for what she did."

"Maybe not, but it is a reason. Sometimes we go down a path because it seems the only way. Your mum came back, said sorry, and we worked things out. I think we're as happy as most."

"What does this have to do with Mum losing her rag about Daniel?"

"Do the maths. Honestly, what's the point of school these days? How old is your little brother?"

"Oh." Pip realised how stupid her question had been.

"Daniel's my son in all the ways that matter. Unfortunately, your Aunt Jane put two and two together – she's sharp enough to cut herself, she is – and now your mum thinks you have too."

"So, what do I do? Say nothing?"

"Yes. Let things calm down and then stay off the topic."

Pip thought for a few minutes.

"So, the computer Daniel was given—" she began.

"Was a present from his real father, yes. He was entitled to know he had a son out there. Every so often, he makes an expensive guilty gesture and then disappears again, but he hasn't the courage to actually meet the boy."

"Will you tell Daniel?"

"Maybe one day, if it's necessary."

"Does Gran know?"

"Yes, so did your grandad. He said a very wise thing once. 'I used to have rambler a bit like our Julia', he told me, 'with thorns everywhere, scratching away whenever I tried to look after it, but I couldn't mind because the beautiful rose-blooms were so precious and fragile. They only came once a year, mind, but worth waiting for'. He was right, she might scratch you if you get close in the wrong way at the wrong time, but your mum has so much to love about her that you mustn't mind. If I can get over this, Pip, you can. She just rambled the wrong way for a bit, that's all, but she came back and she's not going again."

They arrived outside Lyn's house.

"Do you want to come in for a cuppa?" Pip asked. "We have little cups with flowers on."

Her father laughed as he turned off the engine. "Ever the best of friends, eh, Pip?"

~ * ~ * ~

After his time in America, being home with his parents felt like a pleasant break for Gavin. Leaving for university was just weeks away and he spent much of his time revising his mathematics, although he also frequently visited his very pregnant sister, who was getting fed up with the hot weather.

One special surprise came in the form of a pale blue airmail letter from Miss

might sting old wounds, but he was smiling, happy that his family were around him and content.

After dinner, Matthew went out to see his girlfriend (whose existence was news to Pip), Daniel returned to the digital world, Mr Raven decided that a smoke followed by a snooze was a good plan, and mother and daughter went into the kitchen, ostensibly to wash up. Julia opened an under-counter drawer and removed an envelope which she gave to Pip.

"It's the money you lent us for Daniel's uniform and other stuff, plus a bit of interest," she explained.

"I can't take this," Pip objected.

"You must. We shouldn't have accepted it in the first place. Can you get your Mini back?"

"No, but maybe it's for the best." Pip noticed her mother's right hand, two fingers of which looked very bare, save for a pale stripe near their knuckles. "Where are your rings, Mum?"

"Where they should have been long ago. Don't look at me like that," Julia held up her left hand and wiggled her wedding band with her thumb, "I've still got the valuable one."

Pip understood. This was her mother's way of setting things straight.

Later, she turned down the offer of a lift home and walked to Lyn's house following the familiar route she used to take when visiting Sharon. The absence of her old friend loomed in front of her, a spectre of the void. Sharon's letter had left more questions than it answered. What could she be doing that Pip would disapprove of? Drugs? Well, she'd already done that. Prostitution? Unlikely that she'd say she was happy. Pip found herself praying fervently for Sharon's safe deliverance, advocating that the girl's heart was fundamentally good, that she had been a true friend. She was still deep in thought when she entered the house and walked into the living room. Gavin was there.

"Pip?" He jumped to hug her. "You look amazing. What are you doing here?"

"I live here."

"Oops," said Lyn as she came into the room, "I forgot to mention it."

"But this is wonderful," Gavin exclaimed. "Have you any plans for Saturday?"

"I do now," Pip laughed. "We've a lot of catching up to do, and you can drive me around all the garages in the morning, because I might be looking for a car. I've come into a bit of cash."

Pip had doubts about spending her windfall. She worried that Lyn might ask for more rent, but her concern was unwarranted as Lyn hoped for the occasional lift. Also, Simpkins' threat to recoup her training remained a worry, but she decided to deal with that when it arose.

"I have to go now," Gavin sighed. "Is nine-thirty on Saturday OK? We'll visit some garages and then go somewhere nice in the afternoon."

"Sounds lovely. I'll bring a picnic."

Gavin left, to a duet of "goodbye."

"I say, Gav's got a bit handsome while I've been away," Pip said.

"Yes, he's become a good-looking boy."

"Cup of tea before bed?" Pip yawned.

"No thanks, but I have something I want to discuss."

"That sounds ominous."

"It's not meant to. It's just the next room we need to decorate is yours."

"And? It needs it, it's still got Mark's posters up."

"You can't sleep in there while we are doing the work. The obvious room is Sharon's but..."

"You're not ready for someone else to use it?"

"No. Sorry, I can't explain. I'll sleep in there and you have my room."

"That's silly, it's only for a week or so. I'll sleep down here on the couch. I've fallen asleep on it often enough. It's fine, honestly."

"Thanks, my dear," Lyn sighed with relief. "Our Sharon still causes problems even when she's not here. Now, I also want to talk about that employment contract you told me about."

"Don't," Pip groaned, "I worry that they're looking for me with a huge bill."

"Well, don't. I talked to my union rep and she says they couldn't make it stand. In fact, they owe you money."

"I wouldn't want it," Pip stated, "I want nothing from them, but thank your rep for me, please."

"I will. If you change your mind, she'll help you. Not that her union has any clout there, she just likes a fight."

~ * ~ * ~

"I doubt this dealership will have anything in your price range," Gavin told Pip, as he stopped his car on the industrial estate, "and I'm not keen on some of the people who work there."

"They might have a cheap part-exchange," Pip replied, "and don't worry about Tom, we can have fun ignoring him."

"Not just Tom. Mel too."

"I met her a while back," Pip said. "Did you know she and Tom went out? I think he'd just dumped her."

"No, I didn't know, or I'd have warned her after what he did to you."

"What, dumping me?"

"No. The night of the gig at The White Hart, I overheard him arrange to meet another girl. That's why he left you on your own. I confronted him, but he ignored me and then got you to refuse to have contact with me, so I couldn't tell you. In fact, as I recall, he cut you off from all your friends."

Pip wanted to be shocked, but she wasn't. She was angry with herself for ever having fallen for Tom and his mind games.

"I'm sorry," she said, "I shouldn't have let him come between our friendship – but you seemed alright and I thought I was in love. I was scared I'd lose him."

"I'm the last person to judge someone for doing stupid things for love," Gavin laughed.

"That sounds interesting, do tell."

"I will, but later, when we can relax. Not here."

Pip pointed to a young woman leaving the garage. "Look, that's Mel, isn't it? She looks upset, I think I'd better check on her. Stay here if you feel awkward."

Pip lightly cantered to Gavin's ex-girlfriend as he awkwardly tailed her at a more reluctant pace. Mel was in her own world of thoughts when Pip broke through, "Hello, it's me again, are you alright?"

"Oh… yes," Mel replied, and then emotion welled up in her as she screwed her features to prevent herself from crying. "Well, no actually. I've just been fired. I had to tell them, you see, because it will be obvious soon."

"What will be?"

"My baby-bump. Apparently, I would set a bad impression for the customers."

"Why, because you're pregnant?" Pip grew visibly indignant.

"And single. Unmarried mothers don't set the right tone for the establishment, though how anyone is supposed to know is beyond me. I offered to wear a ring." Mel realised Gavin was standing close by. "Hello, Gav. Well, I've got myself into a right pickle. You must be glad you escaped a mess-up like me."

"Never," he replied gently, "I only ever wanted good things for you."

"Yeah, me too," she said, bitter at her life, bitter that he was being nice.

"Is Tom the father?" Pip asked.

A single sudden sob escaped Mel's lips. She nodded.

"He said it could be anybody's, said I'm a slag and that everyone knows it, said I'm on my own, said I should get rid of it... but I couldn't. So, I was a fool then and a fool now."

"No, you are not," Pip insisted. "I want you to wait here for a few minutes, OK?"

She started to walk towards the garage.

"Where are you going?" Mel called.

"They've fired you, so I can't make things worse, can I?" Pip answered over her shoulder. She stormed in the showroom and a salesman oozed into her path, seemingly from nowhere.

"May I help you, miss?"

"It depends. Are you the boss?"

"No, but I can—"

"No was all I needed," Pip told him and marched past. By chance, Tom was standing at the reception desk looking over some paperwork. She pointed at him as if spotting an imposter and crooked her finger to beckon him. "You!" she somehow shouted without shouting. "You'll do."

"Yes, madam, how may I assist you?" Tom was like a rabbit caught in headlamps. The receptionist, an immaculately presented woman of forty, sitting close by, goggled with fascination.

Pip's incandescence was majestic. "I'd like your expert opinion on what kind of a man gets a girl in trouble and drops her, and what kind of a company fires her because she has a bun in the oven while a duplicitous snake, who can't keep his trousers on, stays in his job. Any thoughts, Thomas my dear?"

Tom was dumbstruck – whether because he had no answer, or whether because he was trying to work out what duplicitous meant was unclear. The receptionist, however, had no such problems.

"Who has been fired?" she asked.

"Mel," Pip replied, without breaking eye contact with her former boyfriend.

"Well, that is very interesting," the receptionist stated with a coldness directed to Tom that would make a penguin shiver, "because only two people could fire Mel. Mr Cooper, the owner, who is away this week, and me. Now, unless Mr Cooper magically transported here from Tenerife, or I'm suffering memory lapses, I rather think that someone might have toadied up to his sales manager and got him to make Mel think she was out of a job. Maybe he was planning to tell the rest of us she'd quit."

"I don't know," Tom muttered.

"Well, my little Tom-Tom," the receptionist continued with ill suppressed pleasure, "I am sorry to dash your plans, but let's you and I get something straight. I've known Mr Cooper for twenty-five years and he wouldn't like what's gone on. Mel will be back here on Monday, but you don't have to be. I'm not one to judge, so you'll have your chance to make good, but remember, I decide which customer goes to which salesman and Ford Orions can be taken away from boys with disappointing sales figures. That would be terrible, because someone is going to need to earn lots of money to help with a baby, aren't they, Tom?"

It was a magnificent stampede of words, and several verbal wildebeest had detoured to make sure Tom was well and truly trampled into submission. All he could do was nod, anger oozing from every pore of his skin.

"Now, miss," the receptionist turned to Pip, "how may we help you?"

"I was wondering if you might have any cheaper part exchanges come in? I need an automatic."

"No automatics at the moment, dear, but do pop back any time."

Pip thanked the kind lady and left, hurrying back to Gavin and Mel, who were still awkward in each other's company.

"You've got your job back."

"What?" Mel asked, not daring to understand.

"Your job's still yours," Pip explained. "The guy who fired you couldn't and the people who could didn't." The look on Mel's face showed that things were no clearer. "You're not fired, so you should go back to work."

"But... you're amazing, thank you!"

"It had nothing to do with me, it was your boss on reception. She knows what's what."

After hugging Pip painfully tightly and giving Gavin a relieved smile, Mel hastened back inside, happier than she had been in some time.

"That was a great thing you did, Pip" Gavin said. "I think you're amazing."

"There are plenty that wouldn't agree with you."

"Well, I should have a thing or two to say to anyone who didn't."

A thunder of footsteps caused them to turn. Tom was running towards Pip, focussed on her with tunnel vision. He skidded to a halt, just short of barging into her.

"What are you playing at?" he shouted. "You could have cost me my job!"

"I doubt it," Pip replied, cool as a cucumber, "and that's not why you're upset. You're upset because you got shown up in public."

"Yeah, well what about when everyone hears a druggy slapper like you stuck up for a slut like Mel?"

"They'll think you've got funny taste in girlfriends," Pip retorted. "Come on, Gav, let's go." She turned towards Gavin's car.

"Don't turn your back on me!" Tom shouted, reaching for her shoulder, only to be blocked by the lean body of Gavin. Tom was outraged when he recognised his antagonist. "Oh, it's you – out of my way."

"I think you've said all you need to say." Gavin was resolute.

Tom didn't debate the matter further, but pushed Gavin in the chest, forcing him back a step.

"Get out of the way, that little bitch is getting what's coming to her."

Pip wandered up and peered past Gavin, arms folded.

"The last bloke who thought that got a broken nose," she advised. "Let's just stay far away from each other, OK?"

Tom's fist lashed out, but Gavin pre-empted it and dodged elegantly. A second clumsy swing followed, easily evaded save for a brush of a shoulder.

"I'm about to take the advice of a clergyman," Gavin said, "because I'm tired of this, and of you."

"Yeah, what's that?" Tom taunted.

One of Gavin's fists shot out like a lightning bolt, which Tom saw just in time and managed to parry; but he failed to spot the uppercut on its way from the other hand, which gave him a gentle love-tap under the chin and sprawled him on the ground in a state of confusion.

"He told me to always lead with my left," Gavin explained. "Good advice, I'd say."

"Come on, Rocky," Pip laughed, dragging Gavin away by his elbow.

~ * ~ * ~

Pip and Gavin decided to spend the afternoon visiting the ruins of an ancient castle. Their car hunt proved fruitless, but they were both in good spirits.

"I don't get it," Pip remarked as she shared the sandwiches between them. "If you can box like that, why let yourself get bullied at school?"

"Because I detest violence," Gavin replied. "I can't harm people for myself, but I couldn't let him insult your honour."

"My honour!" Pip snorted into a cheese sandwich. "Oh, Gavin Knight, I could have done with you around so many times over these last years. You live up to your name, don't you? Like a medieval knight rescuing damsels in distress, but I'm more of a serving wench, I'm afraid."

"They are my favourite kind of wench," he laughed as he munched, "because they bring sandwiches. Mind you, they also seem more than capable of looking after themselves."

"I'm not so sure about that," Pip giggled, "but seriously, I half expected to come out of the showroom and discover you proposing to Mel." Gavin's expression brought her up short and her jaw dropped. "You didn't, did you?"

"It seems the right thing to do."

"What, you actually asked her?"

"No, I was working up to it when you came back."

"Sir Gavin," Pip proclaimed in regal tones, "that's the most noble, selfless and above all, daft thing I've ever heard!"

"Yes, well, in the cold light of day—" he began, to justify himself.

"It was eleven-thirty in the morning! There's no lighter bit of day. You don't have to justify yourself, it's marvellous... just so long as you don't actually do it. What would you have done if she had said yes?"

"Married her. Raised the child as mine. Sounds stupid, I suppose?"

"No," she assured him from experience. "No, rash maybe, but not stupid. Beautiful ideas and sentiments can't be stupid. You're a fine man, Gav, a real man, and there aren't many left."

When they had finished eating, they explored the site. The crumbling sandy stone of the castle contrasted with the patchy grass and the gently swaying fir trees behind the old well. The sky was pale blue with a faint grey sheen that you only saw when you stared to the outer reaches of the atmosphere.

They scaled an old stone staircase that once led to somewhere very grand, but now just stopped suddenly at an iron railing high above the ground below; the view was breath-taking, stretching far beyond the limits of their county. Rolling hills, lined with hedges and roads, dotted with trees and speckled with livestock, reached to the horizon, pulling their hearts with a Siren's promise.

"Soon, I'll be going to university in that direction," Gavin said, pointing to a gap between two distant hills where the blue sky shimmered to the Earth; little glints of light were all that could be seen of the cars on the hidden motorway that secretly snaked through the countryside.

"It's hard knowing you're leaving when we've only just found each other again." Pip was not sad, but wistful, thinking of what might have been. Gavin merely nodded; it was too painful to think about.

A tiny brown and cream bird fluttered to land close to them, its feet finding grip in the little holes on the weathered surface of the castle stone.

"Oh, I love wrens," Pip said, "they are so small and plucky."

"Troglodytes troglodytes," Gavin muttered.

"Charming!"

"No, troglodytes troglodytes is the scientific name for a wren," Gavin explained, not realising Pip was joking. "I used to go birdwatching."

"That I can believe," she giggled, quietly so as not to disturb the wren. "But that's a big heavy name for a tiny little bird... I wonder what it wants, I wish I had some food for it."

The wren flew off, as if understanding that Pip was not about to offer sustenance.

"Plenty of wild food for them at this time of year," Gavin said. "Come on, let's go back down."

The steps seemed to be steeper when viewed from above, uneven and full of concealed risk.

"You know why I need an automatic?" Pip asked. "It's because I dislocated my knee and it took a long time to heal, so I couldn't use a clutch." She grabbed his hand with hers. "You need to help me keep my footing. It's time to be a knight-errant again."

Slowly, nervously, they moved down, step by step, inspecting each one with paranoid eyes before trusting their weight to it. Once safely back in the level courtyard, they moved off to look at the old well, not realising that they were still holding hands.

They mutually realised their fingers were interlocked when they stood by the low circular wall that marked the well's perimeter. Neither of them acted to loosen their grip. Gavin summoned years of repressed courage.

"You were always the most beautiful girl at the school," he said, not breaking his gaze into the well's gloomy depths.

"There were loads of prettier girls," Pip laughed. "Sharon for a start. I reckoned you fancied her."

"So much for women's intuition! Anyway, I said beautiful not pretty. They're different, beauty comes from within, it doesn't fade. You'll always be beautiful, because you have a beautiful soul. You never fail people."

"I failed you a few times. What about when you got a bloody nose and your calculator broken? That was my fault. What about letting Tom get in the way of our friendship? I was a shallow, horrid person and I thought you were a computer geek who wasn't interested in girls."

"Well, what do you think about me now?"

"Other than my dad and grandad, I've only admired two men. You're one of them."

"Who was the other?"

"A man called Theo. I loved him, but I couldn't have him."

"There was a girl called Tori in America. I loved her, but it wasn't to be."

"Do you want to know something that may be to your advantage?" Pip asked, suddenly shy.

"Yes, very much," he answered, unexpectedly short of breath.

"I wouldn't mind at all if you were to kiss me, right here, right now."

Still holding hands, he stooped, she tiptoed, and their lips met; man and woman lost sense of time, put painful memories behind them, and recaptured innocence. When they ended their kiss – was it a minute or an hour later? – Pip lowered her heels to the ground and Gavin straightened his back, but they kept eye contact. Only then did she release her grip on his fingers to place her arms around his waist and press her face to his chest.

"That was nice," she murmured. "I'd almost forgotten how it felt."

"What does this mean?" He kissed her head, savouring the scent of her hair.

"I don't know. I'm too broken to know, but I know that right here, right now I'm happy."

Chapter 17

"**A**re you still looking for a car?" Bren asked as she brewed a pot of tea. "Yes," Pip replied, pausing from her ironing to wipe sweat from her forehead with the back of her hand.

"I thought so. Chap down the road from me is selling his Vauxhall Chevette."

"Is it an auto?"

"Yes, he says he prefers them. We were interested in it ourselves, but I had bad news on the job front. Bad for you, too."

"What's happened?"

"The boss has thrown his lot in with that big industrial laundry on the estate. They pick up and deliver to people's houses, so it means folk won't be wanting service washes from this shop. And they'll do ironing too, so there won't be work for you for much longer."

"That's alright, I've got lots of cleaning jobs on. I'll miss our chats, though."

"Tell you what," Bren brightened up, "why don't you come over to ours later? Roy can take you over to see the car and then you can stay for a bit of supper."

That evening, Pip went to Bren's house. The neighbour's car, a gold Vauxhall Chevette, was ideal and after a test drive, Pip paid a deposit and promised to be back the following day with the balance. The meal at Bren's was lamb chops and mashed potatoes, accompanied by a glass of stout to wash it down; it was the obligatory drink for the three adults, while the children enjoyed less malty colas. Pip envied them but drank her stout politely – however, the pudding – tapioca with a spoonful of raspberry jam dolloped in – didn't sit well with it. Thus, Pip gained not only a new car but also a sleepless night of bloated indigestion.

Come the morning, the nocturnal discomfort became a memory and she hurried to the insurance broker for a cover note for the car, and then on to Bren's. The first thing she did after collecting her new pride and joy was take her grandmother for a drive in it. The old lady enthused about how comfortable and spacious it was for a small car, but she soon fatigued and Pip took her back to her room, sitting with her until she dozed off.

Pip's next stop was the hardware store, where she invested in a small set of folding steps, assorted brooms, brushes, dusters, cloths, and a mop and bucket. She carefully stored her purchases in the boot of her car.

An idea had formed in her mind, encouraged by a notice she had spotted that morning while insuring her car at the offices of Jack Stanhope, Insurance Broker. Mr Stanhope was a man of many talents, for he practised as a book keeper, an accountant, an insurance agent, and a wedding car service; the last aspect to his professional life allowed him to own an aging Rolls Royce and claim it as a business expense, although surprisingly few people ever managed to successfully book him.

The entrance to Stanhope's office was situated between two shops on the high street, a butcher and a haberdasher. Its black door featured a prominent brass plaque declaring the business name and services. Pip climbed the narrow staircase to the first floor where the receptionist sat in peroxide and fake leopard skin splendour, unnecessarily touching up her heavy mascara; she mustered the condescension to call through to Mr Stanhope and ask if he could once again spare the time to meet with Miss Raven, and it seemed that he could.

"Back again?" Stanhope asked as Pip entered his office. He was a rotund, balding man sitting, perspiring freely, on a threadbare swivel chair at a large desk in a small room. The leather writing surface was hidden beneath meticulously random piles of paper; it was chaos to any eye except his own, for he knew precisely where everything was. There were two grey metal filing cabinets squashed behind him, with a disinterested Siamese cat lolling across their tops. The walls, not wallpapered for at least two decades, were yellowing, probably a result of years of cigarette smoke. Stanhope gestured to one of two chairs, which looked like they may have been pilfered from the 1950s, signalling that Pip should make herself comfortable.

"Yes, I'm back," she replied. "That sign in reception about a phone answering service, is it still available?"

"It is," Stanhope replied, rubbing his hands together. "I've a spare line coming in on a number I don't use any more – a will-writing service that lacked the longevity of its customers. Are you interested?"

"Could be."

"Thirty quid a week." Stanhope lit a cigarette as if to underline the reasonableness of his offer. He read her reaction. "Alright, twenty-five."

"A week?" Pip laughed and stood up. "Sorry to have wasted your time."

"No, don't go. Did I say the twenty-five includes an office?"

"No, but I don't want one."

"OK, fifteen."

"Ten," Pip offered with undoubtable finality.

"OK, ten," Stanhope huffed, holding his hand out.

"Including the office," Pip stated, just before she shook his hand.

"I thought you didn't want it?" he said, shell-shocked.

"Yeah, but you're not using it, are you?"

"I suppose not…"

"Tell you what," Pip pressed, "make it a fiver and I'll clean your offices for you twice a week for free."

"What, the toilet too?" Stanhope asked, his eyes narrowing with opportunity.

"Yes, the toilet too."

"Well, my customers might like that. You drive a hard bargain, Miss Raven, but you've got yourself a deal."

Back home, Pip used pieces of thick white cardboard and a set of poster paints to create two signs, which she stuck in the rear side windows of the car. Decorated with happy flowers, they read 'Pipsqueaky-clean Cleaning Services' and her new telephone number was underneath.

"Very nice," said Lyn when she came outside to see. "Almost as nice as you've got the garden looking."

"Thank you," Pip said with great satisfaction. "Well, I've really started my own business now!"

~ * ~ * ~

Bren struggled to remain positive surveying the empty launderette. A few machines whirred, but it was nothing to the hubbub of activity when she had started working there two decades ago; in those days of friendships and camaraderie, people, mainly women, would be in and out all the time, stopping for a chat or asking her to watch a toddler while they ran an errand.

She wandered into the back room where Pip was ironing.

"That's your last batch ever," Bren said. "Well, here, anyway."

"It's sad. It's only been weeks, but it's a big part of my life."

"Well, think how I feel, getting the boot after nigh on twenty years," Bren said, close to tears. "They said there'd be some part-time, but even that's not happening now. What am I going to do at my age?"

"Come and work with me?" Pip suggested. "Business partners. There must be loads of work round where you live, we could drop leaflets and drum up business. If we do a good job, we'll build up a reputation. Come on, you know we'd have a laugh together."

"I don't suppose I have much to lose, so why not?"

"Well, don't be too enthusiastic," Pip laughed.

The door to the launderette opened, and a tall elderly man dressed in tweed slowly entered. He walked to the notice board and studied a poster for Pip's cleaning services, unsteadily moving closer, peering until he could read the telephone number. He produced a small brown leather notebook from his jacket pocket and jotted some notes.

"Can I help you?" Pip asked, causing the old man to start slightly and turn to look at her. She gestured to Bren. "That's our business."

"Most fortuitous," the man replied, pushing his horn-rimmed glasses back to the bridge of his long convex nose. "I am seeking someone to undertake household duties which I am presently unable to perform for myself. Nothing difficult, you understand, merely cleaning the kitchen and – er – bathroom facilities, and dusting and vacuuming. My name is Swann, and you are Miss…?"

"Raven," Pip told him. "We'd be very happy to help, Mr Swann."

"How soon would you be able to attend?" A note of anxiety in his voice suggested urgency.

"Two o'clock this afternoon, if you like," Pip said. "What's the address?"

"The Rear Flat, 15b Burrow Gardens. Do you know where that is?"

"Yes, just up from St Michael's Church."

"Indeed, the bells of St Michael's are my Sunday morning wake up call."

"Super. See you at two."

The old man nodded amiably, his grey eyes lingering on Pip, making sure he would remember what she looked like, before he made his slow, dignified departure.

"See?" Pip said to Bren. "Another client and we've not even started advertising."

~ * ~ * ~

Fifteen Burrow Gardens was an imposing red-brick Edwardian building, with tall white sash-windows and a crimson glossed front door; a panel of doorbells indicated that the once great house had been converted into luxury apartments some years beforehand. To the right was a blue, solid gate with '15b – Rear Flat' neatly written in white paint; it led into a narrow passageway running down the side of the big house. The brick wall on the right of the alley had been painted many years ago with a bright mural of intertwined flowers, but the colours were faded from decades of neglect.

At the end of the passage stood a rusted dustbin, and to the left was a white door marked 'Rear Flat'. Pip gave two raps using the brass doorknocker above the letterbox. The catch turned, and the door creaked open. Mr Swann peered out.

"Ah, Miss Raven. You are very punctual. Do come in."

Pip entered the short, narrow, whitewashed hallway, featureless except for a long-neglected vacuum cleaner and five coat-hooks, from which hung a tired greatcoat, an umbrella, and a dog's leash. On the floor were two pairs of shoes, one dark brown and the other black; both bore the well-polished traits of a former military man's care. The only inner door was to the right, and it was there that Mr Swann bade her follow.

A small dachshund came scampering towards Pip, tail wagging happily; she stooped to fuss the creature and received some affectionate licks.

"He's adorable," she said, "what's his name?"

"Oscar."

"Hello, Oscar! You're lovely, yes you are."

Oscar yapped, sharing Pip's sentiments.

"This is our home," said Mr Swann.

His entire domicile was a sizeable lounge leading to a smaller bedroom via an arch with concertina doors. As Pip stood in the doorway, the archway was directly ahead of her, and a small kitchenette was to its left. The living room was dark and dusty. Heavy burgundy curtains hung from just below the high ceiling to the rose carpet on the floor, blocking out any natural light from the window behind save for tiny bright pinpricks in the fabric. The furnishings were classical; two high-backed reading chairs with footstools, a settee with a floral pattern, some rosewood side tables, a mahogany dining table with four matching chairs, several standard lamps, a freestanding gramophone, and an ornate marble fireplace in which an anachronistic two-bar electric heater sat unused. Pip also counted no fewer than eight tall bookcases packed with volumes of varying sizes, and two writing desks, one unused and the other scattered with paperwork. Pictures hung in all the spare space in the walls, right up to the ceiling; landscapes, still-lives, and animal studies, all oils and dark with aged varnish.

Mr Swann said nothing as Pip walked through his small home, although he winced with embarrassment when she entered the sleeping area. It contained a large rosewood wardrobe, a double bed, a bedside table and lamp, Oscar's basket, another electric fire, and several more bookshelves. This area was lighter, with an arched stained-glass window set high in the wall which afforded no view to anyone without a stepladder; beams of red and green illuminated the old man's ruckled, unmade sheets and blankets. A sliding door revealed a small but functional bathroom, which backed onto the kitchenette.

"Where would you like me to start, sir?" Pip asked. She unslung a large bag from her shoulder and unzipped it to access her essential cleaning kit.

"In the kitchen, I think," he replied. "I fear I am on very limited means, so please do not exceed two hours' work."

In the kitchen, Pip realised the size of the task that lay ahead of her. The surfaces had food congealed upon them, spillages were baked onto the electric hob, the oven appeared broken and unused, and the refrigerator smelt rank. At least the washing machine appeared to be new, all crockery and cutlery was clean and stowed neatly away, and Oscar's bowls were well tended. She donned her rubber gloves and set to work on the countertops. Mr Swann settled into one of the nearby wing chairs, flicked on a lamp and began to read.

"What are you reading?" she asked, trying to make conversation.

He closed his eyes, unaccustomed to being interrupted.

"Poetry. Wordsworth, who I believe is sadly lacking from the modern educational syllabus."

Pip smiled and recited from memory.

"'*For oft, when on my couch I lie*
In vacant or in pensive mood,
They flash upon that inward eye
Which is the bliss of solitude;
And then my heart with pleasure fills,
And dances with the daffodils'."

"Most people don't start with the last verse." Mr Swann's pleasure was evident.

"But it's my favourite. It's about drawing peace from remembered beauty. When I'm not with my roses, or reading or writing, it's what I do, even if a room is full of people."

"And you like poetry?"

"I do, very much."

"Then, while you work, I shall read to you."

He was true to his word. As she washed and scrubbed, and polished, he delved deep into the volume before him, sweetening the air with honey-coated verse. However, gradually his voice slowed and quietened until he slumbered into his own blissful solitude; Oscar snoozed too, resting upon his master's slippered feet.

When Mr Swann awoke with a start, he detected the faint odour of lemon detergent. The kitchenette gleamed, and the washing machine hummed quietly. He looked blearily at his watch and discerned that it was six o'clock; his book of poetry lay closed on the table beside him, his glasses folded on top.

Once his spectacles were restored to the bridge of his nose, he observed that the room seemed tidier and less dusty. He nodded, pleased that Miss Raven had achieved so much in just two hours, but satisfaction turned to mortification when he realised that she had left without payment, presumably unwilling to stir him from sleep.

Making his way into the bedroom, he found the bed freshly made, the surfaces dust free, and the mirror on the wardrobe clear and bright. A strange squeaking came from the bathroom, and he slid the door back to find Pip bending over the side of the bath, vigorously removing the yellow-grey tide-mark ingrained on the white porcelain.

"Why are you still here?" he asked, anxious and annoyed in equal measure. "I specifically stated that I could only pay for two hours."

"That's alright," she replied, as bright as the sparkle of the polished chrome taps, "it's my company policy. Two extra hours on the first visit, as a free taster, so to speak. That way, if you still want me to come regularly, then I've got a head start." She was so earnest, that Mr Swann had to believe her. Pip silently congratulated herself on her new policy, limited to just one client. "Anyway, all that lovely poetry you read me had to be worth something."

"You enjoyed it?"

"I did."

"Then we shall repeat the exercise next week, if you are agreeable?"

"I am," she said, turning to finish the bath.

"Miss Raven."

"Yes, sir?"

"Two additional hours would have brought you to six o'clock. It is now more than five minutes past. The bath can wait, thank you."

Pip didn't argue but packed away her materials and allowed Mr Swann to count her payment into the palm of her hand with tremulous fingers.

"Thank you," she said, "would you like a receipt?"

"That is quite unnecessary."

"That's what everybody keeps telling me," Pip sighed, "so why did I buy a receipt book? On my course I was told we had to do invoices and receipts."

"Well, I hadn't realised the serious import of your question," Mr Swann smiled, "I think perhaps a receipt is in order."

Pip ecstatically pulled a blue book and a pen from her bag, and gleefully wrote out receipt number 00001. "Thank you," she said, "you're very kind."

"I rather think that I stand pale in comparison to your own generosity, Miss Raven."

"Most people call me Pip."

"Why Pip?"

"It's short for Philippa. My dad called me Pip, because of Great Expectations."

"Your father is a man of excellent taste," Mr Swann said, "but there could be no doubt about that, given his daughter's nature. My son was a Philip, and my wife and I called him Pip too, for much the same reason, but that was long before you were born, before your father too, I suspect."

Pip sensed it was not the time to ask further, nor to point out that Great Expectations was one of only three books that her father had ever read. Instead she held out her hand, and the elderly man shook it. His fingers were cool and gentle, like a breeze on a hot day that makes you want to climb to the summit of a hill just to feel its full effect.

"Until next week, two o'clock," she said. Oscar bounded over to say goodbye and she knelt to hug him. "And I'll see you too, Mr Bouncy."

She saw herself out, serenaded by barks of adoration.

~ * ~ * ~

Gavin found Pip in the back garden of Lyn's house, wrestling with an obstinate fuchsia.

"We've been invited to a party," he announced.

Pip stood up and brushed her hands on the legs of her jeans.

"We?" she asked. "I don't get invited to parties."

"Don't be so sceptical, when Lucy heard that we were together, she wanted you to come too."

"Lucy? Lucy Barrow?" Pip exclaimed.

"Yes, she and Heather are heading back to uni and they're holding a goodbye bash. I bumped into Lucy earlier."

"Gavin! Lucy and Heather are the daughters of high-flying legal types." Pip wasn't sure why she was so annoyed. "Your dad's a company bigwig, so you fit in but what do you reckon they think of someone like me?"

"They never gave you trouble."

"No, but they never invited me to anything ever before."

"Well, I said we'd go."

"You should've checked!" Pip now knew why she was annoyed. "I thought we agreed that we don't know what this thing between us is – I've been through a rough time and you're on the rebound, but suddenly we're invited somewhere as a couple."

"You're right," Gavin was contrite, "I got carried away. It's just that I've liked you for so long."

"And I like you too, very much. Let's just go slow, OK? So, when is this party?"

"Seven."

"Seven? This evening? In two hours? Well, thanks for all the warning! I haven't even got an outfit."

"Well, I only knew today. Sorry."

"Oh, don't worry," Pip sighed, "I'll figure something out. I need a shower, so come back and get me at six-thirty."

Half an hour later, Pip sat on the edge of Lyn's bed, wrapped in a bath towel, fixing her hair. She was still spending the nights on the sofa, and Mark's room was a mess of decorating materials, so she kept her few clothes and personal effects in suitcases in Lyn's bedroom. She was filled with dread. Heather and Lucy were very particular girls, not the kind who turn up to a party in jeans and a t-shirt. Pip had but one outfit that wouldn't draw comment, but it needed courage to wear again. The shoes were fine; she occasionally wore them for other reasons, liking the boost it gave her in height. The miniskirt was OK, too, especially if she wore some tights this time, but the lilac top was a problem. There was no point asking Lyn if she had anything because Lyn didn't do youth fashion.

"Pull yourself together," Pip told herself. "Make some happy memories and then you can wear it any time." She donned the clothes and added flesh tights and a light cream cardigan.

"Wow!" exclaimed Gavin when she came down the stairs. "You look lovely."

Pip laughed and kissed him lightly on the lips. "Come on, or we'll be late."

Dire Straits' 'Money for Nothing' throbbed into the evening from the open front door of the party house, a large late '30s mock-Tudor building, with a long driveway snaking through the meticulous garden. Gavin strived not to seem impatient as his date repeatedly stopped at the rose bushes that lined their progress, sniffing the blooms and casting a critical eye over their condition.

"When did you become so interested in flowers anyway?" he asked.

"Roses mainly," she replied, dreamily distracted by the plants. "They're my joy."

The hostesses seemed pleased to see them, hugging Pip as if she were a third sister and kissing Gavin as if he were anything but their brother. After a Bacardi and Coke or two, Pip started to believe that she was going to enjoy herself. They went into the living room and danced without inhibition amongst the other guests.

"It's hot," Pip said as she took off her cardigan. She popped up, quickly kissed Gavin on the lips, and pulled him down for a longer follow-up.

Berlin's 'Take my breath away' came on and the slow dancing began; people held someone close to them, moving in synchronicity, sometimes kissing. Pip and Gavin stopped any pretence of dance when Simple Minds began playing.

"We'll never forget each other, will we?" she asked, as the lyrics pressed home.

"Impossible," he replied, feeling her hands reach behind his head and pull him down to her. This was a new level of passion between them, impossible to know when and how they breathed. Pip stepped back, leading him, looking him in the eyes until she felt the wall behind her and they pressed ever tighter, bodies tingling, lips once again meeting.

Gavin's touch travelled from her hands, up her arms, thrilling her. In the background the music changed again and the opening chords of 'Every Step You Take' resonated around the room, just as his hands reached her shoulder. In a quantum instant, every feeling in her switched from pleasure to horror. They were not Gavin's fingers moving past the straps of the lilac top, they were the nicotine-stained bony digits of a foul old man, and she once again smelt his stale tobacco breath.

"Please stop," she begged, "oh, no, please no!"

"Are you OK, Pip?" Gavin broke away in puzzlement.

His voice must have attracted the attention of other people in the room, because Pip saw faces slowly turn to look at her, distorted, full of judgment.

"I'm sorry," she said, her voice tiny and inaudible, "I have to— I can't—"

She ran blindly from the room, up the stairs, frantically looking for the bathroom. At last, she found it and was about to enter when someone asked, "Are you feeling alright?" She turned, twisted in just the wrong way and felt the monstrous pop in her knee. Pip's scream rebounded through the house, stopping everyone in their tracks. People ran to see what had happened, but the bathroom door was now locked. Heather was the first of the hostesses to arrive.

"Who is in there?" she asked.

"Pip Raven," someone replied.

"Pip, Pip, can you hear me?" she called as she knocked. "It's Heather, can you let me in?"

Lucy hurried to join her sister.

"Open up, please, Pip!" she called, with more authority.

The lock clicked, and the door opened. Pip was perched at the foot of the bath, a large towel wrapped around her body, her leg in an awkward position.

"Oh, bloody hell, look at her knee," someone said.

"I think I'm going to be sick," said another.

"Why don't you all just bugger off?" Heather said. "Leave her to me, Lucy, and Gav. Someone call for an ambulance, will you?"

The other people left, and the sound of a 999 call being made travelled up the stairs. Pip's lilac top lay on the floor.

"What's wrong, Pip? It's not just the leg, is it?" Lucy asked.

Maybe affected by pain and alcohol, Pip suddenly started to tell them about Simpkins, about Adam and about Glenda and Charlotte. Three worried faces bore increasingly shocked expressions, tears of empathy and sympathy mixed with anger on her behalf. Heather held her close.

"Lucy, darling, get Pip something of yours she can wear, please," she instructed, but her sister was already on her way and quickly returned with a navy cotton top.

"Gavin, be a dear and push off for a couple of minutes while we help get Pip in shape for the ambulance people. Thanks," Heather said.

"I'm so sorry, Gav," Pip said, her voice faint, "I'm a terrible date. I'm sorry I got upset."

"You have nothing to apologise for," he told her, "but the people that did that to you have. I'll bloody kill them."

Lucy went with Gavin, leaving Pip with her sister.

"Don't say things like that, about killing people," she said. "We all feel it, but don't, because it's not in Pip's nature. You must know that."

"Sorry."

"Don't be," she touched his arm reassuringly. "I'm going to send everyone home – they're a bunch of leeches anyway – will you give me a hand?"

The flashing blue lights of the ambulance were outside and two uniformed medical experts were soon with Pip, while the deflated partygoers made their collective departure.

Later, when the Barrow sisters' parents had returned home, Pip sat propped up on the couch and was being made a fuss of.

"No arguments," Heather insisted, "you're staying here tonight. The ambulance men said you should be back to normal by Monday at the latest, so be our guest for a bit, OK? We've lots of rooms."

"Thank you," Pip accepted. "Gavin, will you let Lyn know, please?"

"Yeah, I'll call her now. May I use your phone, please, Heather?"

"In the kitchen."

As Gavin left, Lucy came in.

"Pip," she said, "my mum wants to talk to you. I've told her what happened to you. She's a solicitor. Those pigs mustn't get away with it, and Mum can help."

"But I couldn't afford to pay her," Pip protested.

"She wouldn't want you to. Mum's got a bit of a bee in her bonnet about this sort of thing."

"Alright," Pip found determination, "I'm not afraid any more."

~ * ~ * ~

"How is your friend Pip's leg, Gavin?" Mrs Knight asked as her son emerged from his slumberous pit and graced the family at the breakfast table.

"Fine," he replied, helping himself to cereal. "She was back at work on Monday."

"She certainly has an excellent work ethic," his father remarked.

"Pip's pretty amazing." Gavin crunched his cornflakes.

"I do wish you wouldn't talk with your mouth full," his mother sighed. "Did you see there was post for you on the hall table?"

Gavin had not spotted the mail, so he bolted down the last of his breakfast and went to collect it. The handwriting was unmistakeably Tori's and his heart skipped a beat; he ran to his room and opened it in private.

'*Dear Gavin,*

Thank you for your letter, it meant a lot to me. Please don't reproach yourself for what happened, it was my dream and my mistake. I was angry with you, but I knew in my heart I was wrong. Miss Lucille wrote me a while back and put things straight in my mind.

You're right, I lost everything, but I am a big girl and knew the risks. Paul is back in our lives now, which almost makes it worthwhile. I don't mind about losing my college fund, but I do mind that I lost you. I never expected you to come into my life and I never dreamt that I could be so stupid as to lose you. I guess when we are angry, we hurt those we love the most. I ended up breaking my own heart and yours too. I am so sorry.

Gavin, I love you. Is there a way back for us? We talked about a long-distance relationship. Would you be willing to forgive me and try?

All my love

Tori'

Gavin sat in a soup of confusion, rereading the letter multiple times. He reacted emotionally and physically, as if the paper in his hand were a part of Tori – he pictured her curly hair brushing the corners of the envelope when she had licked and sealed it and was sure that some of her scent must be infused in its fibres.

But then he thought of Pip. Perfect Pip. They had stepped back from one another since the party and he knew she felt embarrassed and guilty. Gavin needed to talk to her, to understand what she wanted and how she felt about him.

He tried to push the matter to the back of his mind and joined his parents in the kitchen, but was preoccupied and untalkative, contemplating his cup of tea.

"Well, you are a chatterbox," his mother remarked dryly. "I can't imagine how we'll manage for conversation when you're at university."

"Sorry, I was just thinking."

"Well don't exert yourself, son," Mr Knight chuckled, "save your brain cells for your degree."

"I was thinking of having a party." Gavin saw the surprise on his parents' faces and added, "More of a dinner party. Here, at the weekend, if that is convenient? To say goodbye to my friends. Just a few people – Pip, Lucy and Heather, their boyfriends, and the guys from London."

"A dinner… party?" Mrs Knight stifled a smirk. "You're going to cook a dinner party?"

"Yes, I can cook."

"Gavin, my lad," his father interjected, "scrambled eggs with beans on toast, do not a dinner party make."

"I'll figure something out."

"You mean conscripting poor Philippa," Mrs Knight tutted. "No, I'll make a casserole and you can heat it up. You can do baked potatoes and sort out the veg yourself."

"Thanks, Mum. If one of your chocolate cakes was in the fridge, I suppose we could have that for dessert."

"The odds of that are approximately equal to the downstairs of the house having been dusted, polished, cleaned, and vacuumed by Friday... by you, Gavin – no getting Pip to do it, even if she is a professional."

~ * ~ * ~

Pip arrived at Mr Swann's flat at exactly two minutes to two and knocked on the door. He seemed agitated when he opened the door.

"Ah, Miss Raven, I wonder if you would take Oscar for a walk? I have been unable to and he needs to relieve himself."

The weather had been dry and clement all day, so Pip wondered why the dog had not already been taken out, but she happily took Oscar to the nearby park for a pleasant half an hour.

"It's glorious out there, it's a shame you couldn't join us," she said when they returned.

"I should have liked to," Mr Swann replied.

Pip scanned him, her eyes moving down his usual old tweed suit, until she noted the bare tops of his feet, just visible between the uppers of his slippers and the ends of his trouser legs.

"It is rather embarrassing, but I could not get my socks on today," Mr Swann stammered, holding the offending hosiery up. "I was trying again just as you returned."

"I had just the same problem over the weekend," Pip said. "Sit down and I'll help."

"I could not possibly ask you to do that. Above and beyond the call of duty."

"Not above and beyond friendship, though. Please." Pip led an embarrassed Mr Swann to a chair where he allowed her to roll the socks over his bony feet. "I'm going to give you my home phone number. Call me if you need help in the mornings. I could stop off on my way to work. I wouldn't charge. Please, I'd get to see Oscar too."

"Well, if you are sure?" he wavered.

"It's settled," Pip closed the deal. "Is calling me by seven too early? Otherwise I may have already left."

"That would be most satisfactory, thank you."

"Good. Now, I'll crack on with work. Let's see, it's two thirty now, so I'll be out of your hair by half-past four."

"But you walked Oscar for half an hour," Mr Swann pointed out.

"That wasn't work, that was fun. Now, shall I make a proper job of the living room today?"

"Um, could you start in the kitchen? I have not yet had an opportunity to wash up."

"Of course." Pip turned on the water at the sink.

"Where shall we start reading today?" Mr Swann asked, picking up his book. "Byron?"

~ * ~ * ~

Gavin began to panic. There were no potatoes and his mother had specifically said that there were potatoes to be found; all he had to do was wash them, prick them and put them in the oven with the casserole, but that presumed the presence of potatoes and he was becoming increasingly convinced that there were none. Maybe it was a cruel practical joke on the part of his parent, maybe she and his father were at Karen's and all were laughing at his expense – oh, the hilarity that he should be serving up casserole and have no baked potatoes to accompany it.

The doorbell chimed - could it be the first guest come early? He hadn't even finished changing, because he had suddenly realised that there was a potato issue. He tutted and ran to the door, fearing his vegetable-related shame might be revealed before he had even had a chance to numb the humiliation with alcohol.

Alcohol! He had forgotten to get drinks – no wine, no beers, no anything. Crisis was sliding towards disaster.

"It's awful!" he declared as he opened the door to reveal Pip, who was smiling and posing on the doorstep to show off her new electric-blue dress.

"Well, that's charming!" Pip's smile changed to an expression of wounded pride. "What's wrong with it? I spent ages picking it out, just for your effing party." She pushed past him and peered at herself in the hallway mirror.

"No, not you, you look nice."

"Nice? That's not much better than awful."

"Sorry, you look fantastic. It's everything else that is awful."

"Well, that's more like it. What's the problem?"

"Um, no drink. I forgot to buy any," Gavin whined.

"Um, no, you asked me to pick it up and it's in the boot of my car waiting for your manliness to carry it inside."

"Oh. OK, I'll get it now," he muttered, preoccupied by potatoes.

"I don't know what this neighbourhood is like," Pip said, grabbing Gavin's elbow, "and I'm not saying that you don't have a nice pair of legs, but maybe you should put on some trousers first?"

"What?" He looked down in shock; his hairy legs were displayed between his boxers and his socks. "Ah, yes, I was halfway through changing when I realised about potatoes."

"Potatoes?"

"Yes, potatoes."

"You've only just realised about potatoes? Any specific ones, or are you going all Walter Raleigh on me?"

"No, no! The potatoes for the meal, they have vanished – or it's a plot and they were never there. My mother wishing to humiliate me."

Pip became matter-of-fact and marched into the kitchen.

"Don't be ridiculous," she said. "What exactly was the very, very last thing that your mum said, just before she left?"

"That everything was sorted, and I was to put the oven on at 170 degrees for an hour and a half."

Pip opened the oven to reveal the casserole pot on one shelf, and multiple jacket potatoes on another. "Ta da!"

"How did you know?" he asked.

"Either telepathy, or we both know you and your memory," Pip laughed. "You decide."

"I'm not that forgetful!" Gavin protested.

"Says the boy who still hasn't put his trousers on! Come on, let's get you dressed."

"Do you want to come up with me? You could see my Airfix collection."

"Well, if you put it like that..." Pip waggled her eyebrows. As they made their creaky progress upstairs, she asked, "Who's coming tonight?"

"Lloyd and Darren, Lucy and her boyfriend, Heather, she's just broken up with someone, and us two."

Gavin shyly showed Pip into his room and began pointing to various carefully constructed scale models dotted about the place.

"This is my Apollo Eleven," he explained, absorbed by his love for his hobby. "These planes are a Spitfire, a Hurricane, and a Messerschmitt. And these are—"

"Oh, my! You're actually showing me your Airfix!"

"Aren't you interested?"

"I will be once you've put your trousers on."

"Sorry," he apologised, pulling on a pair of black jeans. "There. What's wrong?"

Pip's countenance was one of sadness. She stared at a piece of paper sitting prominently on his desk; the signature at the bottom of the handwriting was unmistakeable.

"Is that a letter from Tori?" she asked.

"Yes," Gavin was contrite and honest, "I didn't know how to answer, I wanted to talk to you. I wanted to understand where we are."

"May I read it?" Pip needed to understand.

Gavin nodded and passed the letter. Pip's soft eyes absorbed the words on the paper and then dripped their import down to her heart.

"She loves you very much," she said when she finished, with a softness that belied hurt. "A letter like that is so… raw. Tell me about her."

"Are you sure you want me to?"

"Yes."

"She's lovely." Gavin sat on his bed, simultaneously guilty and proud. "I was sure she was the love of my life. She is clever, and funny, and—"

"Pretty?"

"Yes. And she's strong, but fragile too – I think she needs me."

"And you need her too?"

"Yes," Gavin said, wretched. "You see, I love her, but not like I love you. You're the perfect woman. I've always thought so."

"I'm not, and when you found that out, you won't find it so easy to love me."

"You've an inner strength that I don't think you realise. Whether it's internal or external, something insulates your soul from the harshness of this world and makes you fearless."

"That's kind of you, Gav, but I'm just as broken and afraid as anybody else – more so. You saw me at that party!"

"But that's just it! Look how far you got by yourself and look how little you needed from the rest of us. Other people's darkness doesn't taint you. It can't reach your heart to poison it. You'll always be self-sufficient."

Pip didn't know how to receive this praise, because it felt more like a curse. It implied she would never need anyone on a spiritual level, and that felt a lonely proposition. If she truly was insulated and independent, then it was imposed on her by events rather than being innate; it was a protective shell resultant from repeated betrayal, dashed hopes, and cruel abuse. She reacted no differently to anyone else - was she to be punished yet more by a life of loneliness? No. Gavin was wrong, she would trust again, she would love unconditionally and freely, but she needed a man who understood that.

"You make me sound like a nun," she said.

"No, you are too passionate, too real, but far above anyone else I've known, and you always have been. I'm almost frightened to love you."

Pip was shocked. Frightened to love her! Had she become so inaccessible, so damaged, so fault-riddled that to love her was too intimidating, even for the gentlest of men like Gavin? Or was it possible that he unknowingly created this barrier because he had deeper feelings for Tori?

"But you do love me?" she asked.

"Yes. I always have, I think."

"But Tori isn't perfect, and you still love her?"

"I do, but I don't know if I trust her. I'd need to know if her anger truly has gone. I'm not trying to two-time anyone. I was going to tell Tori that I'd found someone else, but I couldn't bring myself to write it and I don't know why."

"I think I do," Pip said with a wry smile. "Gavin, you don't love me, not like you do Tori, and to be honest, I'm not sure how I feel about you. You see in me the girl who you knew at school, but she's gone. Perhaps we'd make each other happy, but Tori might make you ecstatic. You need to find out if you two can work it out. Don't make her lose her happiness as well as her money."

"What are you saying? I can't lose you, Pip." Gavin had tears in his eyes.

"You won't, we'll just be how we were before. It's not a bad thing, I'm not hurt, I promise. You see, I don't think you'd have invited Tori up to your bedroom and then showed her your Airfix collection. Don't worry, it's happened to me before."

"But, Tori's in America and I'm in Britain."

"That sounded like you only wanted me because I'm here and she's there," Pip strived not to be angry, "but I am sure you didn't mean that. No, you'll just have to write to her until you can afford to see her. Now, I'm going downstairs while you finish dressing. Then you can get all the drink in from my car, because I really, really need one. Thanks for showing me your Airfix models."

Within seconds, she was on the way downstairs, holding back her tears.

~ * ~ * ~

"Thanks again, Gav, good luck at uni!" Darren and Lloyd shouted as they departed. The party had been so much fun that they had stayed much later than intended, leaving only when Gavin's parents returned home. The two friends hurried into the night, skirting through the streets and using the shortcuts that Darren knew so well.

"That Heather seemed to like you," Darren said. "Did you get her number?"

"Yeah," Lloyd replied, "but I don't know if I'll call. She's nice and all, but I think she just wants to shock her right-on parents by bringing home a working-class black boy. That Pip girl is more my type, but I think she's Gavin's girl."

"I'm not so sure. They didn't seem very lovey-dovey and I think she looked sad."

"Maybe, but Gav's a nice guy, so I wouldn't want to move in on his bird."

"I'm sure he will be eternally grateful," Darren remarked with his usual dry wit. "You're certainly sure of yourself."

"The ladies do love us musicians."

"Well, that's not much use to me!"

Lloyd laughed and patted his friend on the back.

"It's nice here," he said, "you're lucky to have grown up in this town."

"It's not so great when you live here, believe me," Darren looked around with disdain, "and it's worse when it looks like you'll have to come back."

"Are things that bad?"

"Worse. Will's in a job he hates, I'm working in that bloody hotel, and our music's going nowhere. I've got an uncle who'll pay three times what I'm earning if I go and learn plastering with him. Anyway, you're off to Manchester soon, so what's the point of us staying?"

"That's a bit dramatic, mate," Lloyd laughed. "Manchester's hardly the height of excitement."

"You're following your dream – a doctorate, a career!" Darren became emotional. "You don't know how lucky you are!"

"I could say the same to you, growing up here," Lloyd countered.

They arrived at the station – just in time to see the last train pulling away.

"We'll have to doss down at my parents' place," Darren said. He found the walk depressingly familiar, but Lloyd was still taken with the town.

Darren's mother greeted them at the door, pleased to see her son and fascinated by his exotic friend. She bustled around and plied them with food while she made up the spare bedroom. Then she settled down to chat to the boys over a pot of fresh tea at the kitchen table. Her husband returned from the pub, looked at the visitors, picked up his tea, and departed, gesturing that his wife should follow; with a sigh, she complied, returning a few minutes later.

"Your dad wants to speak to you in private." She rolled her eyes. "Nip and have a chat, will you?"

Darren entered the living room, shutting the door behind him. His inebriated father was red-faced.

"So, lad, you like to humiliate us in every way, don't you?"

"How?" Darren had a familiar sinking feeling.

"You and your dark friend through there, coming here like two sick little lovebirds." Darren's father spat his words as if fearful of contamination. "I mean, is it so hard for you to be happy with just breaking our hearts by acting—"

"Gay?" Darren suggested, not caring if he was playing with fire.

"You don't seem very happy to me."

"Jollity is difficult when your dad hates you," Darren etched his words with acid.

"Do you blame me? Turning up out of the blue parading your new lover, a Nancy-boy nigg—"

"Don't you dare use that word," Darren's ire shocked his father who involuntarily stepped back, "not about him. You know something? Lloyd's straight, I wish he wasn't, but he is. But you're right, I love him – I love the music within him, it's… transcendent, like listening to God."

Unsure how to process the words as well as his son's anger, the father swayed. He took a swig of tea, but it was too hot, and scalded his mouth. He swore.

"Yeah, that's about the size of it, Dad," Darren sneered. "You jumped to conclusions because you like finding the worst in me. I met Lloyd trying to help a good man who died because he couldn't bear to lose his daughter, and I bring him here to meet a man who can't wait to get rid of his son. We'll go now, before my way of life or his skin colour disgust you any further."

Darren stormed to the door but was stopped by his father's voice.

"Don't go, son!"

"Why?"

"Because… well, for your mum." The father sank into a chair.

"I'll tell you what, Dad, if you can look past all the things you hate about me and say one good thing, I'll stay."

The older man sat silently.

"Exactly." Darren's heart broke. "It's a bloody shame, Dad."

"Wait! I admire you, Darren… I admire your strength."

Darren was startled – his father was intimidatingly powerful, whereas he was small and thin. Was this drunken sarcasm?

"When I was a lad," the older man explained, "my old ma paid for me to have trumpet lessons. I was quite good. She wanted me to learn the trombone because she liked Glenn Miller so much, but the pawn shop only had a trumpet. I loved the big band stuff, you know, Sinatra, Dean Martin, Nat King Cole, Sammy Davis Junior."

"I didn't know you were musical." Darren overlooked the irony of his father's racism given some of the names on the list.

"I think I'm where you get it from – sorry if that's a disappointment. Anyway, when I left school, I was offered a chance to be in a band, a bit like you are now, but my pa lost his rag. Why be a musician when I could be earning ten quid a week working beside him? I was too scared to argue, so I flogged the trumpet and went to work, met your mum and got busy making you. You've had the guts to stick to your dream, son, and I respect that."

"Drink your tea, I expect it's cool enough by now," Darren said as he opened the door.

"Are you still going?" asked his father.

"Only as far as the kitchen."

When Darren's parents had gone to bed, the two friends sat up talking. It was surface conversation, listing their ten favourite movies, or Stevie Wonder versus Kraftwerk, or Stevie Wonder versus anybody. Then Lloyd became serious.

"We could hear you and your dad talking earlier. Your mum didn't know what to say, other than asking if I found the weather cold here. I said it's not much worse than Lambeth, but she thought that was somewhere in Africa."

"I'm sorry about them," Darren said. "They aren't bad, it's just their world. No black people live here, and I was the only out gay man."

"Are things really so bad in London that you have to come back here?"

"Yes. I'm skint, so is Will."

"Then come up to Manchester," Lloyd suggested. "Finish up your lease and then both come and join me. I'm in halls, but I pay termly so I can move out after Christmas. We can get a flat together."

"Yes please," Darren said, a little too quickly. "So long as you don't mind living with a queer and a weirdo."

"I hope you don't mind living with a Southern Baptist Stevie Wonder fan," Lloyd laughed. "But don't make fun of Will. He's given up a lot for you."

"For our so-called band, you mean?"

"No, I don't mean that. You don't need half the kit you've got, but Will agreed because you wanted it. He trailed around after us looking for a girl that he had never heard of, just to make you happy. He turns up every night you're playing in that hotel and nurses a half of lager that he can't afford, just to support you. You might call that weird, but I'd call it love."

The barbed arrow of reality hit Darren straight in the heart and he flushed. "How could I be so blind?"

"And I reckon you like him too."

"Oh, I do, I have from the beginning, but I never thought he was interested in me. He told me he's gay when we met, but he never made a move or said anything."

"Well, he wouldn't. Will's got no self-confidence. He acts the way he does because of years of not fitting in."

"Are you sure?" Darren asked, frightened that it might not be true.

"As sure as I am of anything. I just wish I could find a girl who feels the same about me," Lloyd sighed. "Not to seem big-headed, but I've never had trouble attracting girls, but they never stick around."

"You've not met the right one yet, then. That's all."

"Thanks, mate," Lloyd smiled. "You'll come to Manchester? Both of you?"

"If it is what Will wants, then yes."

Chapter 18

"Good afternoon, Mr Swann," Pip said when the door to the flat opened, "and good afternoon, Oscar," she added when her smallest admirer arrived at her feet in excited little leaps and bounds. "Oh, Oscar, what a mess you've made on the floor with your toys. Be careful that your master doesn't trip up on them."

She began picking up chewy toys and a ball, hindered by nuzzles and licks from the little dog.

"Hello, my dear," Mr Swann hovered around, almost as excited as Oscar.

"I've got some leather restorer," Pip said, "I thought I'd give the tops of your desks a going over."

"That is most thoughtful," he said, gathering up his papers.

Pip stowed Oscar's toys in a small basket by the door and began polishing the pale green leather of the unused desk.

"It's hard to see under these lights, may I draw back the curtains?"

"I would prefer that you didn't. My eyes, you see."

"Of course. Silly question: why do you have two desks but only use one?"

"The one before you belonged to my late wife. We worked in here together, for many happy years, researching our interests, she at her desk and I at mine. When she passed, I kept hers as she left it."

"That's a lovely pen," Pip remarked, looking at a slim fountain pen that sat beside an old ink pot.

"We bought matching ones on our thirtieth wedding anniversary."

"May I ask when she passed away?"

"My dear Anna left this world more than twenty years ago, in 1965. We were parted far too soon by the evil corruption that is ovarian cancer. She was a pioneer, a musician and composer, but she had little commercial success, for family reasons. I do have some recordings of her playing, if you would care to hear them?"

"I would like that very much," Pip replied, carefully tending to the leather writing surface.

The old man inspected his shelving, extracted a record from a small selection of albums clustered near the gramophone and placed the vinyl disc on the turntable. Over the faint crackle of needle in groove, the first notes of a bow being drawn across a cello's strings transformed the dim room into a place of exquisite sensory delight. The music was so sublime, so transcendent, that Pip immediately felt nostalgic for each phrase as it passed; it gradually overwhelmed her, and she stopped working. The sound was not sad, nor melancholy, yet it touched that very part of the soul that mourns the promise of long-lost people. Even Oscar seemed transfixed.

At length, Pip managed to return to reality sufficiently to move her hand and the cloth it held. The green leather was regaining some of its old lustre and the gold edging glistered in the yellow light, as if the desk was charmed back to life to by its former owner's music. Pip moved to Mr Swann's workspace and repeated the treatment.

Eventually, the music faded and died, and the record player's arm returned dutifully to its rest, but the ghost of the melody lingered. Oscar sensibly realised that everyone was being much too solemn, and deposited his ball at Pip's feet, his eyes willing her to send it to a corner of the room where it may be pounced upon like dangerous prey. She couldn't deny him that simple pleasure and he soon scampered after his toy with contagious glee.

"That was a piece of my wife's own composition," Mr Swann said as he carefully replaced the record into its sleeve. "*The Wild Roses.*"

"Beautiful. Roses are my favourite plant. All kinds."

"Really? Anna's too. I believe cultivating them gave her the strength to face a future without our Pip, through that darkest of times. People celebrated VE day, but not us, for we were burying our boy."

"Was he killed in the war?" Pip asked tentatively.

"No," Swann replied, heartbroken, "Philip was a spastic. Please don't take offence at the word, I know I should say cerebral palsy these days, but it was a scientific term then and still would be had it not been debased by ignorance."

"Some of the people at school used to say it to be horrid," Pip sympathised.

"Children can be cruel and do not know the hurt they cause," Mr Swann said. "When Philip was born, we lived in the big house, but we needed money for his treatment, so we created this flat and moved in here - it is the former scullery and coalhouse. We sold the main property and travelled with our boy, looking for cures, that he might one day walk or speak. I could tell how intelligent he was, and Anna and I read to him all we could."

"You sound like dedicated parents," Pip said.

"Anna certainly was. We travelled to many spa towns to take the waters. She would push his chair to the edge of the pool, and I carried him in. We laughed and splashed, but there was no change. It should have been a sad time, but the love that we three shared and the blossoming of his uncorrupted soul made them Halcyon days. We had very little money, I had given up my job teaching English and Classics at the Grammar School to assist with Philip's care, and there was no National Health Service as we have today, so our hopes for a cure faded with our fortunes. Our boy passed away, aged seventeen, from perforated ulcers, two days before VE Day."

"I am so sorry."

"No, it is I who should be sorry." Mr Swann straightened himself and his jacket. "It was quite wrong to burden you with my private grief, but I so rarely get to speak of my family, and one day soon, no one will remember them or their story."

"I'll remember," Pip promised. "Please don't apologise. Good friends speak of such things to each other."

"Miss Raven, you have a beautiful turn of phrase, please don't waste it. I very much suspect that you have the soul of a poet. Had you been in my class when I was teaching, I would have loved to guide you... though you may not have liked it, for it was an all-boy establishment."

"My trouble is that I might have liked it too much!" Pip laughed.

~ * ~ * ~

Gavin loaded the last of his suitcases into his increasingly dilapidated car. His father circled the vehicle, kicking the tyres, and trying not to look sad. His mother stood, arms folded, simultaneously miserable and proud that her son was leaving for university. There were several long hugs and multiple checks that he had packed all he needed – Gavin suspected that he had been cajoled into taking enough for several years in the Antarctic, let alone a ten-week university term.

"Ring when you get there," his mother said, her voice croaky. Gavin nodded and gave her one last hug. He was nervous, wondering if the whole idea was a bad one. Maintaining a façade of calm, he was about to get into the car, when a figure appeared at the foot of the driveway. It was Pip.

"I brought you a good luck present," she said, handing him a small package.

"You didn't need to."

"You brought me a card on the day I left all those years ago. Do you remember? You believed me when no one else did."

"I'll always believe in you."

"Did you write to Tori?" Pip asked, hoping that he might say he changed his mind.

"I did. I told her I love her, and I want to work things out, but the last time I saw her she had anger in her eyes and I need to know it's gone before we can truly commit."

"Sensible," Pip said, wishing she was less jealous. "Come on, open your prezzie."

Gavin complied, ripping the shiny paper from the gift, which turned out to be a small paperback book. "*84 Charing Cross Road*. Thank you."

"Next time I'm reading my copy, I'll wonder if you're reading yours and I'll smile," Pip said, hugging him close.

"I am going to miss you so much," he whispered in her ear, just managing to stifle a convulsion of emotion. "You know I love you."

"I do," Pip's lip quivered. "Me too. Now, it's time for you to go off and be very clever."

She was joined by his parents waving as the Marina drove down the road. Gavin tooted his horn and monitored the rear-view mirror until Philippa Raven couldn't be seen any more.

~ * ~ * ~

Lloyd was driven to Manchester for the start of his postgraduate life by Angelique. His mother had also come, meaning he had an uncomfortable journey jammed in the back seat up against his cello case for several hours.

Once at the halls of residence, he unloaded the car, supervised by the two ladies.

When he had dumped the last of his luggage on his bed, Angelique's disgust for the standard of hygiene became unambiguous. She ran a disapproving finger over the basin in the corner of his small room.

"They call this clean?" she asked, displaying her powder-coated fingertip to her assembled family. "Let me go and find someone in charge."

"Please don't, I'll sort it." Lloyd imagined his cousin demanding to oversee the merciless disinfection of the entire building.

Angelique tutted and began rubbing the offending porcelain with a damp tissue. Meanwhile, Lloyd's mother was disapproving of the thin, stained mattress that lay upon the bed; she patted it and coughed dramatically, waving her hand to clear an invisible cloud of dust.

Sensing the mattress was about to be carried downstairs and publicly beaten, Lloyd ushered his grumbling relatives out of the building and towards their car.

"Have we no time for a cup of tea?" his mother asked.

"No, Mum, or you'll catch the rush-hour traffic. Stop for tea at a service station, yeah?"

"Service station tea is undrinkable!" Angelique turned back to the halls. "They don't use properly boiling water."

Lloyd's mother took mercy.

"No, we need to be on our way and my boy needs to start his doctoring." She patted her son's arm. "Study, mind! No spending your time cavorting with these half-dressed girls. Have they no decency?"

The last question was directed at a young woman passing by wearing a fashionable leather miniskirt. She was clearly taken aback but was further admonished by Angelique's tutting and headshaking before she could react. With an apologetic smile, Lloyd dragged his relatives to the car.

After tearful goodbyes he returned to the halls, wiping lipstick from his cheeks and forehead. As he neared his floor, the building vibrated with The Beastie Boys' never soothing tones, and by the time he reached his room, it was intolerably loud. His cohabitants were insistent on fighting for their right to party, but it wasn't clear who was providing resistance.

"I'm Zac. Floor party tonight!" said a strange young man in the doorway. He vanished as perplexingly as he had arrived.

"What have I done?" Lloyd's geriatric twenty-two years felt a cavernous age gap. "Hurry up Darren and Will, I'm never going to last three months."

~ * ~ * ~

Pip struggled to carry a large box up the narrow passageway to Mr Swann's flat, barely able to see where she was going. She unlocked the door with her own key and entered backwards, dragging her cumbersome load along the floor.

"Hello!" she called out. Oscar scampered to greet her, nearly tripping her.

Mr Swann sat in his chair, saying nothing and staring into space, unaware of Pip opening the box and not hearing as she continued to speak.

"One of my customers is moving. They've a snazzy new kitchen where they are going, so they don't need this." Pip delved into the box and awkwardly heaved out its contents. "Ta da!"

Mr Swann didn't react.

"It's a microwave," Pip explained. "I know your oven isn't working, so I thought you could use this. The cold weather will be coming soon, and you'll need hot suppers, especially as you've got no heating in here. I'll pop it on the counter next to the fridge, shall I?" Pip didn't wait for an answer, but carried her booty into the kitchen and proceeded to plug it in. "It's like new, and it's got the instruction manual that tells you how to cook all sorts of things." She opened the refrigerator and peered into the icebox. "Maybe I could get you some instant dinners. What sort of thing do you like?"

Her friend's lack of response finally filtered through. He was pale and unmoving.

"Mr Swann – are you alright?"

It was only when Pip's fingers touched the wrinkled skin of his hand that he reacted.

"Oh, Miss Raven, yes, a microwave. How very kind. I must give you some money."

"No need," Pip replied, assessing the old man with narrowed eyes. "They let me have it for free."

Mr Swann progressed to nervous agitation; Pip sensed he wished her to leave, but something made her stay. He was in his dressing gown, rather than his usual shirt and tie, but it was a familiar odour that told her all was not well.

"Would you like a cup of tea?" she asked. He calmed and nodded, so she filled the kettle and turned it on.

"While I'm waiting, I'll give your shower curtain a wipe down," Pip said. "We don't want it all mildewed again."

Before Mr Swann could reply, she walked into the bedroom. The smell of urine was overpowering, and his bedclothes and pyjama trousers were in a dark damp crumple on his mattress. She sensed him behind her, and knew he was beside himself with embarrassment.

"Oh, Oscar," she tutted to the uncomprehending little scapegoat at her feet, "have you been a naughty little doggie and been on your master's bed? Did you have a little accident?" She gathered the sheets and blankets together, taking them to the washing machine. "Don't worry, Oscar, everyone has accidents. Soon these will all be washed and the whole thing forgotten."

The mattress presented more of a problem. Pip sponged it gently with a mild detergent until she was confident that it was only damp from water, but it was nevertheless still very wet.

"It's a lovely day," she observed. "This'll dry quicker outdoors, but the alley's too dark. Is there a door to somewhere behind the living room curtains?"

Mr Swann sank into his chair, trapped in miserable indecision and covered his eyes with his hand.

"There is," he sighed, defeated. "Please draw them open."

Pip complied, tugging the heavy drapes apart and disturbing decades of dust, to reveal ornate French windows and a long, cream-glossed conservatory behind. The glass roof was high at the left wall but sloped down to meet the top of the outer doors set in the fully glazed right-hand side. The roof and windows were dark from years of dirt deposited upon them.

Decayed wicker furniture had allowed someone long ago to sit and enjoy the garden beyond. The place was thick with dust and mildew, spider carcasses and mouse droppings speckled the floor, and curtains of dark grey cobwebs hung low, capturing light as well as prey. There were several ornate pots on the filthy floor, hosting the desiccated remains of once resplendent plants.

Despite the grime, Pip could see the garden – a small, wild, weed-riddled, dilapidated patio courtyard, surrounded by untamed wisteria atop high brick walls. Ivy crept everywhere, its dark green leaves dominating the grey-sandy stone of the flagstones and statues. It had devoured a garden bench, leaving only the shape to suggest the seat's skeletal presence. Towering in the centre of the garden was a huge rosebush, now shaped only by nature's uncaring eye, its prickly branches weighed down by large ivory flowers.

Pip turned the key in the lock; the mechanism was stiff, but yielded, and the hinges creaked when she pushed the glazed door open.

"It was my wife's creation." Mr Swann's voice was as dead as the drapes which now dangled uselessly either side of Pip. "It was her gift to our son's memory. She planted the rose tree on Pip's spot, because that is where he liked to sit on a sunny day."

"That's a lovely idea," Pip said. She answered the kettle's summons and made Mr Swann a cup of tea.

"Anna worked to create that garden for over twenty years," the old man explained, "but when she died, I drew the curtains. Our library was shared, you see, but outside was her domain. I recall it being the hot summer of 1976 that I pulled them back, at last ready to see her wonderful creation again. Instead, I was confronted with the chaos that you see before you. I had failed. I closed them and kept them closed until today. Please try not to think too badly of me."

"I could never think badly of you."

"I cannot bear to look at it!" Mr Swann cried out. "I prefer a damp bed. Please draw the curtains again."

Pip pulled the door shut and tugged the drapes across, blotting out the day.

"It is still early," she remarked, "I'll pull the mattress off the bed, prop it up, and turn on the electric fire. Keep an eye on it, but I'll come back about nine o'clock tonight and get you all set up."

"It's a punishment," Mr Swann sighed.

"What is?"

"Everything. I shut myself away, angry for what I had been denied and not grateful for my blessings. Anna and I were together from 1919 to 1965. That is forty-six years of joy, yet I sulked and wasted the subsequent time. And then you came into my life and I began to look forward to my days again. You are very like her, calm and kind."

"Thank you. That's a beautiful compliment."

"Your efforts earlier to save my blushes were very kind, but we both know that my dog was not responsible," Mr Swann said. "I have to go into hospital very soon for a procedure. It would put my mind at rest if you would be kind enough to feed Oscar and take him for walks."

"Of course."

"I am afraid you see, Pip. More afraid than I was in war. I led a solitary selfish life after Anna passed. What if I do not deserve to be reunited with her?"

"I think you are a good, kind man, who misses the love of his life." Pip knelt beside the old man. "And I think God is a good, kind God, who understands. I see the Reverend Johnson sometimes to talk about things – he listens and isn't at all judgemental. Shall I ask him to visit you?"

"But I have not attended St Michael's for over twenty years."

"You hear the bells on a Sunday, I think that counts. Want me to ask him?"

"Please."

"You go to bathe and dress. I'll make up some lunch for you. Then I'll sort out your mattress."

"No, Pip, my dear. I cannot afford to pay."

"No need, it is what friends do."

~ * ~ * ~

Susanne Barrow was deeply engrossed in her work, writing comments on a legal contract drawn up by one of the junior solicitors in her practice. There was a knock at the door and a secretary entered.

"Miss Philippa Raven is here for her appointment."

Susanne looked up, momentarily unable to place the name until she connected Heather's and Lucy's friend Pip to the more formal Philippa. She picked up a folder from her desk and perused the contents.

"Ask her to come in, please."

Susanne stood up to greet her visitor.

"Thanks for coming in to see me, Pip," she said, handing the young woman a business card. Pip, not wanting to seem unworldly, rummaged in her handbag and produced a Pipsqueaky-clean business flyer which the solicitor received with solemn respect. "I have some news for you. I've been in touch with Mr Reeves, a lawyer who represents the new owners of your former employers."

"OK," Pip said, convinced she was about to be presented with terrible news and that debtors' prison awaited her.

"Mr Reeves remembered you the moment I mentioned your name. It seems his firm had problems tracking you down."

"I had to move suddenly," Pip winced at the memory.

"Well, he was most apologetic. He wanted me to tell you that changes have been made. He spoke to several of your colleagues and they told similar stories regarding bullying and sexual impropriety. Your former supervisor, Glenda, was reprimanded and moved to another position, where she's no longer responsible for staff. She's been replaced by Nicola, who I believe you worked with?"

"I did. She was the only kind person there."

"I hope and believe there were more than just her, but they were afraid of the regime. Your former departmental manager, Mr Simpkins, has taken early retirement. All security guards patrol in pairs and CCTV has been overhauled. The HR team has operational independence under their own board level director with a defined staff grievance procedure, so I am confident that the bad practices that were tolerated have now stopped. I hope you are pleased."

"You hope I'm pleased?" Pip echoed, tight-lipped. "Those people mentally tortured me, they drove me to a point where I believed I had to let a disgusting old man touch me, just to have a peaceful work life. I felt sick every morning, I jumped at every sound, and I was terrified in case I made the slightest mistake. And then there are the rumours about me that I know people will believe, because I have been through it before."

"I understand."

"I'm not sure you could understand. Glenda overseeing a photocopier and Mr Simpkins spending more time with his golf course are hardly punishments – how many other people were treated like me? And nothing's happened to a man who intended to force himself on me, who put his hands on me."

"It's a question of law. There's insufficient evidence for any formal proceedings to stand a chance. Mr Reeves achieved all that he could possibly have, and more." Susanne had silently fervently agreed with every word that Pip had said, and it galled her that sadists and perverts should be able to evade meaningful punishment. "But you're right – it's too little too late in all respects."

"It's hard to explain how what they did affected me," Pip said. "You see, I held myself responsible for a long time – I was a bad secretary, a silly immature girl who'd given off the wrong signals. It was only after talking to other people that I saw how twisted my mind had become. So, I don't blame you for not understanding, I don't think anyone could who hadn't been there."

A tear rolled down her cheek as she spoke and the final few words were whispered with emotion.

"There's more." Susanne slid a piece of paper over the desk to Pip. "Mr Reeves has negotiated a without prejudice financial settlement for you."

Pip examined the offer.

"Five thousand pounds is very generous," her voice was ice cold, "it's a year's salary, but I can't accept it."

"Why not?"

"Because I didn't earn it and I don't want their money," Pip spat the final few words as if they themselves were her antagonists.

"Pip, this money could make your life better."

"My life already is better, thank you. I really don't want to seem ungrateful. You're very kind but it's impossible to explain how I feel about anything that comes from that company."

"You don't have to decide now," Susanne said. "Let me deposit the money in an account with my firm. It could be life changing."

Something in those words brought about a change in attitude. Pip nodded, deep in thought.

"Life changing, but whose lives?" she murmured. She thought hard and came to a decision. "There is something that I would like to do with the money. Please can you help me?"

Pip spent several minutes outlining her wishes.

"You realise that you will be left with nothing for yourself?" Susanne confirmed.

"I do, thank you, but what I've asked you to do is better than money in the bank."

With more thanks, Pip departed, and Susanne Barrow was left alone to muse.

"'How far that little candle throws her beams. So shines a good deed in a naughty world'," she muttered to herself.

She toyed with Pip's leaflet, thinking, admiring the selfless young woman. She picked up her phone, dialled the office manager, and asked him to come up for a quick chat.

~ * ~ * ~

"Pip, this is amazing!" Bren exclaimed. "Barrow & Co called this morning to ask us if we want a contract to clean their offices, and then two other firms rang. We can't cope with all this work."

"We can if we expand," Pip said, full of determination. "We'll take on some help, we know enough trustworthy people. I'll do the admin, but that's what my course was all about. We can do this, Bren, we can have a proper business."

"Shall we go and take a look at our office?" Bren suggested. "We are going to need it now."

It was late afternoon and Mr Stanhope's receptionist was putting on her coat, when Pip and Bren arrived. Her relief was palpable when they continued past her and onto the second flight of stairs and she made a hasty exit, stilettos clacking. Pip and Bren surveyed their office. The room was a good size, but the sloping roof meant that much of the floor space couldn't be easily used.

"It'll be cold in winter," Bren observed.

"Can't be worse than the stables, and I'll bring in a heater. What we need is carpet, desks, chairs and a filing cabinet."

"My Roy might be able to help with all that. He's good at finding stuff. He'll sort it out – didn't you say you were busy with your friend Mr Swann all next week?"

"Not exactly. He's going into hospital and I said I'd look after his dog and do a few other things. I'll be a bit tied up, so I'll get the new help sorted pronto." Pip looked at her watch. "I think we both need to be getting home for dinner."

"Oh, I clean forgot!" Bren slapped her forehead. "Your mum rang earlier, very happy about something. Can you meet the family at The George and Dragon for dinner?"

Pip went to Lyn's, changed into her new blue dress and drove to meet her family at the pub.

"Order whatever you want," her father decreed with regal bonhomie. "I'm having steak! We're celebrating tonight."

"What about?" Pip asked.

"We had a letter from a big legal company." Julia was overjoyed. "Your dad's been left a legacy – five thousand pounds! It's going to make such a difference. I feel like we should make a toast, but I don't know who to."

"To us!" shouted Daniel and he raised his cola high and leaned affectionately against his big sister's arm.

"To us," Pip echoed, sipping her drink with a satisfied secret smile.

Pip collected Mr Swann at the end of his week in hospital. Such a private man had found the noise and hubbub of the ward overwhelming and the lack of privacy miserable, but Pip's daily visits had been oases of calm, as she brought books from his library and reassuring updates about Oscar.

"Thank you once again, my dear," he said as Pip parked in the road near the entrance to his home. "I would have been perfectly content in a taxi, but your company made the trip far more pleasant. I can manage from here. I am sure you have a busy day."

"I'd like to make sure you're settled first," Pip insisted, "and I've got a spot of lunch which I thought we might have together. Unless you are fed up with having people around?"

"Some people, but not you. It sounds delightful."

Once inside, Oscar's elated greeting gripped the old man's attention for several moments. Then Mr Swann noticed the room was cleaner and tidier than he could remember it being since his wife had become ill, and brighter too. There had been no need to switch on the light, for cool, clear, autumnal sunbeams were the sole source of illumination; the curtains were drawn back, and he hastened to the tall glass doors as quickly as his fragile frame would permit.

The conservatory was transformed. The glass panes were clear and glistening, the cobwebs and detritus swept away, the surfaces were washed, and the furniture freshened; the plant pots now hosted brightly coloured flowers, stipples of reds and yellows and orange celebrating his return.

Confused, excited, tremulous fingers turned the key in the freshly-oiled lock and the door swung open without a creak. Inside the conservatory, Mr Swann had a clear view of the garden. The weeds were gone, the wisteria and ivy tamed, and the bench and statues liberated; the flagstones basked in the sunlight, surrounding the glory of the beautifully balanced rosebush.

"Oh, Miss Raven, oh Pip, my dear, what have you done?" Mr Swann gasped. "I cannot afford to pay you for all this work."

"Please, it's my gift to you, to Anna and Philip. I don't want money, just your friendship and happiness. I thought it would be a nice surprise to come home to."

"It is!" A smile returned to his thin lips. "It is as my Anna had it. But surely you didn't do this alone?"

"My dad helped with the outside, especially the conservatory roof. He enjoyed it, we haven't much of a garden at home. And my friends Bren and Lyn gave a hand inside. I hope you don't mind?"

"Mind, how could I mind? You restore my faith in goodness."

Pip was relieved and elated beyond measure.

"Come inside and I'll sort lunch." She bade her elderly friend to sit at one of two place-settings on the newly-waxed and polished dining table and busied herself in the kitchen.

Mr Swann must not have remained seated, because a square package, wrapped in brown paper secured with yellowing string sat on the table when Pip returned. She was curious but said nothing as she set down two dishes of mackerel salad and took her seat. A jug of water sat between them, and Mr Swann used it to shakily fill their glasses. He slid the package across the table.

"This is for you," he said. "One of only two copies I have left. This one has not seen the light of day since it was printed."

The old string and brittle paper gave way to reveal a thick, hardback book. The green fabric of the front cover was embossed in gold letters, 'Swann's Anthology of Verse, edited by A. Swann.'

"After I left teaching, I worked occasionally as a literary editor," Mr Swann explained. "In my spare time, I worked on this. It was published in 1951 and it had some small success in literary circles. Just as the garden was Anna's tribute, this was my memorial to our son. Please look at the dedication, Philippa."

She turned the first two, creamy pages and came to one which had a single printed line.

'*Pip. Ever the best of friends.*'

"It is fitting that something I created for the son whom I lost should equally apply to the woman so like the granddaughter I would love to have had. Would you permit me to sign it for you?"

Pip nodded and slid the volume back across the table. Mr Swann removed his fountain pen from his jacket pocket and carefully wrote, '*To Philippa "Pip" Raven, in fondness and admiration, Arthur Swann.*' He blew lightly on the page to dry the ink, closed the book and passed it back to its new owner.

"I don't know what to say, except thank you." Pip tried not to cry. "I'll treasure it always."

Chapter 19

L loyd was wet and weary. A constant drizzle plagued his walk back to his halls of residence after an afternoon of library research and four hours of cello practice in the morning. He was coming down with a cold, so a warm shower, a hot meal in the cafeteria, and an evening relaxing in his room seemed to be in order. That dream faded as he reached his corridor. Many of his fellow residents milled about, moving between rooms and chatting idly as another party began. Lloyd didn't blame them, but it was bad timing for him.

One of the girls – twiggy of build with a mass of freckles and short copper hair – emerged carrying a plate of pizza which she waved under Lloyd's nose. She was swaying gently, having made an early start on the vodka, so the food was a constantly moving target for anyone wanting a piece, but Lloyd succeeded.

"Thanks, Sally," he said, blowing on the pizza to cool it. "What's all this in aid of?"

"It's Alex's birthday."

"Which one is Alex?"

"Search me," Sally shrugged, with a tiddly giggle. "Who needs a reason for a party? Anyway, I wanted to talk to you about those two blokes staying with you the other day."

"Darren and Will? They're house hunting with me."

"Well, I didn't like the way the tall one looked at me." Sally's head moved like a charmed cobra, as she struggled to maintain a veneer of sophistication over a core saturated in Russian alcohol.

"You're alright, Will won't be interested in you."

"Why not?" She looked down her own cleavage and nearly tipped the pizza off the plate. She snapped her head back up and stared at Lloyd. "He's a man, isn't he?"

"Yeah, and he's also Darren's boyfriend."

"You mean they're poofs?" She snorted with laughter, and two slices of pizza dropped on the carpet.

"Yup," Lloyd replied, taking the plate from her, "so what?"

"So what?" she echoed loudly. "They might have AIDS or something. We all have to share a loo here!"

"Yeah, well you won't have to worry, we found somewhere," Lloyd snapped, returning the plate a little too forcibly.

"Oh!" Sally exclaimed. "You got pizza all over my shirt."

"Sorry, I'm really tired, and your blood alcohol level's three times your IQ, so let's talk tomorrow, OK?"

"OK," Sally smiled, the conversation already receding into a muddled haze. She tottered away down the corridor and into a room. A few moments later a plate broke. "Oh, my trousers!"

Lloyd let himself into his room and finished off the rest of his slice of pizza. He gave up on a shower, not fancying wearing only a towel in a corridor full of drunk students drifting around like vegetarian zombies. He was developing a headache, and the throb of music from outside was grating on his nerves.

"Idiots," he grumbled.

"I hope that doesn't include yours truly?" a nasal voice asked.

Lloyd had not noticed his door open. On the threshold, arms resting on the doorframe, was a small, underdeveloped young man with a disproportionately large mullet clinging to his skull like a greedy gopher. Jeff was not a man to be diverted by such trifling matters as other people's privacy.

"Hi," Lloyd tried to not sound irritated.

"It's Alex's birthday."

"I know. Which one is Alex?"

"The big guy, always in a rugby shirt. We've all clubbed together and got him one of those Strippergrams, you know where a sexy girl sings happy birthday and takes her clothes off. I thought you might like to come and watch with the rest of us."

"No thanks, mate, I'm not in the mood."

"Yeah, well Sally was just telling us about your shirt-lifter friends," Jeff laughed. "Maybe it's catching."

"Yeah, exactly, they're my friends," Lloyd said. "Why would you think I'd want to hear my friends called something like that? Why don't you go and ogle the stripper and leave me be?"

"Alright, Princess." Jeff realised he had pushed his luck too far and made a hasty retreat.

Lloyd slammed his door, flopped onto his bed, and closed his eyes, hoping to sleep his headache away. About half an hour later a confused skirmish in the corridor woke him – arguing and faltering footsteps preceded a loud bang against his door.

"I still want my bloody money!" shouted a deep male voice.

"It was a misunderstanding!" Jeff gurgled.

The clattering continued, moving away. Peering out, Lloyd saw the back of a powerfully built man in a black leather jacket, menacing Jeff into a corner.

"What's going on?" Lloyd shouted. The man turned around and he and Lloyd looked at each other in mutual shock and astonishment. "Sam?"

"You know each other?" Jeff asked, hoping he may escape unscathed.

"Yes," Sam replied, turning back, "but it won't help you. I want my money."

"But we didn't get a stripper!" Jeff protested, ennobled by Lloyd's presence.

"That's not my fault, is it?" Sam snarled. "You booked me. How was I supposed to know Alex was a bloke?"

"Well, how was I to know, Big Sammy wasn't a girl?"

A large hand pinned Jeff to the wall and a fist drew back.

"Calm down, Sam," Lloyd intervened. "Jeff, pay him right now. I can't stop him if he wants to hurt you."

Jeff drew some crumpled notes from his shirt pocket and pressed them into Sam's outstretched hand.

"Run along now," Sam growled, and Jeff scarpered.

Lloyd invited Sam into his room, and the former bandleader accepted.

"What's going on, are you a stripper now?" Lloyd asked.

"My girlfriend, Polly, normally does it, but sometimes they want beefcake, and that's me."

"But why?"

"I ditched the band idea, it didn't work, but this one's sweet. We're getting cash together to buy some gear and then we can supply extras to the punters."

"Sam, it's a no better idea than the band. You're not cut out for the drug business. You look like you take more than you sell. What happened to you?

We found Tracy in London, doing well for herself. She said you and Frank got into a load of debt and he tried to sell her to some dirty movie set-up. Then you all vanished."

"I'm glad she's OK," Sam said. "I did try looking for her but got nowhere. What about Ed?"

"He went to prison – got into a fight with the cops – but I hear he's out now and living with Tracy."

"That sounds like Ed," Sam nodded. "You heard right – me and Sharon quit London, headed north and formed another band, but it was a joke. Then the money guys caught up with us, but I'd got most of the cash together by then and they let the rest go. Not long after, Polly joined the band, Sharon did her nut and ran away with my remaining cash."

"Where did you get all the money from?"

"I pulled in some favours, sold a few things…" Sam tailed off.

"Nicked it?"

"Yeah, well Sharon's surprisingly inventive at that sort of thing. She already had experience of it."

"So, why did she up and off?"

Sam shrugged.

"She's a pretty messed up kid, snorting a bit too much white powder, so who knows what got into her head? Do you mind if I smoke in here?"

Lloyd did mind, but it seemed to calm Sam's nerves. At least the room came with an ashtray.

"Why are you in Manchester?" Sam asked.

"I'm doing a doctorate in music theory."

"Good on you!" Sam was genuinely pleased. "At least one of us is a success."

"I see Darren quite often too. He's moving up here after Christmas."

"Darren?" Sam was puzzled. "How do you know him?"

"Complicated story. Sharon's dad went spare after you lot left. He trawled London looking for her and picked up Darren and me on his way."

"I feel bad about that," Sam admitted. "I thought she'd put it right with her family."

"She won't get a chance now, her dad died."

Sam swore and stubbed out his barely smoked cigarette.

"Shame."

"Do you know where she went?" Lloyd asked.

"Sharon? No. Ellesmere Port, or Liverpool, possibly. She met some blokes from over that way when we were getting the money together. She's probably doing well, and I'm stuck here."

"Why do you do it, Sam? Darren said you were a toolmaker, a proper craftsman, and proud of it."

"Yeah, I liked it, but where would it get me, a two-up two-down and a nice little wife?"

"It sounds better than taking your kit off for a bunch of pissed students."

Sam momentarily seemed angry but relapsed to self-pity.

"I've screwed up, haven't I?" He put his head in his hands.

"But you could go back to what you used to do."

"Yeah, maybe I could." Sam stood up, reverting to a chirpy façade. "I'm going now, Polly's waiting for me at the bike, and it's raining. Say hi to Darren for me."

As he left, a thought struck Sam. He hovered in the doorway.

"One thing about Sharon. Polly said she saw her at the Arndale Centre recently, all done up to the nines but wearing a football scarf. It seemed odd."

"Did she say which club?" Lloyd asked.

"You're having a laugh! Polly wouldn't know and wouldn't care. I'm off - bye."

Lloyd was left alone to ponder the irony of another new lead on Sharon when nobody was looking for her any more.

~ * ~ * ~

Gavin paused writing his essay to look out of the window at the university campus buzzing with student life in the early evening. His building was on a hill at the very edge of the estate, offering a spectacular view but a steep walk home, and his room was comfortable but far from luxurious – a bed, an armchair, a wardrobe, and a desk were the sum total of his furnishings.

He stretched and yawned. His workload was heavy after a few beguiling weeks of build-up, but university life held many tempting diversions. His new friends were always up for fun, and part of him wondered why he was trying to make things work with a girl who lived thousands of miles away; but then he thought of Tori and his heart swelled, for he was hopelessly in love. Her letters, at one point arriving two a week, were so passionate and so open that he already knew her anger with him truly had subsided.

Gavin decided to fortify himself for his studies with a mug of instant soup. He filled his little kettle at his basin, took a soup sachet from the box he kept in a drawer, and emptied its contents into a mug. Waiting for the water to boil, his eyes strayed to the cork notice board above his desk. Beside a year-planner were pinned two letters, one from Pip and the other from Tori. It was nearly two weeks since he had heard from his girlfriend, and he was beginning to worry.

The kettle juddered to boiling point, and the hot water was added to the powder at the bottom of his mug and stirred, creating what the manufacturer assured its customers was soup. A tentative sniff told Gavin that he had selected leek and potato… or possibly cream of asparagus... or maybe chicken. He returned to his work, waiting for the drink to cool. At one point a piece of what seemed to be mushroom bobbed to the surface, suggesting yet another flavour. He prodded the suspicious item with his spoon but learned nothing new.

A knock at his door caused him to tut. He had told his mates that he really needed to study – but maybe he could spare the time for a bevvy and a game or two of pool. He opened the door with an expression of sham irritation but froze in shock.

"Surprised?" Tori asked. "Look at my eyes, lover-boy. Do they look angry?"

Gavin shook his head slowly, fearing he was hallucinating. Tori gave a 'yahoo' more Texan than Bostonian and jumped onto him as if he were a rodeo bronco, wrapping her arms and legs around him and kissing hungrily. The unexpected additional weight caused Gavin to take several steps backwards until his spine met the wardrobe and all that prevented him from sliding to the floor was the closet door-knob embedding itself between his buttocks.

"Mm," moaned Tori in pleasure.

"Mm," echoed Gavin in agony.

Eventually, she detected his whimpering and detached her mouth from his. "Are you OK?"

"Um, could you just get off me for a second?"

Tori lowered her legs to the ground and Gavin extricated the wardrobe from his person.

"Had you forgotten how forward Boston girls are?" Tori asked.

"I've only one to judge from, but Boston girls seem perfect."

"Good answer," she purred.

Gavin closed the door to his room and advanced on Tori, eager to take up where they left off a few moments before. She dragged him onto the bed and this time they didn't break the kiss for a long time.

"Let's go out this evening," Tori suggested when they had completed their reintroduction. "Is there a decent bar here?"

"It's not terrible," Gavin replied. "I'll get your luggage first – where is it?"

"In my room, one floor down," Tori exulted in his surprise. "I'm a student here too, college boy."

"But how?"

"Miss Lucille and her church. They have a scholarship fund for local kids, but when they heard my story, they added me to the list. It's only a contribution to my fees, but my parents are lending me the rest. I decided to study overseas, and a handsome guy I knew had written to me saying this is a good place to study."

"Watch out for him," Gavin growled. "He'd say anything to get you here and he'll do anything to keep you."

~ * ~ * ~

"You made it, then," Bren said when Pip walked into their attic office. Lyn followed, interested to see where her young friend worked. "I didn't sleep a wink. I've never known a storm like it – those winds! There are fences down everywhere and two of the trees in the park were blown over. I thought I was about to wave goodbye to the roof."

"Yeah, it was crazy," Pip said. "Our garden's a mess, and we've got next door's birdhouse in the middle of the flower beds. They said it was a hurricane on the news."

"Did you see Jack Stanhope on your way in?" Bren turned to business. "He was complaining about all the calls they've had to handle from our customers this morning. He said having a clean loo isn't worth the grief."

"Maybe it's time to get a telephone of our own up here," Pip mused.

"Maybe it's time to move somewhere where you don't have to crouch, and the floor doesn't look like a multicolour zebra," Lyn suggested.

"My Roy went to a lot of trouble to get this carpet, and it didn't cost us a penny," Bren defended her corner. "It's not his fault that the bloke he got it off couldn't get all the same colour."

"But why are all the bits long and thin?" Lyn asked.

"Roy's mate works at the railway repairs yard. They're for the aisles up the middle of the coaches."

"You mean the carpet's stolen?" Lyn sounded aghast.

"How can we steal it? We're taxpayers, we paid for it."

Pip was relieved that Bren had to go to a client and Lyn needed to start at the supermarket, which meant the argument had to come to an end. She busied herself alone in the office for a while before she slipped away to visit Mr Swann to check that he and his little garden had weathered the storm.

Oscar bounced to greet her as she entered the flat; by the strangest coincidence she had a dog biscuit in her coat pocket which he munched noisily, watching her with undisguised adoration as she went in search of his master. Mr Swann was in the garden, enjoying the calm of a pleasant autumn day after the tempest the night before, and he seemed almost as delighted to see his visitor as Oscar had been a minute earlier.

"Philippa, my dear, what a delightful surprise!" he exclaimed. Pip was starting to like being called by her real first name now; it was a poetic greeting from a loving friend and no longer carried the suggestion of imminent discipline.

"Hello, Arthur. I'm glad you and the garden haven't been blown away."

"Both quite undamaged, I assure you. A few leaves have been lost, but we are nicely sheltered."

"How about some tea?" Pip suggested.

Once they were settled comfortably at the table, a warm drink and slices of Battenberg before them, Mr Swann started to talk again.

"I had a telephone call from my doctor yesterday, he had the results of some additional tests that he did last week."

"You should have told me," Pip scolded, "I would have come with you."

"Thank you, but I prefer to do some things alone. Philippa, my dear, it seems the surgery that I underwent last month was unsuccessful. The problem is not dramatic, but I fear I shall not be able to manage on my own for very much longer."

"I'll look after you."

"Thank you, but I would not wish you to. You give more important spiritual, uplifting support – because of you, I have joy in my day and have come to believe that I might once again be close to my Anna and my first Pip. I intend to go into a home, but will you still visit me?"

"Of course! My gran's in a nice home, not far from here."

"Well, if it merits hosting your grandmother then it is a palace among care homes. I would be most grateful for its details," Mr Swann smiled and then sighed. "But what will become of Oscar?"

"He shall live with me, and we will visit you together," Pip said, inwardly wondering how to bring Lyn around to the idea.

Relieved, Mr Swann rested back in his chair and looked around him, radiating contentment.

"Perhaps change is a good thing. I have lived in this house since I married Anna in 1919 and in these rooms since about 1933."

"You have never told me how you and Anna met," Pip said, willing him to speak once more of his great love.

"Where to begin, how to explain? It was a miracle that we met, for I had no pedigree. I'm the youngest son of a cooper and a seamstress. I did well at the local church school and won a scholarship to the grammar school. I hoped to do a teaching certificate and return to my own first school to try to help those left behind."

"I think that's very noble," Pip smiled.

"Then the Great War changed everything, and it changed me. I was little more than a boy when I enlisted, full of hope, but I returned an angry man. I was an officer, but only because so many around me had perished. They would have promoted a rat, if it could salute. I returned to this town because my family was here, but Spanish Flu took my mother before I had arrived home. I was dead inside, and I lost faith in anything in this world or any other."

"That's very sad," Pip sympathised, trying to imagine the gentle old man before her as a world-weary soldier.

"One warm day, I was walking along this very road when I heard a piano forte being played, accompanied by a woman's voice purer than I believed possible. It was Anna. I was transfixed by her and her music. She saw me from the window and spoke to me. I think it was love at first sight for us both. The following year, we wed and lived in the house with her parents. We were blissfully happy, and I studied for a Bachelor of Arts in English. They were good times."

"It sounds very romantic," Pip said.

"It was idyllic and continued to be even after her parents both passed away. I took up a place teaching at the grammar school and we began to build our precious library, while Anna studied her music. After a few years, she was at last carrying the child she so ached for, and all seemed perfect. Well, you know the rest."

"She sounds like a wonderful woman. I wish I'd known her."

"Anna was indeed wonderful. Were things different, her musical compositions might have reached a wide and appreciative audience, but as it is, I believe that you and I are the only two people alive who know of a single note that she wrote."

"Would she have wanted fame?"

"Ah, you have the habit of asking the right questions, my dear Philippa. No, Anna would have hated celebrity. She wrote her music for herself, for me, for Philip, and for God, and she cared not who else knew of it. Later, when we were alone again after Philip passed, I came to understand."

"Which is the bliss of solitude," Pip recalled.

"Quite so," Mr Swann sighed, "and now my library will be torn up, for care homes allow their residents to bring a mere handful of books. The owners of the main building will knock down this place and extend the car park for the flats, so my little haven will disappear. My flat is worth very little, I am told, for it has no access other than the passage, no parking, and no central heating. All it has are, thanks to you and Anna, a pretty garden and peaceful memories."

"There has to be an alternative!" Pip exclaimed. "This lovely place can't be destroyed."

"I believe it is called progress, my dear, for who else would buy it?"

"Me," Pip said. "My business is doing well. I could raise the money."

"Philippa, my dear, I am delighted to hear it, but you should be buying a nice house."

"I want a nice little flat full of books and a garden with roses in. And Oscar wouldn't have to move."

"Let us not argue," Mr Swann insisted. "Any and all of the books are yours for the asking, but sometimes things are meant to end. This was created for us to care for Philip because it was all we could afford, and it is right that it should end with us. One day, you will want a family of your own and you would have to sell this flat – then you would realise the imprudence of your generous offer. Oscar will be happy wherever you are, I know that much."

~ * ~ * ~

Pip thought deeply about her conversation with Mr Swann, unable to reconcile herself to the notion that his quiet little corner of civilisation should be lost and that Anna's garden and Philip's memorial should be bulldozed to rubble and tarmacked over.

However, she had more urgent matters to attend to. Gran had asked to be taken to visit her late husband's grave before the winter set in and Pip offered to take her. They set off early one Saturday, initially bubbling with adventure, making up for the lack of a car radio by singing songs together, but as they neared the village, their moods became more sombre. The mornings were dark, the days contracting, and the sky permanently gloomy; but the weather remained dry, though cold.

Pip lost track of how long they stood in the peaceful churchyard, her grandmother speaking softly to the grave. The old lady was increasingly frail, and her skin was as grey as the gravestone that held her unwavering gaze. It was impossible to hear the whispered secrets that passed between two lovers separated by mortality, but eventually the conversation ended, and Gran allowed herself to be led into the warm pub for a hot lunch.

It was no great coincidence that their former neighbours, Jerry and Barbara, should be there too – they had lunched at the same table at one o'clock every Saturday for the last fifteen years. It was good to chat to them, to catch up on village gossip and banish the sombre thoughts of the churchyard.

After their meal, Jerry and Barbara invited them to their home, ostensibly for a cup of tea but really to beak over the fence to see what the new occupants of Gran's bungalow had done to the back garden. Pip's heart broke to see her grandfather's rose trees replaced by a kidney-shaped pond, with reeds around the edge and a jolly gnome perched atop a fibreglass rock permanently fishing the murky waters. Unnoticed, she slipped back indoors and tried to reason herself out of crying; her fingers fumbled with the catch of the locket that she wore around her neck until it opened, and she sniffed the crushed petals inside, desperately trying to find the scent, the last remnants of a blissful time.

"Haven't they done wonders with the garden?" Gran's voice invaded Pip's misery.

"Wonders?" Pip was aghast. "No, they've ruined it— dug up Grandad's roses."

"No, my girl, they have changed it, that's all. Made it their own, and that's a good thing. The garden, those roses, they were his and then yours, but you've both moved on in different ways. The new people have kept it a living part of a home, not a garden of remembrance."

"But Gran—"

"But nothing. Tell me truly, forgetting what was there before, did you like the garden?"

After a delay, Pip muttered, "Yes," appalled by her own truthfulness.

"If they had kept it as it was, your memories of Grandad would be no more real. Any rose will remind you of him, but he'd be pleased that the new people care about the garden."

"Funnily enough, I had a similar conversation with my friend Arthur a couple of weeks back," Pip sighed. "Sometimes things and places have to end when the person who created them leaves, but the sentiment, the feelings, the love that was there can't die."

"That's a bit poetic," Gran chuckled.

"It doesn't mean I have to be happy about what they've done to the garden, though," Pip muttered.

"Ah, that's more like my stubborn Pipsqueak."

~ * ~ * ~

Darren stumbled through the door of the Hammersmith flat, weighed down with several heavy carrier bags that were beginning to stretch and tear.

"Are you there, Will?" he called, kicking the door shut. "I stopped off to get the shopping and missed the bus. I hope you didn't wait for me to eat... Will?"

The sound of spitting came from the bathroom. Darren pushed open the door and found Will harshly defined beneath the humming fluorescent light, gripping the basin and spluttering blood down the drain. He looked up, revealing a swollen eye.

"What happened?"

"I told you we shouldn't walk around holding hands," Will's words were malformed due to pain and swelling, "but you wouldn't listen. I was coming home when the kid downstairs let their stupid cat out."

"What's that got to do with anything?"

"He thought he was going to be in trouble with his dad. The cat climbed on top of the fuse box, so I got it down for him."

"So, that's a nice thing to do."

"Not according to his father, it wasn't. He didn't want the likes of me talking to his little boy. Said it was bad enough they had to live in the same building as us." Will reached into his gory mouth and tentatively touched an incisor. "I think he's knocked a tooth loose. When are you going to understand that this is our life? You were so sure that London was going to be better."

"We'll be in Manchester soon."

"It won't be any different, Darren! You're chasing unicorns." Will stooped and rinsed his mouth from the cold tap. He winced and spat once more, his sputum clearer but still patterned with rosy veins. "Sorry, but when we get there, we can't be public like we've been here, I'm not being chased away again. I just wish we could leave now."

"Then, why don't we? The flat up there is empty."

"Because we don't have enough money," Will explained. "We'd have to pay a month's rent on two places."

"Not if we sold our kit and keep what we really need. That's got to be worth the month's rent and you must know people who'd buy it."

"Yeah, but Lloyd may not have his share of the rent until January."

"So?" Darren persisted. "I'll double up on work. There is bound to be loads of seasonal stuff in the run-up to Christmas. Come on, we could be out of this place in a fortnight."

Silent, Will walked slowly into the living room and flopped onto the couch. He left the light off, relying on illumination from the hallway to see where he was going, and lay for several minutes, shivering and shocked, until he became aware of Darren placing a glass of water and a bottle of painkillers beside him.

"Promise me," Will faced the cushions at the back of the sofa, "please, promise me that we'll keep who we are a secret when we get there. Only Lloyd needs to know."

"I promise."

"Then let's get out of here as soon as possible."

~ * ~ * ~

Mr Swann's bookshelves looked very empty, slowly stripped bare as the elderly occupant sat in his favourite chair and watched the activities with detached interest.

"How many more boxes of these books are there?" Pip's father asked with a world-weary sigh, half in jest.

"Another three, plus this one," his daughter replied. She was placing Mr Swann's selection of records into a large carton. "They're in the conservatory."

Pip discovered an old foolscap envelope squeezed between an LP and the side of a bookshelf. It contained perfectly preserved sheet-music for *The Wild Roses*, including the original pages that bore Anna's meticulous handwriting and composition in faint pencil. A bridge across time formed between her fingertips and the grainy paper beneath them – Anna was pleased her beloved had found friendship after years of solitude.

"What would you like me to do with these music sheets, Arthur?" Pip asked.

"I doubt very much that anyone will be interested," he replied. "I should like to keep Anna's original for myself, but there is no need for anyone to clutter up their homes with the copies."

Having removed the printed sheaves from the envelope, Pip placed it, still containing his wife's original work, into Mr Swann's case, but she slipped the copies into her handbag, unwilling for them to be lost.

"Eight boxes," the old man remarked, contented. "Eight boxes of books you are willing to provide with a home. It is more than I dreamt."

"I wish I could have taken the rest," Pip said, "but Lyn has limited storage space."

"You have selected the cream of the crop, my dear," he assured her, "and the others shall be looked after by the house clearance people. And I am beyond happy that you have agreed to take Anna's desk and pen for your own – the thought of you working at it, writing your letters and stories fills me with joy."

"They're just my silly scribblings," Pip was at pains to explain. "I'm not a proper writer or anything, you know that. I wish I was. I wish I could be all that the desk deserves."

"You are, Philippa. Just have some of the faith in yourself that you instil in others." Mr Swann saw how she struggled to take the compliment and decided to change the subject. "Just think, tomorrow I shall no longer be resident here but shall be neighbour to your excellent grandmother. I do so look forward to meeting her."

"But you must be so sad to go," Pip projected her own misery onto him.

"In some respects, yes, I shall miss this place, but I will get over it as soon I wake up in a warm room with central heating." Mr Swann tapped his temple with a long finger. "However, I am not leaving any memories behind, for they are safely stowed in here. It is many years since I have been on a new adventure, and I am excited about it."

Pip's father strolled back into the room and exhaled wearily. "I'll be getting over to Lyn's, unless there is anything else you need?"

"Can you put that one in my car on your way?" Pip pointed to the box which she had just finished working on. "My keys are on the desk."

"Thank you for all your assistance today, Mr Raven," Mr Swann said. "I perceive your daughter's kind disposition is thanks to you."

"Maybe so, but I'm responsible for a fair bit of her stubbornness too. I'll be back with Pip tomorrow to help move your things to the home."

Lyn had been delighted when Pip asked if Oscar could live with them (she had always wanted a pet, but Bob had never been keen), so Mr Swann took his dog for one final walk before they both moved to new homes the next day.

When she was alone, Pip put on her coat and removed a crumpled carrier bag from its pocket. As quick as lightning, she was in the back garden, clipping at the rosebush and putting the few remaining late autumn blooms into the bag.

"I know what you're up to," her father's voice boomed God-like from the conservatory, "but you can't dig up the plant."

"No, it wouldn't survive," Pip reluctantly agreed. "What are you doing back here?"

"You wouldn't have got far without your car keys. Got enough of them roses?"

Pip nodded, and father and daughter left together.

"I've something else I need to tell you," Mr Raven said. "Your Uncle Ted called the other evening. I thought he was mending fences, but he was having a gloat. Dropped a bit of a bombshell, though – your cousin Charlotte's getting married in the spring."

"Not to Adam?" Pip asked, visibly distressed.

"I think that was the name. Is he the fellow who tried to—"

"Yes!" Pip interrupted. "Did you say anything?"

"It would've sounded like sour grapes. She's my niece and I like it no more than you do, but she's made her choice."

~ * ~ * ~

Mr Swann's move to the home went very smoothly. His room was small but thoughtfully furnished, with a pleasant outlook onto the garden and tucked away in a quiet corner of the building. He unpacked his residual library of books, setting them out on a small set of shelves which had been provided, while Pip arranged his clothes and personal effects.

She then gave him a housewarming gift, a silver snuffbox that she had spotted in the local antique shop; she had polished it until it glistened and filled it with dried petals from the roses she cut from the bush in his garden. Inside the lid, '*Pip*' had been engraved. Mr Swann held the miniature treasure chest to his long nose and detected the scent of his son's memorial.

"Thank you, my dear girl," he whispered, a husky voice and a tremor of his stiff-upper lip the only external signs of a deep bitter-sweet flood of gratitude, memories and emotion.

They joined Gran and several other long-standing residents for afternoon tea in the communal sitting room. Mr Swann was embarrassed when Pip told the assembled party about his expertise in poetry, but it took very little to persuade him to promise a recital later in the week.

Finally, the old man took a private farewell with his beloved dog – yes, they would still see each other, but not in the same way. Oscar sensed the solemnity of the occasion and stayed still to be fussed; then he jumped into his new owner's Vauxhall and watched from the window as Mr Swann waved farewell.

~ * ~ * ~

Pip hadn't slept well since hearing about her cousin's wedding. She oscillated between worrying about Charlotte and being angry with her, as painful memories resurfaced. Oscar sensed her melancholy and positioned himself on the foot of her mattress, ready to be summoned for cuddles, but also sharing his body warmth with her cold feet beneath the duvet. Pip rose as soon as she heard Lyn get up at a little after six in the morning.

The two women shared a pot of tea, staring at their own reflections in the black pre-dawn kitchen windows, grateful for company but not able to vocalise their thoughts.

"I'm thinking I might not put the house on the market for a while," Lyn said. "I don't think I'm ready to go just yet. Mark's busy all the time, so I don't suppose I'd see much more of him, and I've got used to having you about. And Oscar."

It seemed to take ages for the words to filter through to Pip's consciousness. At length, she realised Lyn was waiting for a response.

"That's good news," she said. "I love living here and so does Oscar, don't you?"

The little dog scooted in a happy circle, delighted to be the centre of conversation. A morsel of Lyn's breakfast somehow fell onto the floor and was hoovered up by an excited canine mouth.

"Are you happy to look after Oscar today?" Pip asked.

"You're going to see that cousin of yours, aren't you?" Lyn deduced. "After what she did to you! You're asking to get hurt again – she's made her decision."

"I have to try! Charli needs to hear the truth about Adam. If she doesn't believe me, so be it, but at least I tried."

Pip left almost immediately, driving through the fading darkness into a pale grey daylight. She arrived at the hospital at just after ten, hoping to meet Charlotte after the handover from nightshift to dayshift. It was a preferable meeting place to the flat, (too many bad memories and Adam might be there), but an overworked and exhausted nurse advised that Charlotte had been off ill for several days. Consequently, Pip had little option but to go to her former home. She parked in the familiar car park, climbed the familiar stairs, and knocked on the familiar door.

"Who is it?" Charlotte's voice came faintly from within.

"Pip," she replied, dreading the verbal assault.

"Oh, sorry, I'm not well. Come back another time. I'll call."

That was strange – her cousin was many things, but never meek. Pip dithered on the doorstep but eventually used the key that she had never returned to enter the flat. The smell from the overflowing kitchen bin was the first assault on her senses, but her eyes soon found a worse horror. Charlotte lay on the couch in a stained blue dressing-gown, one leg on the cushions, the other foot on the floor. Her face was a swollen mass of bruises, and she seemed to be experiencing pain when breathing, with one hand constantly pressed to her ribs.

"Who did this, Charli?" Pip didn't need an answer.

"I fell. Down the stairs."

"That's interesting, because I see lots of bruises on your arms, but no scrapes or scratches. I only had a small fall on those stairs, and still took skin off my elbow." Pip saw several dark circular scars on Charlotte's forearm. "And I'm fairly certain that the stairs don't smoke... but Adam does."

"It's my fault. I made him angry, nagging him," Charlotte fretted. "You can't be here, Adam's off today – he's gone to get some fags."

"You need to go to hospital."

"I'll be fine— I'm a nurse, remember? I'll be fine. Please go."

"Charli, you need to leave with me now." Pip spoke with authority.

"I can't, it's my home. I can't just drop everything and go!" Charlotte exclaimed, not seeing the grotesque irony that she should say that to Pip of all people.

"I'm serious," Pip insisted. "We're leaving now or I'm calling the police."

"No point, they're all Adam's mates. His name's on the lease now, so they'll make me let him in and take me away."

"Then we leave, now, together."

Charlotte yielded. She moaned with pain and stood up, resting on her cousin and wheezing.

"Do you think you can get dressed?" Pip asked. "No? OK, let's get some shoes on. Is there anything essential you need to take with you?"

Charlotte grabbed her handbag. Pip found a pair of slip-on canvas shoes for her cousin's bare feet and draped a long raincoat over her shoulders, covering the blue dressing gown.

"Wait!" Charlotte cried just as they reached the door. She opened a cupboard and removed some letters before agreeing to continue.

Their descent was a slow and painful progress, with Pip bearing most of her cousin's weight. Each step was a dagger into Charlotte and her breaths alternated between groans and rasps. At one point, turning on the stairwell, Pip feared her own legs would give way and she experienced an alarming twinge from her knee, but she remained resolute.

Both women froze with horror when they heard the downstairs door opening, followed by horribly familiar lumbering footsteps. They squeezed into an alcove, willing themselves invisible as Adam passed by; a glance to his left would reveal them, but thankfully his eyes didn't waver from the stairs ahead. Cigarette smoke and stale body odour hung in the air. Pip dared not breathe and was sure her heartbeat must be audible. The moment the door to the flat closed, the two women made agonising haste out into the car park.

"Stop!" Pip said. "If he's in the kitchen, he'll see us. There's no way we could reach my car before he caught us."

"What do we do?"

Before Pip could reply, they heard Adam coming back down the stairs. She dragged the door closed.

"Hide by the skip," she hissed, and they crouched among the dustbins, nervously peering out.

Adam burst out of the door and prowled around the cars. A cold clammy revulsion came over Pip when she saw him, and it was reinforced when she realised her business name was stuck in her car window. If he saw it, he would know she was there.

"Stay here," she whispered, "I've got a plan."

Pip waited until the huge man was side-on to them, and then silently moved behind him towards the main entrance to the car park. She was frightened, but felt less vulnerable than at their last encounter, partly because this time she wore a coat, jeans and trainers. That said, Adam was a formidable threat, and she knew that there was no hope of the same element of surprise which she had used last time. At least she had a good chance of outrunning him if it came to that.

"Peekaboo!" she shouted. Adam whirled around.

"You!" he exclaimed. Shock turned to anger and delight at once again having Pip in his grasp.

"Yes, it's just little me," she said sweetly. "Charli's gone. Her dad came to fetch her, but I've stayed around to give you the good news. Don't be scared, I won't beat you up again."

"This time you won't get a chance," he menaced, advancing towards her.

"One step nearer and I'll scream, and this time I'll be heard," she gestured

cooking dinner. Oscar sat at her feet, making a wide-eyed petition for a tasty morsel; by a well-engineered miracle, a piece of sausage fell to the floor and the dog sniffed it with his twitching nose before scoffing it with happy chomps.

"How did things go with your cousin?" Lyn asked.

"I didn't have to do much to persuade her about Adam."

"That's good."

"Not really," Pip sighed. "He'd beaten her so badly she could hardly walk. I took her to her parents."

"Bloody hell! You hear about things like that happening, but…" Lyn trailed off, not knowing where her thoughts were going, except that her Bob would never have laid a finger on her. "Did you go to the police?"

"Charli refused. She says they're all Adam's mates, but I have a plan, which I'll make a start on tomorrow."

"Mysterious," Lyn said, turning the heat off on the cooker. "Did you want some of this dinner? There's plenty spare, if Oscar doesn't get there first."

"Can you stick it in the oven to keep warm, please? I need to make a call first."

When she telephoned Directory Enquiries, Pip trembled with excitement and the numbers she wrote were scrappy rather than meticulously neat as usual. When Theo answered, all she could say was, "It's Pip!" But it was all she needed.

"I don't believe it!" Theo was ecstatic. "When you didn't reply to our letters, I just about gave up hope."

"I moved away." Pip decided now was not the time to give reasons. "I only got the letters today. What's happened between you and Claire?"

Theo's military background showed in his matter-of-fact tone. "Long story made short, it started with a falling out because she and her bloody parents decided Bobbie should go to boarding school back in England."

"Why?" Pip asked.

"Why indeed – it made a mockery of our plans for Jersey. When I said that I left the navy to spend more time with Bobbie, Claire took it personally. Maybe I meant her to, I was angry. We ended up going back and forth at each other, and then your name came up."

"I never wanted that!" Pip detested being dragged into arguments.

"I know – but I was a fool and admitted how I felt about you. And then…"

"And then what?" Pip pushed.

"Then Claire only goes and owns up to having had an affair! I'd seen her having some letters, but she lied and said they were from an old schoolfriend – turned out old boyfriend was more appropriate. She contacted him the last time we separated, about the time I met you, and they continued to meet even after we had so-called reconciled. In fairness, she tried to stop it – that's why she suggested we move to Jersey, but it seems they're in love and I'm a prize sap for believing there was something to salvage."

"No you're not," Pip insisted, "you owed it to yourself and Bobbie to try."

"Maybe," Theo conceded, "but Bobbie was the only reason Claire and I were still together, we both realised. But I can't help being angry about it. At least she apologised for making me break things off with you – she actually really likes you."

"Well, that's nice to hear." Pip's civility masked rage renewed. All that had happened to her since she left the village need not have done – her friend, her support, her rock in a time of need was taken from her by Claire's lies and jealousy. But the storm within her quickly abated and was replaced by longing to hold Theo and to be held by him, to feel his strength and touch and to make up for lost time.

"Things got more civilised when it was all out in the open," Theo said. "We've agreed that Bobbie will live with me and I'll find a day school for her. Claire's coming back to set up home with her new man here in the Richmond pad."

"Sounds like you've got everything worked out." Pip was annoyed but didn't know why.

"Pip, I have to ask you if you've found someone else?" Theo faltered. "I know I've no right to hope, but you must know how I feel about you."

"No," Pip struggled not to cry, "no one else. But things have happened to me, Theo – painful things. I'm OK, but maybe a bit damaged. I'll explain another time, but you may not want to take on what I've become."

"There is nothing I want to do more," Theo promised, "but it's best for both of us to tread carefully. We can go slowly, but I'd like to try if you're willing?"

"Yes," Pip's voice cracked, "I'm very willing."

"I want to see you so much, but I've not found a school, not found a job, and Claire wants the flat in a few days. Her parents will pay the school fees, but I just can't find anywhere I like. I don't want her to go back to where she was before – too many memories and she wasn't happy."

"My brother Daniel goes to a lovely school," Pip ventured, full of hope. "It would be perfect for Bobbie, and you could stay with us until you found a place. I'm sure Lyn wouldn't mind."

Her hopes were met by Theo's excitement. She could feel herself falling more in love with every syllable he spoke, but the stalking dark fear remained: she was too broken, too untouchable to deserve happiness. She pushed such thoughts aside when a bed-drowsy Bobbie was brought to the phone. Predictably, the conversation couldn't end until Mrs Nestyhead was recited to the happy child.

~ * ~ * ~

Pip spent much of the following morning in a curious mix of emotions. The joy from having Theo and Bobbie back in her life permanently tingled through her, but Charlotte's problems dominated her consciousness. After a couple of hours in the cold attic catching up on business paperwork, she visited Susanne Barrow at her considerably better heated offices.

"You were very kind to me before," Pip said, "I can't thank you enough, but I need your help again. Yesterday, I went back to see my cousin Charlotte, because I heard she was planning to marry Adam next year."

"Adam's the security guard who tried to assault you?"

"Yes. I wanted to warn Charli about him. I found her in a bad way – Adam had beaten her. She refused to go to hospital, so I took her to her parents."

"Pip, I am a civil lawyer, and this is a police matter," Susanne stated. "I'm not sure what you think I can do."

"Charli won't go to the police where she lives. She's convinced they're all Adam's friends."

"A security guard for a major company may well have police contacts, but I doubt they go very high up the pecking order. How long ago was the assault?"

"Charli was vague. Three or four days, five at most." Pip pieced together fragments of conversations.

"That's a bigger problem. People may ask why she left it so long to report it."

"She's terrified!" Pip flared. "She'd still be there now, if I hadn't turned up. I know Adam, he plays twisted mind games that make you think black is white. I understand about the police, but I can't let Charli lose her flat while he sits there like a disgusting fat rat, contaminating more people."

"I can probably help with the flat."

"How much will it cost?" Pip asked. "I need to be able to pay you."

"You? Why not Charlotte or her family?"

"They don't have it, and I'm partly responsible. I knew what type of person Adam was and I left it too late to warn her."

"Pip, my dear, it is in no way your responsibility. Anyway, I doubt she would have listened. By your argument, I'm as responsible as you. Get me all the details and I'll see what I can do, no charge. And get a doctor's report on your cousin too. Let's give the police a go."

Susanne was surprised by the sudden effusive hug Pip sprang on her, accompanied by profuse thanks, as a down payment for her services.

With an exultant burst of energy, Pip ran down the stairs and out of the building, savouring the fresh air and the sights and sounds of the town. She couldn't wait to tell Charlotte all about it.

"We are going for a drive, Oscar," she said when she reached her car.

Her canine passenger expressed no objection and rested comfortably on a tartan blanket draped over the back seat. However, after about an hour of travel, he started to make clear that something was on his mind.

"Is it lunch time, by any chance?" Pip giggled.

Her thesis having been confirmed by a yap, she stopped at the next village they passed through and bought provisions in the shop. They strolled away from the main road up a steep narrow street towards the churchyard to have a picnic. Each entrance to the white-painted cottages lining their route had a single flagstone bridge from their front door to the tarmac in front; a narrow drainage culvert gurgled beneath, with fresh water sparkling towards the river far below. Oscar poked his inquisitive nose into the ditch.

"Careful you don't fall in," Pip cautioned, tightening his leash and earning a withering canine stare. "Don't look at me like that, you can't jump in and have a splash. Anyway, I thought you wanted some din-dins."

The mention of food put all thoughts of aquatic adventures from the dog's mind, and Oscar dragged his mistress the rest of the way up the hill to the church and a stunning view across the valley. The rooftops of the village dropped away below where Pip stood, and she could just see the back of her gold car near the shop, then the road, and then verdant fields, defying the December gloom, sloping down to the broad green-brown river that angrily followed gravity's call. The far side of the river valley was lined with deciduous trees, their bare branches stark grey against the dark ground beneath.

The two travelling companions munched their goodies uninterrupted, save for a brief visit from a thin robin redbreast; Pip sprinkled some crumbs from her sandwich, which the robin pecked at, under the vigilant gaze of Oscar. The bird hopped closer and closer, until Pip wondered if she might, oh so slowly, reach out and touch it, but just as her fingers seemed mere millimetres from its trusting head, her dog barked at the feathered intruder and the moment passed in a flustered flutter of wings.

"Why did you do that, Oscar? You scared him away."

A voice from behind said, "I'm surprised he let you get that close, he's a timid one is that robin." Pip twisted to see a grey-haired woman in a long overcoat smiling at her. "He comes here most days but won't stay. I thought he might be about to let you feed him, but I suppose he's too timid."

"He had a few crumbs."

"Did he? Well, that's all you can do, my dear," the lady remarked, and wandered away.

Pip tidied away the picnic, while Oscar scampered around the churchyard, and they then made the return trip to the car. The dog only barely avoided a post-lunch dip in the drainage culvert thanks to the vigilance of his mistress and they resumed their journey without further incident.

The old railway station near Charlotte's home was still bleak and deserted, and a row of crows perched on its roof gazed down on the little gold car as it drove past and onto the estate. Their distant caws serenaded Philippa Raven as she knocked on the door and was met by Aunt Jane.

"How's Charli?" Pip asked.

"Gone home," Jane replied, white with worry.

"What do you mean?"

"Adam's mother came, and I let her talk to Charli, like the trusting fool I am," Jane moaned.

"Glenda?" Pip was unable to pronounce the name without a guttural growl.

"I could hear her talking, saying how her Adam was sorry; how it was all a misunderstanding; how it won't happen again, and how my Charli needed to go home to him and make it right."

"And Charli went with her?"

"Yes."

"Right." Pip turned on her heel, but her aunt caught her elbow.

"Stop, she's made her mind up."

"I can't," Pip insisted. "You don't know what Glenda's like."

"I heard her drip enough poison about you that Charli won't have you near the wedding. She said you prostituted yourself to an old man just to get on in the company."

"That one again," Pip sighed.

"Charli said she already knew and that you were disgusting. Is it true, Pip?"

"Do you have to ask? Even if it was true, even if I had slept with every man in the company to work my way up, why would that make a difference? But since you need to ask, Aunt, the answer's no."

"I'm sorry, dear. I suppose I wanted to believe it because then everything else she said to Charli might be true. I don't think I know what's true or not any more, but I'm sure you're the last person who Charli will listen to. I'll talk to Ted when he gets home, she's our responsibility."

Pip was beaten. She returned to her car and sobbed. A cool nose nuzzled her affectionately.

"Oh, Oscar. Why can't people be as nice as you?"

Chapter 20

Lloyd placed the last of his items into a suitcase and took a final look around his university room while Will waited patiently in the corridor with a box of research papers at his feet. A familiar skinny young woman with short copper hair approached and hovered in the doorway.

"Are you really going?" Sally asked.

"Yes," Lloyd replied, "this is the last of my stuff."

"I hope it's not because you've felt unwelcome. I know I said some stupid things at that party. I was a bit drunk and you caught me unawares."

"Those are the times you might show what you really think, if you're not careful," Lloyd said, "but that's not why I'm leaving."

"That's just it," Sally pressed on. "It's not what I think, it's just all those adverts on TV with the icebergs, and the big tombstone, and 'there is now a deadly disease' stuff. I didn't know what to think, but I'm sure I was wrong."

"I don't blame you," Will interjected, "they're stupid and they don't tell you anything. They scare me."

"Thank you." Sally smiled gratefully.

"The truth is, I'm moving out because I need to concentrate," Lloyd said. "Radio Three are doing a series of programmes on promising new talents and they want me to do a ten-minute piece where I introduce the audience to a piece of music that they won't have heard before. How am I supposed to do that?"

"I'm sure you'll think of something."

"I haven't done yet," Lloyd sighed. "Anyway, that's why I need to be somewhere without constant parties. Not that there are many at the minute – nearly everyone's gone. When are you going home for Christmas, Sally?"

"I'm not," she replied. "My step-mum won't have me in the house, so I'm staying here. It's a bit creepy now everyone else is away."

"Why won't she have you?"

"We've never got on and when I turned eighteen, I was out. Thank heavens for grants, because I'd be in big trouble otherwise."

"No other family?" Will asked.

"No. Mum left when I was eight. I'll be fine here – I turn up my stereo really loud in the evenings and hang out in the library during the day."

Lloyd and Will exchanged glances and came to a mutual understanding.

"Or you could spend Christmas with us," Lloyd offered. "We've got a spare room."

"Really?"

"As long as you don't mind sharing our bathroom?"

"Ouch!" Sally was cut by the words. "That was a bit below the belt. I said I was sorry."

"No, he's being serious," Will laughed. "You won't get AIDS, but you might need a gas mask after Darren's hit the curry house. How long do you need to pack?"

"Ten minutes?" Sally suggested, but then got desperate. "Five?"

"Take ten, I'll let the taxi know." Will negotiated his exit with the cardboard box.

"Thank you," Sally called after him.

"What I forgot to mention," Lloyd said, "is that Christmas morning I sing in my gospel choir and you're roped into coming."

Sally grinned and hurried away to pack a bag. Lloyd waited, thinking how pretty her smile was.

~ * ~ * ~

The Reverend Johnson was particularly pleased with the church nativity display, not because it looked very different to previous years (it didn't), but rather because the number of people who visited it exceeded reasonable expectation. He bustled hither and thither, perfecting the arrangement.

The scrape of the heavy oak entrance door upon the old worn flagstones resonated heavenwards, or at least as high as the arched roof, and the gentle tapping of footsteps told him that he had a visitor.

"Hello, Pip," he said.

The young woman smiled and walked up to the Advent display for a closer look. She picked up Oscar so that he could get a better view, but the dog's ever-inquisitive nose led his long body in snake-like movements of fascination and made him hard to hold.

She returned her canine companion to the floor, "Are you free for a bit of a chat?"

"Certainly." The vicar gestured to the threadbare chairs beside the Mothers Union notice board. "Would you like some tea?"

"No thanks." She sat nervously on one of the chairs. "When I've finished you might not want me in here, let alone drinking your tea."

"Oh dear. You're not about to sacrifice a cockerel or something, are you?" he joked, sitting opposite.

"No, Oscar would eat it first. Which reminds me." Pip produced a biscuit from her pocket and proffered it to the little dog who munched it contentedly at her feet. "What I wanted to talk to you about is very difficult for me. Remember the things I told you about at my old job?"

"I'll never forget."

"People say I'm basically a prostitute… there's a word that I didn't think I ever would say in church."

"Why not?" the reverend asked. "The Bible's full of them, and there are two of them in Jesus' lineage. God seemed to have a lot more time for them than people did."

"I suppose so, but the rumours hurt because they're true. I was terrified of losing my job, I needed money, I couldn't go to my parents or anyone else, and I almost... well, you know."

"Philippa, you did nothing wrong."

"But if I hadn't stopped him? In fact, I still don't know why I did."

"That so many young women, and some boys too, are forced into such things is a stain on our alleged civilisation. You've nothing to reproach yourself for, but even if every lie about you was true, I'd still count you as one of the finest people I know. It appals me that anyone should think badly of themselves because of such things – it's a failure of all churches. I've only one thing to say to you. Sorry."

"Why should you be sorry?"

"Because you believed that you had nowhere to turn, and it didn't occur to you to ask your church for assistance. That is not your fault, it is ours, so I am humbly sorry."

"Thank you," Pip said. "I don't think you'll like the next bit, though."

"That sounds ominous."

"I'm in love with a man who is in the process of getting a divorce."

"Ah, well, the Church of England pretty much exists only because a less than exemplary king wanted a divorce, so you may be on firmer ground than you realise – tell me about the relationship."

"Nothing physical. We met when he separated from his wife a while back and remained friends when they reconciled, mainly just writing letters to each other. Then, he broke our golden rule and told me that he loved me, and we lost touch."

"Any children?"

"One, a lovely little girl, and I adore her. Anyway, he broke off contact but found me again a few days ago. His wife's been having an affair and they mutually decided that their relationship was over."

"It seems on the face of it that neither of you have anything to reproach yourselves for. Look, the Samaritan woman who Jesus met at the well had been married five times and was living with another man, yet He chose her, and she answered; her background clearly didn't trouble Him."

"But—" Pip began but was interrupted by a vicar in full flow.

"But sometimes, people make mistakes. My advice is to go and be happy – I'd say be careful, but you're too sensible to do otherwise."

"I'll take things slowly, I promise," Pip assured him, "but I wasn't worried about the divorce. What I was going to say was that I'm scared that I have such strong feelings for a man that I have kissed exactly once and who I've seen in person only a handful of times – but I feel like I know his soul. Am I being stupid?"

"Ah," the Reverend Johnson felt slightly stupid for opining theology rather than listening to his parishioner. "Love at first sight happens to some and not to others. I've known couples who've been together twenty years and they don't know each other, and yet I knew everything that I would ever need to know about Rebecca on the night we met. Trust your instincts, but tread lightly, and listen to the Man upstairs."

At that exact moment, a long-faced bespectacled man with a receding hairline descended the old wooden steps from the upper gallery, smiled apologetically for disturbing them, picked up a hymn book and returned whence he came.

"I mean God, not Mr Thornhill the organist," the vicar clarified. He gazed thoughtfully towards the lofty perch that housed the musical brain of the church. "Does he ever go home, I wonder?"

However, Pip had stopped listening, instead working herself up to broach her main reason for speaking to the vicar. It didn't take long to explain the story of Charlotte, of her injuries, of escaping Adam's clutches, and how his manipulative mother had persuaded her to return. The reverend listened gravely as the facts were laid out, wincing at the description of the injuries.

"What should I do next?" Pip asked when she finished.

"Nothing," the vicar replied.

"Nothing?" Pip was indignant.

"Yes, you've done all you can. In fact, you're the last person who could help. Other than be there for her if Charlotte reaches out, you must accept that there are others better placed to help. Thanks to you, your aunt and uncle are aware of the situation and I'm sure they are sensible people."

"That's very hard to accept."

"I only know what you have told me, but I do know domestic violence escalates quickly. You've humiliated Adam on two occasions now, so you're a trigger to him. I beg of you to stay away and let other people look after her, at least until you have more information."

"I can't leave her with a... thing like Adam!" Pip was aghast.

"And yet you must, and your reaction says why. You want to help and protect Charlotte, but you also have a righteous anger towards Adam, which I share. I'd gladly thrash the brute and take it up with God when my time comes, but that overlooks the problem that your cousin believes herself in love with him. There's a real risk that the more you try to part them, the more she may cling on."

"So, what are you saying?"

"Trust your aunt and uncle to make the right decisions. In time, hopefully Charlotte will see Adam for what he is."

~ * ~ * ~

"I still can't get used to being on the wrong side of the road," Tori remarked as Gavin drove them through the streets of his home town. She ran the back of her finger down the slightly misted pane of glass in the passenger door, leaving a clear track snaking from the top and exposing the accumulated spattering of raindrops on the outside. "I suppose that I'll have to get used to it, if this is to be my forever home. How do you think your parents will take the news of you proposing to me?"

"How do you think yours will take you saying yes?"

"What, engaged after eight weeks?" she giggled. "Probably not well, but they'll like you. Anyway, you haven't asked properly yet. Popping the question when I'm helping you change your duvet cover is not the height of romance, nor what I am willing to tell my grandchildren."

"You'll be wanting an engagement ring next!" Gavin teased.

"You'd better believe it, buster, Boston girls are forward but very traditional."

"OK, it's our secret until I rustle up a ring and get on bended knee." Gavin briefly glanced at Tori; she was drinking in the varying architecture of the houses they passed and imagining living in one. Wondering what it was about her upper lip that he found so irresistible, he pulled the car to the side of the road and turned off the engine.

"Is this your house?" she asked, looking incredulously at the sign on the front door of the nearest property, which read, 'Fiona Hepworth-Garland. Dance and Deportment for Young Ladies of Distinction'.

"No," he replied, edging closer, "my place is about five minutes from here."

"Then, why have you stopped?"

"Because I can't wait another five minutes to kiss you." He pulled her willingly to him.

"Gavin Knight!" Tori exclaimed breathlessly when their lips parted. "I see my Bostonian forwardness is catching."

"Yup," he replied, shuffling back into the centre of his seat. He turned the ignition key and was rewarded with a loud banging from the engine.

"That doesn't sound right," Tori said.

"Good old British Leyland," Gavin grumbled, turning off the cacophony. "I'll have to ring Dad and get him to come and tow us."

"Well, that's an awkward way to meet my future in-laws!"

"Looks like we'll be keeping our secret for a good while longer, because I doubt I can afford to have the car fixed and buy a ring."

Tori grabbed Gavin's arm and pulled him back to her, kissing him fervently.

"I don't want money, I don't care about a ring, I just want you to love me," she whispered.

As soon as Pip opened the front door of the house, Bobbie's arms were tight around her.

"I missed you so much," cried the little girl.

"Me too!" Pip pressed her face against the mass of blonde curls and then extricated herself sufficiently for a cursory hug from Theo, who leaned over his daughter's head. "My, how you've grown, Bobbie. Come inside, someone's dying to meet you, he's my special little friend."

Oscar scampered up to the girl and formed an immediate bond; within minutes he had presented her with his favourite ball and they were playing a game of fetch up and down the hallway. Lyn emerged from the kitchen and was transfixed by the excited mass of golden curls.

"Where do you want these?" Theo asked, dragging two large suitcases through the door.

"Upstairs and first on the left," Pip replied. "It'll be a squeeze for you two with the Z-bed in there, I'm afraid. I'll be downstairs on the sofa."

"No, no!" Theo protested. "I'll take the sofa. I'm sure you and Bobbie can make things work much more comfortably."

Lyn was still looking at the girl running in her hallway.

"Bobbie," she said. The child stopped short and looked up with big eyes. "Would you like to sleep in my Sharon's room? There's lots more space for you and Daddy in there, and I expect you might find some of her old toys in the bottom of the wardrobe."

"Are you quite sure?" Theo asked.

"I am. Straight ahead at the top of the stairs. It's time it was used properly."

Theo carried a suitcase up the narrow staircase. Pip went to pick up the other and follow him, but it failed to budge. She heaved at the case like a desperate pretender trying to extract the sword from the stone, but red-faced with effort, she only budged it an inch or two.

"Pip, dear, why don't you move the Z-bed into Sharon's room?" Lyn suggested.

"I'll not be beaten!" Pip proclaimed, squirming with effort.

"Let me take that," Theo said, returning from above and picking up the case with one hand and a slight grunt.

"Men!" Pip was determined to be unimpressed by his raw strength and quite certain her heart didn't skip a beat.

"What did I do?" he asked, pausing to look back.

"I had it all in hand," Pip said.

"No, you didn't," Lyn interjected.

"Shh!" Pip hissed. "Whose side are you on?"

"I can bring it back down, if you like?" Theo offered.

"No, no," Pip waved a regal dismissal, "you may as well finish now you've started – and you can move the Z-bed as well! What have you got in that case, anyway? Did you bring your own bricks?"

"Lots of things," Bobbie replied on behalf of her father, "including a surprise for you."

"For me?" Pip's faux anger shifted to badly concealed excitement.

"Daddy! Bring down Pip's surprise!"

"I'm sure she doesn't want to be bothered with that," Theo said, going to Pip's room for the Z-bed. Then his head appeared over the banisters. "Or does she?"

"Whenever, no rush," Pip attempted to sound nonchalant.

"Aye aye!" Theo vanished again. A clattering from above suggested that the folding bed was not cooperating.

"Alright, you win!" Pip squeaked, running up the stairs, followed by Bobbie and Lyn, who carried an insistent Oscar. "Get my surprise – I'll sort the bed."

Pip expertly collapsed the Z-bed and wheeled it through to Sharon's room where Theo handed her a book. She spent several seconds staring at it. Why had they given her a children's book? It was square, with a stiff green cover and a cartoon of a lady with very messy hair... and the title was 'Mrs Nestyhead', under which was written 'by Pip Raven' and much lower down, 'Illustrated by Theo Dickson'.

"I don't understand." She furrowed her brow.

"When we were in Jersey, I started to draw again for the first time in ages," Theo explained. "I did some of these pictures as a surprise for Bobbie, because she loved the story so much, and we ended up doing the whole thing. An old school friend of mine is in publishing, and I sent it through to him. This is a proof copy, if you're willing to give it a go?"

"Give what a go?"

"Publishing it, Pip!" an exasperated Lyn interrupted. "Surely you must have understood that?"

"You're saying someone wants to publish my story?"

"Yes!" Theo, Lyn and Bobbie chorused. Oscar barked too because it seemed the fun thing to do.

Pip remained silent, flicking through the pages of the book, seeing her story brought to life by Theo's quirky illustrations.

"So, what do you say?" Theo asked.

"What do I say?" Pip repeated. "Yes, please!"

This time, their embrace was far from cursory.

~ * ~ * ~

Darren and Will spent a fruitless day traipsing around employment agencies, filling out countless forms and handing out copies of their CV. Back home, the weary job-seekers found Lloyd and Sally relaxing in the living room, listening to Terrence Trent D'Arby on the hi-fi.

"It was a long shot," Will wheezed, collapsing into an armchair and fishing a well-used tissue from his pocket to blow his nose.

"Nobody's hiring in the week before Christmas," Darren said, "but we've got a few days on a function at a football club in the New Year."

"Which one?" Sally asked.

"Search me, I know nothing about the stupid game," Darren snapped.

"Go easy, mate," Will interjected, noticing a flush beneath Sally's freckles, "it's a fair question."

"Sorry," Darren muttered, "I'm just worried about finding the rent on this place."

"I don't suppose you fancy moving in full-time, Sally?" Will asked.

"It's tempting – I'll think about it," she replied. "I have to post some Christmas cards – anyone want to come?"

"Yeah, I will." Lloyd jumped to his feet and followed her out.

"What did you do that for?" Darren grumbled.

"Do what?" Will said. "Oh, Sally. Well, we've an empty room."

"She's an airhead."

"That's not very nice – she can't be that stupid, she goes to uni. And Lloyd likes her, so why don't you?"

"She's so bloody cheerful," Darren grumped. "Look at this place – she's been here a few days and suddenly we have Christmas decorations on everything and a tree that looks like Barbara Cartland's hat stand! We've never bothered with a tree before."

"What's the harm?" Will retorted. "Not everyone wants your entropy-dedicated gothic theme park. I think you're scared that she's going to decorate you next."

As if on cue, Sally reappeared holding some sparkling Deely-boppers and popped one onto her head.

"These were in the Post Office when I was buying stamps yesterday. I thought we could all wear them at Christmas dinner."

Will reverently accepted his and perched it amongst his wayward mop of curly hair, and then took another and placed it with malevolent glee upon Darren's unimpressed brow.

"Take a picture," Darren snarked, "you could send it to my dad."

"Oh, what a lovely idea," Sally said. "I'll nip and get my Polaroid."

"Oh, I like her, she's a keeper," Will said after she had skipped from the room. "Look at you, Santa's little elf."

Darren went to rip off the headband, but realised Will was laughing for the first time in ages. His attitude to Sally changed instantly; if she made Will happy, then she was welcome. He didn't, however, allow his demeanour to betray his change of heart.

"Yeah, it's a Christmas miracle," he grumbled, using his most sardonic tones.

~ * ~ * ~

"I like your little rosebushes, they are very pretty," Bobbie observed as she wandered around Pip's bedroom.

"Thank you. My grandad helped me grow them and they give me lots of lovely flowers," Pip was hunched over an old shaving mirror of Bob's, applying lipstick. "Can you see the spray bottle next to the pot on the left?"

The little girl carefully examined the area around the flowerpots. "Yes."

"Good. Why don't you give the leaves a spray? Not too much, just a bit."

Bobbie concentrated, tongue protruding from the corner of her mouth and head cocked to one side; she squeezed the atomizer and sent a pure mist over the perfectly pruned plants.

"The little one on the left doesn't look well," she observed.

"That's very sad. They all fell out of a window one day, and that one hasn't recovered as well as the others yet."

"How did they fall out of the window?"

"They were trying to escape the tickle monster." Pip launched a sudden attack with her fingers, causing a fit of giggles. They spent a few happy moments in recovery and Pip sensed an opening for an important question. "Bobbie, where do you want to be for Christmas?"

"Here. Why?"

"Won't you miss Mummy?"

"No." Bobbie's head movements became exaggerated, as if she was disturbed by a fly.

Letting the matter drop, Pip stood up and twirled in her blue dress.

"How do I look?"

"Like a film star. I like your hair – it used to be short, but now it's long."

"It's not as long or as pretty as yours. Shall we go and see if Daddy is ready?"

Bobbie stayed put, staring at the floor.

"Mummy tried sending me to boarding school but Daddy wouldn't let her. I heard them arguing, and now they aren't together."

"They both wanted what they thought was best for you, and I'm sure it's not why they split up."

"Then why?"

"Sometimes two grown-ups realise they need different things, but your parents both love you lots. Talk to Daddy about it, and Mummy too when you see her."

"Aren't you going to be my new mummy?"

"You don't need a new mummy when you have such a nice one already. How about you and me being best friends? That's even more fun, because best friends do fun things together, like have sleepovers."

"Ooh!" Bobbie squealed. "Can we have one tonight?"

"I don't see why not. I won't be home very late. You go to bed when Lyn tells you, and when I get back, I'll fetch you and we'll snaffle a midnight feast and sleep on the floor in here. How does that sound?"

A scream of elation followed by a dash out to the upstairs landing appeared to be confirmation. The excited girl danced to her father.

"Daddy, Daddy, Pip and I are having a sleepover tonight!"

"Are you indeed? Aren't you the lucky one?" Theo glanced at Pip, who was standing in the doorway to her bedroom.

"Yes, and we are going to have a midnight feast, so don't let her eat too much dinner," Bobbie instructed.

"I promise to be good," Pip assured them both, with the kind of smile that makes life worth living for the observer.

She and Theo left the house and walked to his car, which was parked in the road outside. He opened the passenger door of the Audi Quattro with ill-concealed pride.

"I hadn't seen your car before," Pip remarked. "It's very posh!"

"Oh, I picked it up after we came back to England."

Theo fired up the engine and revved it, wanting his girlfriend to appreciate the throaty roar as the beast awakened.

"This must have cost a fortune," Pip said, immune to the charms of the mechanical symphony.

"It's not brand new!" Theo wondered why he was justifying himself. "And I have a few quid locked away for a rainy day."

"Sorry. It's just we come from very different worlds," Pip explained. "Every Sunday morning, my dad washes and polishes his car and checks the engine. Twice a year, he does his own service because he's scared stiff of it breaking down – he couldn't afford to replace it. But you can spend thousands and not worry about it, even without a job."

"If the truth be known, I spent much more than was wise," Theo admitted, "but I'd always promised myself one… and I wanted to impress you."

In the darkness, she bobbed across the divide and kissed his cheek lightly enough not to leave lipstick on his face.

"I am impressed. I'm from a place where a car like this is an impossible dream."

"You're an impossible dream come true for me," Theo said. "But speaking of impossible things, I'm never going to find the restaurant if you don't tell me if I'm driving in the right direction."

"Oops!" Pip giggled. "Keep going along here until you come to a big roundabout, take the first exit, down the steep hill and keep going for about two miles. The place will be on the right, up a bit of a track, but you can see it from the road."

"A track, you say?" He smiled in the night. "Perfect for a Quattro."

"I really wouldn't get your hopes up, if I were you."

They had travelled for several minutes in comfortable silence when Theo said, "Thanks for being so great with Bobbie. I'm not sure how much sleep you'll get tonight, she's so excited by your sleepover."

"I don't mind, it'll be like when I was little, and Sharon stayed over. We built dens in my room by stretching a sheet from the bed to my dressing table."

"Do you miss Sharon?"

"I miss who I thought she was, and who I hope she truly is," Pip replied, thinking kindly of her childhood friendship; but sweet nostalgia ends when cruel betrayal lies at the end of memory lane. She snapped her head to look out of the passenger window. "Speaking of missing people, I am worried about Bobbie and her mum."

"Why, has Bobbie said something?"

"In a way. I think she's cross with Claire – she knows about the boarding school idea. She heard you arguing."

"That's harsh. Claire loved boarding school. It wasn't intended to be a punishment."

"Whatever the rights and wrongs, Bobbie's in danger of emotionally blocking Claire because she thinks her mum doesn't want to be with her, and your divorce adds to the rejection. From a child's perspective, it makes sense."

"I've never spoken badly of Claire to Bobbie."

"No, but have you ever spoken positively?"

"I hope so, but I'll make sure I do."

"That's why I think you're the best person I've ever known." Pip reached for Theo's hand where it rested on the gearstick. "Has Claire arrived at the Richmond flat?"

"I haven't heard otherwise, so I'll assume so. I've been too busy to check. I've still not told her we are staying in the same house as you."

"But it's not like we've done anything!"

"No, more's the pity," Theo agreed a little too readily.

"Please be patient, don't rush me." Pip experienced a small surge of anxiety.

"I didn't mean it like that, sorry. I suppose Claire will jump to conclusions anyway, so I don't know why I didn't tell her the full story. And she's hardly in a position to throw stones."

"She wouldn't be the first to jump to conclusions about me," Pip sighed.

"Sorry, I forgot about all the business at your school," Theo said, "but that's ancient history. No one who knows you could believe you were capable of it."

Pip remained mute.

"What's wrong?" Theo asked.

"I'd have agreed with you before you went away, but things happened to me," Pip stumbled over her words. "Now there are even worse rumours about me."

"Do you want to talk about them?"

"Not really, not tonight." Pip fiddled anxiously with her handbag. "You might go off me if you heard them. What is it about me that makes people believe these things?"

"What is it about them, I think you mean," Theo corrected. "They're the ones who delight in rumour, innuendo and half-truths. If any of them want to try telling me one of their twisted stories about you, they'll be counting their teeth on an X-ray of their stomach. You don't need to tell me anything, we've both got a past which we're drawing a line under tonight."

Pip laughed and then squeaked, "That's the restaurant!" She pointed to a building situated well back from the road on their right.

Theo steered onto the track that led up to the old inn, which alas necessitated none of the Quattro's 4x4 capabilities. The surface of the car park was an uneven aggregate and they crossed it arm in arm, partly because Pip was wearing heels, but mainly because it was nice to do so. The establishment had a Dickensian air to it, with old beams on the ceiling and a dark-wood bar with a glittering rainbow of optics behind. Near the large fireplace, a single huge blazing log at its centre, was a restaurant area with well-spaced tables draped with stiff linen cloths. A waitress led them to a quiet corner close enough to the fire to be warm but set a little apart from the other patrons.

Pip had borrowed one of Lyn's coats for the evening. Too large to wear, it nevertheless looked stylish draped over her shoulders. Theo moved to take it from her, and as he did so, his fingers ran along her exposed skin up to her neck; she shivered and gave an involuntary intake of breath.

"Is something wrong?" he asked.

"Nothing at all," Pip replied. "In fact, quite the opposite."

Neither of them had a large appetite that evening due to mutual excitement for their first official date, so they skipped starters and went straight to the main course. They sipped their wine, facing each other over the flickering red candle in the centre of the table.

"I think Bobbie should wake up with her mother on Christmas morning," Pip said, "and you should be there too. It's just a bit of continuity. We can't let a wedge come between her and Claire, none of us want that."

"I can't pretend I haven't given the matter some thought." Theo swirled his wine in its glass and sniffed the bouquet, torn between knowing she was right and not wanting to spend a second out of her company, especially at Christmas.

"Divorce is hard on kids."

"I've something to tell you and I don't know how you'll take it." Theo had a slight quiver in his voice as he leaned across the table and took her hands in his. "Claire and I were never married. We referred to each other as husband and wife because, well, we didn't have better terms and we didn't want Bobbie to suffer – you know how people are about these things, even these days."

"But why didn't you tell me?" Pip managed to ask through her surprise.

"I was embarrassed, worried you might disapprove."

"You know me better than that." Pip pulled her hands from his and sat back. She was not angry as such, but disappointed that she was misunderstood. Maybe Gavin was right, maybe she was inaccessible and unknowable.

"I do, I'm sorry." Theo realised his mistake. "The truth is, I felt a failure. I asked Claire to marry me years ago when she got pregnant and she refused. She said it's an outdated institution, but at the time I thought her father convinced her I was after their money. Now I believe it was because she was still in love with her ex. When Bobbie came along, we just pretended. I should've told you long ago, but it got harder as time went on. Are you very angry?"

Still stunned, Pip took a few moments to think, her brow furrowed.

"I think I am the opposite of angry," she said, "I think I might be very happy. Except..."

"Except what?"

"Except marriage means something to me. Not right now, but one day. Just so you know."

"That's not going to be a problem."

"But I have to go slowly," Pip insisted. "I'm a bit... damaged."

"You seem perfect to me."

"Please don't say that. I'm not perfect."

"OK, how about this? You are perfect for me. Good enough?"

"Good enough," Pip laughed. "Anyway, it's an improvement on prize totty, or whatever it was you called me when we met."

"Don't remind me," he groaned.

"Ah! So now you're saying I'm not prize totty?"

"Quite the opposite," Theo regained his verbal equilibrium, "I should have said officer totty."

"Well, I outranked you, remember, so maybe you're my fancy boy."

"Yes, ma'am." Theo adored her eyes and the way they caught the glint of candlelight.

After their meal, as they strained to see where they were going in the darkness of the now almost empty car park, Pip said, "I think Claire needs to be the one who asks Bobbie to come for Christmas. Don't let it seem like it comes from you, and especially not from me."

"You're sure about this? You and I being apart on our first Christmas?"

"Yes," she replied. Pip's internal wobble externalised when her heel caught in a hole in the rough ground, but fortunately she was holding on to Theo's arm.

"Careful," he said with the tenderness of a truly strong man. "It looks like you need me as much as I need you. I hope you'll always want me by your side to catch you when you fall."

"Then, you don't think I am insulated from you?" she asked, hopeful that he could know the true her, and fearful that he may not like what he found.

"Insulated?" Theo was incredulous. "What could you mean by that?"

"Can you reach me, the real me? Can our souls touch?" Pip begged with a desperation born of self-denial.

"Every time I see your eyes, or hear your voice, or even just think of you," Theo replied. "It's not a question of if they can touch because they're already intertwined, never to be separated. I could never feel the same about anyone else."

Theo kissed her in the invisible night and her cool damp tongue darted to meet his, leaving traces of promise and Liebfraumilch. They were breathless when their lips parted, and they silently continued their walk to the Audi, which stood alone in a less-used corner of the car park. Theo opened the passenger door and waited as Pip climbed in and then walked around the car to the opposite side.

"Don't start the car yet," she said when he was in the driver's seat.

Pip leaned across the silent cabin with newly freed passion and Theo's lips met hers in perfect union; the electricity, the raw emotion, felt like a regenerative force in her still broken soul. How long they kissed was unknown, but they eventually broke off and held each other in the darkness.

"I love you," Theo whispered as he gently kissed her ear. "I have from the moment I saw you at the stables. At last I can say it in person."

"I know." Pip slid her arms further around his body and held on as if she feared being ripped away from him by a tide of misfortune. Maybe she was still too broken to be worthy of love. "Me too."

"What do we do now?"

"Now?" Pip edged back into her seat and put on her seatbelt. "We go home. I have a sleepover date with my best friend."

~ * ~ * ~

On Christmas morning, Bobbie awoke with a shout of excitement and ran from her bedroom in the Richmond flat. She roused her father from his slumber on the sofa by bouncing mercilessly upon him, begging him to wake up so that present opening could begin; trapped inside his sleeping bag, Theo could offer no resistance until he finally wriggled his arms free and bear-hugged his daughter into giggling submission.

Claire came in, tousle-haired and pale from late-night present wrapping. She perched on the edge of an easy chair beside the Christmas tree and picked a large gift which she handed to her daughter. Bobbie tore the paper off and screamed with delight when the box beneath was shown to contain a doll and an accompanying toy pony, which bore a striking resemblance to Polo. Peering over the top of the curls that had bounced ecstatically to her embrace, the mother mouthed her thanks to her now ex-partner as he lay, merman-like, upon the settee.

Gavin also woke early and crept downstairs to the kitchen to make some tea. A creaking floorboard told him that he was not the only one unable to sleep and Tori soon padded onto the chilled linoleum and tiptoed to kiss his cheek. He poured two cups and they carried them through to the lounge where he lit a fire in the old grate. Sitting on the floor cuddled together, they sipped their drinks and watched the orange flames darting between the lumps of coal and grey streams of smoke weaving up the chimney and out into the silent midwinter morn. Slowly the warmth began to radiate, thawing their blood and igniting their hearts.

Hearing his parents stirring upstairs, Gavin seized his moment and reached into his pocket to produce a small velvet-covered box. Tori's questioning eyes flicked between the box and her love as she slowly opened the lid and saw a ring; the jewels signified the modest means of a student, but their value was beyond computation to her.

He removed the gift from its velvet prison and asked, "Which one?" Her left hand was held out and her ring finger-wiggled. "Are you sure?" he whispered, but she had no words, only the bobbing of her dark wavy hair could answer him. "Marry me?" were his last words before she kissed him. Gavin knew himself to be the luckiest, happiest man on the planet, and he didn't care that he had no way to get his car fixed.

In Manchester, the four flatmates were awake at a more civilised hour. After church with Lloyd, unlike any service she had been to before, Sally revealed a rigidly organised schedule of party games, music, drinking and food (an unconventional festive repast of pizza, garlic bread and chocolate yule log), all of which served to give Darren the first happy Christmas since his adolescence.

Pip stayed at her family home, sleeping on the sofa. She and Oscar experienced a similarly rude awakening to Theo when Daniel came careering into the living room at an unearthly hour, trailed by a groggy, but not uninterested, Matthew. Aided and abetted by the little dog, the three siblings created so much noise that their parents were soon obliged to join them for present-giving.

Despite their mysterious financial windfall, money was still tight in the Raven household, and their gifts were meagre compare to those in many other families, save the one expensive present for Daniel that sat under the tree. Pip's parents gave her a coat to replace the one that ended up in a skip, which itself had replaced one that Sharon lost years before.

Pip and Lyn met later at St Michael's for Christmas Eucharist, where they sat side by side in the chilly pews and gave silent thanks that the other had come into their lives. Mark and his fiancée were visiting, so Pip knew Lyn wasn't going back to an empty home.

After a delicious meal in the Raven household, Matthew went to see his girlfriend while Pip and her mother visited the care home. The festive atmosphere of the communal sitting room was enriched by post-luncheon snores, but Gran and Mr Swann were both alert and pleased to see them. Oscar was delighted to be reunited with his former master, and the two old friends were impossible to keep apart until it was time to leave.

In the late evening, when everyone else had gone to bed, Pip had one last secret gift to open; it was from Theo. With Oscar snoozing beside her, she carefully removed the golden wrapping paper and absently flattened it beneath the palm of her hand while she examined the box it had once enveloped. Inside was a gold ladies' watch, which she fastened around her wrist, holding out her arm and watching it glint in the glow from the only lamp in the room.

A piece of paper, almost unnoticed in the box, fluttered to the ground. It was a note from Theo.

'Never another Christmas apart, my love.'

Chapter 21

After a long day temping in a local department store, Darren plodded upstairs to the flat, every step a mountain to his tired legs. He watched the news every day and heard the economy was booming, but the new-found prosperity hadn't reached him yet. Instead, he was footsore and resentful of the unshackled consumerism surrounding him. His relative poverty felt more a punishment than a state of being and were it not for Sally becoming a flatmate, the financial burden might be overwhelming. The front door jammed slightly when he pushed it open, and he helped it on its way with a frustrated kick.

"Hello?" he called out. There was no reply, so he went to the kitchen to see what food there was; half a tin of tomatoes and the remnants of a packet of pasta were all that was on offer.

"Sod it," he muttered, deciding to wait for Will to get home and maybe go to the chippie together.

As Darren entered the living room, Lloyd's and Sally's heads popped up over the back of the sofa, where they were sitting at such a degree of inclination that the rear of the seat had obscured them. Their startled expressions and dishevelled appearance suggested they found each other more interesting than their television programme.

"Didn't hear you come in, mate," Lloyd panted. "We're watching telly."

"But you hate travel programmes," Darren said.

"Sally was interested."

"I think she was more interested in your tonsils, mate. You've got more lipstick on than she has."

"Busted," Sally giggled.

"You two are about as subtle as a steamroller," Darren laughed. "It's been obvious for a while."

A clattering from the front door preceded Will's arrival; he was clearly excited.

"Lloyd and Sally are an item," Darren announced before anyone else could say anything.

"Was it supposed to be a secret?" Will didn't wait for a reply. "I have news. We've been asked to an acid-house party."

"A what?" asked Sally.

"They're huge parties playing cool music held in big old warehouses and the like," Will explained. "It's a really big scene around here."

"That's not music," Lloyd tutted. "Not proper music, anyway."

"It's as much proper music as anything else!" Darren was nettled by Lloyd's superior tone. "Have you ever heard any?"

"Enough. Each to their own, but we all know it's more about drugs than music – everyone high on Ecstasy."

"And?" Darren snapped. "You're sounding like your mother."

"What's so wrong with that? You've no idea what it was like growing up where I did, surrounded by lowlife drug dealers. My mum worked hard all her life and kept me on the straight until I could get out."

"Calm down," Darren dismissed Lloyd's words with a wave of his hand. "It's hardly smack."

"I know what it is!" Lloyd's temper snapped. "I want nothing to do with it. You know how some people are making money at these parties. Do what you want, Darren, but keep it away from me, I've got a career and I'm not ruining it. The cops love to find a working-class black boy in the vicinity of drugs, even pills that are as synthetic as the so-called music."

"Lloyd, you're not being fair," Sally interjected. "You know they like that sort of music, and so do you sometimes, I've heard you. You're stressed, we all know it, but don't take it out on them."

Lloyd took what Sally said on board and bowed his head slightly, rubbing his tired eyes.

"Sorry, Sally's right," he said. "I still can't find a piece of music for the radio station thing and the uni's pressuring me. The deadline's in a couple of weeks. Sorry."

"Us too." Will patted Lloyd's back. "Aren't we?" He shot a look at Darren, who was taking a little longer to dismount from his high horse.

"Yes." Darren found the goodwill to make the peace.

"It's ironic," Will remarked. "Your mate Sam's business model was selling drugs at gigs – it's just been scaled up. Imagine how the poor sod's going to feel when he realises."

~ * ~ * ~

Neither Will nor Darren could believe how many people packed into the disused warehouse, or the shuddering vibration of energy that connected the crowd. They were invited to arrive early, while the party was still being set up, and Will immediately struck up a rapport with the organisers; both men helped in an unofficial capacity, handling some of the tech that didn't need specific expertise.

Darren was standing on an elevated platform when he first spotted Sharon among the sea of writhing dancers beneath the flashing lights. She danced sensuously, arms raised, eyes closed, in chemically induced euphoria, somehow moving slowly and yet in time with the fast beat of the music. A man was with her; he was tall, handsome, muscular, more compos mentis than his dancing partner, and attracting the attention of several of the female revellers – he appeared to be a celebrity of some sort.

As a matter of principle, Darren made a point of being unimpressed. He had no intention of approaching Sharon, who clearly didn't wish to be found, and she soon disappeared amongst the heaving throng of bodies. As brief as her sighting had been, it was equally short-lived in Darren's memory – by the time he was home, he had forgotten the whole thing.

~ * ~ * ~

In early April, Will and Darren were asked to staff another corporate event at a major football club. They turned up wearing white shirts and black trousers, and were assigned to the directors' box, which hosted an elaborate buffet and a bar with free-flowing drinks. Will was designated a greeter, checking each guest's invitation against a prepared list, while Darren took on basic waitering duties, interminably moving anonymously among the guests with a tray of drinks.

A large plate-glass window ran the length of the room, looking patronisingly over the stadium stands to the pitch below. The team were taking part in a training session for the entertainment of the assembled wealth in the directors' box, and one of the more flamboyant footballers performed an ostentatious overhead kick which generated a ripple of applause from a handful of guests who witnessed it. Interested to see what the fuss was about, Darren peered through the window and for the first time in his life, recognised a soccer star – it was the man seen dancing with Sharon a few short weeks beforehand. Anger and resentment bubbled within Darren – although he disdained celebrity, he felt it unjust that Sharon, who had so little talent, should be the one fraternising with the A-list.

"Cheer up, it might never happen," remarked a male guest. "You should see the look on your face, son."

Struggling to keep his temper, Darren almost walked into a woman, whose expensive white lacy top and spandex miniskirt narrowly avoided a tray of drinks being spilled over them.

"Watch where you're going!" she snapped before resuming flirting with a grey-haired man whose once muscular physique had relapsed to a more gelatinous state. His attention was captive to her long legs, accentuated by white stilettoes and stockings, the tops of which were barely covered by the hem of her skirt.

It was the voice that betrayed Sharon – her expensive clothes, makeup and flamboyant hairstyle rendered her unrecognisable. It was clear that she hadn't recognised Darren, but why would she pay attention to a lowly waiter when a club director was absorbing her artificial fascination?

Darren hurried into the reception area to find Will had been relegated to watching and fetching people's coats.

"Sharon's here."

"Are you sure?"

"Of course! Not that she remembered me, stuck-up cow. I just served her a drink."

Will flipped through the pages of the guest list.

"There are three Sharons here. What's her surname again?"

"Wells."

"Not here."

"Look how she's dressed. Do you reckon she is an escort, like Tracy?" Darren spotted another waiter and sidled up to him, gesturing towards Sharon. "Do you know who she is?"

"Yeah," the waiter replied, making sure they were not overheard. "I won't name names but she's the bit on the side of one of the first-team regulars. He's married, so he gets the chairman to invite her – that's the bloke she's all over at the minute."

Darren returned to Will and relayed the information.

"Guests of the chairman are marked with an asterisk." Will flipped through the pages. "Here we are. There's only two women on the list and one of them is Sharon Watts."

"What, like the one off Eastenders? That would be her kind of joke."

"I've an address for her."

"Seriously?"

"Why would she lie? It's where they send the invitations and the freebies."

"I can't believe it," Darren exhaled a long slow breath. "We've actually found Sharon. We'll ring Gavin as soon as we're home – I'll wager he and that girl Pip will be up here before we know it."

Chapter 22

Lloyd woke early, worrying about the deadline for finding a piece of music for the radio programme. He had countless suggestions from his PhD. supervisor, but all of them left him feeling frustrated. This was his big chance and he was having to sift through someone else's second-best options – it would have been easier had he been asked to produce an original composition of his own, but that wasn't what the show was about.

Lying in bed just seemed to be a futile waste of time so he decided to get up and watch breakfast TV. The living room door was half open before he remembered the four guests sleeping in there and pulled it closed again, choosing instead to sit at the small kitchen table. Will had left a half-read copy of NME on the counter and Lloyd flicked through it for want of something else to do, but his mind remained preoccupied.

Pip was disturbed by something but didn't realise it was the door opening and shutting. For a while, she enjoyed lying in the comforting netherworld between sleep and full consciousness and basked in the warmth and weight of Theo's arm which was draped over her. She opened her eyes and saw Gavin and Tori cuddled together still deep in contented sleep.

Unfortunately, she came to realise that sleeping on the floor after a long journey was one thing but continuing to lie there after you are awake is quite another – in fact it was downright uncomfortable. She took great pains not to wake the others as she wriggled out of her sleeping bag, and from under her boyfriend's sleepy embrace, and tiptoed into the kitchen for a glass of water.

"Hi," Lloyd said without looking up, "did I wake you?"

"No, I was just thirsty. Is it alright if I make us a cup of tea?"

"That would be nice thanks."

Pip filled the kettle and eyed her host, sensing something was on his mind.

~ 353 ~

"Do you think Gav and I are doing the wrong thing, going to see Sharon?" she asked.

"Some things aren't right or wrong, you just have to do them," he replied, "but I think I'd do the same if it was someone close to me."

"What's wrong, then? I can tell something's on your mind."

"Just a ton of pressure." Lloyd grimaced. "I'm due to play cello live on radio, but I'm supposed to introduce a piece of lost music the audience won't have heard before. I have to pick one by Friday, but nothing feels right."

"I know a piece that's the most beautiful thing that I've ever heard," Pip said, "and I'll guarantee that no one will know it. I have the sheet music, if you'd like me to send it to you?"

"Couldn't hurt, thanks." Lloyd visibly brightened, though he didn't know why he should feel positive about something that was likely to be the (no doubt praiseworthy) efforts of an amateur.

The knocks and bumps of other members of the household getting up reached their ears and Pip offered to cook breakfast.

"No way, you're the guest," Lloyd insisted, "I'm chef today, and I heard Sally getting up, so she'll lend a hand."

"I could get used to this," Pip laughed as she left to get changed.

~ * ~ * ~

"This can't be right, surely? It's far too posh," Pip exclaimed as the Audi drew to a halt outside an attractive modern house in a broad road of similar properties. Mercedes, BMWs and other high-end cars sat on the driveways, beside manicured lawns and lush shrubbery.

"This is definitely it!" Gavin jabbed his finger on the roadmap. He was nervous about seeing Sharon.

"Someone's home," Theo pointed to the maroon Jaguar parked beside the front door. "You'd better get up there – good luck."

Pip and Gavin walked to the house exchanging anxious looks. The doorbell was answered by a tall, muscular man with cold eyes and a shaved head. He gave a grunt of curiosity and stared at the callers, waiting for their explanation.

"Is Sharon here, please?" Pip piped up.

"You don't look like a customer." The man's voice was as menacing as his demeanour.

Pip was sure that poor Sharon was at the mercy of this thug, no doubt being forced to service up-market clients. What other explanation could there be?

"No, we aren't customers, we are friends of hers," she explained. "Is she in?"

"I know her friends and you aren't one of them, so scram!" The man moved to close the door.

"It's OK, Vince, she's telling the truth," said a familiar voice from the hallway. Sharon moved into view. "You can let them in."

The man reluctantly stepped back, allowing the previously uninvited guests to enter. The heavy front door thudded closed behind them as Pip and Gavin followed their hostess into a large sitting room. The furnishings were on-trend, with a thick carpet and two large plush sofas either side of a glass coffee table. Through an archway into a dining room, a second man sat at the table working on a pile of paperwork. Built similarly to Vince, his black t-shirt gamely attempted to stretch over his enormous biceps.

"Could you give us some privacy please, Terry?" Sharon asked.

"Don't forget you've got clients to see this afternoon." Terry lit a cheroot. The look of icy contempt that he threw at the visitors was haunting – they were cockroaches, spared from being stamped on by the flighty intercessions of an overindulged girl.

"I won't." Sharon fixed him with a pouty sulk until he left.

She settled on one of the settees and gestured that her guests should sit opposite. Sharon lit a cigarette from a silver box on the glass table and sat back, exhaling smoke, comfortable and sophisticated. Her expensive jeans and shirt could only have been more ostentatious if she wore them inside-out to display their designer labels.

"Well, you found me. I thought you probably would, you've never been able to leave well alone, Pip."

Disregarding the barbed comment, Pip whispered a series of breathless questions, "What is this place, Sharon? Who are those men? Do you need help to get away?"

"Oh, you are priceless!" Sharon laughed patronisingly. "You actually think I need rescuing – and is big strong Gav here going to help? You couldn't be more wrong. Vince and Terry are my bodyguards."

"Why would you need bodyguards?" Gavin asked.

"It's necessary in my line of work, especially if you are a woman." Sharon was clearly unwilling to discuss the matter further. "Pip, I told you that I was fine in that stupid letter that I sent to you, so go home and tell Mum and Dad that it's true."

The visitors exchanged a look and shuffled uneasily.

"Sharon," Gavin said slowly, "I have bad news. There's no easy way to say it, but your dad passed away."

A crack in Sharon's façade appeared briefly. Her eyes darted, and her face flushed; she drew hard on her cigarette several times, using it to control her breathing.

"How?" she asked, taking a tissue from a box on a table situated by the arm of the sofa and dabbing just under her mascara line.

"It was a heart attack, very peaceful," Gavin half-lied. "I was with him and you were in his last thoughts. He loved you very much."

Sharon nodded, regaining her composure, drawing sharply on her cigarette once more before stubbing it out into an ashtray, barely a third smoked. She controlled her exhalation through narrowed lips, emitting a narrow stream of smoke that widened and hung about her like an old memory.

"That's a damn shame," she said. "How's Mum?"

"As well as can be expected," Pip replied. "Worried sick about you and missing your dad, but she is strong, she has friends, and Mark of course – he'll be getting married soon."

"More fool him," Sharon snorted, "but he always was the weak one."

"I wouldn't call getting married being weak."

"You haven't changed a bit, have you?" mocked Sharon. "You're still skipping around in your perfect world where everyone is nice – well, I've news for you, life is tough. Don't trust anyone."

"You've no idea about my life, and you taught me about the dangers of trusting people."

"What, because of that joke with the joints?"

"Betrayal, more like!" Pip's eyes blazed. "I was expelled because of you. My life was ruined— no, I was ruined."

"Don't be such a little prima donna," Sharon had always used derision to dismiss Pip's concerns rather than face her own responsibility, but now her old friend saw it for what it was.

"Yes, Sharon, and who is better placed to recognise one?" Pip asked. She folded her arms, crossed one leg over the other, and stared out of the window, her dark hair bobbing with the sharp movement of her head.

Gavin used the lull in the conversation to simultaneously take heat out of the situation and gain more information.

"You've been seen in town with a famous footballer. That must be exciting."

"Oh, him." Sharon drew a contender from a mental list of possibilities. "Yeah, he's a bit of fun, and fit as anything, but I'm only seeing him because I can't stand his bitch of a wife."

Pip maintained her silence, but her head tilted slowly to one side and her shoulder moved a fraction of an inch upwards, as if a spider was crawling on her neck but she couldn't move her arms to brush it away. Sharon observed the inward struggle and smiled.

"I knew you wouldn't approve of my lifestyle," she exulted.

"It's not for me to approve or disapprove, is it?" Pip snapped. "You do what you want, you always did. So, what's your unspeakable job, if you are so keen to shock us?"

Sharon stood up, walked to a wall unit which housed a drinks cabinet, poured a generous measure of scotch for herself, and held up the glass to ask if her guests wanted one; both declined. She stood in the golden rectangle of mid-morning sun on the fuchsia carpet and looked through the patio doors to the garden outside. She sipped her drink, not sure if she was weighing up whether to tell them about her occupation, or if she was still coming to terms with the death of her father.

"I'm a money lender. Vince and Terry are my protection and my enforcers."

"What kind of money lender?" Pip asked, not wanting to believe what she already knew to be true.

"What kind do you think? I've got Birkenhead just up the road from here, with lots of people who a bank won't look at. I give them money up front and they pay me back on the weekly."

"Except they never do pay you back, do they?"

"Maybe... if they won the pools," Sharon laughed.

"Oh, Sharon, that's awful!" Pip exclaimed. "Those poor people—"

"Dangling on my thread? Maybe, but something's got to pay for all this. It's my dues, after wasting all that bloody time and effort on the band."

"You mean wasting time on Sam?" Gavin corrected, also shocked, betrayed and angry.

"Do I? I suppose I do. It took me too long to realise what a loser he is, but when I did, I took what was rightfully mine and left."

"Your share of the loot?" Pip asked with a diamond voice that would cut through anything.

"If you like, and why not? It was my brains, my networking that made it possible. I never set out to harm anyone, but we were desperate. People were going to hurt Sam, possibly kill him, so I got the money any way I could, and when that wasn't enough, I was willing to—" Sharon broke off, reining in her outburst.

"Willing to what?" Gavin asked.

"It doesn't matter. It gave me enough to set up this little business and I'd already met Vince and Terry, so I hit the road running." Sharon gulped down the remainder of her drink and flopped onto the sofa, taking another cigarette. "It gives me a good life."

"Nicking a few quid off Sam isn't enough to kickstart this," Pip said as she looked around her.

"Who's a clever girl?" Sharon showed mock surprise. "Easy answer – the banks might not lend to my customers, but they'll lend to me."

"And you lend it at a massive profit to those poor sods who haven't got anywhere else to turn," Pip scowled. "Is that even legal?"

"But, if there's a recession, or if interest rates suddenly rise, your clients won't be able to pay, but you'll still be on the hook to the banks," Gavin pointed out.

"Well, there had better not be a recession," Sharon shrugged. "Think what you like, I'm not embarrassed about it and if I didn't do it, then someone else would."

"Why stupid?" Pip interjected with an apparent non sequitur.

"What?" Sharon asked.

"Why did you say your letter to me was stupid?"

"Oh, that. Because I know you, Pip. You like people to wear their hearts on their sleeve like the characters in those awful romance novels that you read. So, I gave you what you wanted, dear Philippa. Not everyone's a goody-two-shoes like you, some of us can't be perfect."

"I don't expect people to be perfect, just kind," Pip retorted, stung in her heart. "One of my best friends helped me twice, when I was just a stranger to her, for no reason other than I was cold and wet and had nowhere else to go. She gave me an old coat and a cup of tea and probably saved my life, but she's no saint and neither's her old man. He's a diamond but a complete scally – if something falls off the back of a lorry, he doesn't ask where it comes from, but he sure as hell shares it with his family and friends, and he would never, never betray one of his own."

"But that's just it," Sharon laughed, "my customers aren't one of my own, and neither are you. It's not that I don't care, it's just that I'm going places. In life, you look after number one. I don't care what you think of me, and I don't care why you think I wrote that letter – I'm not the sentimental type, so why don't you trot back home and tell my mum that I am fine, and I send my love, and I'll try to write or something? Goodbye." She stood up, indicating that the interview was over.

"What's that, then?" Pip asked. "You're just dismissing us after we came all this way?"

"I never invited you!" Sharon shrugged and turned her back.

Stunned, Pip and Gavin went into the hallway. Sharon didn't follow, but Terry glowered at them from the kitchen, drying a mug with a tea towel. Pip paused by the door, thinking the Sharon she once knew was gone, replaced by a caricature – and yet, something niggled at her mind.

"Go back to the car and wait for me, Gav," she said. Pip saw him dither and lowered her voice. "I'll be fine. Please, there is something I need to say to her in private."

Gavin complied, and Pip returned to the living room.

"I don't believe you," she said.

Sharon, who was looking out of the window once again, turned around.
"Why?"

"Your purse, the one I gave you. I know what was in it, and there was nothing of value or importance, so why try to get it back?"

"I must be more sentimental than I realised."

"A reminder of home, of me?" Pip pressed.

"Fine, yes!" Sharon flashed. "In some ways I do miss you, and home, and Mum and…"

"Dad?" Pip finished for her. "So why push us away and act as if we couldn't understand you?"

"You couldn't understand, that's why – you least of all."

"What exactly do you think I am incapable of understanding?"

"Being scared and alone and having no money, not knowing where to turn – you can't understand what it's like."

Pip didn't know whether to laugh, cry, or shake Sharon by the elbows, but she actually found gentleness.

"Why don't you tell me what really happened with Sam?" she suggested softly, like a rose petal. "I know you left London because he owed lots of money, and I know you paid it off by getting the cash by any means necessary."

Sharon hesitated, conflicted between an ache to bring the truth to the surface, and an unjust fury with her friend's perceived purity. Yet another cigarette calmed her nerves.

"By any means necessary?" She dragged Pip's words back to mock her. "Just say we nicked it, because we did. We'd almost got enough by the time they caught us, but they're not the kind of people who'll forgive little shortfalls. The bloke who turned up was a funny looking little man, but he had the deadest eyes I've ever seen. Sam was scared stiff and started begging for more time, but the bloke wanted his money, or he was going to send his men in. So, I persuaded him… in the bedroom. The trouble was, Sam wouldn't look at me or touch me after that. A week later, he turned up with a new girl for the band. I saw the light, took all the dosh, and did a runner."

Sharon tried to read Pip's face but was frustrated not to see revulsion in her countenance; she wanted to be asked 'How could you?' and to be castigated as little more than a common trollop, but no such condemnation came.

"It's easy for you, Pip! You've no idea what it's like to see no way out other than to let a filthy old man have his way with you, to have to pretend that you like his foul touch."

"I guess I'm just lucky," Pip responded. Her fingers went to her pendant and she comforted herself with thoughts of the rose petals within.

"But I came out on top," Sharon gloated. "Look around you, I'm beating them at their own game."

"If it's the game you want to play, then well done," Pip sniped, "but I'm not stupid, all this is rented, isn't it?"

"Well, look who found a mind of her own. What's your point?"

"You're in a gilded cage and it won't last."

"Yeah, but it's fun while it does. Then I'll find another gig. Don't you get it? I'm happy – you can't see why, because it's alien to you, but this is frigging fantastic. Totally worth everything."

"Everything?"

"Everything," Sharon insisted. "Water off a duck's back. I'll let nothing, and nobody, define me, don't worry. You're welcome to come and join me, for old time's sake."

Pip's expression was more than enough to decline the insincere offer. "Then I suppose I'm happy for you, I just wish you didn't do it from other people's suffering."

"You're not the Ghost of Christmas Past, come to show me the error of my ways, and I'm not Ebenezer Scrooge needing to be saved, but nice try."

"Think what you like," Pip said. "I'll go now, but one last question – was anything between us real?"

"All of it, but we were just kids then."

"Please ring your mum," Pip pleaded. "I won't tell her anything, but please, for her sake, call her. She's been through hell since your dad passed."

Sharon half nodded. "I don't suppose I'll see you again?"

"Probably not, but I'll be there if you need me," Pip replied as she opened the door.

"Pip!"

"Yes?"

"Still mates?"

"Always. Just not best mates."

Sharon waited until the front door closed before she started to shake. She poured another whisky and gulped it down, slamming the empty crystal glass onto the counter, holding her breath and struggling not to cry, her chest lurching with suppressed sobs. Sniffing, she picked the telephone and went to dial the long-familiar number of her parents' home – but she stopped herself and replaced the handset. Not yet.

Chapter 23

Pip carefully examined the small rose bushes in her bedroom and sprayed them gently with water, as was her daily routine. All three were fully restored to health and blooming brightly and she lightly caressed the damp petals with her fingertips, remembering her grandfather and the happy times they had spent together potting the plants.

Through the window, she watched Bobbie and Daniel playing in the back garden and became so lost in the childhood memories they evoked that she didn't realise Theo was behind her until his hands were around her waist and his lips nibbling her neck; she squirmed with pleasure and leaned her head back to kiss him.

"Are you still coming over later?" Theo asked when they decided they needed to breathe.

"Is that your way of saying you need help assembling your furniture?"

"It'll be yours too, soon enough." Theo took her left hand and kissed the engagement ring that sat upon her finger.

"True," Pip readily concurred, "but we agreed not to rush things. I need to see Lyn happy first."

"Still no call from Sharon? What's it been, eight weeks?"

"More like nine. I'll have to tell Lyn the truth, but I don't know how she'll take it, or how she'll feel about me afterwards."

"It's not your fault, it's Sharon's. Lyn will see that."

Pip nodded but was unconvinced. She and Theo made her way downstairs and into the garden to join the children under the late morning sun. While her fiancé launched himself into an enthusiastic game of chase, she carefully examined her favourite rosebush and selected its finest flower, snipping it free with a pair of secateurs.

"I'm off now," she called, smiling at the children's happy faces, "I'll see you all later."

"You look very smart," Bobbie observed. Pip's long cream cotton dress was inexpensive but had a flavour of Edwardian elegance.

"Why bother?" Daniel said. "You're only seeing Gran and your friend Arthur."

"Ah, but this is a special occasion," Pip replied.

Soon she was in the large communal sitting room of the care home with Gran and Mr Swann. The old man wore his best suit and sat straight backed in his chair, nervous with anticipation. Pip tucked the rose she had brought into the lapel of his jacket, and he lifted it to his nose to savour the scent.

When they were settled, the old man turned on the radio.

~ * ~ * ~

In the auditorium, Lloyd walked out onto the raised platform and looked at the microphone in front of his seat. The coughs and shuffles of the audience faded away as the lights dimmed until he sat alone in a silent circle of light.

In the darkness, his mother and Angelique sat on the edge of their seats, transfixed with excitement and glowing with pride at the sight of Lloyd about to begin the most important performance of his career. Sally was beside them, her palms pressed tightly together, willing her boyfriend success. Darren was there too, watching, hoping, smiling at the good fortune of his friend, but his happiness was complete when, safe in the dark, Will reached across the narrow armrest between them and held his hand. All Lloyd's friends and family held their breath as the musician drew his bow across the strings of his cello, and the first sweet notes filled the auditorium.

Miles away, Gavin and Tori reclined on the sofa of the living room of his family home while the speakers of the hi-fi resonated to the sound of the cello and transported them to such an extent that they forgot to kiss each other for several minutes.

Further away still, Sharon sat in the back of the maroon Jaguar, looking at the back of Vince's and Terry's heads. She felt bitter-sweet that such beautiful music could still exist in the world, until Vince's finger stabbed at the radio and the station changed. Sharon was about to object but thought better of it.

In the care home, Gran smiled amiably at her granddaughter as they

~ 363 ~

listened. Mr Swann was entranced, as if his dear Anna was in the room with him, playing her tune for herself. He pictured the wisps of her fair hair moving as her head nodded and swayed with the music, while her uncertain eyes looked to her Arthur for the encouragement she would surely receive. Oscar sat soberly at his old master's feet and every so often a pale wrinkled hand would reach down and stroke his soft brown fur.

Philippa Raven watched and listened to everything with a restful contentment she once feared she would never know. As it had before, the music swelled over her, pulling the pain from her heart and offering a glimpse of her grandfather in a garden of blossoms with a covenant beyond all understanding. When the last notes faded away to become a perfect memory, the deep voice of the radio presenter spoke.

"And that, ladies and gentlemen, was *The Wild Roses*."

Lightning Source UK Ltd.
Milton Keynes UK
UKHW011940131119
353477UK00001B/26/P

9 781913 264390